Alison Strobel skillfully intersects the lives of three souls bearing the unfair weight of past wounds. Told with care and sensitivity, Alison capably delves into the often misunderstood cocoon of domestic abuse as well as the changing shape — and density — of personal loss. Well done.

Susan Meissner, author, *The Shape of Mercy*

Alison Strobel has penned an important book about a battered woman's psyche and the length God journeys to rescue her. Honest, painful, redemptive, *The Weight of Shadows* is the kind of gutsy novel book clubs enjoy discussing.

Mary DeMuth, author, *Daisy Chain* and *A Slow Burn*

THE WEIGHT OF SHADOWS

THE WEIGHT OF SHADOWS

a novel

ALISON STROBEL

ZONDERVAN.com/
AUTHORTRACKER
follow your favorite authors

ZONDERVAN

The Weight of Shadows
Copyright © 2010 by Alison Strobel Morrow

This title is also available as a Zondervan ebook.
Visit www.zondervan.com/ebooks.

This title is also available in a Zondervan audio edition.
Visit www.zondervan.fm.

Requests for information should be addressed to:

Zondervan, *Grand Rapids, Michigan 49530*

Library of Congress Cataloging-in-Publication Data

Strobel, Alison.
        The weight of shadows / Alison Strobel Morrow.
            p.   cm.
        ISBN 978-0-310-28945-6 (pbk.)
            1. Wife abuse—Fiction. 2. Secrets—Fiction. I. Title.
PS3619.T754W45 2010b
813'.6—dc22   2010006416

Cover design: Laura Maitner-Mason
Cover photography: Erica Shires/Corbis
Interior design: Christine Orejuela-Winkelman

Printed in the United States of America

10 11 12 13 14 15 /DCI/ 22 21 20 19 18 17 16 15 14 13 12 11 10 9 8 7 6 5 4 3 2 1

Dedicated to Claudia Mair Burney,
who lived the nightmare but never lost her spirit.
Thank you for sharing both your soul
and your journey with such brutal honesty.
I am honored to be your friend,
and thankful you like to be mine.
Chat you soon!

ONE

Is it truly a birthday party when the guests don't even know it's your birthday? Kim pondered the question as she slipped on the slacks she'd borrowed from her roommate Corrie. Certainly it was an improvement over eating a store-bought cupcake alone in front of reruns. She'd done that more times than she cared to remember.

The intercom buzzed the arrival of the first guest. She spread her hands over her stomach, willing death to the butterflies that had come to life. She sucked in a deep breath and blew it away as she put on her only pair of earrings and secured her locket around her neck. Fingering the pendant brought to mind memories of the day she'd received it. She replayed them in her mind, conjuring every detail she could as she pulled a brush through her hair: the blanket of snow on the bushes outside, Sinatra serenading the restaurant's customers, her foster parents ordering four desserts for everyone to share when no one could decide what they wanted. That was the last good birthday she'd had.

Corrie's voice rang out over the stereo, welcoming whoever had arrived and bringing Kim back to the present. She bit her lip, debating whether or not to go out yet. These weren't her friends, she wasn't good at small talk, and with only one guest there was no way for her to disappear into the crowd or avoid interacting. Three strikes. She'd better wait.

A pair of black flats, their toes and heels repaired with a marker, were the finishing piece to her ensemble. She gave her red blouse a tug at the bottom and examined herself in the mirror, happy with what she saw. It was possible she wouldn't talk to anyone all night, but at least she looked nice. In fact, part of her hoped no one would talk to her — she'd met a few of Corrie's friends before, and they were all out of her league. The thought of trying to hold a conversation with any of them resurrected the butterflies. She frowned at her reflection as the familiar self-doubt crept in. The less she said tonight, the better.

Kim hated battling the voice of inadequacy that resurfaced whenever she met new people. She reminded herself of the same things she told her Club girls and gave her head a shake to dislodge the negative thoughts. *Your roots may form you, but they do not define you. You are not less of a person because you lack the things most people have. Your worth as a person is not determined by what you have, but by who you are.* When she talked to the girls, she was referencing money, social standing, academic success, the perfect body — the things teen girls usually stressed over. When she gave herself the pep talk, though, she was thinking of family.

The buzzer sounded again, followed a minute later by multiple voices calling out cheerful greetings. *No more hiding.* Kim left her room and joined the party.

Six people had arrived, an equal mix of men and women who had the same casual sophistication as Corrie, though two of the women had a sort of polished hippie look that Kim envied, knowing she lacked the fashion sense to be like them. Her coordinating abilities ended with slacks and blouses.

Three of the guests sat on the couch, paging through one of Corrie's photo albums, while the others were filling their plates with snacks. Kim flashed a smile to the one person who acknowledged her presence, then walked to the kitchen to get herself a drink. She took her time so as not to look as harried and nervous as she felt, and sighed with a small smile when the intercom buzzed again. A bigger crowd meant easier hiding.

Corrie propped open the front door and returned to her conversation. Kim walked to the snack table and began to load a plate with some veggies and dip. She really wanted the chocolate chip cookies Corrie had baked the night before, but she wanted to make a good impression, and these folks looked like veggie people.

The next wave of guests entered, and instantly the party felt more like a party. More talking, louder calls of "Hello!" across the room, and, to Kim's great relief, less sophisticated dress. The last one in shut the door behind himself and handed his scuffed leather jacket to Corrie as he greeted her. Kim couldn't peel her eyes away from him. *He doesn't seem to belong with these people any more than I do. Who is he?*

The guest who had entered with Scuffed Leather Jacket introduced him to Corrie. Kim was too far away and the room too noisy for her to hear any of what they were saying, but Corrie, ever the gracious hostess, made the universal *mi casa es su casa* arm-sweep with a bright smile before carting the coats to her bedroom.

He stood with his hands half-jammed into his pockets and looked around the room. When his gaze neared Kim she ducked her head, though what she really wanted was to look him in the eye, smile and welcome him, and commiserate. When he appeared at her side, she almost couldn't breathe.

"The snack table is my favorite place to hide at a party too," he said. She couldn't tell if he was sympathizing or making fun of her. But his face, when she glanced over at him, was open and honest-looking. There was no twinkle of teasing in his green eyes nor the tug of a smirk at his lips. She laughed faintly and searched in vain for something clever to say.

"My name is Rick, by the way."

"I'm Kim. Nice to meet you."

"You too. How do you know, um ..."

"Corrie?"

"Yeah, Corrie."

"She's my roommate."

"Oh!" His face brightened. "Wow, this is your place?"

She slid her eyes back to her plate. "No. I wish. I just rent a room from her."

"Oh, that's cool." He leaned in a little closer. "It's a nice place, but not my style, you know? A little too ..." He waved the hand that wasn't holding a snack plate. "Calculated. Like those model homes that are so decorated it's like walking into a design magazine."

Kim looked around the living room, trying to see it through the eyes of a stranger. Corrie had added most of the room's contents since Kim had moved in, so the change had been so gradual she hadn't noticed the overall effect. "You know, you're right." She grinned. "I've never thought about it, but you're right." She swirled a carrot stick in a puddle of dip. "It's not really my style, either, but I'll take it over just having a room any day."

"I'm sure you'll have your own place someday."

She laughed a little. "I hope so!"

They crunched on their respective vegetables in silence for a few minutes before Kim got up the courage to speak again. "So who did you come with?"

Rick pointed to the couch with a celery stick. "Guy I work with. Adam. I think he knows Corrie from college or something like that. Life has kinda sucked lately, so he invited me to cheer me up."

"That's a shame. I hope it works."

"It already has."

Kim felt her cheeks heat. She smothered the smile that stretched across her face with a long sip from her soda.

"That's a really cool necklace."

"Oh, thanks." She pulled it along the chain a few times before patting it back into place. "I got it for my seventeenth birthday."

He grinned. "How long ago was that?"

"Seven years ago — today." She almost didn't say it, but his attention was making her bolder. *And it would take a lot of attention to spoil me, so I'm going to get it while I can.*

"No way. It's your birthday?" She giggled in response, instantly wincing inside at the childish sound. "So this is for you, then? This party?"

"Oh, no. Corrie doesn't even know."

"Your own roommate doesn't know it's your birthday?"

She shuffled a little. "Well, we're not really friends, you know?

I've only lived here a few months. I just found the room through an ad. We share space — that's about it."

Rick shook his head. "That's just a shame. So all these people — just friends of Corrie's?"

"Yeah."

"You're spending your birthday with a bunch of strangers. That's just wrong. I feel like I need to go find you a cake or something." She laughed. "No, I'm serious! Did you do *anything* special for your birthday? Did anyone acknowledge it?"

"Well — one person did." She smiled, remembering her conversation with Patricia, the case worker who had shepherded her through the foster system for so many years. "But no, I didn't do anything special. Just went to work like I usually do. But this — " she waved her hand towards the room full of people, "is more than I usually do. Birthdays weren't a big deal when I was growing up."

He didn't ask why not, to her relief. But he asked plenty of other things, and eventually she reciprocated. Over time they migrated to the kitchen, and then to a couple dining room chairs in the corner. When Adam came to say he was ready to leave, Kim was stunned to see they'd talked for two hours.

"I'm really glad I came," Rick said to Kim as he shrugged into his jacket. "I'm glad I met you."

"I'm glad you came too." Her mouth hurt from smiling so much, but she couldn't seem to stop. "I had a great time talking with you."

"Do you think I could take you out for dinner sometime?"

Her heart nearly burst. "Yes, definitely, yes. I'd love that."

Rick smiled and ran a hand through his blond bed head. "Great. I'll call you this week, I promise."

"He's totally not going to call."

Corrie laughed as she spread plastic wrap over the bowl of dip. "What makes you say that?"

"I don't know — I just don't think he will. I don't have luck like that."

"Maybe you will now."

"Maybe." Kim cinched the trash bag shut and pulled it free from the can. "But even if he doesn't, it's okay. I've never had that much fun talking to a guy before. No one's ever even flirted with me before." Memories of her unattractive teen years surfaced briefly but lacked the sting they usually held. Even thoughts of her life until now — nights alone, undeclared infatuations, awkward introversion — weren't as painful. "I hardly knew what to do. But ..." She trailed off, a smile still tugging at her lips, and carried the trash to the door. "If nothing else, it was a perfect way to spend an evening." *And a birthday.*

TWO

"Joshua, Seth wants to see you in his office at four. Are you free?"

Joshua's stomach dropped. "Yeah, I am, Amanda. Thanks." He set the phone back into the cradle and ground his palms against his eyes. This couldn't be happening.

Maybe it's not. He sat up straighter, took a couple deep breaths. *Don't jump to conclusions.* The spreadsheet on the monitor in front of him seemed to glow brighter than normal, and a low-level throb began in his temples. *God, please, not my job too.*

He still had an hour left before the meeting, and at least three hours' worth of work waiting to be done. This was not the time for a pity party. He shook his head to clear away the wild thoughts that threatened to steal his concentration. *Show them why they still need you.*

He got back to work, diligence and fear driving his pace, and at 3:56 p.m. he set his shoulders back and walked down to Seth's office.

Amanda sat at her desk, the phone clamped between ear and shoulder. She waved her hand towards the door, mouthing, "Go on in." With a final fleeting prayer he pushed open the mahogany door and went inside.

Seth was standing at the window, looking out to the parking lot where snow was once again beginning to fall. Joshua closed the door and walked to a chair, but couldn't bring himself to sit. He wanted to face his fate standing. He braced his hands on the back of the chair across from Seth's desk and waited.

Seth's eyes remained on the view. "You know, of course, about the financial struggles we're having."

Joshua smiled, though there was no humor in it. This kind of small talk didn't bode well. "I wouldn't be a very good accountant if I didn't."

"The board wants me to cut ten positions. With three of you down there in accounting — " He shook his head. "It's killing me to do it, Joshua — I hope you never think for a minute I didn't feel sick to my stomach over this decision."

Joshua nodded, though Seth couldn't see, and felt the last flicker of hope die out. "Last hired, first fired, I know. I understand."

When Seth faced him, Joshua saw the haggard look of a man haunted by the less-pleasant aspects of his position. His boss and friend closed the distance between them, and spoke quietly. "I'm not blind to how absolutely awful the timing of this is. I talked with the board and begged them for another few months, but ..." He shrugged. Joshua knew enough of the organization's worries to be able to end the sentence himself. "They actually wanted your position cut by the end of last year, but held back until now because of the ... circumstances. But the budget — I'm sorry, Joshua. I really am."

Seth's compassion made Joshua's heart ache almost more than the loss of his job. "I appreciate it, Seth. *Really* appreciate it. I don't know what I would have done if I'd lost the job in December. It was a rough enough month without that to deal with."

Seth nodded. "We haven't had the chance to talk in a while. How's Madeline doing these days?"

Joshua took a deep breath. "She's doing about as well as expected for a four-year-old. Still dreams about Lara, though; those nights are ... hard, to put it mildly. For both of us." He took another breath as his composure wobbled. *Keep yourself together, man.* "My parents were here for a couple weeks last month and that helped. Hopefully this summer we'll be able to go out there for a week or two. It gets hard being at the house all the time — all the memories — " His throat closed and he looked away, coughing to cover his emotional slip.

Seth grabbed his shoulder and squeezed. "If there's anything Beth and I can do ..."

Joshua straightened and nodded. "Thanks. Just keep praying." Seth nodded and closed his eyes, beseeching God aloud for mercy and blessings on behalf of Joshua and his daughter.

On the way home, Joshua considered Seth's offer for help. He knew he'd get a glowing recommendation from him, and possibly some contacts at other ministries, but other than that there wasn't much he—or anyone, really—could do. He and Maddie were past the meal phase, though the casseroles they'd stashed from friends and neighbors had lasted them nearly two months. He was also past the shoulder-to-cry-on stage, at least in the eyes of the people around them. Apparently six months was considered long enough for mourning the death of your wife.

Lost in thought, he almost missed the driveway to the day care center. When he entered Maddie's room she tossed down the doll she was dressing and jumped into his outstretched arms. He held her little frame tightly, reveling in the scent of baby shampoo that still lingered in her hair from last night's bath, aching for the hole in her life where a mother was supposed to be. *Please, God. Help me.*

"Logan called me a poopyhead today at snack."

Joshua bit back a smile as he buckled her into the carseat. "Uh-oh. What did you do?"

"I told him that was mean and that he should apologize—"

"Good for you."

"—and that he was poopyhead infinity."

He couldn't stop the chuckle that time. "Sweetheart, do you even know what infinity is?"

Her brown eyes blinked up at him. "No, but Serena says it all the time."

He laughed as he shut her door and turned on the car. "It means something that goes on forever."

"Oh. Poopyhead forever!" She giggled and Joshua rolled his eyes as he backed out of the parking space.

"Anything else exciting happen today?"

"No. I want hamburgers for dinner. Can we get some from Rudy's?"

He hesitated, knowing that money was going to be much tighter than it had ever been. *But why not one last hurrah?* "Sure. And Rice Dream for dessert?"

"Yeah, yeah, yeah!" Her sneakered feet kicked the back of his seat as she began to sing along with the children's worship music that was their standard driving soundtrack. Joshua smiled at her in the rearview mirror but the gesture was missed—her eyes were fixed out the window, watching the snowy world pass by.

They ate their burgers in their favorite booth at Rudy's, Maddie peppering their conversation with her preschool knowledge and a barrage of obscure questions. Afterwards, they walked to Sweet-Please, where she chose her usual bag of gummy bears and ate them one color at a time on the way home. These little capsules of normality were becoming more frequent, a phenomenon he'd noticed a couple weeks ago but now feared losing again when the severance pay ran out.

A couple hours later he sat alone in his home office, the baby monitor crackling occasionally with Maddie's shuffling in her toddler bed. He turned his Rolodex slowly, checking each name and wracking his brain for the connections they might have to help him find new employment. He couldn't afford to be picky right now. Anyone who might have any kind of connection—or even know someone who might have a connection—to a company or ministry in need of accountants was worth considering.

The one name that was not in the Rolodex was the one he knew would be the most helpful—in theory, anyway. He said another prayer, hoping he wouldn't become desperate enough to consider asking his father-in-law, George Michalson, for advice. He knew George would be more than willing to help him, but it was the strings Joshua knew would be attached that kept him from making the call.

"God, I need a break here," he muttered as he set the Rolodex aside. "We've been through so much already — Maddie especially. If I didn't have her it wouldn't be so bad, but God ..."

His eyes caught the picture of his daughter smiling at him from the frame on his desk. She'd been having a great couple days, but then, just before bed, had broken down in tears when Joshua had bungled the order of her bedtime routine. "Mommy never forgot!" she wailed as he cursed his wandering focus. He'd held her and cried with her as they were both overwhelmed once more by the pain of their loss. After finally getting her to sleep with extra lullabies, he'd wandered the house, hungry for a connection with the woman he still loved so deeply, and finding it in all the little objects that resided on bookshelves and end tables: a picture frame from their Maui honeymoon, Maddie's first year scrapbook, nesting dolls from their Alaskan cruise, and finally, her closet, where her summer clothes still hung. The tears had come once again when he'd buried his nose in a stack of her T-shirts and found her scent was finally gone.

"I'm mentally fried as it is. To add a job search and the stress of the hospital bills on top of it ..." He eyed the stack that sat in the tray beside Maddie's picture. How would he deal with one more crisis?

SOMETHING HAD TO GIVE.

He'd been sitting at this desk for half an hour while Maddie played in the snow outside with a friend. Saturdays were usually daddy-daughter days, but he'd made some excuses and plied her with the promise of an afternoon filled with Disney princess movies to secure some alone time for himself. First he'd worked on his resume and posted it to a couple websites. Now he needed to lay everything out and see exactly where he stood.

The desk was covered with the bills Joshua had been putting off for weeks, now organized into small, neat stacks by type. If he could figure out how to cut some expenses, maybe they'd be alright. They hadn't been living hand to mouth; his income had allowed them a little wiggle room. Surely there were some luxuries he could sacrifice. But his severance would only cover two months, and though he hadn't acknowledged it until now, the medical bills had been eating up far more of his paycheck over the last few months than he could afford to spend. He needed to cut back on the nonessentials or risk losing his house.

How ironic. Lara had often talked about simplifying, paring down on their "stuff," reducing their carbon footprint. He'd always loved that hippie side of her. And now it was happening, and not only would she not be here to see it, but it was her fatal illness that was causing it.

He picked up the one bill that sat alone and opened it. The total, in bold print at the bottom, made him groan aloud.

Lara's breast cancer looked beatable at the beginning. The doctors threw everything they had at it, and were successful at first. Two months later it resurfaced, but this time in her liver. Again the doctors attacked it with a vengeance, and again they seemed successful. When it showed up in her lymph nodes four months after that, they stopped looking so confident. Their choice of words became more cautious — more *ifs* than *whens*, a lot of *maybes* and way too many *we don't knows*. His insurance through the ministry was far from comprehensive, but neither he nor Lara had a family history of major illness so they'd never cared.

What little savings they'd had was gone almost instantly. What was left of the bill rivaled the cost of an Ivy League education.

He wiped a hand over his face and drew a deep breath. "Okay. You can do this, Miller. Simplify, simplify, simplify. Where can you cut back?"

He opened bill after bill, scrutinized each account, categorized each ATM withdrawal and credit card charge. His fingers danced over the calculator's buttons, and as the next hour ticked away, Joshua came to realize there was not much he could do. In fact, there was only one thing that would make the kind of difference he needed to make.

He set down the calculator and stared out the window. Maddie and her playmate Julie were knocking down the snowman they'd constructed earlier, running full-tilt and slamming into it, collapsing on their backs in the snow and laughing. *Would it be too soon? Would it be too much change?* He sat back and stared at the ceiling, letting out a slow breath. "It's the only way I see, God. Please show me something else — if there *is* something else. But if there isn't ... help her to adapt." *Don't make it be the reason she needs therapy at thirty.* He sat quietly, waiting to see if God offered anything up. All he could hear was the girls' laughter. He closed his checkbook, put the calculator back in the drawer, and went to the kitchen to make the girls a snack and figure out how to tell Maddie they were moving.

JOSHUA AND MADDIE SAT ALONE at the kitchen table. Julie had gone home, much to Maddie's consternation, and now Joshua was looking for the right time to break the news.

"I love the snow." Maddie sat up on her knees and sipped her hot chocolate almond milk. Her nose and cheeks still glowed from the cold, and wet tendrils of her brown hair curled around her ears.

"I could tell. That was quite a snowman you and Julie built."

"Did you see us knock it down?" Her eyes sparkled with mirth. "We ran into it and bam! We fell back. It was *hilarious.*" *Hilarious* was her new favorite word. She'd been using it indiscriminately for days.

"I did see that. Pretty cool." Joshua took a sip from his mug, then shot a quick prayer to God for Maddie's response. "So I was thinking about something today, Mads. You know how we sometimes get sad because something here in the house will remind us of Mom?"

The light died in her eyes and she sat back on her heels. "Yeah. Like the rocking chair."

"Right. The curtains always make me think of her, because she spent so much time making them."

"Or the burn spot on the carpet in the living room."

That made Joshua smile. It had been the result of a candle toppled from the end table while she'd been dancing the polka to amuse a sick, couch-ridden Lara. That memory made Maddie smile as well. "I was thinking today that maybe you and I should find a place to live that doesn't have so many memories. It might make it easier, not having so many things to remind us, you know?"

He watched her, ready to backpedal if he saw panic in her features. Her eyes stayed glued to the napkin in her hand that she'd balled and twisted and then begun to shred. "So we wouldn't bring our stuff with us?"

"Oh! No, no — we'd bring our furniture, and pictures, and clothes. We wouldn't be leaving all our Mommy memories behind. We'd just be going somewhere new, where we can make new memories and decorate things differently. We could make you a princess bedroom, for example."

"Can't we do that here?"

He winced. "Well, technically, yes, we could." He was at a loss. *God, help me!* "But you and I don't need all this space, all these rooms, all this stuff. I promise we'll take anything you want to bring. But I just thought a change of scenery might do us both some good."

Maddie patted the little mound of napkin pieces she'd created. "Would I still be able to see Gramma and Grampa?"

"Of course." *Unfortunately.* "I wasn't thinking of moving far away. Just to a different neighborhood. But still in Ann Arbor. We could even drive back over here and have playdates with Julie."

"Can she come visit us?"

"Sure. And maybe we'll meet some new kids too." *God, let there be kids there, wherever "there" is, that Maddie gets along with and that aren't a bad influence.* "So ... what do you think?"

She shrugged. "I guess it would be okay."

Joshua leaned over and wrapped his daughter in a bear hug. "Maddie, you are my hero."

She giggled. "No Daddy, I'm your princess."

"Yes, that too."

"Can I paint my room pink?"

"Sure."

"And gold?"

"Um, maybe."

Her eyes lit up again and his heart melted. "How about pink and gold *and* glitter! Glitter *in the paint*!"

He laughed. "How about pink walls with a gold-framed mirror and I'll let you paint glitter on your curtains and dresser?"

"Deal."

Joshua heaved a sign of relief as Maddie skipped off to pick her promised princess movie. Pink, gold, and glitter were a small price to pay. *Thank you.*

"So when were you hoping to list?"

Joshua shrugged. "I don't know — soon, I guess."

Scott fixed him with a dubious stare. "And you're sure you have to do this? The market right now —"

Joshua ran a hand through his hair. "I know, I know. The timing couldn't be worse. That house down the street has been for sale for over a year — and it's the same floor plan as ours. But seriously, I have no choice. Unless I land a job in the next month, I'm in trouble. My resume is out there, but I know how things are right now — no one is hiring. My severance won't last long with the medical bills."

Scott looked around the living room. "Well, you guys did a good job on this place. I've been in that house down the street — yours will definitely show better. And at least you shouldn't have a problem finding a new place, given all the stuff on the market."

"I'll start looking this week. Between that and the job —"

"I still can't believe that. I'm so sorry. Wanna become a realtor?" Scott grinned. "I'll hire you to my firm as soon as you get your license. Teach you everything I know."

Joshua laughed. "Too old to teach this dog any new tricks, sorry. Just keep your ears open for me."

"Will do."

Maddie tore into the living room from the kitchen. "Gramma and Grampa are here!"

Joshua's stomach turned to lead. "What?" Maddie sped past him to the door and he looked to his friend. "Not a word about the move."

"My lips are sealed."

Both men stood and Scott picked up his coat. "I'll give you a call this week."

"Thanks. Say a prayer about—"

"Why is there a realtor's car in the driveway?" Alisha Michalson's brash voice preceded her. She appeared a few seconds later through the front door, holding Maddie's hand. "And why is this child outside without a coat? She's going to catch her death of cold."

Maddie's eyes bulged. Joshua bit back a sharp rebuke and kept his features neutral for his daughter's sake. "It's just a saying, Maddie, she didn't really mean it." *Nice choice of words Alisha. Thanks.* "She just ran out to meet you, that's all. And Scott is just a friend." He made introductions and exchanged knowing looks with Scott as he scooted past Joshua's in-laws and out the door. Joshua had forgotten the decal on Scott's rear windshield that advertised his real estate firm. Not that it mattered, since he hadn't told Maddie not to mention the move, and it was only a matter of time before—

"Guess what? We're gonna get a new house!"

And there it is.

"What? What's this?" Alisha's stare bore down on Joshua with the weight of an anvil.

"We're moving. Not far, don't worry, just to a smaller place that we can make our own, right Maddie?"

"I'm getting a pink princess room." She hopped in place with giddy excitement, and Joshua smiled and thanked God for her positive attitude.

"Stop jumping, Madeline, it's not ladylike." Alisha reached into her pocket and pulled out a 3 Musketeers bar. "That's for you, darling. Why don't you go enjoy that in your bedroom and let us talk to your daddy, okay?"

Maddie held the candy bar reverently in her hands, but Joshua reached over and gently took it. "How about we trade this in for some chocolate Rice Dream, kiddo?"

"Okay!"

"You just take our gift from her?" George said, his arthritis-gnarled hands balled into fists on his hips.

"You guys know she's allergic to milk. Why do you keep bringing things she can't have?"

"That's ridiculous, you can't be allergic to milk. You made this up to be difficult and you know it."

Lord, give me strength and love and patience and please *don't let me go off on them.* "We've had this discussion before, there's no point in having it again." He tried to keep his tone even, to not let the irritation he felt with their unexpected arrival and general sour dispositions color his words. He ushered everyone into the kitchen, then scooped some Rice Dream into a bowl and gave it to Maddie with a kiss on the forehead. "Let me know right away if you spill so I can clean it up, okay?"

"Okay, Daddy. Thank you." Cradling the bowl close, Maddie disappeared down the hall, leaving Joshua to defend their castle against the enemy. The three adults moved into the family room adjacent to the kitchen.

"You always make us look bad in front of her." Alisha dropped her ample body into the sofa, which creaked a complaint. George lowered himself into the recliner and waved Alisha's accusation away. "Never mind that. What's this about moving? When did you plan on letting us in on the secret? Or did you hope to slip out without us knowing?"

Joshua sank into an armchair and answered after breathing two slow, measured breaths. "I just decided last night. It's difficult for

Maddie and me to be here when everything reminds us of Lara. We don't need this much space, the mortgage is a bit more than I want to handle right now, and I thought it would be a good time to take another step towards moving on with our lives."

"Moving on?" Alisha laid a hand on her heart. "You're just going to sweep every memory of Lara right out of Madeline's head, aren't you?"

"No, Alisha, of course not. I'm not—"

"Will you get rid of all your furniture, all your pictures?"

"No—"

"Then how will moving help you to move on? That's nonsense. What's the real reason? You *were* going to go out of state, weren't you? To Maine, I'll bet—to that dumpy little town you came from. Lara told us how you wanted to move back there."

Joshua took another deep breath. "No. I was not planning on moving to Maine. Maddie's been through enough without me up-rooting her from the only community she's ever known. We're staying here in Ann Arbor. She'll still go to the same preschool. We'll still see her friends here. We're just downsizing."

George's eyes narrowed at him, and Joshua tried not to flinch. "Bills eating up your finances, eh?"

Joshua sighed. "Yes, they are."

"You know we could help—"

"I know you could, George, and I appreciate it, I really do." *But you couldn't pay me enough to be in your debt.* "I think this move will really help."

"That place you work for doesn't pay you enough. You oughtta find something else."

"I might just do that."

"I would hire you in a minute, you know that."

"And I appreciate that as well. But corporate work would take me away from Maddie even more than I already am. It's hard enough leaving her at school until 5:30 every night; I couldn't take a position that would require sixty hours a week, or even fifty."

Alisha let out a huff. "Then you ought to let me babysit her. Why you send her to a bunch of strangers every day—"

"She loves her teachers, and the kids there."

"But if you want to save money you could cut out a big chunk right there by letting me watch her."

This was slippery ground. Joshua stepped carefully. "Those teachers and children are her friends now. I'd be afraid of ripping her away from them. She's so social—you know how she is—she craves playing with other kids, and there aren't any in your neighborhood. Plus it's school, not just daycare, despite their name." Joshua stood and moved towards the kitchen. "So, what brought you two out here today?"

"Alisha heard a rumor."

Joshua waited. He could feel Alisha's eyes on him while he poured water for his in-laws. "And?"

Alisha's voice betrayed her enjoyment of having dirt on Joshua. "Well, our new neighbor, Gertie, golfs with a woman whose daughter works with you."

"Is that so?" *Uh-oh.*

"Teresa Gillespie."

Joshua brought the drinks in, bracing himself for the inevitable. "Oh yes, Teresa works in human resources."

"Well Gertie said this friend of hers said her daughter said they had to lay off a bunch of people, and that one of them was this sweet guy who lost his wife. And Gertie knew all about Lara because we told her, and she put two and two together."

Joshua nodded, studying his glass.

"Well?"

Joshua grasped his glass tightly. "Well what, Alisha? Obviously you know the news, so why are you trying to bait me?"

"So you lost your job?"

"Yes."

"Were you trying to hide that too?"

He set down his glass so he wouldn't break it. "Yes, actually,

I was. It's not the kind of thing I'd planned on making a big announcement about." He lowered his voice. "Especially since I haven't said anything yet to Maddie. I don't want to upset her; I don't want her worrying. So keep it under your hat, alright? At least around her."

"Even without a job you're not willing to come work for me?" George's face was pinched.

"I already told you, George, the hours would kill my time with Maddie, so no."

"How are you going to provide for her if you don't even have a job?"

"I get two months' severance and already have my resume put together and posted."

"Posted? Posted where?"

"Online."

George scoffed. "You don't find real jobs on the Internet."

Joshua shrugged. "It's a start, and seeing as I just found out two days ago that I was laid off, I think it's a decent one. I'm calling a temp agency in the morning—" Alisha let out a whimper of disbelief, which Joshua chose to ignore, "and I have a list of people I'm going to contact this week. I'm not worried, and you shouldn't be either."

"She's our only grandchild, and the last connection we have to our daughter. Of course we're worried." Alisha patted her heart. "George, we need to do something."

"No, really, you don't—"

"We do, Joshua." George leaned forward, setting his elbows on his knees and fixing Joshua with his narrowed blue eyes. "Alisha and I have been talking about this. Madeline's a bright, beautiful little girl, and we don't want to see her life squandered. She deserves the best—the best education, the best environment in which to grow up, the best of anything she needs. And we're not convinced you're going to be able to give her those things. Especially now."

Joshua's blood ran cold. He'd always known his in-laws disliked him, but never would he have guessed they'd go to this length. He forced himself not to yell as he tried to respond. "What are you getting at?"

"In light of your current difficulties, we think we ought to take primary custody of her."

"How dare you." The words were out before he could swallow them back. Joshua fought to control his voice, lest Maddie hear his anger. "How *dare* you doubt my ability to take care of my daughter. There is no reason—"

"You have no job, you're losing your home—"

"*Selling* my home, not losing it—"

"You have no savings, your bills are piling up—what will you do if she needs medical care, God forbid? You obviously can't be trusted to make the right decisions there; look what happened when Lara trusted you with her health. Or what about school? Certainly you weren't going to enroll her in the public schools, but you can't afford a private school now—"

"Stop!" Joshua barked the command, his fury barely contained. "She is *my* daughter. You have no right to her, and we have no need of your help. Get out of my house."

"Joshua, don't take this the wrong way—"

"Out."

"We have rights as grandparents according to Michigan law."

"Out."

George's eyes narrowed. "You look almost violent, Joshua. That temper doesn't show itself to our granddaughter, does it?"

Fingers of rage closed around his throat. He couldn't catch a deep breath. "Please get out before one of us says or does something we regret."

The two men sat locked in a staring contest. It was Alisha who broke the standoff with uncharacteristic calm. "George, I think we know where Joshua stands on the issue. Let's get going."

They all stood, and Joshua moved ahead of them to the front door and flung it open. He avoided their eyes until George turned and pointed a finger at him. "We love that little girl. We're not going to stand by and see her life fall apart around her because you can't handle things."

Joshua didn't respond. He didn't trust himself to speak. Instead he closed the door and walked on shaking legs to the nearest chair, where he collapsed and held his head in his hands.

THREE

Back at her apartment after a lunch date turned breakup, Debbie tossed her coat and purse on a chair and headed for the fridge. A quart of Ben & Jerry's sat waiting for her in the freezer, and her craving for it had kicked in with the predictability of Pavlov's bells when she'd seen the writing on the wall at lunch with David. She grabbed the container and a spoon, threw the lid into the sink, and dropped onto the sofa with the television remote.

She was running out of fingers on which to count all her doomed relationships. David put her up to eight, so long as she didn't count college. She never expected to become a serial dater, but now she felt like she needed to include a warning with her phone number when she gave it out to a guy. *Please be advised: this relationship will self-destruct in approximately four months.* Truth be told, she was more disappointed in adding another failure to the list than she was about losing David specifically. Not that he wasn't a great guy — but she was starting to think she was fated to be single forever.

The phone rang, making her jump. She jabbed her spoon into the ice cream and grabbed it. "H'lo?"

"Hi sweetheart, it's me."

Oh boy. "Hey Mom."

"Just thought I'd call and see how your weekend went."

"Oh. It was okay."

"That's convincing."

How do moms always seem to know when you're holding back? "David and I broke up."

Her mother *tsked.* "I'm sorry, sweetheart. Are you alright?"

"Yeah, I'm alright. I saw it coming."

"You've had quite the string of bad luck when it comes to men, haven't you?" Her mother's tone proved she didn't think *luck* had anything to do with it.

Debbie wasn't falling for it. "Yeah, I really have, haven't I? It's a miracle I haven't gained forty pounds with all this therapeutic ice cream. If we ever install an elevator at the shelter, I'm dead meat. Those stairs are the only thing saving me."

Her mother's silence spoke volumes. Debbie sighed. "I know, Mom. I know. Believe me."

"I just want you to be happy, sweetheart. I want what God has for you, and I can't help but think you're missing out."

Debbie excavated a cluster of fudge pieces in the ice cream. "It's hard not to lose faith in the whole gender when you see what I see every day. And every time I meet a guy I can't help wondering what, if anything, makes him any different. A lot of the women I work with are smart cookies, you know? And yet ..." She chewed the bits of fudge, savoring the burst of heart-soothing chocolate. "I mean, these guys don't come off as abusers at first blush. You can't just look at them and *know*. White collar, blue collar, clerical collar ... from all walks of life. So how do I know the guys I meet aren't going to be like that? I just don't know if I'm willing to take the chance."

"Debbie." The mother voice kicked in. Debbie braced herself for the lecture. "The work you do at the shelter is commendable. You're making a huge difference in the lives of a lot of women. But you're letting it get to you. I understand what drives you—"

"Mom—"

"—but it's not going to change the past. Don't let your life pass you by, sweetheart. That's all I'm saying. You don't need a new job; you just need a new perspective."

"It's not that easy."

"Did I say anything about it being easy?"

Debbie chuckled. "No."

"Well then. 'All things are possible,' as the verse says. So. Enough of that. What flavor is it this time?"

She laughed. "How did you know?"

"Oh please, are you or are you not my daughter? Mine is Peanut Butter Cup."

"Phish Food."

"I should have known."

"Thanks for listening, Mom."

"Thank *you* for listening. I'm going to assume you did, anyway. And you're welcome. Come to dinner Friday; your father and I miss your face at the table."

"Yes, ma'am."

After they'd rung off, Debbie returned the quart to the freezer and hauled her briefcase to the dining room table. She understood her mother's concern, but she had no choice but to live, eat, and breathe her job right now. The place was falling apart.

THE FRESH BRUISE ON THE YOUNG WOMAN's face made Debbie's stomach churn. "Shelly, get Meredith an ice pack, will you?" The counselor nodded and disappeared into the hall while Debbie began the woman's registration. "Is there anyone you'd like to call? Let them know you're safe and where you are?"

Meredith nodded. "Yes, please."

Debbie pushed a phone over the table towards her. "All we ask is that you not give out this address unless you absolutely have to and you trust them not to tell it to your abuser. We don't want your husband to find out where you are." Meredith nodded, eyes wide, and began to dial. Debbie left to give her some privacy and to gather a toiletry kit, a box lunch, and bottle of water for their new guest.

When she got back to the office, she peeked in to make sure Meredith was done with the phone before entering, then set the items on the table. "I got you something to eat, if you're hungry. And here are a few personal items in case you're not able to get yours today."

Meredith readjusted the ice pack to her jaw and gave Debbie a lopsided grin. "Thank you so much."

Debbie smiled. "You're welcome. I'm so glad you made it here. I'm going to go over some of the basics of staying here at the shelter; feel free to eat while I talk; I won't be offended." They exchanged smiles, and Debbie was happy to see Meredith loosening up with her. "When you're done I'll walk you around and get you acclimated to the dorm. You can stay here tonight, of course, but if you want to continue with us after tomorrow you'll need to meet with a caseworker."

She pulled a folder out of the filing cabinet beside her and gave Meredith a quick overview of the facility rules, chore assignments, activities, and staff. Debbie slid the folder to her, then sat back in her chair. "If you decide to stay, then you'll meet with a caseworker tomorrow who will help you determine your goals while you're here. If you need a job, she'll get you enrolled in the job training program. We also have a number of 12-step groups if you decide you want to join one.

"I know it can be pretty overwhelming to have so much information thrown at you, so I'm going to step out for a bit, let you finish your lunch and look over the information in the folder, and then we'll do the orientation. Does that sound alright?"

Meredith nodded, then her lower lip began to tremble. Debbie slid a box of tissues to her and laid a hand on her arm. "You did the right thing, coming here. I know it might not feel that way, but just trust me for now."

Meredith nodded slightly, dabbing at her eyes with a tissue. "Thank you."

"You're welcome. Enjoy your lunch." Debbie gave Meredith's arm a squeeze and left her to eat. Her own stomach was beginning to rumble, so she went back to her office and pulled out the protein bar she'd stuffed in her purse on the way out the door that morning. Her desk was a nightmare of folders, mail, and random items that needed sorting, and she'd resolved not to leave today until it was all taken care of.

She ripped open the protein bar and sat down to survey the

mess. Chomping on the chewy chocolate concoction, she began to rearrange and sort into piles. She kept an eye on the clock, not wanting Meredith to feel abandoned, and after fifteen minutes decided it was time to head back.

She was on her way when Andi, her programs coordinator, saw her from down the hall and jogged to her side. "Hey, got a minute?"

"Sure, hold on." She stuck her head in the green room. "Meredith, I'll be right with you, okay?"

Meredith smiled cautiously. "Okay, thanks."

Andi pulled Debbie into the kitchen. "I'm on my way out for the day, but I wanted to talk to you before I left."

Debbie's insides jiggled. This didn't sound good. "Okay. What's going on?"

"Well," Andi twisted the wedding ring on her finger. "Devon is getting relocated."

"Oh, wow. Where to?"

"Chicago." Debbie winced, and Andi sighed. "I know, I know—I feel awful, Deb."

Debbie waved her hand. "It's life; it happens. God will take care of us. When do you go?"

"End of the month."

"Wow, that's fast."

"Well, we could push it off a couple more weeks, but going now means—oh, never mind what it means. Point is—I'm sorry."

Debbie gave Andi a quick hug. "A new adventure for you, though, right? List me as a reference on your resume, okay?"

"Thanks, Debbie. You're amazing."

They parted ways, and Debbie stood outside the green room, trying not to panic that she was losing her second staff member in less than a month. *You're seeing this, right God? You know we need these positions filled to stay in operation?*

She took a deep breath to clear her head, then rejoined Meredith. It was time to set her anxieties aside; she had a life to help rebuild.

FOUR

Kim was right—Rick didn't call. He showed up at the salon instead.

She was righting a vase of flowers she'd nearly knocked off the receptionist's desk and trying not to feel put out that another meaningless Valentine's Day was getting x-ed off the calendar when a voice behind her said, "Any of those come for you yet?"

Two hours of conversation had made his voice familiar, and a giddy smile slipped across her face. She was embarrassed at the warmth that spread through her body. Certainly he didn't feel this way when he thought about her.

"Not yet, no." She turned. He held out a bouquet twice as big as the one in the vase, a mix of yellow, red, and orange blooms accented with baby's breath. She gasped.

"Well good, because I'd hate to think I had any competition."

She scrambled for something clever to say and failed. "I can't believe you brought those for me. I can't believe you came here!"

"I hope that's okay."

"Of course, but ..." Her eyes went to her next client who had already started walking back to Kim's station. "I can't really talk now."

"Oh, I understand. What time are you done tonight?"

"Six."

"Are you free for dinner?"

She hoped her joy wasn't too plain on her face. "Yes, I am."

"Excellent. I'll pick you up then."

"Okay."

He handed her the flowers, then gave her a little wave as she turned to go to her station.

"Oh, how beautiful!" her client said when Kim set the flowers on the ledge of her station.

"Aren't they?"

"Are they from a guy?"

She laughed. "Yeah."

Her client's eyes brightened. "I didn't know you were seeing someone."

"Well, I'm not." She smiled. "Yet."

JOSHUA CLENCHED THE PHONE TIGHTER against his ear as it rang. *Be there, be there, be there.* When Adam said hello he relaxed just a fraction. "Hi. It's Joshua."

"Hey man, what's up?"

"I officially hate February 14th."

Adam blew out a breath. "Rough day?"

"Very, for obvious reasons."

"I understand. I'm sorry, Josh. Anything I can do?"

"Just pray for me today, will you? It's been a lousy couple weeks on top of the inherent crappiness of today. Lara's parents are threatening to sue for grandparent rights."

"What?" Adam made a noise of disbelief that brought a small smile to Joshua's face. He'd known Adam since college and had seen the face that accompanied that sound a hundred times. It never failed to make him grin at least a little. "On what grounds?"

"They think I'm moving to take Maddie away from them. And they don't think I can adequately care for her since I've lost my job. They have an idea of what they think her life should be like, and it's not the life I'm giving her — that's what it comes down to."

"That's ridiculous."

"You've got that right. They blame me, too, for Lara's death. So part of me wonders how much of this grandparents' rights excuse is just their way of trying to get back at me."

"Twisted."

"Even more so when you realize they're using Maddie as their pawn."

"What are you gonna do? You and Mads are free to crash here if you need to get away for a while."

Joshua chuckled. "Thanks. I'll keep it in mind; we may need a vacation eventually. But at this point I'm just going to keep doing what I'm doing and pray God doesn't let them get to me too much. I don't want to poison Maddie against them, but it's to the point where I need to send her out of the room every time they come over, just in case I flip my lid. I'm certainly not about to leave her alone with them; God knows what they'd try to tell her about me."

"Seriously. So, any news on the job front?"

"No—I actually signed up with a temp agency Monday."

"Oh, wow, flashbacks to college."

Joshua chuckled. "I know. At least I have some marketable skills this time around. I've already got one job lined up to start Monday. I need something long term—or permanent—quick, if for no other reason than to keep me from stressing myself to death."

"Something's bound to happen. Keep the faith. How's the house thing going?"

"I'm almost done with all the little things I needed to do to get it ready to show. Scott is listing it next Friday. Pray for Maddie—she says she's okay with the move, but I don't know how she'll feel when we actually start packing, you know?"

"Yeah, I know what you mean. We'll be praying for both of you; don't be surprised if it's harder for you than you thought it would be."

The thought made Joshua squirm in his desk chair. "I've been trying not to think about it."

"I don't blame you. Can I ask you a really personal question?"

"Um, okay?"

"When do you think you'll start dating again?"

The thought turned his lunch in his stomach. "Oh man, I have no idea. I mean, I hardly even notice women, you know? I can't imagine actually *liking* someone else again. I suppose I will, but I can't fathom it right now. Why are you asking?"

"Well, I met one of Rebecca's book club friends the other day and thought you two might connect. But if you're not ready yet, that's fine."

The suggestion brought to mind Maddie's recent obsession with mothers. They'd be reading a book or watching television, and she'd point to a character and say, "Where's her mother? Does she have one? Is her mother dead too? Is she going to get another one?" It was this last question that made Joshua's heart hurt the most.

He thought he was doing pretty well, for a guy. Lara had always said he was a good "girl dad." He didn't mind playing tea party or brushing Maddie's hair and fixing it in braids and ponytails. It wasn't his idea of the best time in the world—but he *did* love spending time with the little girl whose face so mirrored her mother's, even more so now that her face was the closest he could get to Lara's.

But there were things he looked ahead to with dread. Needing her first bra. Getting her first period. Starry-eyed conversations about her latest crush. Planning her wedding. These were not events fathers should be responsible for, as far as he was concerned. They lay fully in the territory of the mother-daughter relationship. It wasn't so much his discomfort with those topics that made him fear them. It was knowing that Maddie would be wishing her mother was there and that he could never be all she needed.

Joshua pressed his finger and thumb against his squeezed-shut eyes. "Thanks for thinking of me, I guess. I'll let you go now. I just had to talk to someone for a minute."

"No problem, Josh. Rebecca and I are praying for you guys."

"I appreciate it. Tell her I said hi."

After they hung up, Joshua forced himself to get up and finish working on the caulking he was doing in the bathroom. The sooner he got the house fixed up, the sooner Scott could list it, and the sooner he could move out and move on.

At least, that's what he hoped.

VALENTINE'S DAY WAS ALWAYS DEPRESSING at the shelter. Women

fresh from abuse often suffered from self-loathing along with the hatred they felt for their abusers, so every year Debbie centered that day's group therapy session around loving and forgiving themselves. To try to see themselves as lovable and to identify the traits that made them special and unique were exercises that taxed their emotions but were key for the healing they needed. She implored them to see themselves as Christ saw them, to extend to themselves the grace they were always quick to give to the other women at the shelter. It didn't click for everyone, but for the women who took the discussion to heart Debbie always saw a leap in their recovery.

The irony that she was the one imparting these truths, however, was always plain to Debbie. How long had it been since she'd been able to embrace herself with all her foibles and quirks and extend herself a little grace?

Seven years, actually. Or five, depending on which event she was trying not to think about. Not that she was counting.

Oh, who was she kidding? Of course she was.

When she'd cleaned her desk the other day she'd unearthed a picture of her sister that used to hang on the wall of her office. She'd taken it down when the room was painted last year and never put it back up. It just hurt too much. Gina's bright, sixteen-year-old smile would drag Debbie's eyes off whatever paper she was reading or email she was writing, and she'd find herself staring at the picture until her eyes misted. Now she had it taped on the side of the file cabinet drawer, where she only saw it now and then, only had to catch her breath from grief once or twice a day instead of being transfixed a dozen times a day by those deep blue eyes.

How many more years did she have to endure the guilt? How long did she have to carry around the ache of "if only"? Some good had come of it—Safe in His Arms Women's Shelter was what it was because of the work Debbie had done over the last few years—but despite all the women who credited this place as having saved them, she'd trade it all to have Gina back.

Or to regain just a little trust in herself.

Debbie glanced at the clock and realized she was late for a staff meeting. Cursing herself, she gave the file cabinet door a shove and grabbed her notebook from her desk. Work was good. It kept her mind off unpleasant things.

Kim RETURNED HER CURLING IRON to its bay and took one last look at her station to be sure it was cleaned for the evening. Satisfied, she walked to the closet and pulled out her coat and purse, retrieved a lipstick from one of her pockets and applied a fresh coat to her lips. *Done and done. So scoot! What are you waiting for?*

It was 6:03. She'd been done for ten minutes, but she couldn't seem to get herself out the door. The self-hate and despair that were always hovering in the shadows of her mind were threatening to ruin the night before it had begun. *You don't deserve to be happy, remember?*

But she was so lonely, so desperate to be known, to be intimately connected with somebody. She'd longed for a day like this her entire life. Couldn't she turn off the guilt for once?

The remainder of her day after Rick's visit had been surreal. Valentine's Day had never felt any different from any other day of the year. Obligatory cards in elementary school were the only ones she'd ever gotten, with candy hearts and mini packs of M&M's attached. Being given a whole bouquet of roses was like eating a king-size Snickers on an empty stomach—almost too much to handle, especially after a lifetime-long drought of affection.

She'd spent her breaks compiling a list of conversation topics in case there was a lull. They'd discussed so much at the party it had taken her a while to come up with some good questions, but she needed to have some ready just in case. She hated it when conversation stopped. She was much more comfortable when someone was talking, preferably not her.

She looked at her watch again. 6:04. She huddled deeper into her coat and stepped out to the sidewalk. The strip mall parking lot was bustling—no doubt the bistro two doors down and the Maggiano's on the other side of the lot were booked for the night. She scanned the cars for a moment before realizing she didn't know what she was looking for, but no one seemed to be waiting for her. She tamped down the disappointment that was piling like snow on top of the fire she'd had in her heart all day. *You really thought this was going to happen, didn't you?*

The sky was dark with clouds, and the puddles on the sidewalk outside the salon were frozen solid. She leaned against the building, hands deep in her coat pockets, looking at the driver of each car that entered the parking lot. Her stomach twisted with hunger and anxiety, and she hated herself for being so nervous. She tried to imagine how Corrie would be in this situation. *Calm and unaffected by her date being five minutes late, I'm sure. Her stomach probably doesn't even know how to knot.*

In an effort to distract herself, she thought back to the previous afternoon at the Boys & Girls Club. Only one of the girls she worked with had a boyfriend, the others were grousing about Valentine's Day and bemoaning their singleness.

"Girls, believe me, not having a boyfriend when you're sixteen is not the end of the world. You don't see me panicking and I'm eight years older than you."

"Nobody said it's the end of the world," Kea had said. "It just sucks."

"Yeah it does," said Tandi, her fingers twirling a couple of her long, tiny braids. "'Specially when *other folks* is rubbing it in your face."

"I ain't rubbing it in your face." Egypt had looked wounded. "I don't get to talk about my guy when the holiday comes, is that it?"

"Ladies, please," Kim had said with a laugh. "Let's shelve all Valentine's Day talk for now, alright? I wanted to talk about magazines, anyway."

"Which ones?"

"All the ones at the grocery store check stands that scream about fashion and diets and that kind of crap."

"I hate those," La-Neesa had said, shoving her glasses up her nose. "All you poor white women having to get skinny, must drive you crazy."

Kim had frowned. "Poor white women? You girls don't feel that pressure?"

Joelle had given Kim a sympathetic smile. "Naw, not the same way. I think black men appreciate curves."

Tandi had nodded. "Brothas love a booty."

La-Neesa had laughed and given her a high five. "True that!" Kim couldn't help cracking up.

"I know what you're getting at, though, Kim," said Mercedes, the quietest girl of the group. She didn't speak often, but when she did, the other girls always listened. "Even if the message isn't fitting for our specific situation, it's disheartening nonetheless to see women of any culture being told that they *need* to be a certain way. We should strive to be healthy, sure, but even healthy looks different on different people."

"Well said, Sadie."

"Okay, but Kim, what if being a certain way got you what you wanted?"

"What do you mean?"

Egypt had leaned back in her chair, balancing on the rear legs. "Like, if being ten pounds lighter got you a man. It's a small price to pay, all the dieting and working out it would take, if you got a man at the end of it."

Kim had frowned. "Like the end justifying the means?"

Egypt had thought for a second. "If you say so, sure." The other girls laughed.

Kim had shaken her head. "No, I don't think so. You have to stay true to yourself. If you don't respect yourself, then no man is going to respect you, either. Love isn't an important enough 'end' to justify compromising who you are."

They had been easy words to say at the time. But now, huddled against the salon's façade, panicked that she was being stood up, and having a glimmer of hope that there might actually be a day when someone did love her made her realize she couldn't be so sure that she wouldn't do absolutely anything to get someone—Rick specifically—to love her.

She waited three more minutes before letting herself consider going home. She was going to get frostbite sitting out here—

"Kim!"

She jumped. "Oh—hi!"

Rick jogged up, cheeks flushed. "I'm so sorry I'm late. I feel terrible."

"It's alright, I'm just glad you came."

"I said I would, didn't I?" He grinned. "C'mon, it's freezing out here. This place is a zoo, I'm parked around the corner." He took her arm. "Do you like Italian?"

"I do. I love it in fact."

"I pegged you as an Italian food girl. Have you ever been to Alfredo's?"

Kim couldn't stop the smile that stretched her frozen cheeks. "I've heard about that place! Never been, though, a little out of my price range."

He grinned. "I got reservations at 6:30, so we should get there just in time." Rick steered her around cars until they reached his blue hatchback. He opened the door for her and she settled into the cracked leather seat, relieved to get out of the wind even though the car's interior was no warmer. He slid into the driver's side and started the car, cranking up the heat as soon as the engine turned over. "So how was your day?"

"Significantly better once I knew my dinner was taken care of." She grinned and nearly burst when he laughed. *I'm being witty!* "Usually it's hard working Valentine's Day because people are getting dolled up for special dinners and it just rubs my nose in the fact that I'm not doing anything, you know?" She unzipped her jacket as the heat from her own nerves parched her.

"I totally understand. Valentine's Day is pure torture, I agree.

Well, usually, anyway—this one isn't so bad." He flashed her a smile. She thawed even more.

They arrived at Alfredo's just in time for their reservation. Rick opened the car door for her and took her arm like he had in the parking lot. He even beat the seating host to her chair to pull it out for her. She felt like underdressed royalty.

The waitress came and set a basket of breadsticks between them. "Welcome to Alfredo's and Happy Valentine's Day. Are you celebrating tonight?"

Embarrassed, Kim ducked her head. "Oh, we're just, um—"

"—on our first date," Rick finished, flashing Kim a smile.

"How romantic!" The waitress clasped her hands. "I'll get you an appetizer on the house to celebrate. What can I get you to drink?"

"Do you drink wine?" Rick asked Kim.

"I don't usually, but just because I've never learned how to pick the right one."

Rick picked up the wine list and scanned it. "I'll have a glass of the Barbera d'Alba, and the lady will have the Chianti."

The lady. Kim sat up straighter, intent on earning the title. "Thank you, Rick."

"You're welcome. I hope you like it. I don't know a lot about wine, but I know what I like, and usually other people like it too."

They sat in silence for a minute, and Kim began to panic. Her carefully compiled list of topics fled her memory, and she grew self-conscious under his unwavering stare. She definitely didn't feel like a lady. More like an awkward adolescent.

"You're blushing."

Kim's hands patted her cheeks. "Am I?"

"Yes. I'm sorry—am I embarrassing you?"

"No, no—I mean, I'm just … feeling a little under the microscope. I'll be honest, I don't go on a lot of dates. And I'm not very good at small talk. I thought of all sorts of things while I was at work that I was going to ask you, but now I can't remember any of them."

He flashed a disarming smile that chased away her anxiety. "I don't go on a lot of dates, either. In fact, the girl I just broke up with—Karen—was the first girl I'd ever dated long-term. Not that we were that long-term, but longer than just a couple dates."

"How did you two meet?"

He made a face. "At a bar. Isn't that lame? It sounds lame to admit it, anyway." He shrugged. "She seemed sweet in the beginning, but she changed after a while. Then she started getting all ... I don't know, distant and accusing. Not attractive. And then she left me—*she* left *me!*" He shook his head, a muscle twitching in his jaw. He took a long drink on his water and resumed. "Anyway, having been in a relationship makes it that much worse to *not* be in one, you know? Then you know what you're missing." He stared at the space between them for a moment, then sat up straighter and gave his head a small shake. "Sorry, kinda went off for a minute there."

"I understand. It must have really hurt for her to treat you like that."

"It did." He rewarded her understanding with another ice-melting smile. "Thank you for letting me get that off my chest."

"I'm glad you felt comfortable telling me." She really did. For him to be willing to open up to her must mean he really did like her. She hoped she'd have the chance to show him she wouldn't be like Karen.

The waitress came back with their appetizer and wine and asked for their order.

"I haven't even looked at the menu," Kim said with a laugh.

"I don't need to look," Rick said as Kim scrambled to scan the entrees. "I'll have the pollo parmesan, and the lady will have the ... pollo marsala. How does that sound, Kim?"

"Oh—um ..." she glanced at the description and shrugged. "I've never had it before, but it sounds good. Thanks."

The waitress took the menus and Rick frowned. "I hope that was alright."

"Oh, sure. I've never had someone order for me before."

"I've had that dish here a couple times. It's very good. I really think you'll love it."

She spread her napkin on her lap and picked up her wine. "I'm sure I will." She took a sip and tried not to make a face at its strong flavor. It wasn't the kind of drink she could imagine ever being in the mood for, but she didn't mind enduring it tonight.

Rick set his glass back down. "So how about you?"

"Um, what about me?"

"What happened to your last relationship?"

"Oh, well ..." She could feel the heat creeping back into her cheeks. "Actually, I've never had a boyfriend."

"You're kidding me."

"No." She tried to add a little laugh that said, "What do I care?" but it came out more like a strangled cough.

"I can't believe that! You're so easy to talk to, and so kind, and pretty. Did you go to all girls' schools or something?"

That did make her laugh. "Ah, no. Public school all the way. But when I was a kid ..." She'd never told any of her adult friends about her childhood. The only people who'd ever known had been some of her friends in school, but after high school graduation they'd all gone off to college. She'd liked the fact that no one knew anymore. But she also longed to be so close to someone they'd not only know she'd been in the system, they'd know all the circumstances surrounding her placements, and the names of her social workers, and why the families she'd been assigned to had eventually returned her.

Go for it.

"When I was a kid, I was in foster care. Grew up in it, actually. Which means, by the time I was old enough to date, everyone knew I was weird and didn't have a family, and my clothes were lame, and I seemed to give off this vibe that said ..." She searched for the word. *Unlovable? Worthless? Damaged?* "Uninteresting." The other words suited better, but she wasn't about to admit that to Rick. "Anyway, I got used to being alone and just haven't tried to make myself available."

Rick shook his head, but he was smiling. "I knew there was a reason we connected so well."

"Why? What do you mean?"

Rick leaned in, face shining. "I was a foster kid too."

Her heart stopped. "No way!"

"Way!"

They laughed together at the lame phrase, then Kim said, "But not here in Ann Arbor, right? Because I would have seen you."

"No, not here. Ohio. I moved here to Michigan after I graduated from high school. Worked at Ford for a while, then went to night school for graphic design."

"Wow, good for you."

"Thanks." He looked genuinely appreciative of her encouragement, and Kim felt again the swell of desire to show him she was on his side.

Rick sat back and folded his arms over his chest. "I can't believe you were in foster care too. Whole life?"

"Basically. I was five when I went in. You?"

"Nine. But I was only in for a few years."

"Were you reunited with your family then?" His face clouded and she instantly regretted asking. "I'm sorry, you don't have to answer that. I shouldn't have asked."

"No, you had no way to know, don't feel bad." He took a sip of his wine. "I was, but I shouldn't have been. My dad was a great actor and had everyone fooled. He did all their classes and all the treatment and all the crap the court said he had to do before he could have me back, but he was still an alcoholic and he still beat me like he had before family services removed me. But after being in the system I knew I didn't want to go back — better the devil you know than the devil you don't, know what I mean? I didn't want to get placed with any more foster families. I figured I might as well stay with my dad, who I at least could predict."

"So, your mom wasn't in the picture then."

"Nope. Never knew her. Just dad and me as far back as I can remember."

"I'm so sorry."

He shrugged. "It's life. How about you?"

Kim took a deep breath to calm the queasiness that began whenever she was asked about her childhood. "Didn't have a dad; it was just mom and me. I don't have a lot of memories about her. Most of what I know I found out from my caseworker. When I was twelve they told me she'd been killed in a car accident." She shrugged. "There wasn't any other family to take me, so I had to stay in the system."

"That's so tragic."

She forced a grin. "Yeah, I'd say. Though, so is your story."

Rick took a breadstick and waved it between them. "This is way too depressing for a first date, especially on Valentine's Day. We'll talk about all this stuff again some other time. Agreed?"

"Agreed."

"Excellent. And here comes our appetizer."

They spent the rest of the evening exploring more pleasant topics, and by the time they'd finished dessert Kim felt like she'd known Rick her whole life. It wasn't just the shared experience of the foster system. It was their easy conversation, his openness and frank demeanor, and the dozens of little shared enjoyments—favorite movies, favorite foods. When they left the restaurant, she wasn't surprised when his hand sought and held hers while they dodged frozen puddles in the potholed parking lot.

When they arrived back at her apartment, Rick parked in a visitor space and walked her to the door. "Do you want to come up for some hot chocolate or something?" she asked. "Not very sophisticated, but it sounded better than orange juice, which is about the only other thing I could offer you."

He laughed, his breath clouding the air. "I wish I could, but I think if I did I would find it very difficult to leave."

The look on his face made her tongue-tied. This was the kind of face she imagined on men in the romance novels she read, when they were burning with desire for the heroine. She never thought she'd inspire it. "Well, um, stop by any time."

"I will."

"Good night."

He looked about to speak, but instead his hands reached out and landed gently on her cheeks, and before she could react, he was kissing her.

Her brain felt scrambled. She followed his lead, both embarrassed at her lack of experience and eager to communicate her most definite permission. When he finally backed away, she had to lean against the door to steady herself.

He spoke slowly. "I hope it was okay that I did that."

Kim swallowed and nodded, her brain still fuzzy.

He smiled, his entire face lighting up. "Good night, Kim."

She managed to find her voice. "Good night, Rick."

She watched him walk away, hands thrust into his pockets and shoulders hunched against the wind that was picking up. She fumbled her key into the lock and somehow made her way upstairs despite her shaking legs. She let herself in to the apartment where Corrie sat at the table with papers spread out in front of her. "Wow, you're home late. I was starting to worry."

"Oh, gosh—I'm sorry."

"No problem. Just glad you're okay."

Kim smiled. "Yeah, I'm okay."

Very okay.

FIVE

I don't know how I'm going to do this.

Joshua surveyed the couch where Lara's clothes were piled by season. He'd been all gung-ho when he'd started the project after putting Maddie to bed. But now he could hardly see what he was doing, the memories of Lara in each dress, each blouse, each skirt so vivid in front of him. He had hoped to choose a few special outfits to save for Maddie and then box the rest for Goodwill, but now every outfit seemed special. Even the T-shirts she'd only worn to the gym or while gardening had a handful of memories attached. How could he get rid of any of them?

Am I completely crazy with this move? Can I seriously pack up and leave the first real home we had together? How can I take Maddie away from the one place where she can best remember her mother? It's a stupid idea, isn't it? I never should have considered it. Not that it's too late, I guess, but ...

He sat with a black cocktail dress clutched in his hands, eyes trained on but not really seeing the wedding photo above the mantle. Joshua whispered his lament to God. "But I feel like I'm suffocating here. And when I *do* start dating, I don't know if I could bring another woman here and not feel like she was intruding. Or like I was cheating.

"And as difficult as it is to consider dating again, I'm going to have to, if for no other reason than to find Maddie a mother. She's got me a little nervous about all the mother-talk. She *needs* a mother, or at least a woman in her life, and who is that going to be? Certainly not Alisha. Not my mom, who's a thousand miles away."

He tossed down the dress and stood, pacing aimlessly. "And

now George and Alisha are pulling this grandparents' rights crap! They can't possibly have a chance. I shouldn't be worried about that, right?" He rubbed a hand over his face.

"God, I'm stuck. And I'm scared. Am I doing the right thing? Am I going to regret this?" He looked again at the picture of Lara, glowing in her fairy tale wedding dress. She'd had it specially preserved after the wedding, "in case we ever have a girl and Vera Wang knockoffs are still in fashion." The alternative — staying here, haunted day and night by the ghost of Lara past — was aging him. And he couldn't afford to get older any faster than nature intended, not with a four-year-old to keep up with.

"You're going to have to do some serious work on me, God. Starting now, or else I'm going to end up going to sleep right here on these clothes." He sat again, picked up the cocktail dress, and after staring at it for a while, put it back on its hanger. The dress she'd worn the night he'd proposed. Definitely special.

Kim pulled her makeup bag from her purse, humming along with the music playing over the salon's speakers. She stared at herself in her station's mirror and dabbed her nose with powder. She'd never thought about her makeup after applying it in the morning, but now she never left home without the bag so she could freshen up before Rick picked her up after work.

"Another date, huh?" Emma stopped by, leaning against the counter. "You two are really racking them up."

Kim smiled. "Yup."

"Why don't you just put that on in the morning before you come in?"

Kim whisked the blush brush over her cheeks. "I do. But it doesn't stay fresh. I look all wilted at the end of the day if I do that."

Emma smirked. "A girl goes through that much hassle to look good, it means she's got it bad."

Kim said nothing, but her eyes gave it away. Emma laughed. "Have fun tonight."

They'd gone out nearly every night since their first date two weeks ago. Despite how their evenings started—restaurant, mall food court, take-out, or foraging for leftovers in one of their kitchens—lately they'd all ended the same, with a make-out session that stopped only with the appearance of Corrie or with Kim's begrudging insistence that she be getting home.

She gave her nose a final pat, then rummaged in the bag for her eye shadow. Her stomach gave a little flutter as she swiped the color across her eyelids. She was excited to talk to Rick about the idea she'd come up with that morning for a mobile salon business. She and Suzi had brainstormed marketing and equipment needs over lunch, and it had been all she could think about for the rest of the afternoon. She knew Rick would be able to come up with even more ideas. He had that kind of a mind. Maybe he would be able to help her put a business plan together.

Rick was waiting on the sidewalk when she came out. "Hey you."

"Hey *you.*" He kissed her and took her hand, leading her to his car. "So what are we cooking tonight?"

"You have two choices: homemade pizza or ravioli."

"Pizza for sure."

"Oh good. I wanted to give you a choice but that's what I was hoping you'd say." They chatted on the short drive to the grocery store, then wandered down the aisles, picking up their ingredients. After paying for their groceries, they made a mad dash through freezing rain to Rick's car, where they passed the time while the car heated by engaging in a serious kiss that steamed the windows. Finally Kim thumped Rick's chest with her mittened hands. "I'm hungry!"

"Okay, okay." He grinned. "We'll pick up where we left off after we eat."

Once home, they made their pizza, then sat at the table to eat a nacho appetizer while it baked. "So I came up with this awesome idea today," Kim said after munching a handful of chips. "I want to start a mobile salon business."

Rick froze with a chip halfway into his mouth. "What? Why?"

"I'm getting a little bored, honestly. I like doing hair, and I'm good at it, but I think I'd enjoy the freedom of my own business. Plus, I think I'd be—"

"No, bad idea." He shook his head and dusted salt from his hands. "Don't you listen to the news? The economy sucks right now. It would be a terrible idea to try to start a business. Besides, you're not a businesswoman. You know how much paperwork there is with your own business? The licensing, the taxes—you wouldn't be able to handle it."

Her chest burned with wounded pride and embarrassment. "Well ... but I thought maybe you'd be able to help me. I know I'm not a genius, but between the two of us—"

He laughed, his tone scornful. "Like what, you'd hire me? I'd be your employee? No way I'd want my girlfriend to be my boss."

Speechless, she ducked her head to hide the tears that brimmed and stood to find something to occupy her in the kitchen. She searched for a retort but all she came up with was, "Well then, never mind I guess."

He made a noise of frustration and came up behind her. He wrapped his arms around her waist and rested his head on her shoulder. "Sweetheart, look, I'm sorry. But seriously, you're better off staying where you are. I'd just hate to see you get disappointed when it didn't work out."

Kim sniffed and shrugged him away. "I can't believe you don't have more confidence in me. If you had come to me with the same idea, I would have been totally supportive and would have offered to do anything to help you."

"Kim, I said I'm sorry. What else do you want me to say?"

"I want you to say, 'Hey, great idea, let's go for it!'"

"So you want me to lie? You want me to set you up for failure?"

"How do you know I'd fail?"

He let out a terse laugh. "Look, Kim, the fact that you think this is a good idea shows that you don't know what you're talking about.

Trust me, it would fail." He wrapped his arms around her again, pulling her closer despite her resistance. "I'm just looking out for you, Kim. I care about you. I don't want to see you hurt."

He's just looking out for me. He cares about me. She soaked up his words, trying to soothe her wounds with his sentiments. He smiled when she allowed herself to relax in his embrace. "But see, this is a great example of why we work so well together. We balance each other out, we're each strong in different ways. I know more about business stuff than you do, but I'm sure there will be situations in the future where you can help me out."

He kissed her and she tried to let go of the anger and hurt that were still simmering in her heart. She had to admit he was right—she didn't have a mind for business. And she could see how it could be weird—for both of them—if she was his boss. *Though if we went at it as equal partners . . .* She pushed the thought away. The economy would still be in shambles, like he'd said. Best to just put the whole idea to rest. *Get over it, move on, don't ruin the rest of the evening with pouting.*

"Thanks for wanting to take care of me," she said when they broke their kiss.

"You're welcome. How could I not? You're beautiful, you're sweet, you're so good to me—taking care of you is the least I could do."

"I'm not just some rebound girl now, am I? You are fresh from another relationship, you know. I've heard stories about these kinds of things."

"Not on your life." He tightened his arms around her, kissing her again. "I couldn't ever leave you. You're all mine."

Shawnee popped her head into Debbie's office. "A new guest just arrived. Do you have time to process her or should I see if Candice can do it?"

Debbie looked at her watch. "I'll do it. Get her comfortable and grab a box lunch for her if she needs it. Let me know when she's ready."

Shawnee closed the door behind her and Debbie sagged in her

seat. She knew how much was already on Candice's plate. Hers was no less full, but she had to be careful not to burn out her remaining staff now that Andi was gone. *Just don't let* me *get burned out either, God.*

She picked up another resume from the stack, scanning it for the skill-set she needed for their fund-raising and grant-writing position. It was one of the few parts of running the shelter for which she had no competence, and it wasn't the kind of job she could divvy up amongst the other staff. It was also one of the most important positions, since it was the one that kept them in business.

The applicant's resume was lacking in too many areas; she set it on her reject pile and took another with a sigh. There were so many jobless people in Ann Arbor, but none of them had the training she was looking for.

Shawnee returned, handing Debbie the new arrival's intake form. "She's not hungry, Deb. She's ready for you."

"Thanks Shawnee, I'll be right there." She stood and pulled her notebook and a welcome packet from her desk drawer, then said a prayer as she made her way to the green room. *Speak to this woman, Lord. Speak through the staff and the other women here. Open her eyes to her worth as your creation and to your existence. Break the cycle of abuse in her life.* She grabbed a bottle of water for herself from the kitchen, then walked into the green room and lost her breath.

The young woman couldn't have been more than twenty, but it wasn't her age that struck Debbie with such force. It was her face, her eyes, her build—all striking in their resemblance to Gina.

Debbie reached out a hand to her sister's doppelganger and hoped her shock was not plain on her face. "Hi Stacia, I'm Debbie. Welcome to the shelter." Stacia shook her hand quickly, then returned her arm to her midsection, holding onto her middle as though her insides might fall out. "I'm so glad you made it here today." Debbie sat down and opened her water, then took a long drink before meeting again the dull stare of those sapphire eyes.

Stacia spoke so softly Debbie had to lean in to hear her. "I haven't slept in a few days. He was manic and made me stay up with him. I'm really tired. Could I maybe take a nap somewhere?"

Debbie's heart ached for the young woman. She handed her the welcome folder and helped her gather her things, then ushered her to her dorm room, explaining that they could go through her orientation later. After she got Stacia settled into her room, Debbie made a beeline for her office, where she shut the door and collapsed in her chair.

She looked just like her, God. Deep breaths kept her from crying, but her thoughts were overtaken with the last conversation she'd ever had with her sister.

"Look Gina, it's your own fault. If he's hurting you and you're not breaking up with him, then you have no one to blame but yourself."

"It's not that easy, Deb. Why are you being so judgmental?"

"I'm not, I'm just calling a spade a spade. If you're not happy, get out of the relationship. I don't see why that's complicated."

"Because I love him!"

"You're seventeen, Gina. What on earth do you know about being in love?"

"Mom and Dad met when they were fifteen."

"Yeah, but Dad never hit her. How can you love someone who hits you?"

"If I'd wanted a lecture I would have called Mom. Can't you just listen and help me like a sister is supposed to?"

"I am listening, *and I am* helping. *I hear you saying your boyfriend hits you. I'm helping you by telling you to get your head straight and leave him. What else do you want me to do?"*

"I should have known better than to expect any sympathy from the golden child."

"Oh please, Gina, don't pull out that old song and dance."

"Just forget it. Good-bye."

"Gina, come on, don't hang up— "

But the line had already been dead.

Debbie rubbed a hand over her eyes and murmured a prayer

aloud in the silence of her office. "God, I'm trying to redeem myself here. I know I've asked for forgiveness a thousand times. I know you've already given it. I'm sorry it doesn't seem to stick. But did you have to throw Gina's virtual twin in my face?"

She wiped tears from her cheeks and blew her nose, then sat up and chugged half her water. She wasn't going to do anyone any good if all she did was throw herself a pity party. She had a shelter to run, and right now it was two staff members short of optimal. Until Stacia awoke, she'd make it her mission to find some potential hires, and then she'd pour herself into getting Stacia well.

Maybe it would heal a little bit of the hurt.

SIX

Kim had forgotten she was supposed to be miserable.

The last three months had been pure bliss. Meeting Rick had changed her life. She hadn't picked up a romance book in weeks, and not just because she didn't have time to read anymore. She'd even lost a few pounds, the result of dinners left cold on the plate while their conversation meandered from one random subject to another. She was happy. She was loved. Finally, after a life of independence and solitude, she was loved.

But the morning of their three-month anniversary she awoke in a cold sweat, those haunting eyes staring at her from inside her mind, the ungodly scream echoing in her ears even when the pillow was clamped over her head. She huddled beneath the sheets, trembling, knowing she'd had her fun but now it was over. She'd had twelve weeks of respite from the dream. Now it was back, along with the guilt that squeezed her chest and soured her stomach.

If he knew . . .

She shook the thought from her mind. If he knew, he would leave her. How could he love someone who was so cold-hearted?

The self-loathing she had worn like a stifling winter coat for the last seven years enveloped her once more. She didn't remember losing it, but Rick's attention and ardor had slipped it off when she hadn't been looking. Now, as she looked in the mirror above her dresser, her face seemed altered, stark. The bright eyes and perma-smile that their relationship had given her were gone. This was who she really was. And when Rick found out, he would be gone.

"I'm so stupid. Stupid, stupid, *stupid*," she muttered, the words hissed through clenched teeth. Her sins scrolled like film credits through her mind, reminding her of reality. She should have known better than to think anyone's love could change who she really was.

Kim sat on the edge of her bed, fists clenched on her knees, head bowed by the weight of guilt and anger that were stronger than they had ever been. And now they were compounded by fear—fear of losing Rick, fear of her secret being discovered. Her stomach roiled, her chest squeezed. *You're going to lose it all. Rick, security, peace—all of it, gone.* She felt like she was suffocating, like she would explode. She didn't know what to do. She needed a release, to let out the pressure of her self-loathing before she went crazy.

Her eyes landed on her desk and the paring knife she'd used to slice an apple the night before. She snatched it up and swiped it across her fingers before she could think about it.

It was like slashing a tire. The intensity of her emotions slowly deflated as blood welled up from the cuts. She panted, drawing ragged breaths as though she'd run a mile. And over it all, sweet relief.

She sank onto the bed again, hand open and trembling in front of her, and stared at the wounds. The buzz in her head dissipated until all she heard was her own breathing and the birds singing in the May morning sunshine. It was a miracle. Why hadn't she done this before? After all these years she had a way to ease her pain.

Though now she had a new problem. Her fingers were bloody, the sting was intensifying, and she had to be at work in half an hour. How was she going to do hair with her hand like this?

Knowing her own medicine cabinet was empty of bandages, she ran to Corrie's bathroom and discovered three boxes of them in various sizes. She pulled four from the standard-size box and fumbled them out of their paper packaging. Once they were all in place, she brought the wrappers to her own bathroom trash can, then went to the kitchen to fix breakfast.

Sitting calmly and eating her bowl of cornflakes just seemed wrong. Everything felt surreal, like she'd woken up in an alternate universe. Her hand pulsed with each heartbeat, the dull pain reminding her of her transgression. *What will I tell everyone? And how am I going to wash hair?* She concocted a story to explain her injury as she ate and resigned herself to asking one of the other girls to do the shampooing for her clients.

When she arrived at the salon a little before ten, she saw a vase of roses on the table. A small white envelope was propped against it, her named scrawled in purple pen. She opened the envelope and slid out the small card that read, "Happy anniversary to my Kim. See you tonight. Love, Rick." She pocketed the card and fingered one of the rose's velvety pink petals. *I don't deserve him.*

"What's the occasion?" Rumiko asked as she passed by. "I saw the delivery guy drop them off."

"Our three-month anniversary." She smiled a little. "He's so sweet."

"Wow, three months already? You in it for the long haul, you think?"

"I don't know. But I don't want to jinx it by even thinking about where it might go, or how long it will last. I'm just going to enjoy it while—"

Rumiko grasped Kim's wrist. "Kim, your fingers! What did you do?"

Kim made a noise of irritation, gently pulling her hand away and curling her fingers in to hide the bloody bandages. "I'm such an idiot. I fumbled a knife and grabbed the blade instead of the handle when it was falling."

Rumiko tsked. "You poor thing. You alright?"

"Yeah, it's fine, not even that deep."

"Well that's good."

Kim took one more sniff of the roses. "I need to get my station in order. See you later."

She turned her attention to her station, praying Rumiko didn't notice how Kim couldn't look her in the eyes.

"BABY, WHAT DID YOU DO?"

Rick held Kim's hand in his, examining the bandages that were now grubby and pulling away from her skin at the edges. "Just being klutzy and stupid. I'm fine."

He kissed her palm and patted her hand back into her lap. "What were you doing?"

She rolled her eyes, then turned them to the menu. "Dropped a knife and grabbed for it, but I grabbed the blade and not the handle." She flashed him a rueful grin. "Told you I was a klutz."

He laughed a little. "Yeah, that *was* stupid." He opened the wine list and scanned the pages, then set it aside in favor of the menu. "You have to have the duck, I hear it's amazing."

She wrinkled her nose. "Duck? I've never had it before. I think that's a little too close to reality for me. I think I'll have a filet."

"Well, I was going to get a filet, so we'll get you the duck and then we can share."

"Rick, I—"

"Have you decided what you'd like?" Their waitress appeared tableside, smiling, then looked to Kim. "For you, miss?"

"I'm going to have the fil—"

"The duck," Rick said. "She'll have the duck, and I'll have the filet, medium rare please. And a glass of Pinot Noir for me and Australian Shiraz for her."

Kim frowned, but waited until the waitress was gone to speak. "Rick, that's not what I wanted. And you've gotten that wine for me before and I didn't like it, remember?"

Rick narrowed his eyes slightly. "You didn't give it a chance last time. I think you'll like it this time around. It's even better with duck than it is with chicken. And like I said, we'll share."

"Why didn't you get the duck then?"

"Does it matter who gets what, if we're trading anyway?"

Kim huffed. "Well, if I don't like the duck, then yes, it matters, because then what am I going to eat?"

"Look." Rick waved his hand, batting at the angry words that hung in the air between them, then took a deep breath and sighed.

"I'm sorry, I'm sorry, Kim. I just really thought you'd like it, that's all. I should have just kept my mouth shut."

His countenance drooped, and Kim felt like crap. *Way to ruin the mood, Kim.* She reached across the table, hand held out in a gesture of surrender. "I'm sorry, too. I always like the things you order for me, I should have just trusted you. Don't be mad, okay? I'm sorry if I spoiled the night."

Rick tipped his head side to side, as though considering her apology, then took her hand and gave it a squeeze. "It's okay, babe. I forgive you. My emotions always go a little haywire when big things are going on—and, I consider today a pretty big thing."

She smiled. "Yeah?"

"Absolutely. Three months? That's, like, the relational equivalent of two years these days." She laughed along with him, relieved he didn't seem mad anymore. But then he sobered. "I have to admit, I feel a bit on edge, too, because I'm a little nervous."

"Nervous? About what, our anniversary?"

"No, no, not dinner." He released her hand and sat back a moment, then cleared his throat and leaned forward again, taking her hand once more. "Kim, I'd like to ask you something."

Her heart began to race. "What?"

"I know it might seem a little soon, but ... I've never felt like this about anyone before. You're amazing. I feel like I've known you forever."

Her mouth went dry. "Me too."

He looked relieved. "Good." He stared at her for a moment, then said, "Would you move in with me?"

"Oh. *Oh.* Really?"

"Yeah!"

"Oh—Rick, I don't know, I've never even thought about living with someone."

"Well, think about it!" He sat back, grinning. "It would be perfect. We'd be able to see each other so much more. No more slinking back home late at night, no more having to worry about your roommate walking in on us." He wagged his eyebrows and squeezed her hand.

Her laughter sounded nervous to her ears. She hoped he didn't hear it that way. "Rick—I'm so flattered. I can't believe you asked."

"It's the most logical next step. We're practically living together as it is, with all the time we spend together. Why not make life easier for ourselves?"

It made sense. Of course it did. And yet she felt on the edge of panic at the thought. She had already grown anxious the two or three nights that she ended up in bed with him, worried that she'd end up like her mother—pregnant and alone. If they were living together, how much more often would they test the reliability of her birth control? And when they broke up, which was bound to happen eventually, she'd be homeless.

The light in his eyes faded as her answer took longer in coming. "I thought you'd be excited about this. I thought you'd be as happy about it as I am."

"Rick, I'm sorry—"

"I love you, Kim. Seriously. I love you. And I thought you loved me too."

"I do—"

"No, no you don't." He let go of her hand and sat back, crossed his arms over his chest and glowered at her across the table. "If you did you'd say yes. Why would you not want to live with someone you love? With someone who loves you? Unless there's someone else."

Kim's jaw dropped. "Someone else? Of course there isn't, Rick. That's ridiculous."

"Then prove it. Prove that you really love me. Because I'm not in this relationship just to have fun, Kim. If you're not committed, then I'm gone."

A tornado of emotion was ripping her apart. Of course she loved him. Never in her life had she thought she'd find someone who felt this way about her. But they'd only been together for three months, and she couldn't deny the concern she felt at the proposition. But was it enough to risk losing him?

"Okay." *It's just cold feet.* "Of course I want to move in with you. You just … took me by surprise, that's all. I wasn't expecting it." She shut her mouth to stop the rambling, then drew a deep breath. "Let's move in together."

His eyes lit up and Kim knew she'd done the right thing. She loved that she could make him so happy.

"It's gonna be awesome, waking up next to you every morning," he said, eyes dancing, his smile nearly pulling right past his cheeks. "Can you get out of your lease early? Let's do it next weekend." He continued to talk but she didn't hear him. Her mind was racing with the realization of what she'd just agreed to.

It didn't take long for Rick to realize she wasn't as wrapped up in the idea as he was. He stopped and gave her a cautious look. "Already rethinking things?"

Don't do anything else to ruin it. "No, no, I'm just — overwhelmed. It's a lot to think about." She forced a smile and took a sip of her water to occupy her nervous hands. Her wounded fingers began to throb.

"I understand, baby." He squeezed her good hand across the table. "We'll make a list. The actual move shouldn't be too bad; it's not like you have a lot. And you don't have to do everything all at once. I'll help you out however I can." He gazed at her, his head shaking slightly. "How did I get so lucky?"

Kim felt a blush creeping into her cheeks. "I could ask the same thing."

"We're quite a pair, aren't we?" Rick laughed and settled back in his seat, looking happy and content. Kim pushed down the niggling concern that itched in her chest and let herself be drawn in by his good mood.

Everything will be fine. You'll see. Better than fine, even — you'll be a family.

"Hey Corrie, I need to talk to you a minute."

A few days had passed since Kim and Rick had celebrated their anniversary, but Kim kept missing opportunities — sometimes on purpose — to talk to Corrie. Rick was getting impatient, though, and Kim didn't want to make him mad. Resigning herself to the path she was taking, she stayed up late to wait for her roommate to get home so she could talk to her about moving out.

"Do you have a minute?" she asked Corrie when she finally walked in.

"Sure, as long as you don't mind if I eat. I'm starving. What's up?"

Kim followed her to the kitchen and leaned against the counter. "I know my lease isn't up for another three months, but I wanted to see if it would be alright with you if I moved out early."

Corrie turned from the fridge with a look of surprise. "You're moving out? Where to?"

"I'm moving in with Rick."

Corrie's eyebrows arched. "Really? Wow."

Kim chuckled. "Yeah."

"You guys have only been dating for, like —"

"Three months."

"And you're moving in together now. That seems really ... fast."

Kim bristled inside but tried not to show it. "Well, when you know, you know, right?"

Corrie shrugged slightly and turned back to the open fridge. "Can't argue with that." She pulled leftovers from a shelf and said, "Adam asked the other day if I knew how it was going with you two. He seemed ... concerned."

"Adam — the guy Rick works with? Why would he be concerned?"

"I don't know. He mentioned something about Rick's last girlfriend, and how things got pretty crazy at the end, or something like that."

Kim huffed. "His ex was a drama queen."

"You met her?"

"No, Rick told me about her and their relationship. She dumped him."

Corrie nodded. "Ah."

This conversation was not going at all like she'd hoped it would. "I don't think Rick and Adam are very close friends. I wouldn't trust his view of things." She stood a little straighter. "Besides, Rick and I have a lot more in common than he did with his old girlfriend. We understand each other a lot better."

Corrie seemed to consider this, then shrugged. "Well, good luck then. Why don't you give me rent for next month and we'll call it even."

"Sounds fair. Thanks for letting me out of the lease early."

"No problem. When do you think you'll move?"

"Probably Sunday, since the salon is closed."

"Okay. Hand me that towel, would you?" Kim pulled the towel from the drawer's handle and held it out to Corrie, who frowned as she looked at Kim's arm. "There's something on your sleeve. A stain or something." She leaned over and pointed to the long white sleeve where a small dark red spot had formed.

Kim gasped, covering the spot with her hand. "I had a—a bandage on, it must have come off." Trying not to look panicked, she pushed away from the counter and headed for her room.

"What did you do?" Corrie called. "That's a weird place to get hurt."

Kim pulled up her sleeve in the safety of her room. "Yeah, it was ... at work today. Collided with the receptionist. She had a—a box cutter, after opening a shipment of product." The lie coalesced from her racing thoughts and she tried to pass her demeanor off as irritated rather than alarmed. She muttered—loudly, so Corrie would hear her—about hoping she hadn't ruined her work shirt, then shut the door and stripped off the shirt to examine the wound where she'd cut herself an hour earlier.

The bandage hadn't come off—it was just too small. Blood had oozed from beyond the gauze. She grabbed another bandage from the box she'd bought and put it in place of the first, though it didn't appear to be bleeding anymore.

More guilt and shame compounded the guilt and shame she lived with all the time. What if Corrie had caught her? What if it had been Rick who had seen it? But she knew she couldn't stop. Not yet. For now, the relief she gained from each slice outweighed the risks.

She just had to be more careful.

SEVEN

Joshua stepped into the kitchen just in time to hear the phone ring. It was his realtor, Scott, with news of an offer on the house. Joshua knew he had to jump on the opportunity but wasn't ready to pack up and leave the house so soon. He hadn't found another place for he and Maddie to live yet, and with temp positions as his only income now, he was loathe to take time from his job hunting to start house hunting.

After hanging up with Scott, Joshua logged into the websites where he'd posted his resume and searched for half an hour for new job postings, but as usual there was nothing.

I don't remember praying for patience or faith, Lord. What's up?

The classifieds from Sunday's paper were still on the corner of his desk, so he read through them again, this time allowing himself to consider anything that made more than minimum wage and didn't sound like something college kids did on their summer vacations. *It doesn't even have to be a new career. Just a job that will pay the bills. C'mon, God, throw me a rope, here.* But even as he scanned the listings he knew there weren't any for him there.

The temp jobs weren't coming as often as he needed. He couldn't afford many more days like this—days spent at home, staring at the computer, begging God to put his resume in front of the right person. He was doing everything he could, but with unemployment so high, he knew the only way he'd find a job was by God making the connection.

"This is nuts." He stood, running his hands through his hair and staring out the window. He had an hour before he needed to pick up Maddie. As much as it hurt his pride, it was time to start going after any full-time job that would get him a paycheck. Who cared if it was minimum wage? A little money was better than none.

He opened the classifieds once more and started at the top. He skipped the first three ads, which asked for experience in their field, then called the next six. Each one ended the same way—"Thanks, but you're overqualified." He didn't care if their jobs were "beneath" him—but they did.

He called a few more before leaving to pick up Maddie but only got more of the same. When he arrived at the preschool, a woman he'd never seen before was waiting near the front door, talking on her cell phone. He didn't recognize her as one of the usual moms, and he couldn't help overhearing her phone conversation.

"But I'm leaving Wednesday for New York. I can't do it! Are you *sure* none of the others could be trained for it? Not even Tammy? . . . Alright, well, post an ad, then."

Joshua was dying to break in and ask what kind of ad they were going to post, but gave the woman a brief smile instead and passed her to enter the building.

He was tying Maddie's shoes when the woman appeared behind him. One of the girls came running from the dress-up corner, shouting, "Aunt Lori! Where's Mom?"

"Hey kiddo! She got stuck in traffic coming back from Detroit and asked me to come get you. Go get your things and I'll talk to your teacher."

"Who is that?" Maddie asked the girl.

"She's my aunt. She owns a store that makes sandwiches that are *so good.* I go there sometimes with my mom and we get to eat for free!" The girls ran off together to their cubbies to retrieve their backpacks, and Joshua felt a prick of hope. A sandwich shop? He could do that.

When the woman came back to the door, Joshua smiled at her. "Your niece says you own a sandwich place?"

"Oh, yes—Zelman's Deli on Detroit Avenue."

"Really! I've eaten there before, and your niece is right, that was a good sandwich."

She laughed. "Well thank you."

"I couldn't help but hear you on the phone when I came in—it sounds like you've lost an employee?"

She sighed. "Yeah—one of our managers quit without giving us any notice. Usually I'd just step in, but I'm going out of town for two weeks, and my business partner is already covering for another employee that just had surgery. It's been messy. The joys of owning your own business, right?"

An idea began to form in Joshua's mind. *But she'll think I'm a lunatic.* He waffled as she gathered her niece and ushered her out the door, praying for guidance. *What have I got to lose?*

Joshua pulled Maddie down the hall to the door, and caught Lori as she was settling her niece into the car. "I've got an idea for you. This is probably going to sound bizarre, but I'm going to take a chance here, just hear me out." He took a deep breath. "I just lost my job, I've been looking for weeks for another one, and not only do I like sandwiches, but I'm pretty good at making them. And I'm a very, very quick learner. Oh—and I have managed a café before, though it's been ten years, but I'm at least somewhat familiar with the position. You sound swamped and short on time to find someone, so if nothing else I can fill the position until you're able to find someone else."

She stared at him open-mouthed, then laughed. "Well, um ..." She studied him for a moment, eyes narrowed. "Do you have a resume? References? Just so I can check up on you, make sure you're not crazy?" She grinned.

Just being taken seriously made him want to hug her. "Yes, I do—tell me where to email it and you'll have it in half an hour."

She nodded, then dug a business card out of her wallet. "Send it along, and then why don't you stop over in the morning. Say, around nine?"

He held out his hand and they shook on it. "I'll be there."

DEBBIE NEEDED A SHOULDER TO CRY ON.

It was one of those days when she was *this close* to throwing in the towel. From the minute she'd stepped through the door she'd had nothing but stress and bad news. It was only noon on Wednesday, but she felt like it was five o'clock on a Friday at the end of a really awful week.

It had started with the ledger she'd found on her desk when she'd arrived that morning. She'd placed an ad in the paper the day after Harold told her he'd be leaving, confident the position would be filled before the retired volunteer actually left. But the ad was still being run, Harold was officially gone, and the ledger was there, taunting both her math phobia and her faith. Three open positions now—how long could they operate like this?

Seeing the giant black book on top of her already cluttered desk had sent her into a frenzy. She'd scrapped her morning plans and hauled out the folder of resumes she'd been meaning to go through. She had previously organized them into job categories, but sadly there weren't many in the accountant pile. She called them all—but they'd all balked at either the background check required by the shelter or the lack of benefits that came with the position. Not to be deterred, she swallowed back her mistrust of online job sites and tried to browse resumes on the first site that came into her head. But when she saw the price of membership required to look at job seekers, she groaned and promptly closed the browser window. If she'd had any idea what column to look at inside the ledger, she might be able to justify the expense, but deciphering their finances was like trying to read morse code without a key.

She continued to stare blankly at the stack of resumes until a knock came softly on her door. Shawnee poked her head in with a look of concern. "There's someone here to see you. Maria Guerrero—ring a bell? She said her sister Marisol had stayed here about six months ago?"

Debbie thought for a second, then nodded. "I remember her." Frowning, she stood and followed Shawnee to reception. Her gut told her she already knew why Maria was here. She wasn't the first family member to come to Debbie for an intervention, and it always strained Debbie's ability to keep a professional distance when it happened. It was hard knowing that a woman who was so close to physical and emotional freedom had walked right back into abuse.

Maria told the story Debbie had expected to hear. Marisol had fallen for the sweet talk, the promises, the blatant lies that were the hallmark of the manipulative abuser. The honeymoon period that ensued led her to believe he had truly changed. But as soon as she let her guard down, life returned to the horror that was their normal.

"Last night it was worse than it has ever been," Maria said as she twisted the tissue Debbie had given her. "*Agradezca a dios*, her neighbor heard Eduardo yelling and Marisol crying, and then not crying, and he called the police. Eduardo, he ran away before they came, and now she is in the hospital." Her tears ran unchecked. "She was happy here. I know she will listen to you. Please, will you talk to her?"

"Where is she now, Maria?"

Maria's eyes brightened at the question. "University Hospital. Room 412."

"Give me ten minutes and we'll go together, okay?"

Maria clasped her hands and let out a burst of enthusiastic Spanish. "Oh *gracias*, Ms. Truman! *Si, si*, I will wait here for you."

Debbie left Maria and went back to her office to get her purse, then tracked down Shawnee. "Pray for me," she said to her as she handed her the to-do list she hadn't gotten to. "And for Marisol. I'll have my cell but you know how they are about cell phones in hospitals. I'll put it on vibrate, and if I don't answer I'll check voicemail ASAP."

Her last stop was Stacia's room. Her sister's look-alike sat on her bed, folding clothes. "Hey Stacia, how's the packing going?"

Stacia flashed a rueful smile. "Oh, is that what I'm supposed to be doing?"

"Nervous?"

"Um, yeah."

Debbie sat beside her. "That's understandable. It can be tough leaving a place where you feel safe, even when you're equipped with new skills you didn't have before."

"I keep telling myself I'm not the same person I was before I came here. I've learned so much — but I guess I'm just worried the new me isn't going to be any stronger than the old me was." She bowed her head, concentrating on the T-shirt in her hands, but Debbie knew there were tears threatening to spill.

"Listen, I need to go out for a bit, but when I get back you and I can debrief a bit if you want, go over your plan of attack, pray together — whatever you need, okay?"

Stacia swiped at her cheek with the T-shirt. "Thanks Debbie."

"No problem. See you in a bit."

Debbie said a prayer for her as she walked back to the green room, knowing Stacia would be one of those women Debbie would not be able to stop thinking about, worrying about, praying about. She ached for all the women that came through the shelter, but some of them got to her more than others, their stories or person-alities seared into her memory like a brand. She felt good about Sta-cia's progress, despite the reservations the young woman had. She doubted a sister or mother or friend would be coming to the shelter in a few months' time, asking for an intervention as Maria had. Her thoughts turned back to Marisol as Debbie reached the green room, where Maria was murmuring in Spanish, eyes closed as she fingered a rosary of amber beads. Debbie gently knocked on the door frame to announce herself. "I'm ready when you are, Maria."

"Ah, *gracias.*" She stood from her chair and kissed her rosary be-fore slipping it into a black velvet bag and tucking it into her purse. Debbie watched the motions with a twinge of jealousy. Sometimes she wished her Protestantism provided her with something like a rosary for days like today, when she felt like her faith was slipping through her hands and she was just so tired. Maybe being able to hold onto something, to weave her fingers through the string of beads and clutch them like a lifeline, would help her feel more grounded in her faith.

As Debbie and Maria approached Marisol's room at the hospital, they heard voices arguing in rapid-fire Spanish. Debbie got a gnawing feeling in the pit of her stomach, and Maria confirmed her fears when she hissed, "Eduardo." Debbie ran to the nurses' station, jabbing a finger towards Marisol's room. "That's Marisol's abuser in there. Call security, and the police."

Debbie remained outside while the shouting continued, now with Maria's contribution ringing through the halls. Debbie didn't understand a word, but she was confident she knew the gist of the conversation. Threats sound threatening in any language.

A nurse and a security guard soon appeared and led a steaming but compliant Eduardo out the door. Debbie dragged a chair beside the bed and was finally able to get a good look at Marisol, who was weeping quietly, eyes squeezed shut. A large bandage was taped above her eyes. Bruises mottled her face, and two on her throat made Debbie particularly sick. Her right arm was in a cast. Debbie didn't want to imagine what other injuries were hidden beneath her hospital sheet.

"Marisol? It's Debbie Truman, from Safe in His Arms Shelter. Do you remember me?"

Marisol's eyes flew open. She gasped, then began to cry even more as she reached out with her uninjured hand to grasp Debbie's sleeve. She took the tissue Debbie offered her, and dabbing her eyes, she spoke. "Maria told you what happened?"

"Yes."

"Why?"

"She's hoping I can convince you to leave Eduardo."

Marisol closed her eyes and sighed. "Oh Debbie. I wanted to. I tried to! But ..."

Debbie waited for an explanation that never came. "But what, Marisol? He nearly killed you. I can see the bruises from him choking you. What's keeping you with him?"

She began again to weep, and Debbie sat back in her seat, intent on not letting her frustration show. *Show me what to do, God. Tell me what to say.*

They sat in silence for a few minutes before Debbie's phone shimmied in her pocket. She slipped it out and saw the number of the shelter on the display. "Marisol, I need to check my voicemail. I'll be right back."

"That is okay, Debbie. You do not need to come back up. *Gracias* for coming to see me. You are an angel."

"You're sure you don't want to talk some more?"

"*Sí,* I am sure."

Debbie nodded. "Okay then. I'll be praying for you, Marisol. You're welcome to come back to the shelter if you need to."

"*Gracias.*"

There was nothing else for her to say or do. It was not Debbie's battle to fight, but the look on Maria's face gave Debbie some hope. She stood and gave the woman a ginger hug, then left.

Out in the parking lot, she dialed her voicemail and listened as Paula relayed that a pipe had burst in the kitchen. She groaned as she slid behind the wheel of her car and slammed the door shut. *Great. I wonder if that ledger has a mental health vacation fund I can dip into.*

Her stomach rumbled. She looked at the clock on her dashboard: nearly eleven o'clock. Crises always made her hungry, and she knew she'd unravel if she didn't get something to eat before returning to the shelter. She spotted Zelman's Deli while waiting at a stoplight, and remembered that Paula had recommended it once as a catering option for a fund-raising event. This would give her a chance to check it out. She pulled into the first parking spot she saw and nearly ran to the door.

The scent of fresh bread just about drove her to her knees when she walked through the door. She got in line and fixed her eyes on the menu on the wall behind the counter.

"Next in line, please."

Debbie stepped up to the counter, eyes still on the menu. "Man, I am so hungry but I just cannot decide."

"If you like turkey I'd go with the club," said the man behind the counter.

She smiled at him. "Sold."

He returned the smile. "That was easy."

She laughed. "I'm starving. You could have offered me a boot and I probably would have agreed."

He pulled a slice of cheese from a container in the counter. "Here, before you get sick."

"Seriously?"

"Absolutely. It's really gonna back things up if you faint." He winked.

She laughed. "Thanks. I appreciate it."

"Not a problem. Let's get this sandwich made so you can have a proper meal." He dressed up her sandwich to her liking and added a cup of fruit salad. She caught herself watching him as he worked and chastised herself. *Don't even think about it. Your track record is so bad it should be illegal for you to even* talk *to a man right now.*

"Okay, here you go." He slid the tray across the counter. "Cash or charge?"

"Charge, please." She handed him her credit card and took a sip of her iced tea.

He tapped on the keys of the register, frowned, tapped again, muttered, tapped again, and sighed. "I'm sorry, give me just a minute here."

"No problem."

He went through the same routine, his frustration plain on his face. He sighed. "I'm sorry. It's only my second day on the job and I swear this machine has it in for me."

Debbie eyed her lunch. "Looks like you've got the food part down pat. The sandwich looks delicious."

He flashed a quick smile. "Thanks. I've got a preschooler, so my true expertise lies more in the peanut butter and jelly realm, but the basic skills have transferred." His face brightened as the register finally displayed her total. "Ah! Here we go." He swiped her card and handed it back. "At my last job I just moved money around on paper. It's a whole different world actually dealing with it."

Debbie's ears perked. "Moved money around on paper? What did you do?"

He looked almost embarrassed. "Oh — I was an accountant."

She took the receipt and pen he offered her. "Are you serious? What made you quit?"

"I lost my job, actually. Downsizing."

"Oh wow, I'm sorry."

"Thanks." He pushed the tray towards her and smiled. "Here you go. Go eat that sandwich before you start to hallucinate."

She laughed, but her mind was churning. "Thanks. Hey, look — are you still interested in working as an accountant? Or have you found your true calling behind that counter?"

His eyes widened. "No — I'd definitely go back into accounting if I could find a job."

She stepped a little closer, lowering her voice. "We're a Christian non-profit — "

He held up a hand. "So was my last employer."

She straightened and smiled. Beaming, she pulled a business card from her wallet and handed it to him. "Send me your resume."

"Consider it done."

"Excellent." She smiled and pulled the tray from the counter. "Thank you so much, um — "

"Joshua. Joshua Miller."

"Right then. Thank you, Joshua. I'll keep an eye out."

"Thank you — "

"Debbie Truman."

"Thank you, Debbie. Enjoy that sandwich."

She carried her tray to a table, hope igniting in her spirit. *An accountant! At the deli! Sometimes you crack me up, God.* She stole another look as she bit into her sandwich. *I wouldn't mind crying on that shoulder.*

Kɪᴍ's ᴄᴏɴᴠᴇʀsᴀᴛɪᴏɴ ᴡɪᴛʜ ʜᴇʀ Cʟᴜʙ ɢɪʀʟs proved more delicate than she'd expected.

She'd always made it a point to be open and honest with the young women she met with. They'd heard enough lies in their short lifetimes, from fathers who promised to always be there but then left, from teachers who said they could be anything and then steered them away from the college track, from a culture that said sex equaled love and you had to give one to get the other. Even if she wasn't perfect and made a lot of mistakes, they deserved to know there was someone they could go to who would shoot straight with them.

But now she was about to do something she'd never expected to do: move in with a man without being married. She wasn't exactly morally opposed to the practice. She just hadn't ever thought she'd do it, mostly because she hadn't thought she'd ever have the opportunity. But a few of her girls were being raised by single moms, and she knew those girls struggled without the love of a father. She always counseled them against "playing house" with a guy until there was a wedding, so how was she going to tell them she was doing it without looking like a hypocrite?

"So how's Riiiick?" Egypt asked once they were all there. She drew out his name in a purr, eliciting laughter from the other girls and a mock glare from Kim.

"He's fine, thank you."

"How long you guys been together now?" Kea asked. "Two, three months?"

"Three."

"You love him?" This from La-Neesa.

Kim's eyebrows shot up. "Um, wow."

"That's personal, La-Neesa, don't ask her that!" Mercedes thwapped La-Neesa on her skinny arm.

"She don't got to tell if she don't want to," La-Neesa said. "She knows she can tell me to shut up."

"It's alright Sadie," Kim said. She thought for a moment, then shrugged. "Well, honestly, I've been wondering that myself lately. I've never been in love, so I don't know. Everyone always tells you you'll know, but I'm not sure if I believe them. I *do* know that I've never met anyone else like him, and that he makes me tremendously happy, and that I think about him all the time. If I don't love him yet, I think I will eventually. Like, right now it might just be infatuation, but I think that can grow into love if it's given the chance and if the person is right for you."

Egypt sighed. "That's so romantic."

Joelle rocked back in her chair. "If he asked you to marry him, would you?"

"No. Not yet." She'd thought about that, too, since she'd thought he was proposing the night of their anniversary when he'd asked her to move in with him. Later she'd pondered what she would have said if he had indeed asked her to marry him. She had a feeling she would have said yes, and then later regretted moving so fast. "I think, down the road, we could get married. But right now there's still too much we don't know about each other. I mean, it's only been three months."

"Yeah, but then you'd have a family," said Joelle. Kim had been open with them about her foster system childhood so they knew she could relate in some ways to their broken home existences. "Don't you want to get married soon so you can finally have a family? You've told us before how much you want that."

Kim shrugged. "You're right, Joelle. I do want that. But at the same time, I don't want it to fall apart, either. I want that family to always be there, so I need to make sure I'm giving it the best possible chance to succeed. Marrying before I really know him isn't setting myself up for success; it's just taking a risk."

"You could move in with him," Egypt said. "Like, give it a trial run, see what it's like. That way you can still bail if it don't work."

"But you know how she feels about cohabitation," Mercedes said. "Remember when La-Neesa's sister moved in with that guy, and he broke her heart? *And* she got pregnant and ended up having an abortion? Kim said that was exactly why she wouldn't want to live with someone before getting married."

Curse Mercedes and her steel-trap memory.

"How is your sister, La-Neesa?" Kim said, grateful for the tangent.

La-Neesa sighed. "She's alright most days. But she's still real depressed sometimes."

Kim wrapped an arm around La-Neesa's shoulder. "I'm sorry to hear that."

Egypt leaned in. "Hey, that reminds me — did you hear what happened to Shawnelle?"

Kim frowned. "Who's Shawnelle?"

"A girl we know at school," said La-Neesa.

"Wait a minute, wait a minute," Kim said. "We're not going to start gossiping about someone who isn't here to defend herself. Besides, I wanted to get back to what we were talking about Monday when Kea brought up the subject of dieting. We didn't get to finish that discussion."

The girls were eager to jump back into the conversation that had been cut short by the end of their last meeting, and Kim breathed an inward sigh of relief. But guilt niggled at the back of her mind for the rest of the meeting and into the evening when she arrived home. She might not have voiced a lie herself, but she had allowed them to think she still disapproved of living with a man before marriage, and that was just as bad. What was she going to do when they found out?

She sat on her bed after dinner, staring at the moving boxes Suzie had given her and trying to summon the will to do some packing. She'd been excited about moving all week, but now she felt deflated and a little bit depressed. The joy was gone from the move, and she felt lousy for lying to her girls. How was she going to dig herself out of that one? The thought of breaking their trust in her made her ill. She had to own up sooner rather than later — the longer she waited the worse it would be.

The familiar chaos in her stomach made her chest tighten. Her anger at her cowardliness, her guilt from her lie, being reminded what an awful person she was at her core—it all rose up before her like a tsunami. Hot tears blurred her vision and rolled down her cheeks. Her throat squeezed. The voices that screamed her shortcomings grew louder and louder until she cried out loud, "I'm sorry! I'm sorry," hoping they would abate. But when they didn't, her panic grew even more.

The chaos in her veins pounded to get out.

She scrambled from the bed and yanked open her dresser drawer. She reached beneath the plastic organizer box filled with socks and pulled out the paring knife she'd come to prefer. Once on the bed again, curled atop her pillows in the corner, she balled her hand into a fist and drew the knife across her forearm again, then again. Three parallel lines of red stood out against her pale skin. Her breathing slowed and the chaos calmed as she watched the blood welling.

The world was dark outside her window by the time she unfurled herself and set about bandaging her cuts. She didn't know where the time had gone. Her mind felt empty, her body lethargic. She looked at the boxes standing ready for her belongings, and the sight just made her sad. How pathetic that her whole life could be packed up in six boxes. One quickly learned the futility of clinging to material goods when living in the foster care system, and even after being out six years she still lived a spartan existence. She'd felt like a drifter, like she had no roots. Rick's apartment, on the other hand, was a cluttered mess of mismatched objects—couch and armchair from two different sets, garage sale bookshelves, and a lamp more suited to a grandmother's living room. What would it be like to live in rooms that were fully furnished, with overflowing end tables and bookshelves and enough clutter to get in the way? She wondered if he'd let her redecorate. She'd never tried to decorate a room before.

By ten o'clock she'd managed to pack up her winter clothes.

Hangers swung empty on the rod in the closet and the dresser drawer made a hollow thud when she closed it. She taped the box shut and labeled it in marker on the side, then crawled into bed, her clothes still on and teeth unbrushed. Her head had begun to pound. It was one of those nights when she felt a hundred years old.

EIGHT

Kim was up before daybreak on Sunday morning. She pattered about the apartment with light steps so as not to wake Corrie, checking the front closet for forgotten jackets and umbrellas and winter gear. She carted her findings back to her room and dumped them onto the stripped bed to fold before cramming them into a box. Rick wasn't picking her up until ten, but by eight she was standing in the center of an undone room.

She sighed and sank onto the bed, kicking her feet and looking at the sealed boxes. She felt energized today, though it had taken a day to shake off the funk she'd been in a couple nights before. The bandage on her arm was no longer necessary, but she wore a shirt with three-quarters sleeves to hide the cuts that looked like the work of an angry cat. She'd picked up a few more shirts like it yesterday. They drew fewer comments than long sleeves in the warm spring weather.

The phone rang. She jumped, then scrambled to grab it from the base on the floor before it woke Corrie. "Hello?"

"Kim, hey, it's Patricia. I got your message last night — sorry I missed your call."

Usually a call from her old caseworker brought a smile to her face, but today it brought butterflies instead. "Oh, that's alright."

"So you're moving! What prompted this? I thought you liked living where you are."

Kim took a deep breath. "Actually, I am happy here, but … I met someone. Back in February, actually. And we've been dating ever since. And he asked me last week if I'd move in with him, so … here I go!"

The beat of silence before Patricia replied made Kim's heart sink. "Wow," she finally said. "Well—congratulations. How did you guys meet?"

Kim kept her tone light. She didn't want Patricia to catch even a hint of hesitancy on her part. The closest thing Kim had ever had to a mother was Patricia's presence in her life, and it wouldn't take much persuasion from her to sway her feelings. But losing Rick was more important now than Patricia's opinions. Patricia was a remnant of Kim's past. Rick was her future. "He came to the party my roommate had on my birthday. He's a graphic artist, and he was in foster care for a little while, too, so we really understand each other in that respect. But anyway, he's a great guy, and he treats me like a queen, and we have *so* much fun together, and moving in together just feels right. I'm excited." *Please be excited for me.*

"I'm glad to know you're so happy, Kim."

"Thanks."

An uncomfortable break followed, only a couple seconds but feeling like whole minutes. Kim cast about in her head for a new topic. "So, um, you got my new number, right?"

"Yes, yes I did."

"Okay. Good."

"And how are things at the salon?"

"Still good, thanks. I was thinking about training to be an aesthetician, too, and starting a mobile salon service." It seemed like a good thing to tell Patricia, despite the fact that she'd given up on the idea. But maybe Patricia wouldn't think badly of her for moving so fast with Rick if she knew Kim wasn't throwing her life away on some guy. So what if she wasn't pursuing the mobile salon—it didn't mean she wouldn't pursue *something* new. Eventually.

"Hey, that's a great idea! Good for you. What does Rick think about it?"

Kim scrambled. "He's, um, he's a little concerned it'll take up so much time that we won't get to see each other much. Which is another reason I'm moving in with him." Though it hadn't been until she said it. But regardless of what new path she considered, it made sense, now that she thought about it. "Between the salon and Club and training, I would be pretty busy. But it would be worth it."

"That's true. That would be a great job during the prom and wedding season."

They spent the rest of their conversation brainstorming more ideas for the business, and by the time they rang off Kim was fired up about the idea once more. *I'll put more thought into it, do some more research, before bringing it up with Rick again. He just needs a little convincing.* She tore into one of her boxes to get a notebook so she could write down the ideas they'd come up with, then sprawled on the floor and flipped through it, looking for a blank page.

She'd had this notebook since just after graduating from the foster system. Leafing through it was a trip back in time: notes about cosmetology school, the personal budget she'd drawn up after starting her first salon job, lyrics to a song she'd heard on the radio and loved.

As she turned the pages slowly, reading each one, she let her mind wander through her history. Then she saw the letter. She'd forgotten all about it, hadn't thought of it in years — five years, actually, given the date in the corner. As she read it, the day she'd composed it came back to her in vivid detail — the thunderstorm that had been raging outside, the way she'd jumped at every clap of thunder, the piercing pain in her heart she'd tried to alleviate through her words.

> *Dear Saundra,*
>
> *I've been wanting to write this letter a long time, but wasn't sure how I would ever find you to send it. But then I saw the article on Bradley in the paper and I figured out I could just send it to his office in Denver. I hope it gets to you okay.*

The letter went on to update Saundra of her graduation from foster care, her entrance into cosmetology school, and her temporary job at a grocery store. She asked a few questions about Saundra's family, and then moved on to her real reason for writing.

*I really just wanted to thank you for taking me in. I don't think
I ever said thank you when I was living with you, and I know I
didn't say it when I went back into foster care because I was too
mad at the time. I know no one ever wants the older kids. They
always want the babies that don't come with all the emotional
baggage. But the older kids are the ones that really need a family,
even if it's just for a few years. So thank you for taking a chance on
a teenager and for letting me see what a real family is like.*

*There's actually another reason I'm writing. There's something
I need to get off my chest, because it's been eating at me for a long
time now. Remember when I took the car out that one night and
got the front end banged up, and I said I hit a deer? Well, that's not
exactly what happened....*

Kim remembered sitting on her bed, desperate to spill the entire
story but unable to put pen to paper. She wanted so badly to tell
someone, and Saundra O'Riley—being so far away, so far removed
now from everything—seemed like the best person to tell. Besides,
it had been her car that Kim had been driving. But she never finished the letter.

The O'Rileys were a sweet couple to Kim and their two adopted
children. They'd chosen Kim when she was fourteen, two weeks before she started high school. By then, Kim had been in three other
foster homes. The first family treated their four foster children as
slave labor, and the next one had been great, but the farm they had
lived on had not been—that was when they discovered Kim's se-
vere allergy to hay. The last set of foster parents before the O'Rileys
had wanted to adopt her, but she had refused based on their pen-
chant for turning their adopted children into religious zealots.

Before all of that, Kim had actually had a mom.

When Patricia had arrived with the O'Rileys to meet Kim, she'd
been wary about trying another family. Part of her kept hoping
she'd get lucky, but mostly she was tired of the back-and-forth between group homes and families. A new family meant new rules
and new environment, another awkward period of feeling like she

was on loan from some human library—here, try this one out, see what you think. Only the knowledge that this family was looking to eventually adopt made her at all interested in leaving the familiarity of the group home. Plus, they had one adopted daughter already, who was three years older than Kim, and that made Kim feel a little better—they'd pulled the trigger with someone else; maybe they would with her too.

Saundra O'Riley worked part-time as a secretary, but she was always home when Kim got back from school. Bradley O'Riley was a trial lawyer, and for a little while Kim had a bit of a crush on him. He was handsome and tall and funny, though more serious when he was on a case. He didn't talk much about the trials he was involved in, but she always knew when they were over because he started telling jokes again.

When she turned sixteen the O'Rileys offered to help her get her driver's license, and also announced that they'd proceed with adoption if she wanted. She couldn't believe her luck; usually foster kids didn't get to drive because it was rare to find a family willing to take on that much responsibility. But it was clear by that point she was a good fit with the O'Rileys. She said yes to the adoption.

Not long after she began driver's ed, Saundra's sister and brother-in-law were arrested for drug use. Natasha, their seventeen-year-old wild child, was in danger of being placed with the state because none of their other relatives would take her. Saundra and Bradley stepped in, inviting her to stay with them temporarily. Nothing was specifically said to Kim, but she knew the plans for her adoption would be shelved until Natasha was gone.

Kim ripped the letter from the notebook and crumpled it to a ball. She had enough on her mind without dragging all this back up. The last person whose face she wanted hovering in her mind's eye today was Natasha.

"Wow, really? That's all you have?" Corrie stood beside the boxes Kim had piled near the front door.

"Pathetic, isn't it?"

"No — I'm impressed. And a little jealous, even. There are a lot of benefits to being able to travel light."

Kim sighed. "It just reminds me that I've never settled any-where. I really hope that changes now."

Corrie folded her arms and opened her mouth as though to speak. It took her a moment before she finally launched in, her gaze resting on the boxes but occasionally flicking up to Kim. Kim had never seen Corrie uneasy before. "I know we haven't known each other very long, and that we're not close or anything. But, I don't want to hate myself later for not saying something. I'm still a little worried about you, Kim. I just have a bad feeling."

Kim avoided Corrie's eyes when they finally fixed on her and busied herself with smoothing out a bubble in the tape holding one of the boxes shut. She didn't want her last conversation with Corrie to get nasty, but she also didn't want to get into a discussion on the subject when Rick was on his way over. "I appreciate the concern, honestly. But seriously, there's no reason for it. And — not to sound rude or anything — but it's not like you really know me. And you certainly don't know Rick."

Corrie was silent for a moment, her eyes trained on the boxes. "I suppose that's true. I'm sorry I didn't try to get to know you better."

Kim let out a little laugh. "Oh Corrie, we're so different I don't think we'd ever figure out how to be real friends. We worked well as roommates and I'm fine that that's all we were. I'm not your kind of people."

Corrie was about to reply when the intercom buzzed. Kim's stomach lurched as she reached for the button. "Hello?"

"Hey, I'm looking for a new roommate; know anyone who might be interested?"

Kim laughed louder than necessary to show Corrie just how excited she was about this move. "I'm all packed and ready to go!"

"Awesome, let me up."

Kim hit the button that opened the foyer door and turned back to Corrie. "Thanks again."

Corrie gave her a small smile. "You're welcome."

A knock on the door made Kim's heart leap into her throat. She pulled it open and grinned. "Hey stranger. Move my boxes and I'll pay half your rent."

"Sounds like a good deal to me." He gave her a kiss and smiled at Corrie. "Been nice knowing you. Thanks for your hospitality."

"You're welcome. Take care of her."

Kim bristled but tried not to show it. "What am I, five?" She forced a laugh, then hoisted a box in her arms and followed Rick out the door.

Kim's stomach fluttered the whole way to Rick's apartment. She noticed things she'd never seen before: the way the cluster of maples at the end of the building made a perfect shady picnic spot, the paint peeling from the gutters, the handprint cutouts in a window that belied the presence of children. *My new home.*

Rick parked the car at the end of the building, then leaned over and kissed her. "Welcome home, baby."

She gave him a smile, though her face strained with the effort. "Thank you."

"I'll go prop open the security door and unlock the apartment." She watched him go up the short stairs and disappear into the building, then got out and popped the trunk to retrieve the first of the boxes. When he returned with a boot to jam the outer door open, she went inside and turned left, following the short hall to his end unit.

She'd wondered if he would change anything in anticipation of her arrival, but it looked the same as it usually did. The dingy white walls looked more stark in the day, and the dust that sat on most surfaces glittered in the sun that was shining in the living room window. *Bachelors. Do they ever clean?* She walked past the small kitchen and into the bedroom where two dresser drawers were open and empty. She sucked in a breath to steady her nerves and set the box on the bed. She'd only ventured in here a couple times, since they spent most of their time on the couch on the nights they stayed in and cooked. It didn't matter where she concentrated her focus, however—the bed was the only thing she seemed to really see.

They'd started sleeping together after their fifth date. It hadn't been the mind-blowing experience she'd hoped it would be, but the feeling of belonging to someone, of being enmeshed wholly and completely with another person, was exactly what she'd been hoping for. When his arms were looped around her waist, hugging her tight to him beneath a quilt on the couch, she stayed as still as possible to avoid breaking the spell. When the clock on the wall read 1:00 a.m. she had to force the words "I should go" from her mouth.

But when they'd been living apart, their schedules only allowed for so many opportunities for intimacy. Knowing how much easier it would be to find those opportunities now, she worried about falling pregnant. She felt funny talking to Rick about birth control, and had gone on the pill after their first month together even though he always had condoms at the ready. She didn't know how to bring up her fears without disappointing him—she was fairly certain limiting sex would not go over well—and she didn't want to disappoint him.

You're being paranoid. Condoms and the pill together are a contraceptive Fort Knox. Don't say anything to ruin this.

They were done unloading the car in mere minutes, and when they closed the apartment door after the last trip in, he dropped his box on the floor and pulled her into a hungry kiss. "I'm so glad you're here."

"I'm so glad to be here."

"I love you, Kim."

The words melted the resistance she'd felt all day. "Rick, I love you too."

He kissed her again, then said, "Let's get you settled in. I want you to feel at home."

He hung her clothes in the closet while she put her toiletries in the bathroom. Then he put her folded clothes in the dresser while she unpacked her desk drawers box onto the living room floor and separated the items into piles. "Can I have a desk drawer?"

"Of course. Bottom one is cleaned out."

She carted her things into the room and began to set them into the drawer, noting she'd need to buy some sort of organizer so things weren't just sitting in a heap at the bottom. As she was getting up to go back into the living room, she heard a muffled voice. "What did you say?" she called.

"I didn't say anything."

She frowned. "Then you have a ghost."

He laughed and came into the room with her. "What?"

The voice sounded again, as well as another with it. "That! What is it?" She looked in the closet, expecting to see a hole to the outside.

"Oh—it's these walls, they're thin as paper. You're hearing the neighbors."

She stood still, head cocked towards the wall. "Wow, really?" She moved to the wall and set her ear to it. "They're talking about a movie. I can hear practically every word!"

"Shh, they'll hear you too, you know."

She clapped a hand over her mouth and giggled.

"Now you know why I use the other room for the bedroom. Can you imagine how much it would suck to live in one of the interior units?"

"Seriously."

She followed him back to the living room. "I need some lunch. You?"

"Definitely. I'll cook if you want, and you can finish putting your things where you want them."

She smiled and wrapped her arms around his neck. "You're such a doll."

"Right back atcha." He planted a kiss on her nose, then wandered into the kitchen, whistling as he pulled food from the fridge. Kim felt herself relaxing into her new reality and chided herself for her reservations. She unpacked her boxes as Rick prepared their meal, letting her imagination meander through the possibilities for their future as she integrated her belongings into their new home.

The afternoon was filled with errands, and they spent the early evening cooking a celebratory dinner that ended with champagne and strawberries. After dinner they sat on the couch watching re-runs until the news came on. "I have an early appointment in the morning," Kim said at ten as she stretched and stood. "I should probably get to bed."

A light ignited in his eyes. "I was hoping you'd say that."

It was as though a dam broke inside her. Fear flooded her heart and the confidence she'd felt for most of the day was washed away in a tidal wave of regret.

Tears spilled to her cheeks, which made her feel even worse. Now she'd ruined everything. "I'm sorry, Rick, I don't know what's wrong with me."

He took her hand and pulled her gently to the bedroom, then sat down on the bed and tugged her next to him. She kept her eyes to the floor, embarrassed. "Can you tell me what's wrong?"

I feel like I should run out that door and not look back. I feel like I'm about to step off a cliff into nothing. I feel like I'm about to make the worst mistake of my life—and that's saying something. "I—I don't know."

"Is it just stress? The move, all the changes?"

She sniffed. "Maybe."

"Is it because we're not married? I mean, I didn't think that was a big deal to you, but maybe it's a bigger deal than you thought it was."

She sniffed and shook her head. "I don't think that's it. I don't know what it is, Rick, honestly."

He was quiet for a moment. "Maybe you don't feel safe."

Her breath caught in her throat. "That's it. That's exactly it. And I don't know why! I mean, this is *you* we're talking about." She leaned against him, inhaling the heavenly scent of his cologne. "You love me. You're taking such good care of me. Why shouldn't I feel safe?"

He slid off the bed and knelt in front of her. "Maybe because you don't know if you can trust me to always be there for you. Who in your life ever has been?"

She nodded, relieved that he understood. "That's true."

"So maybe if I can show you that I'll always be there, you won't feel so unsafe."

She smiled. "Yeah, maybe. But I already know in my head that you will—any ideas how we can get the message through to my heart?"

He stared at her for a moment, studying her, then a slow smile spread across his face. He reached into his pocket and pulled out a ring, then held it before her. "Marry me, Kim?"

Her eyes went wide and her words left her. She stared at the ring open-mouthed. "Oh. Oh, Rick."

He laughed and took her hand. "That a yes?"

Her mind clicked and whirred as all the reasons she'd amassed for not wanting to get engaged yet went missing. She saw before her the ideal she'd longed for her whole life. There was no way she was turning it down. "Yes!"

He slipped it on her finger and sprang up, tackling her while she laughed, and said, "We're engaged? Seriously, we're engaged?"

"We are!" He kissed her and she kissed him back, her emotions overrunning the disquiet in her spirit. She allowed herself to be pulled into him, body, mind, and soul, until she was lost in his kiss and oblivious to time.

An hour had passed by the time they disentangled and curled together beneath the sheets. Moonlight through the blinds threw stripes across the room, illuminating scattered clothing and sleepy faces. Kim raised her hand and held it in the shaft of light, examining the sparkle of the gold-set solitaire. "Thank you."

"You're welcome."

She giggled. "This is crazy."

"Sometimes you've gotta walk on the wild side."

"When should we do it?"

"Hm—I thought we just did."

She socked him in the arm as he laughed. "You nitwit. When should we get married?"

He held her close, nuzzling her shoulder. "I dunno—July?"

"Like, next year?"

"No, next month."

She sat up. "Are you nuts? We can't plan a wedding in a month!"

"C'mon—Fourth of July, fireworks on our anniversary every year. It would be a blast!"

"It'll be just as big a blast next year as this year. Between our work schedules and my time at Club, there is no way we could do everything in a month. Let's say next year, Fourth of July, a huge barbecue somewhere afterwards where we can watch the fireworks. Maybe Whitmore Lake or something like that." She hunkered back down and giggled again. "I can't believe we're engaged."

He rolled over, propping himself up on an elbow. "So tell me something about you I don't already know."

She sighed. "Well, I'm afraid of ants."

He cocked an eyebrow. "Ants? For real?"

"Yes. Hate them, hate them, hate them. They scare the crap out of me."

"Why is that?"

"Well, when I was little, in my first placement, my foster mom was watching some horror movie with giant ants in it, and then later that week we had ants in the kitchen and I thought they'd get all big like the ones on the TV. And then that night I had a nightmare that I was cleaning the kitchen and the ants were everywhere, and they got into my rubber gloves and started eating my hands."

Rick laughed and swore. "Yeah, I can see how that would give you a phobia. What do you do when you're outside and see them on the sidewalk?"

"I step on them. It's not so bad outside, but if I find one in the house—panic city."

"I'll remember that. No ants in the house."

She laughed. "Thank you. Now your turn."

"Alright, let me think. Oh, here we go: when I was fifteen I ran away from home for a weekend."

She laughed. "Just the weekend?"

"Well, it was supposed to be for longer than that but my hiding place was found."

"What was your hiding place?"

"The library."

Kim shook her head. "I don't believe it."

"No, it's true. There was this one meeting room that had a little storage closet, and hardly anyone ever used the room. So I hid in the closet at night until two hours after closing—I didn't know how late the staff stayed—and then I went to the staff room and ate some of the snack food they had down there, and then I went to sleep back in the meeting room."

"So how did they catch you?"

His smile was sheepish. "I forgot the library didn't open on Sundays until noon, and I waltzed out of the room at ten-thirty. Some of the staff was there to do work before opening the place."

Kim cracked up, then threw her arms around him. "You poor thing! Great plan, though. I wonder how long you could have gotten away with it."

He settled onto his back, hands under his head. "I was only going to stay there for a few days, while I researched where I wanted to go. I was going to hitchhike to wherever it was I decided on."

"Hitchhike in this day and age? It's a good thing you got caught, then." She settled down beside him, staring at the ceiling. Everything felt surreal. She'd never been so close to someone, never felt so vulnerable and protected all at once. A shiver in her soul told her it was too good to be true, and she focused all her will on quelling the familiar anxiety that was threatening to erupt. She couldn't cut herself, not right now, not here. She still had to sort out where to keep the knife and bandages, what Rick's work schedule was, when she was safe to do it.

Her voice was barely a whisper. "Do you have any secrets that eat you up inside?"

She'd thought maybe he'd fallen asleep, his response was so long in coming. "Yes."

"Do you ever wish you could tell someone who you knew wouldn't care? Or at least wouldn't ... tell anyone else?"

He rolled to his side and slipped one of his arms across her waist. "All the time."

She forced a small smile. "Wanna trade?"

He cleared his throat, waited a moment, then said, "The reason I ran away from home was because I tried to kill my father. But it didn't work."

She remembered all the stories he had told her about his father — the beatings, the rage, the drinking. "Oh, Rick. What happened?"

"I just reached the end of my rope, you know? He was passed out drunk one night — or at least, I thought he was. I spilled some vodka on the floor, then lit one of his cigars and a napkin and dropped them on the puddle so it would look like he'd fallen asleep smoking. Not the most efficient or foolproof method, but I couldn't bring myself to actually *do* something to him, like stab him, despite the fact that I'd been dreaming about it for years."

"The police didn't suspect you? *He* didn't suspect you?"

"Well, I had this friend who knew everything my dad did, and his parents knew, too, but I begged them not to report him because I didn't want to go back into foster care. I went to my friend's house and they let me hide out there. They covered for me, said I'd been there since dinner. But the smoke woke him up; his clothes got singed a bit, and he got a few burns on his hand, but that's it. He didn't report me because he was never really sure it wasn't his fault. Plus, he knew if he said anything to the police, I'd just tell them what he did to me, and he'd get arrested too." He shifted, rested his chin on her shoulder. "He beat me within an inch of my life, and that's when I ran away."

Kim shook her head. "That's awful, Rick. I'm so sorry."

He shrugged and snuggled closer. "It's history now. He really is dead, good riddance, and I've moved on." He nudged her with his chin. "So what's your secret?"

The moment of truth. Here was her chance to unburden herself. Could she really do it? Could she finally lay down the weight she'd been hauling for the last seven years?

She took a breath, let it out, tried again and couldn't. Rick chuckled. "C'mon, it can't be as bad as mine. I tried to kill someone."

She felt the rising of the pressure in her veins, the thumping of her heart that seemed to shake the bed. "Yes. But I actually did."

NINE

Kim was running out of excuses. She was also running out of shirts.

The last two weeks with Rick had been about as blissful as an orphan could ever hope for. He let her rearrange the furniture and even replace a few of his oddball items, making the apartment feel more pulled together and less like a bachelor pad. They fell into a rhythm of cooking and cleaning and errand-running. And it turned out to be very nice to wake up next to someone—almost as nice as it was to go to sleep next to him.

Yet Kim had cut herself more in those two weeks than she had since starting the practice. There was a new fear she didn't know how to handle: the fear of losing the best thing she'd ever had. It compounded the guilt she still carried, even after the confession of her secret. In fact, the guilt was worse with the passing of every heartbreakingly wonderful day she had with Rick. She couldn't win.

So she cut. Her arms were a mess of lines. Fresh red, fading pink, healing white, covered in unseasonably long sleeves. Her wardrobe began to draw comments. She complained a lot about air-conditioning.

The girls at Club were easy to fool. They knew she came straight from the salon, so she told them the manager had the A/C jacked up high so she was always cold. Most of the girls at the salon said nothing, though she could tell Emma was suspicious. "Girl, it's gonna be ninety today," she said at the end of the first week Kim had spent with Rick. "Aren't you hot?"

Kim shrugged, making it a point to look her in the eyes for at least a moment. "Rick is so hot-blooded, the apartment is always freezing. I dress for how it feels in there, and then I forget to change clothes before I come to work. The heat feels good, actually—I finally get to thaw!"

The second week she was more difficult to put off. "Kim, I sweat just looking at you. What's the deal?"

"I told you, Emma, Rick keeps the apartment really cold."

"Yeah, well, we don't keep things cold here—and I've seen you break a sweat more than once this week. At least keep some light-weight stuff at your station or something."

Kim scrambled for a reply but found nothing. Emma pounced on her silence. "Kim, I'm getting a weird vibe from you lately. Is everything alright?"

This time Kim didn't have to force the eye contact. "It is, Emma. It's ... it's amazing. Everything about him, about living with him.... I never thought I'd have something like this."

Emma smiled, though Kim could tell it was guarded. "I'm happy for you, Kim. Just—" she shrugged. "I don't know. Just tell me if anything is wrong, okay?"

"Thanks, Emma."

Emma gave her a squeeze before returning to her station and Kim scurried back to hers before she broke down in tears. The stress of hiding her cuts became one more reason to do it.

It only took a few weeks for the honeymoon to end. One week-end toward the end of June, Rick was invited to join some of his co-workers for a poker game. He claimed to have been a card shark in high school, and as he left the apartment he promised Kim a treat with his winnings. "You're pretty confident for someone who hasn't played in a few years." she'd said.

He shrugged as he pocketed his wallet and headed for the door. "I used to be nearly impossible to beat. There's a lot of strategy; most people don't know that. You don't just play your cards; you play the other players. The guys I'm playing tonight don't know what they're doing. I can almost guarantee it."

She was just getting ready for bed a few hours later when a slammed door announced his return. Kim called out, "How'd you do?" and heard the refrigerator door open and shut with a bang, but no response to her question. She went to the kitchen where he was opening a beer. "So? How did it go?"

He threw a bottle cap into the trash, his head down. "I lost."

"Aw, baby, I'm sorry." She went to him and kissed his cheek. "Don't be too sad, sweetheart; it's just a game."

"I got *nothing*. The cards were rigged, I swear." He took a long swig of his beer, wiping his mouth with the back of his hand. His eyes were stormy.

"S'okay love." Kim kissed his cheek, then wagged a finger playfully. "It was karma. That's what you get for being overconfident. But if you don't win next time, I'll have to find someone else who knows when to hold 'em and when to—"

His hand moved so fast she had no time to react. The sting of the slap across her face made her gasp. Tears sprang to her eyes and her hand flew to her cheek as she stared at him in shock.

He looked as stunned as she did. They stood still, eyes locked on each other, until he set down his beer and pulled her into a tight embrace. "Kim, I'm so sorry. I'm *so* sorry." His voice cracked. She had no words, her mind was a tangle of shock and fear. "Kim, please forgive me. Do you forgive me? I can't believe—Kim, I'm so sorry." He gave her one final squeeze, then stood back, still holding her by the shoulders. "I always swore I'd never hurt the people I love. But the thought of you leaving me—it freaked me out." His voice shook as he spoke. "Do you forgive me? Please forgive me, Kim."

She swallowed hard, forcing the lump from her throat, and croaked out a response. "Yes. Of course I forgive you."

He wrapped her in his arms again, then gently kissed her throbbing cheek. "Let me get a cool washcloth for your face." She allowed him to lead her to the bedroom and set her on the bed, then watched as he went about ministering to the fallout of his anger. After a few minutes of applying the cold cloth to her face, he pulled back the sheets and tucked her into bed. "Unless you want me to come to bed right now, I'm going to just go and unwind for a little bit in the living room. Is that alright?"

"Sure, that's fine."

"Okay." He planted a soft kiss on her forehead. "I love you, Kim. Again—I'm so sorry."

She gave him a small smile and reached out to hold his hand. "It's okay, Rick. I forgive you."

He smiled and kissed her again, then left the room, shutting the door behind him as he left.

KIM WATCHED THE CLOCK FLIP to midnight. Rick had snuck in half an hour earlier, slipping into bed and keeping close to his edge of the bed. Kim faked sleeping until she heard his light snore, then flipped her pillow and huddled deeper under the sheet despite the warmth of the evening.

Her face had stopped stinging soon after he'd slapped her, but her mind had raced relentlessly. She'd given him everything she had to give. Her secret. Her virginity. Her independence. Her trust. He owned her now, and until tonight she hadn't minded.

But now ...

She sighed and rolled onto her stomach, pulling the pillow over her head and squishing it around her ears. She didn't want to over-react. This relationship was the most precious thing she had. It was worth taking her time to assess the situation and its ramifications.

In a sense, the situation was straightforward: Rick had hit her. Well, *hit* was maybe a bit of an exaggeration. He'd slapped her. Certainly it had been spontaneous—he hadn't come home with the intent of taking his frustration out on her.

And in his defense, she had provoked him. It had been cruel of her to suggest, even as a joke—perhaps *especially* as a joke—that she would leave him for someone else, particularly when his pride was so wounded from his loss. How would she have felt if he'd in-sinuated such a thing to her?

And she had to remember the years he had been abused by his father. An experience like that wasn't easily left behind. It was a miracle he had turned out as normal as he had.

She sighed and rolled to her side, staring at the ring on her hand. She should have kept her mouth shut. She had only herself to blame.

THE NEXT MORNING RICK WAS gone before she awoke. She took her time readying for work, lingering over a bowl of cereal and sorting in vain through her clothes for a new outfit that would hide her cuts but not look as unseasonable. She was dismayed to see a faint purple spot on her cheekbone when she finally shuffled into the bathroom for her shower. *Well, that's what makeup is for.*

Kim felt heavy and gloomy, like a cartoon with a rain cloud above her head. She sat under the shower's spray for too long as she let her thoughts wander, then had to rush to get to the salon. She made a mad dash to her station to ready it before her first client and barely got it all done in time. Helen Toll entered just as she finished preparing her combs, and Kim walked her to the station as the elderly woman launched into a story about her granddaughter and the new boy she was dating. Mrs. Toll was just the client she needed to start with today. She demanded little from Kim besides nods and clucks of sympathy and the occasional "Oh my goodness, *really*?" It gave her time to compose herself and clear her mind.

"... so I told her she should just tell that boy exactly what she thought. It's never too late to be honest, but it's more difficult the longer you wait."

Kim's attention snapped back to her client. "Yes — yes, that's good advice. Very true." She stole a glance at her face in the mirror to make sure the heat in her cheeks wasn't visible. She could still see the faint dark spot beneath her makeup. "So what did she say?"

Mrs. Toll sighed. "Oh, I think she just humored me. It makes me sad, it really does. She's such a precious girl. I don't want to see her mired in a relationship where she can't be herself." She sighed and smiled at Kim in the mirror. "But no one listens to us old biddies." She chuckled. "I think she thinks men hadn't figured out how to be conniving back when I was her age!"

Kim laughed along with her, though her heart wasn't in it. She continued to set the curlers in Helen's wiry silver hair and gently nudged the conversation into more comfortable waters.

Mrs. Toll related another story while Kim finished setting the rollers and walked her to the dryers. After setting her beneath the dryer's helmet, she cleaned her station and went up to the front to wait for her next client.

Bette smiled. "My, aren't we all dolled up."

"Am I?" Kim tried to look surprised.

Bette squinted at her. "Seems like, anyway. Normally you do your makeup so lightly you can barely tell you've got any on. What's the occasion?"

Kim waved her hand as she glanced down at the appointment book. "There isn't one. I must have overdone it. I didn't get to bed until late last night, and the shadows under my eyes this morning refused to be tamed." She pointed to the book. "My next is in ten minutes, right?"

Bette double-checked the book. "Yep."

"Okay, I'm going to run next door. I'll be right back."

"Next door" was a mini-mart where the stylists often grabbed a midday snack or coffee. Kim rarely went there, wanting instead to hang out with her friends between their appointments. But she didn't feel like she could sit at her station like she usually did, and she didn't feel like socializing with the other girls, especially if Bette had noticed the extra makeup today.

She strolled the aisles, stopping only in the limited office supply section where her eyes snagged an X-acto knife. Her arms began to tingle just seeing that silver blade. Why hadn't she thought of that before? She could have left Corrie's paring knife where it belonged.

She slipped one off the hanging display and took it to the front to pay. She took her change and walked back to the salon, her mind not at all on her client but on her purchase and when she could break it in. She could feel the itch in her soul that preceded a cutting session. It inflamed the anger towards both Rick and herself that had been simmering since last night. She had clients all morning — how would she make it until afternoon?

She was combing through her client's wet hair when Bette came by. "Phone message for you." She handed her a pink slip of paper, then began to chat with her client, a friend of hers. Kim glanced at it and the itch began to burn.

Rick called. Wants to take you to lunch. Call to confirm.

Bette looked at Kim. "I can call him back for you if you want. I know you're booked solid until lunch."

"Thanks Bette. Yeah, I'd appreciate that. I'm open at one; tell him he can stop by then."

"Will do."

It was a long three hours. She had to fight to keep her concentration on what she was doing. She left Mrs. Toll under the dryer too long, though the sweet woman didn't even notice or seem to mind when Kim gushed her apologies. She mixed the wrong combination of colors for a client's highlights, thankfully catching it at the last minute. She was a jangle of nerves by the time her last client before lunch left. The image of the blade in her purse loomed large in her mind's eye.

She pulled off her apron and draped it over the back of the chair, then grabbed her purse and went out to the sidewalk to wait for Rick. He was just crossing the parking lot when she came out, and for the first time the sight of him didn't send a shiver of happiness through her.

He smiled and placed a kiss on her unblemished cheek. "Hey babe."

She stared at him, confused. She'd been expecting a sheepish greeting, a little less spring in his step. "Hey."

"You're ready to go?"

"Um, sure. Where to?"

"You can pick, I don't really care."

She suggested the first place that came to mind. "I don't know. Maybe Salsa?"

He nodded. "Sounds good." He took her hand and began to chat as though there was no giant elephant balanced between them. She only half listened as he recounted some workplace drama. Her mind was preoccupied with recalling the details of the night before to assure herself they had actually happened. By his demeanor one would think it had been just a dream. Her free hand slipped up to her cheek to check the bruise, to make sure it hurt.

She was actually surprised when it did.

Maybe I'm wrong for thinking he should still be penitent. After all, he *had* apologized—many times, in fact. Was it really necessary for him to apologize again? If their roles had been reversed, she'd probably be mad that he was still holding on to his anger and expecting more groveling twelve hours later.

Just let it go. Don't dwell on it.

By the time they reached the restaurant Kim had managed to at least pretend she was glad they were having lunch. Honestly, she didn't want to talk to him right now, but she felt guilty for feeling that way and was careful to make sure he didn't know it. The waitress took their menus and refreshed their drinks, but once they were alone Kim focused her attention on the chips and salsa to keep herself from looking irritated. It was taking more energy than she had to mask her annoyance.

"Kim."

She looked at Rick, schooling her features to remain neutral.

He leaned in, reaching for her with his gaze. "Kim, I just wanted to apologize again."

She sagged slightly in her seat, relieved that he hadn't developed some kind of selective amnesia. "Thank you, Rick. And I forgive you, again." She smiled a little, but Rick's face beamed.

He reached down into his pocket and pulled out a small, flat box. "I got you a little something." He slid the box across the table, and Kim couldn't help grinning. "If you don't like them we can take them back and get something else. But I thought they'd match your ring nicely."

She took off the lid and gasped. A pair of solitaire diamond ear-rings sat on black velvet. "Oh my goodness." She pulled out the card and held them up in the light. "Oh, Rick, they're beautiful."

"You like them?"

"Oh, yes. They're perfect. Simple but lovely." She pulled them from the card and put them on. "Do they look okay?"

"Gorgeous."

She sighed. "I'm sorry, too, Rick. I shouldn't have said what I said. If our roles had been reversed I would have gotten mad too."

Rick came to her chair and kissed her. "Forget it, sweetheart. This is all behind us now, right?"

"Right."

"Good." He sat back down and reached for her hands across the table. "What do you say we start planning that wedding?"

TEN

Today will be the day, right God?

It was the same prayer Joshua had said each morning for the last two weeks. He was bound to be right eventually. At least, he hoped so.

He'd sent in his resume weeks ago, but still had not heard from the woman he'd served at the deli. He was grateful for his job, but Lori was pressing him to join their staff as a permanent member, and he knew it wasn't where he wanted to be long-term. But if not here, then where? No one else was calling for interviews, no other jobs were falling into his lap. Meanwhile they were living on a shoestring and still waiting for the house to sell. The person who had made an offer changed his mind, and two open houses later they still had no new offers.

Joshua pulled into the lot behind the deli and parked. Before going in, he closed his eyes and prayed for Scott, who was showing the house to someone that morning. *Please God, please let it sell soon. And then show me where to move!*

Maddie was still unclear on the concept of their relocation. They had boxed up some toys and clothes and books to declutter the house, and she asked every week when they could bring them back out. She'd also gotten it in her head somehow that one day they would simply up and move, so many mornings she greeted him with, "Are we leaving today? I don't want to move yet!" Sometimes she followed it with tears, sometimes just a sad face that looked all the more pathetic when on a child.

Joshua rubbed a hand over his face and hauled himself out of the car. Lori was already in the kitchen when he got into the deli. "Oh good, you're here," she said. "Sit with me a minute." He followed her into the office and sat on the ancient desk chair in the corner. Lori perched herself on the edge of her desk and sighed. "Okay, so, we got a resume for the manager position, and she looks like a perfect fit."

His stomach sank. "Ah."

"Are you sure you won't reconsider? Because I would still prefer you over training someone again."

Joshua managed a smile. "I'm flattered that you consider me such a good employee, but—I just don't think it's where I'm supposed to be."

She nodded. "I understand."

"So when will you hire her?"

She sat back a bit, folded her arms over her chest. "Well, we haven't even interviewed her yet. But I'm hoping we can get her in here by Wednesday."

"Wow. Three days?"

"Five with the weekend."

"True."

"I feel awful, Joshua."

He chuckled. "Don't—I'm the one turning down the job."

"I know, but still."

"Yeah." He shrugged. "Gotta do what I've gotta do."

But an hour later, he felt the panic setting in. It was Friday— where would he find a job on a weekend? On his lunch break he called the temporary staffing agencies he'd worked with, but there weren't any positions open for him. He told them to reactivate him in their system and prayed he'd get a call Monday morning.

He was on his way to pick up Maddie when his cell rang. "Hey, it's Scott," said his realtor. "We got a bid!"

Joshua wasn't sure if he should be excited or not. "Is it any good?"

"Only thirty thousand under asking price."

Joshua groaned. He'd already lowered the price once. Thirty-thousand lower than that was a painful loss—but it was a solid offer, and he wasn't going to turn it down.

"Alright then. Let's go for it."

He hung up and gripped the steering wheel. "At least one thing seems to be working out."

He picked up Maddie and let her chatter all the way home, then asked her over a bowl of Rice Dream, "So how about if tomorrow we go to look for a new place for you and me to make our own?"

She licked her spoon, eyes down. "You mean a new house to live in?"

"Yeah."

She took another bite, then nodded. "Okay."

He ruffled her hair and kissed the top of her head. "I love you, Maddie."

"I love you too, Dad. Will God and Mom know where to find us when we move?"

He smiled. "Oh yes. God knows where you are all the time; you never have to worry about him losing you."

"What about Mom?"

"I'll bet Mom sees you too. And she knew Ann Arbor pretty well; I don't think she'd lose track of us."

"Okay, good. Because I told her we were moving and she said she wanted to come."

These kinds of talks made him uncomfortable. He didn't know what was normal and what signaled some kind of issue. He didn't know much about how children grieved, but talking to—and "hearing"—the deceased seemed like it could go either way. "What else does Mom say?"

"She says she loves me. And she sings 'If You're Happy and You Know It.' And she told me God is bigger than our house."

He relaxed. "Wow."

"Yeah. And she said to watch out because you like to give me too much Rice Dream."

He laughed. He had to. It was either that or break down and cry.

Saturday morning Joshua snagged the paper before even getting dressed. He spread the classifieds and real estate sections on the dining room table and scoured them for condos. He was disappointed to see so little in his price range. *At least it won't be an exhausting day.*

After calling and making appointments to view a few of them, he woke Maddie and fixed a special pancake breakfast to put her in a good mood. He showered while she ate in front of Saturday morning cartoons, then dressed himself and her and pried her away from the television. "House hunting time, kiddo! Shoes on and let's vamoose."

"I'm not a moose."

"No, you're right — you're a caribou."

She giggled. "Hey Dad?"

"What sweetheart?"

"Can we get a dog when we get the new house?"

He froze halfway out the door. *Where did that come from?* As he buckled her in, Maddie told him that her classmate Christopher got a dog when his family moved. Joshua assured her he'd think about it.

He drove to the first apartment on the list, his mind buzzing between what his priorities should be when looking for a new place and the ramifications of getting a dog. If it helped Maddie to adjust better, maybe it would be worth the extra expense.

The first apartment turned out to be a great disappointment. Run-down and dodgy — "classic cabinetry and fixtures" turned out to be code for "haven't been updated since 1979" and the neighborhood gave him the creeps, even in the daylight. He hustled Maddie out the door and on to the next unit, which was a significant improvement. The only downside was the distance to Maddie's school. It hadn't looked bad on the map, but now that he'd driven it he knew it would tack on at least fifteen minutes to their morning drive, and they already had problems getting there on time.

The third and fourth condos were passable, but nothing that excited him. By the time they were back on the road he could tell Maddie was reaching her limit. "One more, kiddo," he said. "Then we'll head home."

He pulled into the parking lot of the last apartment of the day and saw the *For Rent* sign in the window of the lower unit. It was one in from the end, with a bland view of the parking lot. He could see the telltale signs of children a couple windows down—faded construction paper sun-catchers in windows, smudgy handprints low on the glass. There was a greenbelt between the building and the parking lot, with lush grass and a beautiful maple at the end. He could see Maddie running around with her friends there—maybe with the kids down the way.

He pressed the intercom button and announced himself, then ushered Maddie through the security door and down the hall. A middle-aged man opened the door and welcomed them in. "Thanks for stopping by," he said.

Joshua smiled and looked over the apartment. "So—tell me about the place."

The man handed him a flier with information about the unit and led him and Maddie around the rooms. It didn't boast a lot of amenities, but it was clean and had been kept up well. And unlike the other places they'd seen that day, he could imagine the place with their furniture, their knick-knacks, their belongings strewn around in the slightly sloppy way they tended to live. It was cozy, but friendly. His spirits began to rise.

"It looks like there are some kids down the hall," he said. "Do you know how old they are?"

The man nodded. "Oh yeah. Carlotta and Jorges Jiminez. Nice folks. They've got three kids—two boys and a girl. Not sure of the ages, but not real old—I think the biggest is maybe seven?"

Joshua smiled. "Sounds promising."

"Yeah—there are others in the building too. Carlotta knows 'em all. See 'em running around on the grass when the weather's nice, or in the snow."

They finished their tour and Joshua shook the man's hand. "I appreciate you letting us look around. I'm not quite ready to move just yet; we're trying to sell our place right now. But once I know that's taken care of I'll give you a call. I really like the place."

"Glad to know it. I think——"

There was a muffled sound of someone shouting. Joshua looked out the window, then at the man, who looked sheepish. "What was that?"

"That was the neighbors. Walls are a little thin."

It was a small flaw in an otherwise perfect find. He promised the realtor he'd call with his answer and ushered Maddie back to the car.

He pulled into the garage just as his phone rang. "It's a done deal, Joshua," said Scott. "Congratulations, you've sold your house."

Joshua let that sink in for a moment, then nodded. "Good. That's really good. Thanks, Scott."

"So what do you think? Time to start looking for a place, huh?"

Joshua smiled as he unbuckled Maddie from her seat. "Actually the timing couldn't be better," he said. "We just found a place today."

Kim and Rick sank into wedding planning bliss after putting the slapping incident to rest. Rick conceded to waiting a year, and Kim conceded to making it a small affair——an easy concession to make since neither of them had many friends. Kim splurged on bridal magazines, studying dresses and invitation templates in her spare time. Rick occasionally peeked over her shoulder and added his two cents, but for the most part left the planning to her.

The incident faded from Kim's mind along with the mark on her face, and for the next few weeks she felt once again like she had everything she could ever want. The haunting face returned regularly to her dreams, however, and her X-acto knife rarely stayed in its hiding place long. She'd become an expert at hiding the scars and bandages from Rick——he didn't care how undressed she was for sex, and she justified the long sleeves on a tendency to always be cold. It helped that he kept the apartment like a meat locker. She was thankful for that small advantage.

She weathered a few close calls with the Club girls, however. They were an intuitive bunch. One particularly hot afternoon they were sweltering in the gym where the A/C had busted, and when Kim didn't push up her sleeves despite the sweat dripping down her neck, Mercedes skewered her with her intense stare and said, "Kim, you're going to overheat if you don't change shirts or something. Why are you always in long sleeves?"

Kim made an excuse about not having anything to change into and switched the subject as quickly as she could. But Mercedes wasn't buying it; she could tell. She gave them a fictitious reason why she had to leave as soon as Club was over to avoid being cornered by her, then crossed her fingers that Mercedes would forget by the next time they met.

She had also avoided telling them about the engagement, going so far as to remove her ring before their meetings. It wasn't that she thought there was any reason why they shouldn't be engaged—she just didn't want to send a message to the girls that quick engagements were a good idea. They were surrounded by women who had jumped into relationships with hardly any thought to their futures. She wanted to give them a different model to follow. Even if it meant fudging a little.

But she did highlight for them all the healthy aspects of her and Rick's relationship, to show the girls the kinds of things they should be looking for in a boyfriend. Like how he watched out for her, always wanting to know where she was going and when she'd be back so he'd figure out sooner if something had happened to her. Or how he tried to make her life easier, even in little ways—like how he ordered for her in restaurants or told her what to make for dinner so she didn't have to come up with something on her own. And how, when they fought, he always apologized.

Not that they fought often. Actually, they never fought at all. The most negative interaction they'd had was the night he'd slapped her. Before then, and since, life with Rick had been perfect.

So when he hit her again, she was just as surprised as she had been the first time.

Again, she had only herself to blame. Rick came home from

work in a bad mood, complaining about his boss who had criticized his work for the third time in the past few weeks. Kim tried to just listen and be supportive, but the solution seemed obvious to her. "Why don't you just sit him down and ask him what he expects? I mean, it just sounds like you're both misunderstanding each other and not communicating clearly. He obviously has an image in mind that he's going for—"

"Wait a minute. You're taking his side?"

"No, honey, I'm not taking sides at all. I'm just saying you should—"

"You have no idea what business is like, so don't tell me what I should do."

She cocked her head and put a hand on her hip. "Rick, you're being unreasonable."

He backhanded her across the mouth. The inside of her lip split on her teeth; she tasted blood on her tongue.

"Don't disrespect me! If you're going to be my wife, you should be supporting me, not trying to tell me what to do." He shook his head, ran his hand through his hair. "Why do you make me do stuff like this?"

She'd run into the bedroom, locking herself inside and throwing herself on the bed to cry. Fuming, she asked herself why he had done this again, but then realized he'd told her exactly why. And he was right, of course; she knew it before the tears had dried on her pillow. Why hadn't she just given him a hug, told him his boss was a jerk, like other girlfriends did? Why did she have to try to fix problems that weren't hers?

When she emerged from the bedroom he wrapped his arms around her and apologized. She cut him off. "No, sweetheart, you were totally right. I should have been more supportive. I haven't had a lot of practice at being someone's girlfriend. I'm still learning. Forgive me?"

He kissed her and held her close. "Of course, of course. And I'm sorry I let my anger get the best of me again. I'm working on it, I promise."

She forgave him, and the next day a box of chocolates and roses were delivered to her at work. When the girls at the salon asked what the occasion was, she said, "He just loves me." Because he did.

Right?

The third time wasn't her fault—at least, she didn't think it was. Despite his humiliating loss at his first poker night, Rick had continued to join the group every week, and one night in late June it was his turn to host. She had planned to disappear so she wasn't in the way, but Rick wanted her to make snacks for the guests, so she hung out in the kitchen putting together hot dogs and nachos while the men played cards. When she brought a plate of food to the table Rick wrapped an arm around her waist and held her tighter than necessary. "These better be good, woman."

She bristled as the other men laughed along with him. One of them, however, smiled at her and nodded. "Thanks for the snacks, Kim. Usually our girlfriends and wives go into hiding when we get together. It's nice to have someone cooking for us."

Her wounded pride was somewhat soothed. She smiled in gratitude. "Thank you. I'm glad to do it." She wormed her way out of Rick's grasp, which had gotten tighter, and shot him a look of annoyance as she went back to the kitchen. After preparing more food for the men, she disappeared into the bedroom to read. Their raucous laughter and groans of defeat sounded off and on for another couple hours, and when she heard their activity winding down she put her book away and got ready for bed. She heard the front door lock as she emerged from the bathroom and was preparing to get into bed when Rick came into the room.

"So what was that about?" he said. His eyes were dark and his face set with tense anger.

"What was what about?" Her stomach knotted as she thought back over the night, trying to pinpoint her transgression.

"Give me a break, you knew what you were doing—if I hadn't been holding on to you, you would have thrown yourself into Chris's lap."

"What? Rick, I have no—"

He slapped her hard across the face. She cradled her cheek in her hand, staring at him in open-mouthed shock. "Don't lie to me. You made me look like a fool in front of them."

"Rick, I didn't, all I did—"

He backhanded her. "Shut up! Stop trying to make excuses."

She backed into the bed, fell onto the mattress, and scrambled up onto her knees to avoid being lower than him. He seemed taller, menacing. She'd never seen him like this.

She put her hands up, trying to stop his advance. "Rick, I swear, listen to me. I was just saying thank you. That's all! I wasn't trying to flirt—"

He grabbed her wrist and pulled her forward off the bed. She screamed, catching herself on the floor with her other hand and wrenching her arm in the process. He yanked her to her back and leaned down, his red face just inches from hers. "Don't ever do it again, do you understand? Don't ever look at another man like that again." He straightened, still staring down at her. "He wouldn't want you anyway. A religious guy like him would never love a murderer."

Her breath caught in her chest. The throb in her wrist and shoulder and the burn in her cheeks were forgotten in the face of his cruel comment. He spit one last insult at her as he left the room, slamming the door behind him.

Her wrist and shoulder throbbed. She hoisted herself onto the bed and eased herself between the sheets, then burst into tears that seemed to bubble up from all the way down in her gut. But it wasn't the pain that brought on the crying. It was the fact that Rick had thrown her guilt and sin—the secret she had shared with him, believing he would help her bear the weight—back in her face like a weapon. And the fact that he was right.

Who else would ever want her besides Rick? She was lucky he hadn't kicked her to the curb as soon as she'd spilled her story. She was a murderer—a worthless, cowardly killer who didn't deserve half the blessings she had received.

For once she didn't long to carve her grief in her arms. The ache in her body was punishment enough. And as she laid in the bed, shivering despite her long-sleeved pajamas, it dawned on her that she had gotten what was coming to her. She had run for seven years, putting up with the nightmares and the guilt, but now she was paying for her sins. Karma had finally caught up.

She closed her eyes against the dark, willing sleep to come. But as the truth sank in that she was finally being punished like she deserved, her fear slowly melted into relief.

KIM AWOKE TO PAIN. She sucked in her breath as she hauled herself upright and out of bed, biting her lip to keep quiet so she didn't wake Rick. Her reflection in the bathroom mirror told her she'd be spending a lot of extra time on her makeup that morning.

Her aches eased a bit under the hot shower spray, and once she was toweled off and dressed she didn't feel too badly. She ate breakfast in silence, her mind churning through the events from the night before and continuing to process the realization she'd had that was already easing the guilt she had carried for so long.

Her makeup took twice as long as usual to apply. Both cheekbones sported purple blooms that fought to be seen beneath foundation and concealer. As the powders layered thicker and thicker Kim knew there was no way she'd be able to hide the bruises well enough to fool anyone. The girls at the salon would be all over her asking what had happened. She had Club that afternoon as well, and those girls would sink their teeth into any kind of personal drama and not let go until they were satisfied with the story.

So what's my story?

Giving up on hiding her injuries, she chucked the foundation and concealer back in the bag and continued with the rest of her makeup. As she brushed on blush and dabbed eyeliner, she concocted a cover for her bruises and practiced how she would say it so as not to encourage more questions. Her wrist and shoulder were still sensitive as well, so she took that into account as she crafted her tale. When she was done, she rehearsed a few times so the explanation would sound natural.

She didn't make it past the reception desk before Bette and Rumiko were clucking over her face. "Girl, what happened? You poor thing!" Rumiko said as she winced at Kim's face.

"Oh Kim!" Bette said, her voice low with concern. "That looks painful."

Kim nodded a little and sighed. "Yeah, it is a little bit. But not too bad. Rick and I were rearranging furniture last night, and he's got this really tall bookshelf that's heavier than it looks." The girls groaned in sympathy, and she waited to see if more description was necessary.

"A bookshelf fell on you?" Rumiko shook her head. "Oh man, that makes my skin tingle! Oww!" She gave a little shudder and tottered away on her high heels.

Bette wrinkled her nose. "Wow, really—a bookshelf?"

"Yeah. Wrenched my wrist and shoulder a little too. It's not terrible, but I'm not looking forward to how they'll feel by the end of the day." She made a face of mild irritation and then changed the subject. "So has anyone brought up the Fourth of July party for this year? It's next week and we still haven't set anything up."

"No, not yet." Bette pulled her date book from her purse. "What time did we all meet last year? I can't remember."

"Some of us did dinner beforehand, around six, then met at the park at eight. Should we just do that again?"

"That sounds fun, sure. I'll let the others know. Significant others are invited?"

"Of course." She glanced back at her station. "I need to get set up; my first appointment is going to be here any minute." Kim went back to her station, sighing with relief that she'd passed the first test. She'd called in sick at the Club before coming in to work so she wouldn't have to face the girls that afternoon. She couldn't deal with them right now, and if she waited a couple days the marks might be faded enough that they'd never even see them.

Her first client arrived before she finished prepping. Full of apologies, she led the woman back to the sinks to wash her hair, and by the time she was wrapping the towel around the woman's dripping hair her wrist and shoulder were throbbing. She clenched her teeth as she combed through the woman's long, thick tresses, then made an excuse that allowed her to go back to the supply room to massage her wrist and arm.

She took a few deep breaths. *Penance. This is your penance. It's hardly anything considering what you did. Grin and bear it.* She went back out to her client and apologized yet again, then did her best to concentrate on her work and not on the pain.

It was a long day. Her shoulder screamed if her arm was up for more than a few seconds at a time — a difficult position to avoid. Lunch couldn't come soon enough, and her only consolation was that her day at the salon ended in two more hours.

Suzie came back to her station just before her first post-lunch appointment. "Rumiko told me what happened, you poor thing. How are you doing?"

Kim put on a brave face. "It's going alright."

Suzie wasn't buying it. "You don't look alright."

"I don't?"

Suzie gave her a small smile. "Want something for the pain? I'm sure I've got some Tylenol or something in my purse."

"No, that's okay. Thanks though." This was all part of the punishment. She just had to learn how to deal with it. It was the least she could do.

But, by the time she got home, she'd decided six hours of near-constant agony without painkillers was plenty. She popped three ibuprofen and crawled into bed. *Don't worry, you have a lifetime to ramp up your tolerance.* Twenty minutes later, the medicine kicked in and the pain began to ease. She fell asleep with a smile on her lips.

KIM AWAKENED TO THE SOUND of the door closing. Her eyes flew open. She looked to the clock and saw it was already five-thirty. She struggled to sit up without using either arm and sat on the edge of the bed for a minute before standing. Even with the ibuprofen the pain was still there, and now she felt groggy from her nap.

She shuffled out to the living room and found Rick on the couch. "You're not at Club?" he asked through a mouthful of chips.

Hello to you too. "I canceled."

"Oh."

She waited for him to ask why, or to say anything at all about last night, but he went back to watching the sitcom rerun he had playing on the television. She went to the kitchen and pulled a package of hamburger patties from the freezer and a box of instant mashed potatoes from the pantry. She fixed dinner in silence, but found herself keeping an eye on him, stopping what she was doing and holding her breath in anticipation whenever he shifted in his seat. When he failed to address her, she went nearly limp with relief and resumed her cooking with renewed attention to detail so that everything about the meal was exactly the way he liked it.

She waited until a commercial break to announce dinner was ready, having spent the last three minutes setting the table and arranging the food on his plate as though she were auditioning at a fancy restaurant. He shut off the television and came to the table, kissing her lightly on the cheek before sitting down. She waited again for him to acknowledge the elephant in the room, but he acted as though nothing was different.

"Mm, great burger, babe."

"Thanks."

"How was your day?"

"Um, it was ... fine." *I'm not bringing it up if he's not.*

"Good, good." He shoveled coleslaw into his mouth and flashed her a smile as he chewed. She didn't know whether to brace herself or relax, but she answered his smile with a brief one of her own and began to eat. He talked about his day, about a movie he'd seen an ad for and wanted to take her to, about completely normal and mundane things that left Kim wondering if she'd dreamed her injuries into existence.

When they finished she picked up his plate along with hers, then nearly dropped hers when her wrist gave out. She gasped in pain and set the plate down sharply on the table. He frowned. "What's wrong? You alright?"

She looked at him askance. "My wrist hurts."

"Really? What did you do?" The look on her face seemed to jog his memory. "Ohh. From last night. Right." He drained the last of his beer and picked up the plates. "Here, I'll get those." He cleared the table while she sat in stunned silence. "Yeah, I'm sorry about that, babe. I think I had a couple too many beers last night. I'll try not to do that again." He came back to the table to retrieve the rest of the dishes and planted a kiss on her temple. "You look really tired. Why don't you go to bed and I'll take care of the dishes, hm?"

"Oh. Okay. Thanks."

She wandered back into the bedroom and changed into her pajamas. It wasn't even seven yet, but she felt like she could sleep until noon the next day. She swallowed another dose of medicine and laid herself down with care so as not to aggravate her shoulder. Before she fell asleep, she realized he hadn't given her a gift.

BY THE FOURTH OF JULY her face was fine. She'd gotten a brace for her wrist and learned how to cut and style with her elbow against her body to keep her shoulder from getting too much of a workout. Nothing else was ever said about the incident, and Kim had come to not only accept that it had happened, but to actually appreciate it. For the first time in months, she'd had no desire to cut herself. Her arms were healing well, and besides the faint scars left from some of her more industrious slices, there was little to indicate anything had ever happened. She was almost ready to venture out in short sleeves again.

During the afternoon of July third, Kim and her friends spent their free time planning the next evening's festivities. Emma and Rumiko made an executive decision to replace a restaurant dinner with a potluck picnic and put together a sign-up sheet for assigning the dishes. When Emma came around to Kim, she waved the sign-up and said, "What can I put you down for, girl? Got a secret potato salad recipe you wanna break out?"

Kim laughed and continued to wrap her client's hair in foils. "Not so much. But you can put us down for it anyway. I know where I can get some that's really good."

"Great. Anything else you want to bring?"

"I'll bring a couple two-liters, too. That alright?"

"Sure thing." Emma made the notes on the sign-up. "Alrighty then, tomorrow evening, six o'clock at the park. Bette said to look for the three oak trees when you get there. She's going to stake out a place there early in the morning so we have a place to sit."

"Sounds fun. Thanks, Emma."

"You're welcome. Is Rick coming?"

She grinned. "Yeah, though he gave me some eye rolling when I told him about it. I promised there would be other guys there— Mitch is coming, right?"

"Yes, but only because I promised to make cupcakes for dessert."

"Ooh, good one. That'll make Rick happy too."

She was nervous about her friends meeting Rick, and vise versa, but was also a little relieved it was finally happening. Her salon friends were the only friends she had, and while she didn't do much with them outside of work, they still meant a lot to her. They'd all ribbed her when she'd shown off her ring, saying she'd bought it herself since they'd never met the man. But given recent events, she'd been afraid to introduce them, afraid they wouldn't measure up in his eyes.

On the way home that afternoon she picked up a couple quarts of potato salad and some Coke from her grocery store. On a whim she tossed in a frozen pizza for dinner and ice cream for dessert. It had been awhile since they'd had either one, and she didn't feel like cooking. Rick was a fan of homemade meals, and while she didn't mind cooking, it was not among her favorite things to do. She had a feeling that, if Rick could have his way, she'd have a hot dinner coming out of the oven half an hour after he got home every night, like some 1950s housewife. She figured it was an attempt to have something he was denied during his childhood—framed that way, she didn't mind at all.

They ate their dessert over a game of Scrabble, which he won by a landslide. "Spelling never was one of my strengths," she admitted. "But you've got to admit I didn't do too bad given I had so many vowels."

"I'll give you that, yes." He scraped the last of the triple fudge from his bowl. "Hey, it's only eight o'clock—wanna go to a movie?"

She smiled as she stacked his empty bowl in hers and took them to the kitchen. They never went out in the evenings. "Sure! What should we see?"

"Trevor said 'Dead to the World' was good. I'll check the times and see where it's playing." He picked up the phone and began to dial.

Kim wrinkled her nose as her vision of laughing the evening away at a romantic comedy faded to black in her mind. "That's the scary horror one, right?

"Yeah."

"I'm not really a horror movie kind of girl. I'll have nightmares."

"You already have nightmares; maybe this'll give them some variety."

"Rick!"

He began writing down times and places on a notepad by the phone. "Oh come on, Kim, don't be a wuss. It's a movie, it's not real."

She didn't bother replying, because she knew it wouldn't change anything. That was another thing she'd learned.

They drove to the theater with the windows down and the radio blaring a hard rock band Rick liked. Kim cringed every time they pulled up to a stoplight and got dirty looks from other drivers. Rick never seemed to notice. They joined the mostly male crowd just before the previews started, sitting six rows from the front on the aisle—or at least, Rick was on the aisle. Kim was stuck beside a greasy teenaged boy with the stink of cigarette smoke wafting off him.

They leaned their heads back as far as they could to take in the entire screen when the previews started. Action flick explosions nearly blinded her at this distance, and every preview seemed to have at least two. She had a headache by the time the movie started. She closed her eyes and leaned against Rick's shoulder, but he shrugged her off. She sighed and hunkered down in her seat, trying not to get too close to the teenager so Rick wouldn't think she was trying to flirt with him.

Half an hour into the movie she was as disturbed as she was willing to get. "I'll be back later," she said as she hopped over his lap and into the aisle.

"Where are you going?" he hissed.

"Bathroom, and then ..." She waved her hand vaguely. "I don't know. I'll be back later."

He waved her away and she ran to the door, the sound of a woman's blood-curdling scream following her through the doors and raising goosebumps on her arms. After visiting the washroom, she walked down the hall, passing the doors to the theater where Rick was, and turning into the next one down instead, where a romantic comedy was playing.

She hadn't watched a movie in ages, either at home or in the theater. She snuck to an empty aisle seat, feeling conspicuous sitting amidst the couples and groups of girlfriends that filled the seats around her. She sank down in the seat, eyes half shut from the headache, and watched the typical story unfold. She kept waiting for the heartwarming moment, the "awwww"-inspiring climax, the warm, fuzzy feeling a good romantic comedy always gave her, but when the heroine finally got her man, Kim just felt underwhelmed. When the lights went up, she felt as empty as she had when she came in.

Relationships are nothing like that. She'd always known movies didn't reflect real life, but she'd never seen a romance while actually in a relationship, and now she realized just how far off the mark Hollywood was. She shuffled out the door with the rest of the crowd, then back into the theater where Rick was. She was just in time to see a severed head come rolling down the stairs of the haunted house. She groaned as she walked back to her seat.

Rick glared at her when she sat back down, as did the teenager who had sprawled his long legs into the space in front of her seat. Rick didn't speak to her until the movie had ended. "Where were you that whole time?"

"I told you I was going to go out for a while. I got a headache being this close, and the movie was freaking me out. I went next door to 'Love and Marriage.'"

Rick snorted. "Was it as lame as its title?"

"No. But it wasn't what I was hoping it would be."

"Those kinds of movies are such a waste of time. They're never realistic. They just set women up for disappointment."

It was Kim's turn to snort. "You've got that right."

Rick either didn't catch her meaning or else didn't care about her disillusionment. "That's why I like movies like 'Dead to the World.' They're completely over the top and don't try in any way, shape, or form to be realistic."

She opened her mouth to reply, but gave up. She didn't feel like arguing, and she knew there was no point. She let him lead her back to the car, feeling glum and moody and dissatisfied with the evening.

Oh well. At least they had the picnic tomorrow.

Kim was up before Rick the next morning. She had never been able to sleep in on her days off, but Rick had no problem tacking on an extra couple hours when he didn't have to work. She tried not to be jealous as she drank her coffee.

Three children decked out in patriotic colors skipped past the window, followed by their hand-holding parents. Kim recognized them as the family that lived down the hall. Their kids were always out playing on the greenbelt during the day. They looked friendly, and she sometimes imagined what it would be like to have a child and get together with women like her for playdates. Not that they planned on having kids anytime soon.

She watched the family as they tromped through the grass towards the sidewalk. The little one tripped and began to wail; the mother picked her up and kissed her hair as they followed the rest of the kids. Tears formed in Kim's eyes, and she drew away from the window in surprise. It had been a long time since a display of motherly love had made her cry.

She drained the rest of her coffee and went to take her shower. Rick was awake when she got out, and she made him breakfast and joined him at the table while he ate. "So what's the plan for the day?" she asked as he finished his waffles. "I figure if we left here by 5:45 we'd get to the picnic by six, though the parking there might be a little dicey, so maybe 5:30 is better in case we have to walk far."

He pushed his empty plate away and shook his head. "Yeah, I've changed my mind. I really don't want to go tonight."

Kim frowned. "What? Why not?"

"I'm just not in the mood to meet a bunch of strangers. And I'm not that into fireworks."

"But I really want my friends to meet you—and for you to meet them. And it's a potluck; they're counting on me for some of the food."

"What, that potato salad I saw in there? They can live without it."

"Well, and the drinks."

"A couple bottles of pop aren't going to be missed."

She sighed. "Well look, if you don't want to go, that's fine, but these are my friends and I want to hang out with them. I've been looking forward to this. I'll just go alone."

"No, stay home with me. We can rent a movie or something, maybe go to dinner."

"Rick, I don't want to stay home, I want to go out."

"No."

She stared at him. "No? Like I'm twelve and you're my father?"

He took a moment to reply and she knew she was on dangerous ground. "No," he finally said, "like I'm your fiancé and I am a higher priority than your friends."

He had her there. She fought tears as she grabbed the plate and carried it back to the kitchen to wash. "Fine. I'll call Emma. Maybe she can come pick up the food at least."

He shrugged. "Whatever. We'll go out tonight, get some dinner and bring in a movie."

"Sure, whatever you want." Her voice was flat.

"Aw, c'mon Kim, don't be like that."

"Like what? Like I'm disappointed? Well I'm sorry, but I am. And I don't think that's unreasonable, seeing as I've had these plans for awhile now and you're suddenly pulling them out from under me."

"Well I'm sorry if you were expecting me to just follow you around like some hungry puppy."

"I never expected that! What would make you even think that? All I'm saying is that I want to go out with my friends. If you don't want to, then fine, don't. But I'm not some slave to your fancy. If I want to go out, I'm going to go out."

It didn't matter that she knew how this was going to end; she couldn't help pushing a little and asserting herself. The tension in her belly coiled like a cobra, preparing for the onslaught that was sure to come.

She saw it in his face first. How his eyes narrowed, how his jaw seemed to jut a fraction further. "Don't push me, Kim."

"I'm not pushing you, Rick. But I'm going tonight."

"No you're not." The words were bullets dinging her flimsy armor. "You're staying home."

They stared at each other over the kitchen counter. How far did she dare to go? She breathed hard through her nose, her chest heaving as though she'd sprinted a mile. "No."

He sprang from his chair, and it was instantly clear to her she'd made a mistake. She was trapped in the kitchen. She shrieked as he lunged and grabbed her, his fingers digging into her arms.

He dragged her to the bedroom and threw her on the bed, then slammed the door behind him. "*No?* You told me *no?*" She scrambled across the bed and jumped to her feet on the other side, where she was trapped once more. He shoved the bed, roaring, and it slammed into her knees, pinning her against the wall. He clambered over the lumpy mattress and grabbed a handful of her hair, then yanked her face back to his when she tried to slide away against the wall. "You *never* tell me no. *Never*. I tell you to come to me, you do it. I tell you to lie down, you do it. I tell you you're gonna cook me a seven-course meal, you do it, because you are as good as married to me, and when a husband speaks, his wife listens. Got it?"

"Okay, okay!" He gave her head a shove, then let go of her hair and crawled back over the bed, leaving her to struggle out from behind the bed and collapse on it, shaking.

It was all her fault, as usual, and she knew it. He'd even told her flat-out not to push him, and she had. What had made her defy him?

She mopped the tears from her cheeks with the bedspread and pushed herself upright. Her head throbbed, though her knees didn't hurt like she thought they would. She pushed up her sleeves and saw blue bruises where his fingers had gripped her. The sight made her cuss. She'd been so close to wearing short sleeves.

"Kim, where were you last night?"

"I'm so sorry, Emma. I just wasn't feeling well. I was going to call you but by the time I decided not to go, I figured you'd already left. Did you guys have enough pop?"

"Yeah, we were fine. Are you okay now? What was wrong?"

"A stomach bug, I think. I woke up feeling a little off, and it just got worse as the day went on. I slept alright last night, though, and I feel better this morning." She shrugged. "Just one of those weird things. I'm glad it's gone now, though. I have Club tonight."

She went back to her station, surprised at how easily the lie had rolled off her tongue. She hadn't given it much thought beforehand. She was getting good at it.

The other girls were glad to see her doing alright and added their sympathies to Emma's. The day passed without incident, and after her two o'clock appointment she cleaned her station and went to Club.

She played pool with Kea and Tandi as they waited for everyone to arrive, then they claimed a corner in the learning center and sprawled on the floor.

Mercedes was the first to notice. "Kim! That ring! When did you get engaged?"

Kim groaned in her head and put on a smile while scrambling for a response as the girls grabbed at her hand and inspected the diamond. "Yesterday," she lied. "Under the fireworks." The girls let loose with a collective "Awwww!" and assaulted her with questions.

"So when's the wedding?"

"Next July. Probably on the Fourth."

More dramatic sighs.

"How did he do it? What did he say?"

"He waited until the first firework explosion, then took my hand and slipped it on my finger and whispered, 'Marry me?' "

"That's so romantic!" they chorused, which sent them into a giggling fit.

"Can we come to the wedding?"

"Egypt!" Mercedes glared at her. "That is so rude."

"What? I'm just asking."

"And what if you're not invited, you're gonna make her say it to your face right here and now?"

"Ladies, please." She smiled. "We're going to keep it small, so I don't know if I'll be able to invite you or not. But it's a whole year away, so we'll just have to see when we get closer to the date."

"So you two gonna do it then?"

"Kea!" The other girls all chastised her together.

"Hey, she always says we can ask her anything, so I'm asking."

"That's a little personal, Kea," Kim said.

"Ah ha! So you are," Kea said, smug.

Kim rolled her eyes. "Moving on ..."

"I'm never getting married," Mercedes said. "I don't want some man thinking he's the boss of me."

"It's not like that when you're in love," said La-Neesa. "You're both equal. No one is the boss. Right, Kim?"

"Well, yes, that's the way it's supposed to be." She hoped her discomfort wasn't obvious on her face.

Tandi stared at Kim. "So how did you know he was the one, Kim?"

"There's no such thing as 'the one,'" Mercedes said. "It's mathematically illogical."

"What are you talking about math for?"

"If everyone only had one person they could be in love with, then what happens when a few people make a mistake and go with the wrong person? Then it throws it off for everybody."

La-Neesa snorted. "Well that would explain why there are so many divorces."

"She has a point," said Joelle.

"We're totally off-topic," said Tandi. She turned back to Kim. "Let me rephrase: how did you know you wanted to marry him?"

"Because ... because he loves me." They didn't look convinced, so she plowed ahead. "He loves me, and I love him. We understand each other — we were both in foster care, so we both understand what kind of messed-up histories we have and are willing to make allowances for each other when our baggage gets the best of us. We're a good match, personality-wise." She shrugged. "We just work well together."

The girls looked at her, unimpressed. "That isn't nearly as romantic as I thought it would be," said Egypt.

Kim saw the opportunity for a good life lesson. "Let me pass along a little wisdom, woman to woman," she said, eliciting snickers. "What you see in the movies, and on television, is not how love really is. There aren't strings playing in the background. It doesn't fade to black when you kiss. In between the sweet moments is just … life. And sometimes life is messy and very unromantic. So don't go through life looking for the guy that makes you feel like bursting into song, like you're living in a musical. Look for the one that you don't mind being with when things are boring, and when you've got the flu, and when you're arguing over what to do that weekend. If you still want to be with that person after those times, then you've found someone worth marrying."

She let that sink in for a moment, then promptly changed the subject before lightning struck her down.

ELEVEN

Joshua hadn't expected to tear up as he pulled out of the driveway for the last time. He was glad Maddie was staying at a friend's house for the day—he hated to get emotional in front of her. They'd already shared a box of tissues that morning as he'd dressed her for her playdate. He'd hoped it would be less traumatic moving everything as-is rather than boxing it all up first, but just hearing she'd be coming home to a new house and not to this one had brought on a meltdown. Her distress had triggered his own tears, and they'd cuddled together for awhile and wept.

At least she'd expressed some acceptance of the new place. He'd taken her to the apartment a couple times to familiarize her with the property and neighborhood, and they'd chosen the paint for her walls the day before. The last time they'd been there, Carlotta from down the hall had come out with three children to say hello and welcome them to the neighborhood. Maddie seemed to get along with the middle child well, and that night at dinner she had thanked God for "the kids at the new house" during mealtime grace. As he drove the route from old home to new for the last time, he prayed that Carlotta would be a positive influence in Maddie's life, and that the other children that lived in the complex were as friendly and well-behaved as hers.

Joshua did a mental read-through of his move-in checklist as the rented truck bumped along the road. Utilities switched over and turned on—check. Change of address forms submitted to the post office—check. New address listed on Maddie's school and doctor records—check. Keys to the old house left under the mat for Scott to pick up this evening—check. And in the back of the truck, the last of their possessions.

He was grateful for the graciousness of the folks helping him move, some of whom he hadn't talked to in months. They were people he'd met at the Bible study he and Lara had attended the year before her death. He hadn't gone back since she'd died, but he and Maddie still attended the church, and people from the study continued to send him the occasional email and extend offers of babysitting and meals. Those families jumped at the chance to lend a hand with the move. Two of the women had gone over earlier in the morning to clean the apartment and start painting Maddie's bedroom. Another had come to pack up the food in the kitchen and get it restocked in their new home, and then informed him she'd make some dinners to freeze while the others packed and unpacked. He'd managed to pare down their collection of material goods and donate a mountain of furniture and clothing to the Salvation Army, so it had only taken two trips to transport all the things they were bringing. The men had made quick work of loading the truck, and by noon he and Maddie were officially moved out of the house where their family had begun.

When they arrived at the condo, the smell of fresh paint wafted from the smaller of the two bedrooms and mingled with the palate-teasing scent of lasagna. Eyes dried and focused on the future, Joshua helped the men unload the furniture from the truck and set it up inside. His things looked wrong in their new locations — too big in some cases, and too awkward in others. It felt like a bachelor pad until one's eyes caught sight of the baby handprint plaque on the bookshelf or the shocking pink in the bedroom beyond the living room.

He stood in the spot where the kitchen opened up to the living room and surveyed all he could see from there — which, because the place was so small, was nearly everything. "It doesn't look like a home, does it?" he said to Heather, who stood in the kitchen stirring a sauce on the stove.

"Scatter some clothes on the floor and track in some mud — that usually does the trick."

He laughed. "Yeah, that's probably the issue—I'm no good at keeping house; it's never this clean."

"Give it time. It'll take awhile to settle in, but I'm guessing it'll feel like home much sooner than you think." She grinned. "And it'll be a lot easier to keep tidy!"

"Hey Joshua, we're done in here," called Angie from Maddie's room.

He went in and was overwhelmed by the color. "That is one amazing shade of pink. I don't know how she's going to sleep in here. I feel like my heart rate goes up just being in here."

"Girls will be girls, eh?" Angie glanced around the room.

"Let us know if she changes her mind on the color. Or if you do, for that matter," said Stacy, Angie's painting partner. "We wouldn't mind redoing it for you if need be. Or even sponging over with something lighter to soften it up a bit."

"Thanks for the offer. I may take you up on that."

"So when will she see it?" Stacy asked.

Joshua looked at his watch. "I told her I'd get her before dinner—I'll probably go over in half an hour or so. Everything's about done, and what little is left I can take care of myself. I can't thank you all enough for helping me with this. I couldn't have done it on my own."

Angie wrapped an arm around his shoulder and gave him a brief squeeze. "We're happy to help, Joshua. And you know we're here when you need anything."

Not much later, his friends began to collect their scattered belongings and file out the door. Before going to pick up Maddie, he did a walk-through of the condo, examining each room, straightening pictures on the walls and books on the shelves. While he was grateful for all the help, he was also a little disappointed there wasn't at least *some* work left to be done. He needed something to keep him busy, keep his mind occupied. The rush of paperwork and ruthless pruning of possessions over the last couple weeks had given him a necessary escape from the reality of the move. But now it was done, and there was no running from the emotions that tumbled together in his heart.

He took a deep breath and quickly left for the car before he could give too much thought to the one person he wished was there to really make it feel like home.

MADDIE WAS JUST FINISHING HER BREAKFAST when the doorbell rang. Joshua peeked out the peephole and saw Carlotta's two older children shuffling back and forth in front of the door.

"Well, hi there," he said to the two grinning faces.

"Hi, Mr. Miller," said the girl, whom he guessed to be about seven. He searched his memory for her name and came up with Hannah. "Zak and me were gonna play outside. Does Maddie wanna come with us?"

Maddie came running to the door at the sound of Hannah's voice, then pulled up short and hid behind Joshua's leg.

"Hi Maddie!" said Zak, grinning. He was the one Joshua had guessed to be about Maddie's age. "Come outside with us!"

"My mom has the window open, and she watches us through the patio," Hannah said. "You can do that too. We play out here all the time. We have a ball and jump ropes, and I have my doll."

"I don't have a doll," said Zak. "But I have a dinosaur."

Joshua suppressed a chuckle. "That would be my choice too." He ruffled Maddie's hair. "Want to get your doll and play, sweetheart?"

She was quiet for a moment, then raced off for her bedroom. She returned with her Cabbage Patch baby and Joshua walked the group of them out so Maddie didn't change her mind as he knew she might if he wasn't there.

He stood by the security door and watched as the kids fell into a game Carlotta's children had invented, the rules of which Joshua didn't catch, but Maddie seemed to be enjoying herself. He opened the door to go back in and nearly ran into a young woman coming out.

"Oh, I'm sorry," he said, stepping aside. "Didn't mean to almost knock you over there."

"Not a problem," she said. Then she smiled. "Wait a minute—I think you're the new neighbor. You're in #4, right?"

"Yes, I am. Joshua Miller, pleased to meet you." He stuck out his hand. She seemed to pause a moment, then grasped his hand and shook quickly. "That's my daughter, Maddie—the one with the pink shirt."

"Aw, she's so cute." She smiled, watching the kids. "I'm Kim Slone, by the way. I live in #2 with my boyfriend, Rick Allen."

"Oh, so we really are neighbors," Joshua said. "I'm surprised I haven't heard you yet. I remember the old owners saying the walls were pretty thin."

A shadow seemed to cross her face. "Yeah, well, we don't use the room that is right next to yours. It's more storage, really, and we stay mostly on the other side, in the other room."

"Oh, okay. I gotcha." He smiled and nodded. "Well, I don't want to keep you. Seemed you were in a hurry."

"Just on my way to work. I'm a stylist at A Cut Above, over on Sixth."

"Oh, good to know. Maddie's hair has never been cut, and it's probably about time I took her somewhere—do you do children's hair?"

"Sure! Bring her in anytime. She's got gorgeous hair."

"She does—just like her mom's." He held out his hand again. "Nice to meet you, Kim. Hope you have a good day."

She shook his hand again, even more briefly than she had the first time. "You too, Joshua. See you around."

He watched her walk across the lawn to the sidewalk and disappear past the building. He combed a hand through his hair and went back inside, trying to figure out the red-flag feeling he had about her.

Once inside he opened the sliding glass door to the patio. He could see the children running around, Maddie trailing behind them, and the sight made him smile. Hopefully these new friends would make the move easier on her.

Confident that Maddie was comfortable with her new playmates, Joshua went back to the living room to face the mess. The vacuum bag had chosen last night to burst while he cleaned the half box of cereal from the floor that had scattered when Maddie had tripped. He'd been too exhausted to deal with it right then, and the dust had settled over the coffee table and sofa during the night, while most of the cereal still lay on the floor. Two piles of laundry that hadn't gotten done before the move lay on the floor near the utility closet that housed the stacked washer and dryer. The few boxes they'd used in their move were piled like giant blocks near the door, waiting to be flattened, and the dishes from last night's dinner were still in the sink. He felt bad that in living there less than forty-eight hours they'd managed to trash the place. But being in a new space messed with his routines. Hopefully by the end of the week they'd be back to normal.

He hadn't been in long when he heard Maddie yell, "Gramma!" Joshua's stomach constricted. He'd hoped to avoid another meeting with them until he felt more settled into the neighborhood, knowing they would not approve of the location. He wanted to hide in the bedroom but knew the sooner he faced them the sooner they'd be gone, so he took a deep breath, prayed for graciousness, and went out to meet them.

"You're letting her run around a parking lot unsupervised?"

"Hello to you, too, Alisha, George." Joshua let the security door shut behind him and forced his hands into his pockets to avoid crossing them confrontationally over his chest. "Maddie, were you in the parking lot?"

"No, Daddy, just on the grass."

"We weren't in the parking lot, sir," said Hannah.

He looked to his in-laws and raised his eyebrows. Alisha frowned. "Well the parking lot is all of five feet away. They might as well be in it."

"They're perfectly safe where they are, Alisha. Hannah's mom tells me they play out here all the time. We're both keeping an eye on the kids; I can see them from the kitchen window."

"A lot of good that will do you when some drunk comes careening across the lawn."

"Or when someone walks through and snatches her out of thin air." George nodded to the street that bordered the property thirty yards away. "That road goes straight to the freeway."

"George, she doesn't play out here alone, and there's nowhere to stop a car on that road." Joshua shook his head. "And Alisha, you've got a more vivid imagination than Maddie does. We lived on a *street* and you never worried about cars 'careening across the lawn.'"

"That's because you lived in a decent neighborhood where people knew how to drive properly."

Joshua took a deep breath, then held up his hands in surrender. "I'm not going to argue about this anymore. Do you two want to come in and see the place, or do you need to get going?"

Alisha narrowed her eyes. "I want to see where my granddaughter is living."

Joshua sighed. "Fair enough. Come on in." He turned to open the door and groaned. "I forgot the keys."

"We're locked out?" Alisha sounded alarmed.

"No, no—I have the patio door open, I'll just hop the fence."

George huffed. "People can just climb into your house?"

Joshua made an effort to keep himself calm. "No, George, 'people' cannot climb into my house. *I* can climb into my house because I left the patio door unlocked. I'm still getting used to the fact that there's a security door, so I leave the patio door unlocked just in case. I lock it when we leave the house."

"But this isn't the kind of neighborhood where you want to broadcast the fact that just anyone can waltz through your back door."

"I'm not sure I understand what kind of neighborhood you think this is. It's not Cell Block A, you know. There are normal families here—families like Maddie and me."

"The exception, I'm sure," Alisha said under her breath.

Joshua took a deep breath and forced a smile. "Would you like to hop the fence with me, or shall I go open the security door?"

It was a little snarky, but compared to what else he'd resisted the urge to say, it was the epitome of respect. He vaulted the railing and went inside, counting slowly from one hundred as he walked down the hall to the security door. He led them back to the apartment, leaving Maddie in the company of her new friends. "I'll give you the grand tour," he said, putting friendliness in his voice and trying to turn a corner with his attitude. "Kitchen here, as you can see, with a well-stocked pantry and a freezer full of home-cooked meals." He ushered them into the living room. "Our main hangout. You'll have to excuse the mess; it was a little chaotic here last night and I was too wiped out to deal with it." He pointed them to Maddie's room. "The kingdom of pink. Maddie chose the color herself, as though that's not obvious." He pointed back to his bedroom. "My bedroom, which also has access to that patio."

For a moment Alisha and George seemed disconcerted. He watched them wander the place, searching through it as though looking for clues. Then Alisha marched out of his bedroom with a look of triumph on her face. "Maddie's bed is in your room."

Joshua shrugged. "So?"

"That's completely improper. She should have her own room."

"She does. She doesn't want to sleep in there yet."

"So you let her dictate to you how she wants to do things? Where is your parental authority?"

Joshua's jaw clenched. "I let her have a say, to a degree, in things that affect her. We've only been here two days; she's still getting used to the place. Can you blame her for not wanting to sleep alone in a new place? Have some compassion, Alisha."

Alisha shook her head. "I can't imagine it's healthy for a young girl to sleep alone with her father."

The camel's back was dangerously close to giving out. "She has her own bed, Alisha, and I'll ask you to stop right there with what you're insinuating. Don't ever question my propriety with my daughter."

George put a hand on Alisha's arm. "I don't think she's implying that you would *do* anything. Just that it might be considered a little questionable."

"Well, seeing as Maddie is *my* daughter, and I don't have a problem with it, then other people's opinions don't really matter, do they?" He raked a hand through his hair, feeling close to exploding. "I wish I understood why you're so desperate to prove me incompetent. I wish I understood why you hate me so much."

Neither of them would look him in the eye. He shook his head and motioned to the door. "I don't see this visit getting any better. I'll give you a call later in the week and arrange a time when Maddie can come visit for the day."

George frowned. "You're kicking us out?"

"No. I'm trying to nicely convey that it would be better for this meeting to end now, before anything is said by either of us that is later regretted."

Alisha's chin jutted into the air. "Come, George, let's go. I can see we're not welcome here."

Joshua didn't bother contradicting her or seeing them out. He just shut the door behind them and went into the bedroom to watch their interaction with Maddie before they left. He wouldn't put it past them to fill her head with propaganda when he wasn't looking. He'd call to set a date for Maddie to go to their house for the day, but he'd make sure she didn't actually go. There was no way he trusted them alone with her now.

He watched them emerge from the security door and call Maddie from her playing to come say good-bye. Alisha bent down to give Maddie a kiss, then began to talk to her as she pulled a candy bar from her pocket and held it out to her. Then Alisha glanced back at the patio and did a double-take upon meeting Joshua's stare. She straightened up, patted Maddie on the head, and turned away to stalk off to the car. George kissed Maddie's cheek, then followed his wife. Maddie ran over to him and handed him the candy bar. "I can't have this, can I?"

"No kiddo, sorry."

"Why do they always bring food I can't eat?"

"Because they refuse to believe you're actually allergic to milk."

"But why?"

"Great question, Maddie. I don't know."

"Gramma looked mad when they left."

"I know, honey. Did she say anything angry to you?"

"No, she just looked angry in her eyes."

He ruffled her bangs. "We just need to pray for them, okay?"

"Okay. Can I go play now?"

"Of course."

He watched her race back to Hannah and Zak, then settled himself into a deck chair. Suddenly he didn't want to let her out of his sight.

"READY, SET, GO!" With a squeal, Maddie took off from beneath the preschool awning, running through the rain to the car. Joshua was right behind her, trying to keep the umbrella above her as she dodged puddles on the sidewalk. Once they reached the car he tossed her into the seat as she giggled. "I'm so wet!"

"*You're* so wet—what about me?" Joshua secured the carseat harness over Maddie and shut the door, then jumped into the front seat, wiping rain from his face and hair. His head was throbbing, thanks to the storm system that had moved in overnight. He'd been in pain all day, despite the pills he'd taken. He couldn't wait to get home and lie down.

Maddie sang as they drove, respecting his request that he not have to converse until they got home. The windshield wipers stuttered with each pass, a minor irritation that grew more annoying with each mile. By the time they got back to the apartment Joshua was ready to yank the things off their holders.

Someone was standing under an umbrella at the security door when he reached it, Maddie in his arms and both of them getting drenched. "I've got a key," he said, setting Maddie down. "Who are you here to see?" He still didn't know many neighbors, but he didn't feel right just letting someone in without at least asking.

The woman looked at a note in her hands. "Joshua Miller."

He unlocked the door and opened it wide. "That's me. Come on in." They all ducked into the hall and shook the rain off their jackets. He stuck his hand out to shake hers. "And you are?"

"Natalie Cohen. I'm a caseworker with DHS."

"DH—wait a minute, as in Department of Human Services?"

"Yes."

His headache disappeared with the shot of adrenaline that entered his bloodstream. His hand gripped Maddie's tighter as he asked, "Forgive me for being blunt, but why are you here?"

She smiled. "We received a call this morning, and I'm just following up. May I come in?"

He froze. What was the better thing to do? Let her in so she could see nothing was amiss—but then what if she found some random thing that he never would have guessed would cause a problem? But if he didn't let her in, wasn't that admitting to some kind of guilt?

"A call—from whom? About what?"

"We were told the home might be unfit for a child, and that there may be—," she checked the note again, "inappropriate sleeping arrangements."

He fought to control the fury that rose from his gut. "You've got to be kidding. Let me guess—the caller was Alisha Michalson?"

"I don't know. The call was made anonymously."

He snorted. "What a coward." He unlocked the door and swung it open. "Come on in and I'll put your mind at rest."

The three of them walked into the condo, and Joshua pointed in the direction of the living room. "Please, feel free to look around."

"Thank you, Mr. Miller." She walked into the living room and looked around, then strolled into both bedrooms while he peeled off Maddie's slicker and gym shoes. She returned and looked back to him with her eyebrows raised. She looked amused. "Did you know I was coming?"

"No, I had no idea. I've been at work all day, Maddie has been at preschool—we were just getting home. Are you surprised it's not a disaster?"

She chuckled. "Well, not entirely surprised, given your reaction when I told you. But this isn't even cluttered, much less hazardous to anyone's health. And I see nothing inappropriate about a child's bed being in the parents' room. People do it all the time when they live in one-bedroom apartments."

He knelt down to Maddie. "Do me a favor, kiddo. Go hop into your jammies since your clothes are wet, and I'll come get you when Ms. Cohen and I are done talking, okay?"

"Okay. Are we in trouble?"

"No, love, we're not." He kissed her head. "Off you go."

Maddie ran to her bedroom and shut the door. He sighed and motioned to the couch. "May I talk with you a minute?"

"Of course."

Joshua rubbed his hand over his eyes. "My wife died almost a year ago. She was the only child her parents had. They haven't been handling it well at all, and then a few months back they declared me unfit, in their eyes, to be raising Maddie, and said they were going to fight me for grandparent rights and possibly custody."

"That's why you think they're the ones that called?"

He shrugged. "No one else has been here but them. We just moved here a few days ago, and they saw it for the first time yesterday. It *was* a bit of a mess—Maddie had spilled some cereal, the vacuum bag exploded—but I cleaned it all last night. I'm not a messy guy, but Maddie is a typical four-year-old, so it's not immaculate around here, but it's certainly not dirty enough to endanger anyone."

She nodded. "I understand, Mr. Miller."

"So … everything is alright?"

She smiled. "Looks fine to me. I'll put a note in your file explaining the situation. I can't guarantee we won't have to come back out—we do have to investigate every call we get—but at least whatever agent is sent out will be able to see that you were cooperative and that there may be extenuating circumstances as to the motive behind the call."

He heaved a sigh. "Thank you so much. Man, I can't tell you what panic set in when you said you were from DHS."

She chuckled as she stood. "I can understand that. I'm relieved to see there don't seem to be any problems here. While it's frustrating that agency resources are wasted on calls like this, I have to admit it's a bright spot in my day to visit a competent parent and happy child."

He walked her to the door and saw her out, then shut it, locked it, and leaned his head against the frame. *Breathe.*

He swallowed back bile and gripped the doorknob, counting to calm himself. To think his own in-laws had stooped this low—he knew they were serious about wanting Maddie, but he had no idea they'd go so far as to try to get DHS involved. Had they really thought that small amount of mess was enough to make the agency suspect neglect? Or that Maddie's bed in his bedroom would lead them to consider abuse?

He stood at the door, hanging onto the doorknob with a white-knuckle grip until he was sure his rage had simmered down to a less dangerous level. He didn't want to go off in front of Maddie about her grandparents, or give her the impression that anything was amiss. She didn't deserve to have that kind of stress loaded onto her small shoulders.

He pulled two servings of frozen lasagna from the freezer and tossed them into the microwave. "Hey Maddie, come on out. I've got dinner almost ready."

She trotted out in her pajamas and slippers. "Daddy, my hair is wet and it's all cold and icky on my neck."

He took a kitchen towel off its hook and knelt down. "Come here, I'll fix it." He gathered her hair in a ponytail and squeezed the wet ends in the towel. "Thanks for getting your pajamas on all by yourself."

"Who was that lady?"

"She was just someone who came to check and make sure we were all moved in okay."

"What does 'inappropriate sleeping arrangements' mean?"

He stifled a groan. "It means ... she wasn't sure if your bed was big enough because you're getting so big. Those little beds can't hold you if you weigh too much."

"Oh, okay."

He rubbed her hair, then slung the towel over his shoulder. "I think that's a little better, eh?"

"Thanks, Daddy. Can I color until dinner?"

"Sure, but that only gives you a couple minutes."

"That's alright." She hopped into the living room and pulled out her coloring book and crayons from the toy chest under the window. Tears welled in Joshua's eyes as he watched her.

How could they think he'd just let someone take his daughter?

He swiped at the tears before Maddie could see them, then pulled two tumblers from the cabinet. He went through the motions of preparing dinner, but his mind was elsewhere, trying to remember the name of the lawyer he'd met at his last job. He had a phone call to make.

TWELVE

"So are you going to the Redken Symposium this year?" Rumiko wrapped a towel around Kim's neck and lowered her head to the basin. "Las Vegas is calling my name for sure."

Kim chuckled, closing her eyes as the warm spray soothed her head. "I don't know. I'd love to go, but I'm not sure I'll have the money."

"Girl, you need to try. I went the last time and it was awesome. Not to mention—hello, it's Vegas!" She massaged Kim's scalp and lathered the shampoo in her hair. "Stay up all night, go dancing, play the slots—please, please come!"

"I'll try," she lied. "But if I can't you have to promise to teach me everything you know when you come back."

"Of course I will." She rinsed the shampoo and pumped conditioner into her hands, then smoothed the product through Kim's hair. "Man, your hair is really growing fast. I can't believe how long it is."

"Huh, really? I guess I haven't noticed."

"Yeah, you haven't been doing much with it lately. I've noticed a lot of ponytails."

Kim winced inside. She knew she should be doing more with her hair—it was, after all, the best way to advertise what she did for a living—but she just hadn't had the energy lately to do anything more than tie it up.

"So you want me to cut it different this time? You could try going short, then you wouldn't have to do much. Your face would carry a short cut really well."

"No, I don't think Rick would like that."

Rumiko scoffed as she rinsed out the conditioner. "So? It's your hair."

"Yeah, but he's the one that has to look at me."

"So do the rest of us, but you don't see us dictating your hair-style now, do you?" Kim rolled her eyes and Rumiko chuckled. "Okay, whatever. You're done, you can sit up." She led Kim back to her chair and draped the plastic cape across her chest. "So just the usual half-inch trim, then?"

"Yes please."

Rumiko combed out Kim's hair, chattering away about the color class she'd taken earlier in the week. Kim had wanted to attend too — usually she and Rumiko went to all their continuing educa-tion classes together — but Rick hadn't wanted her to spend the money. She'd tried to explain to him that she needed these classes, but he'd blown her off. "It's hair. How much new stuff can they come up with to do with it, really? It's not rocket science." She'd consid-ered defending her profession, but knew there was no point — it would just escalate into another boxing match.

Rumiko pulled her comb up and snipped with her scissors. "You should see the new applicator," she said. "It's completely — " She stopped, frowned, and leaned in to peer more closely at Kim's hair. "Um, Kim?"

"What?"

Rumiko drew her comb horizontally across Kim's hair, then lifted the layer she had created and handed Kim her hand mirror. "Look at the hair under here. Do you see it?"

Kim angled the mirror to get a better view. Her eyes widened. "It's wavy. My hair is getting curly?"

Rumiko stared at her in the mirror. "Your *hair* is getting *curly.*"

Kim lowered the mirror and stared at Rumiko. "Oh my God."

Rumiko dropped her voice lower. "When was your last cycle?"

"It was ... um ..." She bit her lip, calculating in her head. "Like, a month ago? The middle of June? But it was really short, like not even a day ..." Her voice faded as reality struck.

Rumiko put a hand on her shoulder. "You need to find out, like, now. I'll cut your hair later; go down to the drug store and get a test." Kim sat, dumbfounded. Rumiko tugged her arm and ripped apart the Velcro on the neck of the cape. "Go!"

Kim stumbled from the chair and grabbed her purse from her station. She was halfway down the sidewalk to the drugstore before her emotions caught up with her. She wiped tears from her cheeks and sniffed. *I can't be pregnant. I can't be. What will Rick say?*

She almost ran the rest of the way to the store, and once inside, she bumbled down the wrong aisle three times before finding the section of pregnancy tests. She grabbed the one that required the shortest amount of waiting and took it up to the front. Her hand shook as she laid it on the counter at the register and pulled out her wallet. She expected some kind of comment from the cashier, but the woman merely scanned it for the price and dumped it into a bag. Kim signed the receipt with a signature that looked nothing like it usually did. She power walked back to the salon and tossed her purse onto the chair. She flashed the bag to Rumiko, who flashed back crossed fingers.

Once inside the bathroom, Kim ripped open the box and read the instructions twice to make sure she did it right. Then she stood, her back to the test, unable to make herself watch it as it developed. She counted to one hundred, then turned and saw a little pink plus sign.

WHEN RICK CAME HOME, Kim had dinner laid out on a fully-set table, complete with candles and wine. "Well this is an unexpected surprise," he said as he dropped his keys onto the pass-through counter. "We win the lottery or something?"

Kim pulled out his chair and motioned for him to sit down. "No, no—not quite." She poured a glass of wine and sat down beside him. "But I do have some good news."

He leaned back, drink in hand, and smiled. "Well? Lay it on me, I'm dying of suspense over here."

Hands clutched in her lap, face aching from the perma-smile she'd been sporting all afternoon, Kim took a deep breath and gushed, "We're going to have a baby!"

Rick set down his wine. "What?"

"I'm pregnant."

"You're pregnant."

"Yes!" She laughed. "Can you believe it?"

"But, we've always …"

She shrugged. "Nothing is 100 percent." Her smile faded for the first time that day. "You're not happy?"

"Well, I just … I wasn't expecting this." He picked up his wine and swallowed half of it. "Wow."

They sat in silence for a minute until Kim couldn't stand it anymore. "I need to know what you're thinking. Are you upset? Are you nervous? Are you … what are you?"

He stood and began to pace. "I don't know, Kim. I'm not exactly happy—this wasn't the plan at all, right?"

"Well, right, but—"

"And where are we gonna put a baby?"

She chuckled. "We have a whole room that we don't use—"

"Yeah, yeah, but we're not cut out to be parents. We've hardly had parents, how do we know what to do? We don't!"

"We'll watch a lot of Cosby and *Family Ties* reruns."

He stopped pacing and frowned at her. "This isn't funny, Kim."

"Rick, relax." She stood and went to him, wrapping her arms around him. "This is amazing! This is our chance to reverse karma, you know? The world screwed us over when it came to family, but we'll make it right, we'll be the best parents any kid has ever had. We'll do for her all the things no one ever did for us."

"Um—'her'? Do you already know it's a girl?"

She rolled her eyes. "I had to say something, so I said her."

"When will we know what it is?"

She shrugged. "I don't know. I have to find a doctor. I don't even know for sure how far along I am." She wrinkled her nose. "I feel so guilty — the wine I've drunk, the food I've eaten. I haven't been taking any vitamins or anything."

Rick removed her arms from his waist. "Alright, well, enough about all this. I'm hungry. What did you make?"

Kim served up the lasagna and garlic bread she'd purchased on the way home from work and refilled Rick's wine glass, then filled her own with water. She was aching to talk baby things — registries, names, nursery décor — but Rick dominated the conversation and babies were never a part of it. Whenever she tried to bring it up, he'd wave a hand and say, "Later. I can't think about that right now."

As they were getting ready for bed, she tried again. "So I'm going to find a doctor tomorrow. Do you want to come to the appointment with me when I go?"

He scoffed. "Are you kidding me? No way."

She frowned. "Well, fine, but you don't have to sound so disgusted by the suggestion."

"Kim, this whole thing is so far from what I want right now that the very mention of it is making me sick." His voice held the note of warning she had come to recognize as a precursor to a slap, or worse. She lowered her eyes, ashamed at her need for him to be as happy about this as she was. "Just leave me alone about all this, alright? I need to figure out what we're going to do."

She couldn't sleep that night. She lay in bed, hands resting on her belly, thinking about all that was going to change. How long could she work on her feet all day? Her back had already begun to ache, though she hadn't realized why at the time. How would they pay for the birth? She had no insurance, and while Rick had some through work, she wasn't on the policy. The baby could be, but that wouldn't take care of the hospital stay or prenatal appointments. And she'd need maternity clothes. And vitamins — she had to get those tomorrow.

She rolled to her side and pulled the covers over her head, overwhelmed. There was so much to consider, so much to do. *If only Rick were more supportive.* She longed to nestle against him and cry into his chest, feel his strong arms around her and hear his voice whispering that he'd take care of everything.

"Hey."

She jumped at his voice. "I thought you were asleep."

"No, I was thinking."

"About what?"

"Maybe you could get an abortion?"

She sat straight up with a gasp. "What? No! How could you even suggest that?"

"Relax. It was just an idea."

"Just an idea? Killing our baby? Nice, Rick." Her voice broke with emotion as she threw back the covers and grabbed her pillow.

"It's not a baby yet. Where are you going?"

"I'm not sharing a bed with someone that callous." She stomped out of the bedroom and slammed the door behind her. Beginning to cry, she grabbed the chenille throw from the end of the couch and laid down. She buried her face in her pillow, not wanting Rick to know how much he'd upset her. She was already fearful of him taking offense at how she'd abandoned him.

But he wouldn't do anything when I was pregnant, would he? She wrapped her arms around her middle and wiggled deeper into the cushions. She wanted to disappear into them, into something, just her and her baby alone together. She pictured the baby curled in her womb, recalling photos she'd seen of fetuses in utero, floating in their watery homes, looking like jarred aliens. She grinned a little and was filled with anticipation for her first doctor's visit. She'd get her morning appointments rescheduled and go first thing. She'd cancel at the Club, too, so she could go get some maternity clothes. The grin grew to a smile as she realized her clothes had been tight because of the baby and not because of how much she'd been eating lately. So many little things made sense now — her fatigue, her sore back, how emotional she'd felt. Such a tiny little thing inside her, but such a big impact it was already having.

Her mind roamed the fields of her imagination, dreaming of

tiny baby clothes and images of herself with a blanketed bundle in her arms. She fell asleep humming lullabies.

KIM SLEPT LIKE A ROCK on the couch, and when she awoke Rick was already gone. It took a moment for her to remember the events of the previous day, but when they all snapped back into place, she felt giddy and light with excitement. She called into the salon and left a message for Bette to cancel her appointments, then called the Club to cancel for the afternoon. After showering and eating—during which she thanked the universe she wasn't having morning sickness—she headed out to the free clinic.

There were only five people ahead of her when she arrived. She picked up a magazine and sat in the corner, as far from everyone else as she could. She'd never worried about her health before, but now that someone else was depending on her, she didn't want to take any chances. Who knew what illnesses people were dragging in with them today?

When her turn came up an hour later, she followed the nurse back to be weighed and have her vitals checked. Then she was led to a room where she changed into a paper gown and waited another ten minutes for the obstetrician, a thin, energetic woman with gray in her hair and an aura of kindness. "Well I see you're pregnant!" she said as she sat down. "How do you feel about that?"

Kim smiled. "I'm excited. It wasn't planned, but I'm still excited."

The doctor wrote on Kim's chart. "Is the father aware of the baby?"

"Yes, he is."

"And what does he think of all this?"

Kim sighed. "Well, I don't think he's thrilled. But I just told him last night—I just found out yesterday—so once he's had some time to let it sink in, I'm hoping he'll be more into it."

"Have you given any thought yet to what you plan to do?"

Kim frowned. "What do you mean?"

"Well, you have a few options. You can keep the baby, if you're prepared to deal with the responsibility. You can put it up for adoption. There are a lot of families out there who would love to raise a child but can't have children of their own. Or you could—"

"I'm keeping it."

"Are you sure?"

"Yes. Absolutely."

The doctor nodded and made a note in her chart. "Well, if you begin to have a change of heart, please let us know and we can set you up with the proper resources." She glanced up, then frowned. "What's all this here?"

Kim looked to the spot where the doctor was pointing and felt her insides go cold. Her scars. "Oh—my stupid cat." She forced a chuckle. "She went nuts. We were at the vet. She hates the vet."

She held the doctor's gaze, hoping her features looked as neutral as she was trying to make them. "Hm. Well. Might want to have someone else take the cat in while you're pregnant, just to be safe." She made another notation on the chart. "And you can't change the litter box while you're pregnant, either. The dust from the litter can cause toxoplasmosis."

"Oh, okay, good to know. I'll have Rick do it then."

"Rick? Is that the father?"

"Yes."

"Ah." She made another note. "Alright, let me see if we have all this correct, then, okay?" She double-checked the information Kim had given the nurse, and Kim relaxed again. It was a good thing she'd stopped cutting. There was no way the doctor would buy that story for long.

With the paperwork finally complete, the doctor set the chart aside. "Alright then. Let's do an internal ultrasound and see if we can better determine how far along you are." Kim laid down and fixed her eyes on the small screen. The doctor moved the wand, stopping to type something on the ultrasound computer now and then, and then stopped. "Hello, baby."

Kim squinted at the screen, then gasped as a little leg kicked. "It looks like an actual baby already!"

The doctor chuckled as she clicked and typed again. "It looks like you're measuring at about twelve weeks and five days." She pulled a small round chart from her pocket and consulted it. "That puts your due date around January 15th."

"So ... is it alright? Is it healthy?"

"As best as I can tell right now, yes. It still has a lot of developing to do; we'll know more at your twenty-week scan." Kim concentrated on the screen as the doctor used her pen to pinpoint a specific spot. "That's the heart. See how it's pulsing?"

Kim gasped. "It's got a heartbeat!"

"Sure does. Beating at about 136 beats a minute."

"Is that good?"

"Completely normal." She printed off a few snapshots, then cut one off and handed it to Kim. "Baby's first picture."

Kim stared at the grainy black and white image. "I can't believe it."

"Hard to imagine, hm?" The doctor helped Kim sit up, then turned the lights back on in the room. "We'll get you started on some vitamins, and I'll give you a list of foods to eat and avoid. We'll want you to come back once a month until you're in the last trimester, around thirty weeks. Then we'll do appointments more frequently. Do you have any questions?"

Despite the way her thoughts were buzzing, Kim couldn't come up with any. "I don't think so. But ... everything is alright, right?"

The doctor smiled. "Everything is perfect."

After making her next appointment, she caught a bus to the salon. Her next appointment wasn't for another hour, but she didn't want to go home to an empty house when she had so much good news—and a picture—to share.

She floated into the salon, waving the grainy printout. "Look at my baby!"

Bette squealed. "Let me see!" Her eyes grew wide. "Wow, look at that. Amazing."

Emma came and looked over her shoulder. "So what did the doctor say, Kim? Is everything alright? The baby looks like you, by the way."

They laughed and Kim plopped down into one of the reception area chairs. "Everything is just fine! I got to see the heart beating. Can you believe it?"

Rumiko, who was in the middle of touching up a client's roots, called from her station, "What did Rick say last night, Kim?"

"He was shocked."

"No surprise there. So were you."

"He was kind of ... not excited. But I think he just needs some time to think about it."

Emma raised an eyebrow. "What if he decides he's not cool with it?"

"Oh, I can't imagine he'd be like that."

Bette sighed. "That happened to my sister. Her boyfriend just— *pfft*—up and left when she found out she was pregnant. Like, *really* left. She never heard from him again, never figured out where he even went." She smiled. "But then she found the guy she's married to now, and he's a gem, so she was better off for it in the end."

Kim rolled her eyes. "That is *not* going to happen to me. Don't worry."

Emma's expression was one of concern. "I hope not, Kim. But you and Rick haven't been together all that long. You really do need to think about what you'll do if he leaves. Or kicks you out, seeing as the apartment is his."

"At least you'll know where he is," Bette said.

"You can live with me," Rumiko said.

"Or me," said Emma.

"Or me, though you'd have to sleep on the couch," said Bette with a grin.

"Guys, come on. Rick's not going to break up with me, or kick me out, or anything like that. Trust me. I know him. He loves me, and he just needs some time to get used to the idea of being a father. I can hardly believe it myself, and I'm the one that's pregnant."

She kept a smile on her face so her friends wouldn't worry, but inside she began to panic. What if he *didn't* want the baby? Or her, for that matter, once she had it? What if he did kick her out?

"I'm going next door for a snack. I'll be back in a little bit." She stood and walked outside, drinking in the heat before plunging back into another air-conditioned space that made her skin prickle. She leaned against the building, eyes closed, and let the sun melt away her anxiety. Stress wasn't good for the baby. She had to try not to worry about things she could not control. *If Rick leaves me, it'll be okay. I'll figure it out.* She continued to chant this in her head as she entered the mini-mart. *It'll be okay. It'll be okay.*

She wandered the aisles for a moment, letting her eyes fall on random items. She saw the X-acto knives hanging in the space where she'd found hers not that long ago. She hadn't touched it in weeks. Hopefully she wouldn't need it again, at least not for the purpose she'd bought it. After perusing her options, she pulled a bottle of water from the refrigerator case and a bag of cashews from the snack aisle. There was a basket near the register with fresh fruit in it, and when she went up to pay she picked up an apple as well. She was suddenly famished and couldn't wait to get back to her station so she could eat.

Back at the salon, she propped the ultrasound picture on her mirror, then sat in the chair and opened her water. The information the doctor had given her said to drink ten cups of water a day. She had never been a fan of water, so she was going to have to really work at that. Once she started drinking, however, she realized how thirsty she'd been. The bottle was half empty by the time she set it down.

"Thirsty much?" asked Suzie from her station next to Kim's.

Kim laughed. "I hadn't even noticed being thirsty. Guess I was though, huh?"

"I was like that when I was pregnant. I had never thought about being thirsty before then, and then suddenly I couldn't shake the feeling, no matter how much I drank."

Kim frowned. "You have a kid?"

"Well, I had a baby, but I gave it up to be adopted."

"Oh — wow."

Suzie smiled, and Kim was relieved to see it was genuine. "It was for the best. I'm glad I did it. I wasn't ready to be a mom. I was only nineteen, and my boyfriend was a jerk, though I didn't realize it until I was pregnant and he tried to force me to get an abortion."

The client in Suzie's chair clucked her tongue in disgust. "Men, I swear."

Rick's words rang again in Kim's ears. "What did you do?"

"I kicked him to the curb and my mom helped me pick a really nice couple to adopt the baby. They went to our church and my mom knew they'd been trying to adopt. I still get to see him every once in a while. They send me pictures on his birthday."

Kim shook her head. "Wow. I never knew."

Suzie shrugged. "I don't talk about it much. It was six years ago. I've moved on."

Kim hadn't considered adoption — just like abortion, it hadn't even crossed her mind when she'd seen that positive test. What if she couldn't handle being a mom? What if Rick was right, and they didn't know what they were doing? Maybe she *should* think about it.

"So, do you ever think you'd made the wrong decision?"

Suzie shook her head as she squirted mousse into her palm. "No way. It was hard to do, to go through the pregnancy and then hand him over to someone else. But when I think about my life now and how different it would be with a kid, I know I did the right thing. It hurt, but it was worth it. I had to think about the baby, too, you know? Not just me. He deserved a family that knew what it was doing, not some teenager who had no job or aspirations beyond the coming weekend. I would have loved him — I do love him — but

I couldn't provide for him the way they could. He's way better off with them."

A family that knew what it was doing. I couldn't provide for him the way they could. The words made Kim's heart ache. Maybe she was just being selfish. A baby deserved more than she could give. And she certainly didn't deserve something as perfect and beautiful as a new life to nurture.

She chugged the rest of her water and ate her apple in silence, listening to the conversations around her and the music playing over the stereo. Her thoughts were a mess, as were her emotions. Now she didn't know what to do. If Rick had been excited, then she wouldn't doubt herself so much. But what if he never came around? Emma was right, she needed a backup plan.

I can't believe I'm thinking this way. Kim stood from her chair and chucked her apple core into the trash. *A backup plan? Why on earth would I need that? Rick loves me, I* know *he loves me, and after everything we've both been through there's no way either of us could leave the other.*

The other girls just didn't understand Rick's and her relationship. It was way more complicated than they could fathom, given their shared foster experiences, and Kim's crime and necessary punishment. She could never share with them what happened at home, because they wouldn't understand the need for it. They just wouldn't get it. And it was the same with the baby. They didn't understand the bond she and Rick had. How could they?

Taking a deep breath, she rested her hands briefly on her stomach and sent the baby happy vibes to counteract the negativity she'd been feeling. She had to be careful, the things she thought and felt—she didn't want to contaminate this innocent life.

Kim's first appointment was due in ten minutes, so she stocked her station and took a bathroom break before perching herself back in her chair to wait. Her thoughts tried to tug her towards creating a backup plan, just in case, but she refocused herself on the materials given to her by the doctor, reading over and over the "Nutrition for the Second Trimester" sheet and meal planning in her head.

It'll be okay. They just don't understand. It'll be okay.

BY THE END OF THE DAY, Kim was exhausted. She hadn't felt this tired before. The thought of the twenty-minute walk home made her want to cry. She hated spending money on the bus, especially twice in one day, but if it spared her an emotional meltdown she figured it was worth the cost.

She almost fell asleep as the bus bumped along the roads towards the apartment. When she caught herself nodding off, she shifted in her seat, sat up straighter, and began to think of names for the baby. David, Henry, Jonathon — she liked classic, strong names for a boy, especially with Allen as a last name. But for a girl, romantic names like Juliet, Charlotte, and Genevieve made her smile. She wondered what names Rick would come up with. She selfishly hoped he'd leave it up to her.

The bus let her off two blocks from the house — farther than she felt like walking, but still better than having to walk the entire way home. She continued to consider names as she walked, trying to recollect heroines from her harlequin novels and men from American history. Cosette. Samuel. Colliope. Joshua. Skye. Daniel. Alexandria. She had to admit she liked thinking of girl names better.

The apartment complex came into view, and her stomach turned. She didn't want a big confrontation with Rick. She just wanted him to be as happy as she was. It was already five-thirty; chances were he'd already be home, so she couldn't make another nice dinner to smooth things out between them. She felt bad for what she'd said and done last night, and while she didn't think it had bothered him that much — she'd have gotten a slap at least if it had — she still worried there would be a wall between them tonight if she didn't do something to make amends.

Rick's car was in the parking lot when she turned the corner.

She took a deep breath, squared her shoulders, and entered the building with her head high and her apology prepared.

But when she opened the door, all her words melted away.

"Hey sweetheart! You were later than I thought you'd be." Rick kissed her and took her hand, pulling her into the living room. "I have a surprise for you. Sit down. Can I get you something to drink, some water maybe? You really need to make sure you're drinking enough water, especially with the heat the way it has been lately." He backtracked to the kitchen and filled a glass for her, then led her to the couch and handed it to her. "Okay, are you ready?"

She let out a nervous chuckle. "Um, I guess so—"

"Okay, close your eyes." She obeyed, steeling herself though she didn't know why. She heard shuffling noises, then Rick said, "Surprise!"

She opened her eyes to a stroller overflowing with packages. "Oh Rick!" She jumped to her feet and threw her arms around his neck. "Thank you so much. Thank you *so* much!" She kissed him hard to show her appreciation, then pulled away to examine the gifts. "I can't believe this," she said as she unpacked the presents. A body pillow, a book about pregnancy and birth, two maternity shirts and a skirt, and a heartbeat listener. She giggled. "You know it's going to be awhile until we can actually use this, right?"

He shrugged, grinning. "It looked like something you might enjoy. I figured we might as well get it now."

She smiled, her anxiety gone, and hugged him again. "Thank you. I'm so glad you're more excited. I knew it would just take a little time to sink in. Oh! Look what I have!" She grabbed her purse from the table and pulled out the ultrasound picture. "That's the baby, right there. I got to see the heart beating. Can you believe it?"

Rick squinted at the picture, frowning, then swore under his breath. "It really does look like a baby, huh." He dropped it to the table and wrapped an arm around her shoulder. "What do you say we go out to eat? A little celebration dinner."

Kim felt like her heart would burst with happiness. This is what she had hoped for, even if it was a little late in coming.

He drove her to Alfredo's, the site of their first date. While waiting for their meals, Kim told him about the doctor's appointment and the excitement her salon friends had shown.

"I'll bet your Club girls will go crazy, huh?" he asked.

Uh-oh. She hadn't even thought about telling him. "Yeah," she said, eyes focused on a breadstick. "Yeah, they'll go nuts. Girls always love babies."

"You know," Rick said after a few minutes. "Your job is going to be really hard to do when you're pregnant."

She sighed. "Yes, I've been thinking about that today. I'm sure it's just from the emotional up-and-down I've been through in the last twenty-four hours, but man, I was exhausted by the end of my last appointment. I couldn't wait to get home. I took the bus—did I tell you that? I think I'm going to have to, at least in the evenings. I can probably manage the walk there okay. It'll be good exercise."

"I don't know, Kim—I'm not sure you should keep working."

She laughed. "What? Rick, I have to work."

"No you don't."

"What do you mean, no I don't? How am I going to pay my share of the rent and bills?"

"Well ... you don't have to."

She scoffed. "Oh, come on."

"I'm serious. We're engaged, and frankly, as good as married— the only difference a wedding is going to make is that we'll have a piece of paper to prove it. And a husband should provide for his wife, right? What kind of man would I be if I made my wife work while she was pregnant when she really didn't have to?"

"But you don't 'make' me—I like what I do."

He waved a hand impatiently. "I know, I know, but that's not the point. The point is that you're already tired after only half a day of working, and you've got a long way to go. It's going to get a lot worse. And it could be bad for the baby, couldn't it, for you to be on your feet all day?"

She frowned. "Oh—maybe. I don't really know. I guess it could be."

"Yeah," Rick said, shaking his head. "I really think you need to just stay home. The expenses for two people aren't all that much more than they are for one—more water and food, mainly, and if we started planning our meals more carefully we could save some money there."

"So, you really think I should just quit?"

"The sooner the better. Think how much better you'll feel, being able to sleep in, not being on your feet all day."

She gave him a half-smile. "That does sound nice."

He smiled. "See? I really think this is for the best. And don't worry about the money, Kim. We'll make it work, I promise."

Kim tried to keep her spirits up through the rest of the meal, but the thought of leaving the salon made her heart ache. She loved the women there. She'd been there for years now, and had built up such a loyal client base—how would she tell people like Mrs. Toll that she was leaving?

No negativity for the baby! She spooned another bite of tiramisu into her mouth and shook off her gloom. *Time to focus on the positive, like how lucky I am to have a fiancé who wants so much to protect me and provide for his family. Just like a good husband and father should.* She couldn't get over how much better off this baby would be than its parents. All the bad family history stopped with them. This baby would heal them.

THE FOLLOWING DAY WAS A rough one at the salon. She broke the news that she was leaving, and the girls all begged her to reconsider. Even Suzie, the only one of them who had ever been pregnant, promised it wasn't as bad as Kim thought it might be, and reminded her that she could just reduce her hours and keep making a little money.

"I'm touched that you're all so sad that I'm leaving," she said. "But really, I think this is for the best. And Rick needs to see that he can support his family. It's important to him, and because of that, it's important to me too. We're both feeling our way through this, trying to do what's best for us and for the baby, and we don't have a lot of experience to go on because our families were so absent from our lives. He needs to prove to himself that he's not his father, and I need to prove to myself that I'm not my mom—that I can devote myself to my man, and my child, and not freak out from the responsibility." This last bit came to her as she was talking, and she had to admit it made sense. Plus it sounded a lot better than, "Rick really wants me to quit, so I'm quitting." That argument made sense to her, but she knew it wouldn't make sense to them.

"But how are you going to save enough for your mobile salon?" Rumiko asked as they dined on sandwiches at lunchtime.

Kim wasn't about to admit the idea had been shelved long ago. "The possibility of that is so far down the road now—I'll figure something out eventually. This baby needs a mama—no daycare for us! Maybe when she's in school I'll start working again." Yet another lie added to the pile. Her aptitude for storytelling was beginning to bother her.

Between appointments Kim went through the schedule and wrote down all her regular clients and their phone numbers. She wanted to cancel them personally, and recommend one of the other girls to them based on their personality and the kind of treatment their hair required. She knew how attached women—and even men—could get to a hairdresser. Stylists played confidante, counselor, and pal, sometimes all in one appointment, and clients trusted you with something intimate and personal that could not always be easily fixed if you botched it. She hoped their concerns of working with someone new would be alleviated, or at least lessened, if they knew Kim had personally considered their needs and the strengths of the other stylists at the salon.

Despite how her back ached, Kim walked home that evening, taking in the landmarks and scenes that had become familiar over the last couple months. She decided as she strolled that she would go back to the salon and visit at least once a week — she'd go crazy alone in the house all day long, and she missed her friends already. Not that it would be quite the same — she wasn't going to sit there for the entire day and make conversation in bits and pieces between the girls' clients. But it would be better than not seeing them at all.

She still hadn't figured out what to do about her Club girls. She knew she had to tell them soon, though — who knew how long she'd be able to hide the pregnancy? But she had a lot to explain, and she feared she would turn out to be another bad example for them to follow. Not that it *was* a bad example — it just looked like one from the outside. She sighed. It was so difficult being in a complex relationship.

When the parking lot came into view, she saw the man she'd met a couple weeks ago. He was getting his daughter out of the car — she smiled at the girl's gorgeous ringlets, and at the sight of a father and his little girl. *Maybe someday that will be Rick.* Though it was hard to imagine him with a girl. A rough and tumble boy might be more his speed.

The little girl took off running once he set her down. She headed for the maples, rounded one of them, then came back, slamming into her father. They both laughed and he bent to say something to her. She took off running again. When Kim got closer she could her him counting. "... Eight, nine, ten, eleven, twelve — c'mon, Maddie! Almost there! — fourteen, fifteen ..." Maddie slammed into him again and he cheered. "Sixteen seconds! Man, you're getting fast. That was almost a record." He saw Kim and smiled. She smiled back, and the little girl looked to her and stepped behind her father.

"Oh Maddie, you remember Miss ... Kim, wasn't it?"

Kim smiled and gave a little wave to Maddie. "Yeah. Hi there."

"You remember Miss Kim. She's the one that cuts hair. We met her right after we moved in." He looked back to Kim. "I see you walking a lot. Let me know if you ever need a ride. I don't go right past your salon, but I get pretty close."

"That's really sweet, thanks. But today was my last day."

"Oh." He frowned. "I'm sorry."

"That's alright. I quit. I didn't get fired."

He chuckled. "Oh, good. I was feeling really bad for you for a minute there. Moving to a new salon?"

She beamed. "No, I'm pregnant."

"Hey, congratulations! Yeah, I'll bet all that standing would take its toll after a while. When are you due?"

"Not until January, but I'm already pretty tired these days."

He nodded. "Yes, I remember when my wife was pregnant with Maddie. She would take two naps a day and still sleep nine solid hours at night."

Kim laughed. "Well, I'm not that bad yet. But at least I can take the naps now if I need them." She looked back towards Joshua's patio. "I haven't met your wife yet, have I?"

"Ah, no—she's not here; she passed away last year."

Kim's hand flew to her mouth. "Oh my goodness, I'm *so* sorry."

His smile was kind. "Don't feel bad, you couldn't have known." He mussed Maddie's curls and smiled. "We're getting along alright though, right kiddo? She met the kids down the hall—the Jiminez family. Do you know them? They're really nice people. The kids are real sweet."

From the corner of her eye, Kim saw Rick's car pull into the lot. "I haven't met them yet, but I've seen them and their kids." She waved to Rick as he got out of the car. "It's cute how they all play out here together."

"I hope the noise doesn't bother you," Joshua said. "I know they end up right in front of your place too."

"Oh, it doesn't bother us at all. We're gone most of the day anyway. Though I guess I'll be home now, but I don't mind the noise." She nodded to Rick, who was coming up the walk. "Joshua—it's Joshua, right? This is my fiancé, Rick."

Joshua stuck out his hand to shake. "Nice to meet you Rick. Joshua Miller. We're your neighbors in #4."

Rick shook Joshua's hand, and Kim felt a niggling fear in the back of her neck at the look in Rick's eyes. What had she done wrong now? "You just getting home?" Rick asked Kim.

"Yes. I stayed a little later to clean out my station and say good-bye to people."

Rick nodded, then turned back to Joshua. "So how are you guys liking the place?"

"It's nice—an adjustment, but so far it's been good. I was just telling Kim about the family down the hall with all the kids and how much Maddie likes them." He pointed behind him to Maddie, who was chewing the end of a lock of hair and gazing out at nothing as she leaned against her father. "Maddie, can you say hi to Mr. Rick?" She looked at him briefly, then ducked away. Joshua chuckled. "She's four—and if that doesn't mean anything to you now, it will someday, I hear." He smiled. "Fatherhood is amazing. I hope you enjoy it as much as I do."

Rick smiled. "I'm sure I will. We're pretty excited." He wrapped an arm around Kim's shoulder and squeezed. She felt his fingers digging into her arm and tried not to wince. "We should get in and get some dinner. Nice to finally meet you."

"You too. Congratulations again."

Rick turned Kim with him and walked her to the security door. He didn't say a word as they walked down the hall. Fingers of anxiety clawed at her stomach. Usually she knew what had set him off, but this time she had no clue.

Rick slammed the door behind them, grabbed her wrist, and yanked her to the bedroom. "How long were you out there with him?"

"Just a few minutes! They got home just as I did."

"Don't let me catch you talking to him again, do you understand me? I saw the way he was looking at you."

Kim's jaw dropped. "What? No, no Rick, you misread him, he was just being friendly!"

"Is that what you call your behavior too? Just being friendly?" He slapped her cheek. "If I hadn't gotten home you'd have been in his bed by now, you filthy whore." He raised his arm to slap her again and she raised up her hands in defense. His fingers wrapped around her wrist and he wrenched her onto the bed. "That's not even my baby, is it? Whose is it? Is it his?"

He drew his fist back and she shrieked. "It's yours! I swear to God it's yours!" She curled inward. "Don't hurt the baby, Rick, please! Hit me all you want, just don't hurt the baby!"

His blows fell like rain, and she tried to cry as quietly as she could. She couldn't risk Joshua hearing her. The part of her brain that was detached from it all, the part that was able to think about grocery lists and conversations from earlier in the day while Rick meted out her discipline, noted that he had been wise to bring her into the bedroom instead of staying in the living room.

When he was done he left her alone in the bedroom, and she shook with pain and silenced sobs and fear. Blood from her nose stained the bedspread. Pain shot through her body from a dozen different places. But as she unfurled herself, gasping and wincing, she felt nothing but relief. The baby was still safe.

THIRTEEN

Joshua paused, frowning. There it was again. The last time he'd heard it he'd thought it was his imagination, or the children outside. But this time he was sure the shriek he heard was next door.

The skin on his neck prickled. He'd gotten a bad vibe when Rick and Kim had left. Something about the look in Rick's eyes gave him a check in his spirit. He'd acted friendly enough, though he'd made it clear he didn't want to sit around talking for long. When the security door closed after them Maddie had finally come out from behind him, saying, "I don't like that man." Joshua had almost admonished her for such an uncharitable comment about someone she barely knew, but then he remembered something Lara had said once about never ignoring a child's instinct. "I know what you mean," he'd said instead.

He knew, he just knew, it was Kim he'd heard and that Rick had hit her. His stomach clenched and he forced himself to leave the bedroom and go back into the living room where he turned on the television. He saw Maddie on the floor, coloring in a notebook, and made a note to keep her from his bedroom whenever possible.

He set about making dinner, but his thoughts kept returning to his neighbors. *What am I thinking, 'just keep Maddie from the bedroom'? She sleeps in there. And shouldn't you do something about it? You're not just going to let him do that to her, are you?* His thoughts were so far from his task he fumbled the vegetable peeler three times. *What should I do God? That poor woman— and pregnant! Though not for long if her fiancé keeps that up. Oh, God, what should I do?*

Maddie's voice snapped him from his prayer. "Daddy, what's for dinner?"

He took a deep breath, refocused his attention on the vegetables in front of him. The thought of eating fifty feet from the source of the shrieking made him ill. "I've changed my mind, I don't want to cook. Let's go out."

When Joshua and Maddie returned from dinner, the hallway and apartment were silent. He opened the door and made a bee-line for the bedroom to check for neighbor noise, but even an ear to the wall revealed nothing. His eyes fell on Maddie's bed and he frowned. *I need to get her sleeping in her own room.*

During her bath, Joshua broached the subject. "So what do you think of moving your bed into your bedroom tonight?"

Maddie shook her head. "Nuh-uh. I like sleeping in your room."

He smiled. "I like it, too, but that awesome pink room is just going to waste."

"No it's not. I play in there all the time."

True. "Well, regardless, we need to move you back in there pretty soon, okay sweetie?"

She sighed, swirling the water with a small rubber cow. "But I don't want to. I'm afraid of it."

Joshua thought. "Well, how about if I slept in there with you a few times?"

Maddie grinned. "You can't fit in my bed! You're too long!"

"That's right," he said, laughing, "but I *could* sleep on the floor."

"Like camping out?"

"Sure."

"Could I camp out too?"

"Well, yes, I suppose."

She slapped at the water. "Can we build a fort?"

"Um—"

"And roast marshmallows!"

"Not in your room, no. No fires allowed."

"But we *can* build a fort?"

He sighed. "Sure. Why not." He figured he could get used to the pink. He hadn't been looking forward to sleeping in his room tonight anyway.

But that evening as he read books to Maddie under blankets draped over chairs, he felt the urge to be in the bedroom, listening, as though his presence would prevent it from happening again.

And the next time it did happen, what would he do? Could he bring himself to ignore it? Ignore the way his skin crawled and his adrenaline surged, the way her cry pierced his ears from four rooms over? No, he had to do something. His conscience would never let him be if he sat by and did nothing.

But what *could* he do? Pound on the wall? Break their door down and demand that Rick stop? He didn't look like a big guy, but who knew what he was capable of when provoked?

I just need to call the police. Though Rick would know who did it—who else would hear them? The walls might be thin, but the ceilings seemed to be pretty solid; Joshua had never heard the people in the unit above them. And if he *did* call the police, and by some weird coincidence his in-laws heard about it, then it would just be more fuel to the fire. They already thought the neighborhood was sketchy. Knowing them, they were checking the police blotter for activity in his area.

But what if Maddie heard them and told George and Alisha herself? Or what if he tried to get involved and Rick went after *him*? There were a number of ways that scenario could end, and all of them ended with Maddie living with George and Alisha, at least for a time. And in his mind, any time with them was too much.

He felt like a coward not doing anything. But he had a child to think of too—this wasn't just about his personal safety. Maybe he'd just wait and see. The next time he ran into Kim, he'd look closely for bruises, and if he felt like the time was right, he'd ask if there was something he could do.

He just couldn't take any risks right now. He couldn't do anything to jeopardize Maddie.

DEBBIE WAS HOLDING ON TO the frayed end of her rope with a death grip, but it didn't seem to matter. The shelter was falling apart at the seams. They were down to a near-skeleton crew for a staff, and with her in charge of the ledgers she had a feeling she was practically throwing money away. Somehow the place was still running, and she credited that to the dedication of the people she worked with—and God sparing them from too many new admissions.

That, however, broke her heart. There were scores of women who needed a place like Safe in His Arms—but the shelter wasn't equipped to help them right now. She prayed God simply diverted them to another shelter, or to a friend or a family member or *someone* who would help them get untangled from their abuser. The thought that they might be stuck and suffering kept her up at night.

She had done everything she could—taken on more hours, more responsibilities, and even taken a pay cut to make the books balance. She hadn't told anyone yet that their finances were barely hovering above the red. She couldn't put that on her staff on top of everything else. But now, tonight, as she looked over the budget for the tenth time, she realized she might as well tell them. That way it wouldn't come as a complete surprise when they had to close.

A drop of strawberry ice cream plopped onto the table beside her laptop. She sighed and wiped it up. "That would be the icing on the cake, wouldn't it—gumming up your computer with ice cream?" She disgusted herself sometimes—a lot more lately than usual. She'd consumed her weight in desserts in the last month and it showed. It was the only outlet she could find to deal with the strain she was feeling.

At their weekly staff meeting she decided it was time to let them know that their need was desperate. Maybe God would hear their prayers—he'd apparently stopped listening to hers.

"Debbie—why didn't you tell us before that things were this bad?"

The others murmured in agreement with Paula. Debbie sighed. "Because you were all working so hard already. I didn't want to burden you with it. I'm the director, it's *my* job to worry about the shelter, not yours."

"Okay. So—it's money that's the problem, so we need to brainstorm some fund-raising ideas and figure out where we can cut costs, right?"

"Well ... yes, that is part of the problem. But only part. We have three positions unfilled right now, and that's killing us, too—especially the accounting position. I am *not* the one who should be handling the accounts and the budget, but it wouldn't be proper for any of you to do it, either. We need to get that position filled as quickly as possible."

Paula frowned. "So that guy didn't work out?"

Debbie looked to her, confused. "What guy?"

"The guy you said you were going to call, like, back in May."

Debbie felt like an amnesia patient. "I don't know what you're talking about."

"You don't? You said you'd talked to some guy who was going to send in a resume. He worked at, like, a restaurant or something. I think it was the day you went to the hospital to visit Marisol."

The light bulb went on. Debbie smacked her forehead. "I can't believe it. I *cannot* believe I'm that much of a moron. The water heater broke while I was gone, and when I got back I was so wrapped up in all that I completely forgot about him."

"Well, did he send in his resume? You would have seen it if he had, right?"

"I would have, you're right." She frowned, thinking.

Paula shrugged. "Maybe he changed his mind."

"I doubt it—he seemed pretty eager to get out of the deli and back into accounting."

"Maybe something else came along."

Debbie sighed. "Maybe. Man, that's so frustrating."

"Maybe you should call a temp agency."

She propped her head in her hands. "You're right, you're right." She heaved a sigh. "Alright kids. Time for some serious prayer. I'll call a staffing place and see if we can get at least a couple of the positions taken care of, and we just need to pray that God brings the right people here and that we get the money we need to continue operations."

Shawnee placed a hand on Debbie's arm. "And then I think you need to go home."

Debbie laughed. "Yeah, right."

Tammy, one of the counselors, arched her brows. "When was the last time you *didn't* come in to work?" Debbie tried to answer but couldn't remember. "I thought so. You need a mental health day, bad. Let's pray, and then the lot of us are going to bodily remove you if you don't remove yourself."

They were true to their word. She was escorted to her office to pick up her laptop and purse, then directed to her car. They were right to make her leave, and she knew it, but the thought of all that needed doing made her antsy.

She was halfway out of her parking spot when an idea came to her. "Please, God, let him be there," she prayed as she pulled out into the street.

By the time she reached Zelman's Deli, she was shaky with hunger and nerves. She walked in and her heart sank — she didn't see him behind the counter. *Maybe it's just his day off.* She shot another prayer to heaven as she got in line.

"Next!"

Debbie stepped up. "Turkey and avocado on wheat — and is there a manager I could speak to?"

The sandwich maker pulled a loaf of wheat bread from the basket behind her. "Sure. Hey Lori, customer wants to talk to you," she called towards an open door at the end of the shop.

"I've got a sort of weird question for you," Debbie said to the woman that emerged. "I was here back at the end of May, and I got to talking to one of your employees. He told me he had been an accountant—"

"Oh, yes, Joshua."

Debbie's heart thunked. "So you know who I'm taking about?"

"Oh sure, about this tall, brown hair, late thirties?"

"Yes! Is he working today?"

"No, he doesn't work here anymore."

Debbie's heart flopped. "Oh no. Do you have a way of getting in touch with him?"

"Sure, I have his contact information — but I'm sure you understand why I can't just give that out."

"Of course, of course — but if I gave you *my* information, would you be willing to pass it along?"

The woman shrugged. "Sure."

Debbie pulled a business card from her wallet. "Remind him that we talked back in May, that he said he was going to send me a resume. Tell him to call even if he ended up with another job."

Please let it work out with this guy, she prayed as she ate. A bubble of hope floated through her chest, but she tried not to think too much about it. No point getting excited over it — she'd learned the hard way that men had a way of letting you down. She never thought she'd think it, but God was starting to fall into that category too. *Here's your chance to prove yourself, God. I have no right to ask you to validate yourself to me, but I'm asking anyway. You know how badly I need you right now. Show me I can trust you.*

Guilt spread through her at the prideful thoughts. She apologized as she finished her sandwich and headed home.

Now she *really* needed that ice cream.

JOSHUA HUNG UP THE PHONE and stared at the note he'd dictated from his voicemail. *Is this finally it, God?* He picked up the phone again, trying not to get his hopes up, and called the number he'd written down.

The phone was answered. "This is Debbie."

"Hi, Debbie, my name is Joshua Miller. I just got a call from my old manager at Zelman's Deli, saying you were in looking for me today —"

"Oh, yes! Hi! I'm so glad you called. I hope you'll forgive me for tracking you down like that, but I really felt like I needed to try to find you and just be sure you didn't want the job."

Joshua frowned. "Wait—what makes you think I don't want it?"

"Well, I never got your resume."

"You're kidding! But I sent it the day we spoke!"

She laughed. "Oh man, the post office did us wrong. So does that mean you *are* interested?"

"Seriously? The position is still open?"

"Not only is it still open, we're in desperate need because I've been the one in charge of the books, and I don't know what I'm doing at all."

Joshua gripped the phone tighter, fighting the urge to jump on the table and shout. "Name the time and place for the interview and I'll be there."

"Well, not to sound too desperate, but how about the Java Stop on Fifth and Park in half an hour?"

His mind raced. What would he do with Maddie? "I can do that," he said, still thinking. "I may have to bring my daughter, but I think I can keep her occupied long enough for us to talk."

"That's fine, I completely understand. I'll see you in half an hour then."

"Sounds great. Thanks, Debbie."

After they hung up, he indulged himself in a celebratory whoop that brought Maddie running. He knelt down and hugged her. "Daddy's very happy," he said, "but we've got a change of plans for the evening, kiddo. We're going to pack up some fun things for you, like your connect-the-dots book and your paint-with-water set and your doodle pad, and we're going to go to a coffee shop so that I can meet with someone, okay?"

Maddie hopped in front of him, picking up on his excitement. "Okay! Can I bring my crayons?"

"Yes. Let's go pack it all up in your backpack, okay?"

Once Maddie was situated, Joshua changed his clothes and took a few minutes alone to pray for the interview. *Let this be it, God. Please, please let this be it. I'm so tired of worrying about money and feeling like I'm failing my daughter. Let this be it.*

They got to Java Stop ten minutes late. He felt like an idiot for underestimating their travel time, but he hadn't taken the rush hour into consideration. He ushered Maddie into the shop and scanned the tables for a familiar face. When he spotted a woman staring at them he took a chance and approached her table. "Debbie?"

She stood and shook his hand. "Thought that might be you. Nice to see you again, Joshua."

"And you too. This is my daughter, Maddie."

Debbie smiled. Maddie did as well, something Joshua was pleased to see. "It's nice to meet you, Maddie. What did you bring in your backpack?"

Maddie pulled on the zipper and yanked out the paint book. "You just use water, so it's not so messy."

Debbie laughed. "I remember those! I used to do them all the time. The water always turned green."

Joshua chuckled as he set Maddie up at the table. "It still does. You good to go, Maddie?"

"Yes, thank you."

Debbie smiled at Joshua. "She's adorable."

"Thanks, I think so too."

"Do you want to get yourself something to drink or eat before we start?"

Joshua glanced at the bar. "You know, if you don't mind, I think I will. I'll be right back—okay kiddo?"

"Okay."

Joshua bought a bottle of water and tried not to stare at Debbie while waiting for his change. Maddie was chatting to her about something, a rarity for her when it came to adults, and Debbie seemed to be interested—or else was faking interest very well. Either way, he was grateful.

He sat back down with his water. "Alright. I'm ready when you are. Maddie, Ms., um—"

"Oh, it's Truman, but she can call me Debbie, I don't mind."

"Debbie and I are going to talk for awhile, and I need you to concentrate on your art, alright?"

"Okay."

He smiled at Debbie. "Fire away."

She chuckled and pulled a clipboard from her bag. "I'm sorry again for the snafu—though I guess it's the USPS that should be apologizing. Since I didn't get your resume, would you mind giving me a rundown of your qualifications and past accounting experience?"

Joshua pulled a resume from the folder he'd carried in. "Thought this would be helpful. But I'll elaborate on it a bit for you." He cataloged his responsibilities at the three accounting jobs he'd held since college. "... and I was there until February of this year. They were downsizing, I was the least senior of the accountants, so ..." He shrugged. "Since then I've just done temp jobs wherever I can get them."

"Like Zelman's Deli."

He chuckled. "Yes, which wasn't all bad, despite being completely out of my range of experience. We ate pretty good for a while there, didn't we kiddo?"

Maddie grinned. "Daddy makes really good sandwiches."

Debbie chuckled. "He does, Maddie, I agree. I enjoyed mine quite a lot."

"So if you need anyone working in your kitchen, I could do that, too," he said, grinning. "Being a single dad has taught me the art of multitasking. I'll make lunch for the staff for no extra pay."

Debbie chuckled. "Well, that would put you at the top of my list, if I had one—unfortunately, this job seems to drive applicants away." She put down her pen, her face losing its cheery countenance. "I have a feeling it's the benefits—or rather, the lack of them—that sends people running. The pay is not that great, though it could get better if we got some more funding. Our insurance package is bare bones, and with a child, I don't know how you'll feel about that. If we could get more grants—"

"You need a grant-writer?"

She gave him a wary smile. "Don't tell me you've done that too."

"Well, honestly, no. But a good friend of mine at my first job was, and I helped him out now and then, so I saw the ins and outs of the process. I would be willing to go through a class or training program or whatever you do to learn how to do it."

"It would mean an awful lot on your plate."

"I could do the grant-writing at home. It would allow me to be home with Maddie more. Evenings and weekends, I could work on that, and then do the accounting at the shelter during the week." He spread his hands, a magician showing off the rabbit he'd just pulled from his hat. "Problem solved. See, your team absolutely needs me."

Debbie shook her head, grinning. "Sure you weren't a salesman at your last job?" She sat back, studying him. "You're getting my hopes up, Mr. Miller. Let me tell you a little bit about us, and you can think about whether or not we're the kind of place you'd like to work.

"We're a nonprofit shelter for abused women. We house up to sixteen women at the facility and serve another ten to twenty through a day program. We are a Christian organization—though our clients need not be—and we do incorporate those beliefs into the counseling plan. We currently have a staff of eight, though we're down by three. The accountant position is forty hours a week, but you can spread those hours out however you'd like, though I would prefer you to be at the office from at least ten until two during the week—that seems to be when I'm most likely to have time to meet with you if necessary. The grant-writing is technically a part-time position, but if you really want to take it on until I'm able to find someone to fill it, I'd be fine with you putting into it whatever hours you're willing to.

"Given the nature of what we do, we would need to complete a background check on you and obtain fingerprints before granting you the job." She stopped, tapped her pen to her chin briefly, then nodded. "I think that's it. Provided you pass the background check, the job is yours if you want it."

Joshua nearly dropped his water bottle. "Are you kidding? I absolutely want the job."

She looked like she was going to cry. "Thank you, God, I am *so* relieved!" She clasped the clipboard to her chest, a smile splitting her face, and it looked to him like she'd gotten five years younger in the space of three seconds. "You have no idea what a weight that position has been on me. I still use a calculator to do basic math; I should not be in charge of a budget or a ledger. I'll get your background check run tomorrow, and as soon as that's done and your fingerprints clear, you're free to start."

He nearly kissed her. "Thank you, Debbie. Thank you very, very much." He looked back to the pastry case. "This calls for a celebration for both of us, by the sounds of it—my treat, please."

"Normally I'd decline but you're right, this is worthy of celebrating. If I could get those other three positions filled I'd be dancing on the tables."

He bought carrot cake for Debbie and himself and a fruit cup for Maddie, who awarded her painting to Debbie. When they finally left, Joshua found himself looking for a reason to stay longer, and when he got home he realized he'd spent the whole drive thinking not about the job, but about his new boss.

He shook his head as he walked Maddie up to the building and into their home. *It's the job you're happy about, you idiot, not her. You're just grateful.*

Even still, he couldn't wipe the smile from his face.

FOURTEEN

FOUR MONTHS LATER

Kim awoke in a stripe of sunlight that fell across the bed. She stretched and smiled and loitered under the covers until her stomach began to rumble. "Hungry in there?" she asked her belly as she stood. "Pancakes this morning, definitely. What do you think?"

Rubbing her hands over the mound beneath her shirt, Kim hummed as she cooked and planned her day aloud. She loved talking to the baby, loved the thought of her learning Kim's voice and recognizing it when she was born. Kim tried to get Rick to talk to her tummy, but he'd rolled his eyes at the suggestion and walked away without a word. She'd been a little disappointed, but not that surprised. She'd seen his annoyance when they'd learned it was a girl and not a boy. At least he couldn't pin that on her.

She ate her pancakes with her feet up on the coffee table, eyes glued to the television. Her morning schedule was tied to the television programming — breakfast during the morning news, shower and dress and back in time to watch *Cosby Show* reruns, take a walk around the block and be home in time to watch *Family Feud*, then make lunch and eat in front of *Jeopardy!* After that she usually took a nap or ran errands, depending on how she felt, and then made dinner to be ready when Rick got home at five-thirty.

She hadn't been to the salon in a couple months. She no longer felt like one of them. She missed too much gossip, too much news, too much life to connect with them the way she once had. She'd gotten more and more fearful of them discovering the quirks of her relationship with Rick, knowing they wouldn't understand, and so she avoided their calls. It made her sad, but she tried not to think about it too much. It was just better that way.

She still met with her Club girls, and that saved her from feeling like a complete hermit. She had waited until her belly was obviously bigger to tell them about the baby—and that she was living with Rick—and while most of the girls had been nothing but excited for her, Mercedes and Kea had been critical of her decisions.

"You're always telling us not to give up our independence, not to hang all our hopes on a man or rush into relationships, but then you go and do all those things and say it's okay."

Mercedes rolled her eyes at Kea as she slouched lower in her seat, glowering at Kim. "It's called being hypocritical."

"Yeah, hypocritical. I don't get what the difference is between you and us. It's like you think you're smarter than us." Kea's head was bent, and she wouldn't look Kim in the eyes as she spoke. It broke Kim's heart to know she'd disappointed her and Mercedes so much.

"Kea, I have more life experience, so in that way I *am* smarter. But I don't think I'm any more intelligent. And maybe I shouldn't have been so adamant about those things when I said them. I just see so much potential in you—and in you, too, Mercedes—in *all* of you. I just don't want to see you follow in the footsteps of your moms and aunts and sisters who threw away their futures."

"But why would we be throwing our futures away if we did what you're doing, and you're ... just living your life?"

She had tried to answer, but found she couldn't. "I'm sorry, girls. Maybe you're right. But I swear I wasn't trying to imply that I'm in some way better or smarter or anything like that." Kea had come around eventually, but Mercedes had left the meeting early and not come back for two weeks. When she did, she joined up with a different mentor. Kim tried not to feel guilty for creating the double-standard, but she'd ended up cutting herself once to deal with the anger she felt.

It had been the first time she'd cut since Rick had started punishing her, but since her belly had grown noticeably he'd stopped hitting her at all. On the one hand she was glad, for obvious reasons. But the part of her that needed a release, a way to ease the guilt and fend off the face that haunted her dreams, would sometimes push her to get mouthy with him, to test his resolve, to try to trigger his anger so she could bear the suffering she deserved. It was a testament to his self-control and compassion that he kept himself from lashing out at her, and she was always grateful for it after the urge passed. But then she'd realize the danger she was inviting on her innocent baby, and her self-loathing would eat at her until she simply had to find an outlet. So she would push at Rick and the cycle would begin again.

Kim put her breakfast dishes away and took a shower, then sat to watch *The Cosby Show*. She was filing her nails and not paying much attention to the commercials until one caught her eye and made her cry.

A young woman sat amongst a gaggle of sisters and friends, opening presents to reveal tiny baby clothes. Everyone *oohed* and *ahhed* as she held up each precious outfit. The sentiment of each greeting card—the product featured in the ad—brought smiles or tears both to the women on the television, as well as to Kim. When the spot ended and the show began, Kim found she couldn't concentrate because her heart was so sad.

This baby would have no celebration. Kim would have no honoring as a new mother. There would be no silly party games, no finger sandwiches and stork-adorned cake, no pastel gift bags holding miniature hats and socks and pajama sets. There were no women to share their experience and advice, no birth stories told in a one-upping fashion. There was no one in her life right now with whom she could share this experience and look to for advice as the day grew near, and when the baby came home there would be no stream of visitors bearing casseroles and begging for a turn to hold the new bundle of joy.

Kim wiped tears from her cheeks and mopped her nose with a

tissue. This was hardly the first milestone of her life that would pass unnoticed and unrecognized, and she'd stopped shedding tears over them a long time ago. But she thought she'd reached a new phase in her life where her experience matched up more closely with those of "normal" people—people who had grown up in a regular home with a family and a caring community surrounding them. She thought she'd finally be able to leave behind the foster kid identity. But once again her isolation slapped her in the face, and this time she was not the only one affected. Not that the baby would know the difference—but to Kim it was just like bringing the child into the same stark existence in which she herself had grown up: solitary and unknown.

Kim snapped off the television and stood. She had to do something to show her baby how much she was loved—and something to raise her own spirits. She couldn't bear to mope all day and expose the baby to all that pessimism. She grabbed her purse and keys and left, heading for the bus stop. She knew exactly where to go.

The strip mall housed one giant box store after another—home goods, electronics, discount clothing, and her destination: the baby store. Kim was instantly cheered when she entered it. The sight of all the gentle colors and practical gadgets brought a smile to her face. She pulled a shopping cart from the corral and launched straight into the clothing.

Now don't go crazy. She had no idea how much money they had in the bank. They didn't even have a place to put baby clothes once she bought them. But she told herself she didn't need to get much today, just a few things to perk herself up and honor the little life she was growing.

Kim wound the cart through the displays, unable to control the urge to reach out and stroke every hanging outfit, every blanket, every bib. She selected a package of rainbow-hued bodysuits, a three-piece sleeper set, a flowered blanket so soft it made her want to cry again. A pack of socks, a couple of hats, and three pairs of knit pants to match the bodysuits went into the cart as well, and then, though she'd always hated the look on other people's baby girls, two elasticized hair ribbons with a giant silk flower attached.

Humming along with the music playing over the store-wide stereo, she meandered into the aisle of bath things. She pulled a ladybug-themed towel and washcloth set from the shelf, then baby shampoo and lotion. The next aisle held baby-proofing products; the one after that, diaper bags. Despite her attempts at frugality, every aisle held something she knew she needed, and she didn't see the point of waiting until the last minute to buy any of it when she was already here. This wasn't the kind of activity Rick would enjoy, so she'd end up doing it alone anyway.

By the time she reached the back of the store, she knew she had to call it quits. The cart was almost full, and she had to somehow wrangle it all home on the bus. She wheeled her purchases up to the registers and relished placing each item on the belt.

"It looks like you had fun," said the cashier as she scanned her items.

"I did! This is our first, so we need a lot."

"Congratulations!"

"Thanks."

When the cashier handed her the receipt, Kim made a point of stuffing it into her purse without looking at it. It didn't matter if she'd spent a little more than she'd planned. Like she'd told the cashier, they needed a lot of things. It was unavoidable. And besides, she'd had fun, and it had been awhile since she'd had fun.

Standing at the bus stop, Kim realized she did not want to go home. Her days were all running together—she never did anything, never went out. This was the first time in months she'd ventured away from her usual destinations. And she wasn't even tired—it seemed a pity to waste all this energy. When her bus came she let it pass and boarded instead the bus that would take her to the mall.

When she arrived, she realized she hadn't taken into account the three loaded bags of baby things. By the time she got into the mall, she was exhausted from lugging them along. She made a slow but steady beeline for the customer service desk. "I don't suppose I could leave these here while I shop, could I?"

The woman behind the counter smiled and took her name. "They'll be right here when you get back," she said as she placed them along the back wall. "And if you need help taking them out to your car, just let us know."

Kim thanked the woman and set off for a brief wander, her spirit light. When her eye caught a maternity store, she had no choice but to enter. The sale they were having was too good to pass up, so she picked up some clothing for herself.

When she left, her stomach began to rumble, and her nose caught the scent of the food court above her. She took the elevator up and got a snack from a sandwich shop, then ice cream for dessert, relieved that so many places took credit cards these days since Rick never gave her any cash.

She was in front of Nordstrom's when nature called. After visiting the bathroom, she discovered a "woman's lounge" where a mother was nursing her baby. The plush armchairs beckoned to her, and she sank into one with a moan.

"How far along are you?" the woman asked, nodding with a smile to her maternity store bag.

"About seven months."

"Your first?" Kim nodded. "Congratulations. This is our first too."

Kim smiled. "She's beautiful. We're having a girl too."

"All my friends are going on their second kid, and all the ones with girls told me they're great until they're three. We'll see if it's true."

All my friends. A stab of envy—or was it heartburn?—made Kim shift in her seat. "The teenage years will be interesting too."

The woman laughed. "I know—I keep thinking about what a drama queen I was back then and wondering if she'll be as bad as I was." She hiked the baby onto her shoulder to burp her.

Kim was intrigued by the nursing. "I haven't thought about whether or not I'll breastfeed. Has it been hard? I don't know anything about it at all."

"Eh, it was a little trying at first, but it's so much easier overall. Never have to worry about cleaning bottles, or running out of formula, which is insanely expensive anyway. I joined La Leche League and it really helped. You should join; you'll learn a lot. And the women there are so friendly and helpful."

Friends! Kim wanted to hug the woman. "I've never heard of it, but I'll definitely join. I don't have any friends with babies, and I don't have any female relatives, so I'm really in the dark."

The woman frowned. "I'm so sorry—that must be really hard. I'll give you my number, if you'd like. I live over near the university. I'd be happy to help you out with anything—I could give you a ride to an LLL meeting if you wanted. I'm Jillian, by the way."

Kim couldn't smile big enough. "I'm Kim. Thank you so, so much, Jillian. I would love to get together, and go to that meeting too."

"Great! If you've got a pen we can trade phone numbers." Papers and pens were found and numbers exchanged; then they talked for a few more minutes until Jillian needed to leave. Once alone in the lounge, Kim leaned her head against the plush chair back and closed her eyes. *A perfect ending to a perfect day. I'll just rest for a minute and then go home.*

She awoke to the rattle of a cleaning cart being pushed down the hallway into the bathroom. She jolted upright and looked at her watch. It was already four o'clock.

"Oh no." She shoved herself out of the chair and took off towards the center of the mall where her bags were waiting for her. She didn't know the bus schedule; she had no way of knowing when she'd make it home. If she didn't have dinner ready . . .

"Can I get my bags, please? And do you know when the #5 North bus comes next?"

The concierge looked up the schedule in a binder with maddening slowness. "Three minutes."

"Thanks." She took off at as much of a run as she could muster, her bags slamming against her legs and into the people she brushed past. She burst through the doors to the outside, her lungs aching, begging the baby not to be distressed and willing her body not to react poorly to the sudden exercise.

She spotted the bus approaching the stop. She still had a hundred yards to go.

Please! Please wait! She waved at the bus, hoping to catch the driver's attention, but she could see the doors closing and knew she was out of luck. She came to a stop on the sidewalk, tears welling in her eyes, legs trembling. She sucked in the hot air and began to walk. *Think. Think. What other bus comes this way? What other route is there to get home? Maybe I should just take a taxi.* She didn't know what would be worse at this point — to be late and not have dinner ready, or to add yet another unexpected expense to the list. Neither would make Rick happy. *You idiot. You stupid, stupid fool.*

Too antsy to decide or even to think straight, Kim continued walking to the bus stop, but turned around twice to catch a cab instead. The second time she stuck with that decision, figuring Rick wouldn't know about it until he looked at the bank statement, whereas he'd know a lot sooner if she didn't have dinner prepared on time. She flagged down a cab as it pulled away from the curb heading towards her, and almost cried with relief when it pulled over.

She gave the driver her address, then sank back into the cracked leather seat and gulped deep breaths as she thought about how to put together a quick dinner. She mapped out a plan of attack for chicken parmesan, hoping she'd be at least half done by the time he came home. She'd just tell him she'd fallen asleep without setting an alarm.

When the taxi pulled into the parking lot, Kim pulled out her wallet and gave the driver her credit card. She gathered her bags, signed the sales slip, and was just closing the door to the car when she saw Rick pull in an hour early. Her mind raced for an excuse, but there was no explaining away the bags in her hands and the fact that she was just getting home. She mustered a smile as his eyes met hers, waved, and tried to look unconcerned as she leaned against the wall next to the security door.

"Hi sweetheart," she said as he approached. "You're home early—how was your day?"

"Where have you been?" Frowning, he smacked the bags so he could see the names. "This all baby crap?"

"Some of it, yes, and some clothes I needed. All necessities, I promise."

He opened the door and she followed him in, a glimmer of hope igniting in her chest. Mild annoyance—all that worry and all he showed was mild annoyance. He could be so unpredictable sometimes.

He shut the door behind them and grabbed the bags out of her hands. He upended them each in turn, spilling the contents to the floor. "Receipts?"

"In my purse." She pulled them out, fumbling them with fingers that didn't want to work properly, then handed them over before kneeling to straighten the mess.

He cursed and the receipts fluttered to the floor beside her. "You spent over three hundred bucks!"

Her breath caught in her throat. "I—I did? I didn't realize—"

He hauled her to her feet, his fingers a vice on her arm. "Of course you didn't. Because you don't think. You never think." The crack of his hand against her face rang in her ears. "You think I work all day just so you can go spend my money on crap like this?" A fist this time. "I knew that baby was a mistake—three hundred bucks!"

His fist found her solar plexus. Her breath was gone, an explosion of pain doubled her up and sent her to the floor. She hugged her middle, her mind screaming words that her mouth couldn't form and her voice couldn't create. "I can't believe I thought I could trust you." His foot kicked at her shoulder, then her abdomen. Her breath returned and she howled, writhing. "I should have known you were too stupid to trust with a credit card."

Kim curled on the floor, sobbing. Her entire body was rigid, waiting for the next blow, but it never came. She heard the zipper on her purse, the unsnapping of her wallet, and then both fell to the floor beside her. She peeked through squinted eyelids. The spaces where her credit card and bank card had been were empty.

He walked away, muttering to himself, and she forced herself to her feet and limped into the office where she locked the door behind her and sank to the floor.

It's my own fault. It's my own stupid fault. Pain pulsed all over her body, and nausea roiled in her stomach. She shuddered with pain and fear, waiting for Rick to bang on the door and demand she come out. Her eyes locked onto a digital clock that sat on the desk. She watched the minutes pass and felt the panic leaving her body, replaced by the leaden weight in her stomach of adrenaline and tension settling out of her system.

Her hand drifted from cheek to jaw to shoulder to stomach, assessing the extent of each injury. Nothing was broken as far as she could tell, but she ached all over and knew it would be days before she could sleep comfortably.

She inched to her feet, straightening slowly, and pulled a blanket from the closet shelf. The office chair wasn't the best place to curl up, but it was the only option besides the floor. With her legs crossed on the seat, she wrapped the blanket around her body and closed her eyes after checking once more that the door was locked.

She was almost asleep when her abdomen twinged. It was just enough to make her sit up straight and unfold herself in the chair. She rested her hands on her belly. *What's going on, baby?*

Another twinge, stronger this time, with the familiar ache of a menstrual cramp. She froze, fingers spread over the baby, willing it to move, to tell her somehow that she was alright.

Another twinge. And another. Each stronger than the last.

She stood and opened the door. Rick was coming out of the

bedroom, remorse etched in his features. "Kim, baby, I don't know what came over me."

"I think I'm in labor."

It was the first time she'd ever seen fear on his face. "What? How do you know?"

"I just do. We need to go to the hospital."

"Are you sure? Maybe we should just wait and see if—"

Another cramp, strong enough this time to make her gasp. She grabbed his arm. "Now, Rick. We need to go now."

KIM HAD NEVER BEEN TO A HOSPITAL. She'd watched enough episodes of *ER* to have an idea of how they worked, but the unfamiliarity combined with her fear made her want to run back to the car and hide. The thought of her precious girl being born too early was the only thing that kept her at the admissions desk.

Rick stood beside her, his hand clenching hers. They'd said nothing to each other on the way to the hospital, but the look he gave her as they walked up to the emergency entrance said plenty. *Keep your mouth shut.* She'd practiced her story in her head while Rick drove—*I was cleaning the baby's room and the closet organizer collapsed on me*—until she began to believe it had actually happened. All her stories ended up that way. Figments of an imagination so desperate she forgot they were empty lies.

"How can I help you?"

"I think I'm in labor, but I'm only seven months."

The nurse handed her a clipboard and nodded to the dingy plastic seats in the waiting area. "Someone will come out for you real soon. Just sit over there and start filling out that paperwork."

They sat together, and Rick took the clipboard as another contraction made her wince. "Here, let me fill it out." She closed her eyes and pictured her baby. *Stay in, sweetie. Stay in, it's too early to come out. Stay in for Mama, okay?*

A nurse called her name from the doorway into triage. They stood, but the nurse shook her head. "Just Kim for now, sir. When we're done checking her out we'll bring you back."

"But I'm the father. And Kim's fiancé."

"I know, but that's the policy. She'll only be back there a few minutes." The nurse plucked the clipboard from Rick's hand and ushered Kim into the hallway where a wheelchair awaited. Kim sat down, suddenly scared.

The nurse wheeled her into a room with cubicles curtained off from each other. She rolled Kim into one of the cubicles and helped her onto the table. "We're just going to take a look with the ultrasound, see what's going on, take your vitals, that sort of thing, okay?"

"Okay."

The sonogram showed the baby healthy and moving, a sight that brought tears to Kim's eyes. The belt wrapped around her abdomen showed the contractions were in fact the real thing, however, and the nurse called to the maternity ward that she had a patient to admit. After hanging up she turned to Kim and fixed her with an unwavering stare. "Tell me about your bruises."

She feigned confusion for a brief moment, then appeared to catch her meaning. "Oh, right — we were working on the nursery. The closet has so much junk piled in it, and I was trying to pull something off the shelf and the whole stupid thing collapsed on me. Rick told me I should have just let him do it, but you know how it is, you can never trust a guy to do it the way a woman would. Their idea of cleaning—"

"Okay, okay." The nurse waved her hand, impatient. "Look, this is your chance to protect yourself and your baby. Just tell me you don't want him in the ward with you and we'll take care of it. You won't even have to see him. We won't blame it on you, we won't tell him you said anything, we'll just tell him it's policy." The nurse glanced at Kim's left hand. "You're not married yet, right?"

"Right. But—"

"Perfect." The door opened and another nurse stood waiting for Kim. The triage nurse looked back to Kim, eyebrows raised. Her voice was soft. "I know you're scared, sweetheart. We can help you through it, though. Just give me the word."

For a brief moment, "yes" was on the tip of her tongue. But she just couldn't seem to say it.

Her gaze faltered, falling away to the chart the nurse held. "I don't know what you're talking about."

She heard the nurse sigh, then she detached the belt from Kim's waist and helped her off the table. "The fiancé is in the waiting room," she told the maternity ward nurse as she handed off Kim's chart. Then, to Kim, with resignation in her voice, "Good luck, sweetheart."

The nurse pushed Kim's wheelchair back to the waiting room and called for Rick to join them. He jumped from the chair and was beside Kim in a heartbeat, clutching her hand in his and staring hard into her eyes. She knew the question they were asking, and she tried to silently convey reassurance as they entered an elevator.

The nurse brought them to a laboring room, and the doctor on call came to give her an exam. "Seven months, eh? Taking your vitamins?"

"Yes, every night."

"Good girl." He studied the monitor where the contractions were measured and made a note on her chart. "The baby is checking out fine. We'll give you some terbutaline and see if that helps with the contractions. If we can't get those under control we'll need to keep you until we're confident they've stopped."

He patted her leg and left and was soon replaced by a nurse who brought in the syringe of terbutaline. "Hello there," she said, chipper in spite of the circumstances for Kim's visit. "Have you ever had a terbutaline shot?"

"No."

The nurse made an apologetic face as she swabbed Kim's thigh with iodine. "It burns, I'll warn you right now. And it might make you feel sort of jittery—racing heart, that sort of thing. That's normal." Without ceremony or warning she jabbed the syringe into Kim's leg. "We'll keep an eye on you and see how this works. If it doesn't help in the next thirty minutes we'll do another one."

Kim tried to smile despite the fire in her leg. "Sounds great, I guess."

The nurse returned a smile of her own. "Are you hungry? Can I get you a snack?"

"That would be great, thanks."

The nurse left and Rick walked to the door, checking left and right into the hall before coming back to the bed. "So now what?"

She sighed, her head beginning to throb. "I don't know."

Rick's eyes caught hers. "How did you get those bruises?"

Her jaw dropped. "How did I—oh." Why was her mouth suddenly so dry? "That—that shelf in the nursery closet fell on me."

"Right. Right." He nodded slowly, as though the memory was coming back to him, then released her gaze and stared stonily out the window. Her mind picked up the story again, shoring it up. *That stupid shelf. I should have known it would come down on me. It's been hanging on for months; it's a miracle it took this long. It's just my luck that I'd be under it when it finally let go.*

The nurse returned with a giant plastic mug of water and a handful of packaged saltine crackers. "Here you go. And if you need anything you can page me with this little button right here." She pointed to the remote that hung off the bed. "Or just holler down the hall. The nurse's station is two rooms down. I'm Jill, by the way."

"Thanks, Jill."

"No problem. Be back in a bit."

Kim took a deep breath and pressed her head back into the pillow. "Could you open the crackers for me? My hands are shaky."

"Yeah, sure." Rick tore open the package and handed her the crackers. "So what do you think—are you going to be alright?"

"Sure. *I'm* not the one we need to worry about. It's the baby that is at risk here." *Not that you care.*

Despite the story she'd drilled into her memory, Rick's words came back to her. *"I knew that baby was a mistake."* She chewed the crackers with more force than necessary, calling on the pain it kicked up in her jaw to help drive away the thoughts that were trying to get her attention. She couldn't deal with them right now.

Rick took a package of crackers for himself and sat in a chair near the window. "Want me to turn on the TV?"

"Sure."

He located the remote and began to flip through the limited stations, finally landing on a football game without asking if she cared. She tried to concentrate on the game and ignore the warnings her heart was trying to send her. More crackers, more water, more contractions on the monitor, though less frequent and intense than when they'd first arrived. When Jill came back in with the doctor, she brought Kim a Styrofoam container of red Jell-O. "I know none of this is very filling, but if this next shot works then you can have something more substantial. Until then we need to keep you on easy stuff like this. How are you feeling?"

Kim took another deep breath. "Jittery, like you said I would. My hands are sort of shaky and I feel really anxious."

Jill nodded as the doctor made notes on her chart. "Par for the course, I'm afraid."

"I'm encouraged by how much things have slowed down here," the doctor said. "Hopefully it'll only take one more dose. I'll be back in another thirty minutes to see how you're doing."

After the second injection lit her leg afire once more, Kim found it harder to keep at bay the thoughts that had been creeping into her mind since arriving at the hospital. She stared at Rick, oblivious as he watched television, and wished he would leave. If only the options the triage nurse had given her hadn't been so extreme — if only she'd offered to send him home and tell him to come back tomorrow, so she could have some time alone. That would have been perfect. It wasn't that she wanted him to leave completely. She just needed time to think, and it was getting harder and harder to do that with him around.

Thirty minutes came and went, and when the doctor returned he didn't like what he saw. "They're still coming, and haven't slowed down any more. I'd like to admit you overnight so we can keep an eye on you and make sure we're able to get this under control." He looked to Rick. "Why don't you go home, Mr. Allen. If things pick up again we can give you a call, but I doubt they will, and trust me, you don't want to sleep on that chair tonight if you don't have to. Save that experience for when your wife comes back here to deliver."

Before he had a chance to argue, Kim added her own argument. "You've got work in the morning. This isn't worth missing it for, and if you sleep here you won't feel rested enough in the morning. I'm just going to be sleeping anyway." She smiled, assuring him their secret was safe.

Rick frowned, and Kim knew he was weighing his options — stay and risk looking controlling, or go and risk her spilling their secret.

"We'll let you two talk it over," the doctor said, ushering Jill out to the hall and pulling the door partially closed.

"It's alright," Kim said. "Honestly, it's fine. Go home."

Rick ran a hand through his hair. "I'm sorry, Kim."

"I know. Go get some sleep. I'll call you when they're ready to release me."

Rick stared at her, and she felt like he could see all the way to her soul. Her jitters multiplied. "Stop it," she said, trying to smile. "Are you trying to burn a hole in my head with that look?"

Rick sucked in a breath and let it out with a whoosh. "Alright. Fine. Feel better." He pulled his jacket from the back of the chair, then kissed her. "Call me if you need anything."

"I will."

He kissed her once more, then left the room.

Kim stared at the doorway, waiting for him to reappear. Surely it couldn't be that easy? He'd be back, if not immediately, then within an hour or two, certainly.

But with each minute that passed while she was blessedly alone, she felt some of the anxiety slip away. Jill came back now and then to check on her, bring her more simple treats, and later another shot of terbutaline. But despite the continuing contractions, Kim had a sense of peace about the baby. It wouldn't come anytime soon; she knew it. It was just buying her time alone, creating a reason for her to stay in the hospital and, more importantly, for her to be alone without Rick.

She needed to think.

Jill left again and shut the door behind her. Kim turned off the television, which she'd kept on to distract herself with until she was ready. There wasn't silence, per se — the monitor beside her beeped now and then, pages for doctors could be heard in the hallway, and there were groans of a woman in labor in the room next door. But there was silence enough for her to listen to her heart and hear what it had been trying to tell her all evening.

Rick did not want this baby.

She'd known it, deep down, since the night she'd told him, but he'd worked hard to convince her — and maybe himself — that it wasn't true. But she couldn't pretend anymore that they were in this together the way she wished they were. He was in because she was, not because he wanted to be. The things he'd bought for her when she first found out had been attempts to smooth over his first negative response — not an expression of how eager he was to become a father. He'd never expressed interest in coming to her appointments, even when she knew they'd be seeing the baby on the ultrasound and learning the sex.

He hadn't been able to hide his disappointment when she'd come back from that appointment, either. If it had been a boy, maybe he would have managed to rouse some interest. But a girl wasn't enough for him. He hadn't even tried to be happy for Kim, who was over the moon at the thought of a little girl to dress in pink and adorn with barrettes. Instead he'd sneered at her joy, "Better hope she doesn't take after you." Kim had tried to let his unkind words roll off her back, but instead they stuck in her heart and twisted her elation to fear. What if she did?

But now, in the almost-silence, she allowed herself to face the truth that Rick did not love this baby. And if he did not love her, then he wouldn't treat her nearly as well as he treated Kim. The baby was innocent; she didn't deserve the beatings like Kim did, and Kim couldn't bear to think of her suffering at Rick's hand for her mother's crimes.

Her tears flowed from a deep place, burning and aching as tight sobs squeezed her chest. She knew what she had to do, and were it not for the little life inside her that needed her mother to protect her, she would never even consider it. But it was her only option.

She had to leave Rick.

By morning Kim's contractions had stopped. Her last shot of terbutaline had been administered hours ago, but the doctor had insisted she stay long enough for them to be certain they weren't going to start up again. It was nearly 3:00 p.m. by the time he gave her the okay to go home, and nearly 4:00 by the time Rick arrived to pick her up. "Take it easy for a week," the doctor had told her. "Pelvic rest, feet up as much as you can, no housecleaning if you can help it, and try to stay home. After that, just pay attention to your body and try not to push yourself too much. And of course, come back if the contractions start again."

She'd agreed, though she knew the contractions were done until the baby was ready to come. They'd served their purpose. Kim had her plan.

Now she was jittery because of her own thoughts. When Rick commented on her bouncing leg in the car, she blamed the trace bits of terbutaline still in her system. *You've got to calm down. You can't use that excuse for long.* The chastisement was quickly followed by a more sly thought: *Not that you'll need excuses for much longer.* One week. Just one more week. When planning last night she hadn't realized the doctor would prescribe the week of rest, and it had deflated her a bit to know she couldn't move ahead with things like she'd expected to. But a week wasn't that long, and it still gave her plenty of time to get settled somewhere else before the baby came.

Rick had turned on the charm the minute he'd walked into her hospital room, and Kim was determined to resist it. Not because she didn't believe it—there were times when he truly was wonderful to be with, far more of them, in fact, than times when he was not—but because it was going to be hard enough leaving him when she still loved him and knew he was trying to make her happy. Letting him soothe her heart would only make it that much more difficult. But even once they were home he kept it up. He came around to her side of the car and helped her out, then hooked her arm through his as they walked to the door. "So, I've got a surprise for you," he said as he unlocked the security door.

"Oh?"

"Yeah. I didn't go to work today."

She raised her eyebrows in surprise. "What? Why not?"

"Because I had something else I wanted to do."

She chuckled. "So you just up and played hooky, huh?"

He led her down the hall to their apartment. "Well, I told the boss about you and he was pretty quick to let me off for the day."

"So what did you do instead?"

He grinned as he unlocked the door. "Follow me and you'll see."

She followed him through the apartment, shuttering the memories that popped up of what had transpired there almost exactly twenty-four hours ago. He paused before the closed office door. "Close your eyes."

She obeyed and heard the door open. "Surprise!"

The first thing she saw was a pastel quilt of pink and lavender flowers. It was draped over the side of a white crib that was pushed against the far wall. Her incredulity grew as she noticed the matching area rug on the floor and the changing table that sat beside the window.

"Now, I know you probably had all sorts of decorating ideas already figured out, so if you don't like the quilt and stuff we can take it back and get something else. I just wanted to have it all done up for you, so you could see what it would be like. I didn't think it would look as impressive with just the crib and furniture."

She didn't know what to think. "Rick, it's beautiful. I can't believe you went through all this trouble."

He took her hand and led her into the room. "I thought we could paint it too—maybe bring the quilt to the hardware store so we can match the colors. I almost never use this desk anymore, so we could sell it, maybe get a rocking chair to put here. I don't know what to do with everything in the closet, but if we organize it a little better we'll have some room to hang clothes, or we could put a dresser in there. Baby clothes are little, they don't need that much room, right?"

Kim wiped tears from her eyes and squeezed his hand. "I just can't believe you did this. I love the quilt. I love the crib. It's exactly what I would have chosen."

He pulled her into an embrace, his head resting atop hers. "I'm so glad you like it. I—I'm not good at this kind of thing."

She knew he wasn't referring to decorating. It was his way of apologizing, like the earrings and other gifts earlier in their relationship had been. But rather than allowing herself to dwell on the manipulation they represented, she focused instead on how he had chosen something for the baby and not just her. He could have gotten her a necklace, or a watch, but instead he'd decorated the nursery.

Maybe she'd misread his sentiment for the baby after all.

FIFTEEN

Joshua watched as Rick ushered Kim from their car toward the security door. He saw bruises on Kim's face that hadn't been there a couple days before when he'd passed her in the hall. It made him sick to think of what Rick was doing to her—and even more sick to know he was doing nothing about it.

That night after Maddie was in bed, he decided it was time to do something to let Kim know he was willing to help her. If something were to happen to her, or to her baby, he'd never be able to forgive himself for not stepping in sooner.

But what to say? How would she react if he just told her, point blank, he knew Rick was hitting her and that he could help her leave? Would she be offended? Would he ruin the fragile connection they had? And what if she said something to Rick?

The next morning Joshua flagged Debbie down in the hall. "Hey, do you have lunch plans?"

Debbie had looked surprised at his question. "Well, no—why?"

"I've got a bit of a problem on my hands, and I wanted to get your opinion."

Concern was plain on her face. "It's not about the budget, is it?"

"Oh, no—it's a personal issue, not related to the shelter, though it may concern the shelter indirectly at some point." Confusion replaced concern, and he sighed. "Sorry, I don't mean to be so cryptic. I can explain it all at lunch—if you're willing, that is."

Her smile made Joshua smile too. He didn't often see one on her face. "Sure, I'll come to your office when I finish the group therapy session, around 11:30."

"Great. Thanks." He watched her as she walked away, unaware

that he was even doing it. He holed himself up in his office until lunch, alternating between work and idle thinking. More often than not his thoughts went to Debbie, and each time he became conscious of it he chastised himself. *Focus, buddy; you don't have a spare minute, not with two jobs.*

When lunch came around he had to resist the urge to take her somewhere elegant and expensive. He knew how hard she worked, how much of a burden she carried for the women there and the success of the shelter. Wrinkles were already etching themselves at the corners of her eyes and mouth, and even makeup couldn't disguise a perpetual look of intensity. He found himself wanting to be the one who helped her figure out how to relax.

This disturbed him.

"So, did you have someplace specific in mind?" she asked as they walked out to his car.

"Um, no, not really," he lied.

She sighed. "I've had to make too many decisions today, I don't have it in me to figure out lunch. Take me wherever you want. I like pretty much everything but Thai."

He smiled. "I'm not a big Thai fan myself. Mexican okay?"

"Sure."

Once they were settled into a booth and their orders had been taken, Debbie sat back and grinned. "So I'm dying to know more about this personal problem that sort of but not really affects the shelter."

Joshua took a deep breath. He almost didn't want to talk about it now, knowing how stressful her morning had apparently been. "Well—I think my neighbor is being abused by her fiancé."

The smile fell from Debbie's face and she leaned forward, intensity flaring once again. "What makes you think this?"

"The bruises, the occasional yelling I can hear through the wall."

She winced. "You're sure it's not the TV you hear?"

"Well, no, I'm not sure, but I just have this feeling, you know?"

She nodded, looking sad. "Yes, I do."

"What's worse is that she's pregnant. I can't remember when she's due, sometime soon, I think. And I'm pretty sure she has fresh bruises, so I don't think he's laying off because of the baby." He shrugged. "I don't know what to do. I'm hoping you have some suggestions."

"Wow, that's a tricky situation. I get the sense you don't know either of them very well."

"Maddie and I moved in a few months ago, and I've only talked with Kim a few times. She won't stop and talk to me unless I talk to her — I think she got in trouble for talking to me once, and I try not to engage her because I don't want to stir anything up. But on the other hand, I want her to know there's someone she can trust and turn to if needed. I've only talked to Rick twice. He seems nice enough but I just sense there's an edge there. Frankly, I avoid him when I can."

Debbie nodded. "That's probably for the best. It's entirely possible she 'got in trouble' for talking to you. He may see you as a threat, someone Kim could choose over him, his competition. But rather than going *mano a mano* with you and proving himself to be the better guy, he exerts his control over her — blames her for trying to seduce you, or for making you come on to her. He's afraid to lose her, but instead of being the best guy she knows so that she doesn't want to leave, he intimidates her, tells her no one else would ever want her, so that she feels like she has no choice but to stay with him."

Joshua shook his head. "That's messed up."

"Very. He's not a healthy person. There's something broken there, big time."

"Must be on her end, too, to stay with someone like that and believe the crap he tells her, right?"

Debbie swirled a chip in a puddle of salsa on her plate. "Actually, no — many fairly normal, mentally healthy women end up in abusive relationships. You'd be surprised. I've met college professors, entrepreneurs, socially vivacious, *smart* women who were sucked into a relationship with a man who systematically broke them down, convinced them that they didn't deserve better than what they were getting, that no one else would ever love them. It doesn't happen overnight, and sometimes the abuse is so infrequent that the women don't even think it's abuse. They blame it on a bad mood, on a lousy circumstance, and think it won't happen again. Then, when it starts to happen more frequently, they're so used to writing it off that they don't see it for what it is. Sometimes they get out in time, sometimes they don't." She munched her chip, then shrugged. "Though sometimes it *is* a matter of two broken people coming together and one of them dominating the other. But regardless, the end result is the same."

Joshua pinched the bridge of his nose. "Okay, so what do I do? What *can* I do? My fear is that I'm going to get involved — I'm in a tight spot right now with my in-laws, who want to get custody of Maddie, and honestly, I'm scared of something happening that makes it look like I don't provide a safe home for her. What if I help her and Rick finds out? What if he comes after me? Maybe I'm overreacting, but Maddie's all I've got."

Debbie gave him a sympathetic smile. "I understand your concern. Obviously you'd have to be very sure he's not around, and it's best if no one is around to witness the two of you talking so he's not able to elicit information from anyone. Then, just let her know she can come to you if she needs any help. Don't be pushy about it, but let her know you're worried about her, and why, and that you're there for her if she needs help. If you're comfortable with it, offer her the option of storing some getaway stuff at your place, like some clothes, any personal documents she has like her social security card or birth certificate, so she can contact you if she decides to get away and she doesn't have to go back to that apartment to get them. Other than that ..." She shrugged. "The decision is hers in the end. She has to come to grips with the logical end of this relationship and decide if she's willing to stay in it that long or not."

"But what if she doesn't see the danger?"

Debbie's face was pained. "Then there's nothing you can do."

"HELLO, DEAR."

Debbie laughed. "How did you know it was me?"

"Because no one else would call the house at 9:30 on a Friday night."

"Yeah, guess you're right about that."

"So what flavor is it tonight?"

"What?"

"The ice cream. You never call on weekends unless you're stressed about something, and if you're stressed you're eating ice cream; ergo, what flavor?"

She groaned. "Seriously? I'm that predictable?"

"A mother knows her child."

"Hm. I'll take your word for it, but only because it means I'm not entirely transparent. And it's mint chocolate chip."

"Ahh, one of my favorites. Now I have a craving."

Debbie chuckled. "Come over and I'll share."

"Oh heavens, it would be nearly my bedtime by the time I got there. I wouldn't be safe to drive home. You know me. So anyway, what's on your mind?"

Debbie spooned more ice cream into her mouth, then said, "I'm a head case, aren't I?"

"We all are in our own way."

"Yeah, I know, but seriously, I have issues. I'm a glutton for punishment."

"Oh Debbie, now what makes you say that?"

"How many men have I dated in the last five years?"

"Ah. Hm."

"Precisely."

"So if you're feeling like a glutton for punishment, that must mean there's another man in your life?"

Debbie squirmed in her chair. "Well, not exactly. But sort of.

The new accountant at the shelter, Joshua — we went out to lunch today."

"Oh my, dating an employee? That's new."

"No, no, it wasn't a date, Mother. He wanted my advice. He thinks his neighbor is being abused, and he didn't know what to do. But ... I've *noticed* him, you know? He pops up in my thoughts. I remember stupid details about him like what he wore to work yesterday, stuff like that." She scooped a pattern in the top of the ice cream. "And after lunch today I couldn't stop thinking about him! And then it dawns on me that I've done this *how* many times? And each time I screw it up. How could I possibly, *possibly* do it to myself *again*?"

Her mother's voice held gentle reproach. "Because you're a woman who wants love in her life. It's not an anomaly, you know."

Debbie let out a groan. "But I don't *want* to want love in my life! I want to be independent. I want to be self-sufficient."

"No. You don't want to get hurt. You don't want independence — you want security. You don't want to be self-sufficient — you just don't want to get messed over by someone. It's healthy to want to avoid those things, but you take it to an extreme because you assume every man out there is going to treat you like that, instead of realizing that *that* is the anomaly. Your view is skewed by all the instances of abuse that you see."

And by my own misjudgment that I can't let go of. Debbie stuffed another spoonful in her mouth to avoid answering. "Hm."

"And I think there's probably some guilt there, too, about Gina. You think you owe her something, and you're afraid to have anything in your life that is going to distract you from paying her back."

The ice cream was forgotten. Debbie sat silent on the couch, her mind racing. "How did you figure all this out?"

"I told you, sweetheart. A mother knows her child."

"Why didn't you tell me this five boyfriends ago?"

Her mother chuckled. "Why does it take some of the women at

the shelter years before they finally leave their abusers? They're not ready to face the truth."

"So you thought I was ready?"

"You're listening, aren't you?"

Debbie sighed. "Yeah."

She could hear her mother's smile through the phone. "So there you go."

"I wonder why I'm ready now and I wasn't before."

Her mother chuckled. "I think you know why."

"What? Why?" Then the light bulb went on. "Oh."

"So let me know when you two go out again. And Debbie?"

"Yeah?"

"Don't forget your ice cream."

"Hey Adam, it's Joshua."

"Hey man—how you doing?"

"Pretty good, actually."

"Great! We haven't talked in a while—how's the new job?"

"The job is great. But I don't know what I'm going to do about my boss."

"Aw, man—is he a jerk or something?"

Joshua laughed. "That's the problem. *She* is great. Wonderful, in fact."

"The boss is a she? Wait—do you mean a wonderful boss, or a wonderful person, or—"

"Yeah, more like a wonderful person. A really wonderful person."

"So, wow, you really dig her then?"

Joshua heaved a sigh. "Well, it's funny. I'm not all starry-eyed or anything. It's a completely different feeling than it was when I met Lara. But, I think so, yeah."

Adam let out a holler. "Josh, man, that's great!"

"I think it is. It is, right? I mean, it's not too soon, is it?"

"Do *you* feel like it is? I think that's kind of your call. It has been over a year. Or—it's *only* been a year. Which does it feel like to you?"

He didn't hesitate. "It's been over a year. I didn't think I'd feel that way, but I do. Maddie and I have moved on — literally — and … well, I can't deny that I really like her."

"So are you gonna ask her out?"

"Well — eventually, I guess. We work together, though."

"So?"

"Really?"

"What, you're gonna pass up the woman that brings you out of mourning just because you work with her?"

"Um — no?"

"That's right."

"Okay, so … I'm going to ask her out."

"Excellent idea."

"But what about Maddie?"

"Sorry, man, that's out of my realm."

Joshua sighed. "It's been a long time since I asked a woman out."

"Flowers and dinner have worked for the last hundred years. I'm guessing that would be a safe bet."

A little knock on the door interrupted his thoughts. "Uh-oh, Maddie's awake. Gotta run."

They hung up and Joshua opened the door. "Hey baby, what's up?"

"I don't want to sleep in my bedroom alone."

"No problem, sweetheart." He picked her up and carried her to his bed, laying her in the space where Lara once slept. "You know, I've missed having you in here with me. I'm so proud of how well you're sleeping in your own room, but sometimes I get lonely."

"Me too."

He gave her another squeeze before tucking her in. "Pray again?"

"Okay."

"God, please watch over us tonight, give Maddie happy dreams, and give us both a good day tomorrow. We love you and thank you for all the blessings you've given us. Maddie, is there anything you'd like to add?"

"No."

"Okay. That's it, God. In Jesus' name, Amen."

"Sing too."

"Oh Maddie—"

"Please?"

He sighed. "Alright. *Amazing Grace* or *Be Thou My Vision?*"

"Amazing Grace."

He doused the light and sat on the edge of the bed, then began to sing the song he'd sung so often he could do it while his mind wandered. Tonight it was Debbie's face that filled his mind, their lunch and her advice, which led him to pray that Rick would behave tonight and spare Maddie the sound of Kim's pain. *Save her and that baby, God, and if you want, you can use me to do it. But if not me, then someone, God, please. Don't let him …*

He couldn't bring himself to finish the thought.

KIM SHIFTED ON THE DESK CHAIR and rearranged the blanket around her. Her body didn't fold well into the chair anymore, but the living room didn't give her the distance from Rick that she needed. She just wanted to get away for a little while.

She'd had insomnia the first night back from the hospital, and tonight she just wasn't tired enough to go to bed. It was as though her mind started moving faster once the sun went down, and by bedtime she was so full of thoughts that needed mulling and lists that needed making that she couldn't shut down and sleep. She knew if she went into the living room she'd get sucked into something on TV and not get everything out of her head that was keeping her up, and Rick would hear the TV through the wall and get mad anyway.

This weekend they were going to buy paint for the nursery. She couldn't wait to paint the room, a job that had fallen to her since Rick didn't like the smell. Not that she minded. It gave her something else to do with her day, though she couldn't start until her week of rest was over. She reached into the desk drawer and pulled out paper to make a list of paint supplies she would need.

With those thoughts out, her mind had more room to dwell on the baby. While in the hospital she'd seen a full-color picture in a brochure of what the baby looked like at this stage in its development. Its face had stunned her with its humanness. She'd never considered a baby to be real before it was born, and even the ultrasound pictures hadn't quite convinced her. But that image had completely changed her view of the being inside her, made her more real, more fathomable.

Kim stood and walked to the crib. Staring down at the flowered sheets on the mattress, she imagined herself singing to her daughter, rocking her in her arms, then lying her down to sleep. She didn't like the thought of leaving her baby alone in a room so far away from her at night, but she didn't think she'd be able to convince Rick to let her move the crib to their room. Maybe she'd make up for it during the day by holding her while she napped. It's not like she had anything else to do with her time.

Her thoughts drifted to what her baby would be like. Would she be a good sleeper? A good eater? Would her hair be blonde like Rick's or brown like hers? Whose personality would she have? Rick's creativity? Kim's sensitive heart? Would she make the same mistaskes Kim had made?

No. She will be good—kind and caring to the core. She won't have the reasons Rick and I have for our mistakes. She won't face those kinds of trials. Her eyes teared, and she mopped them with the corner of the blanket. Her mistakes had weighed heavily on her lately. She couldn't bear to think of passing them on to the baby.

A sound on the other side of the wall made her smile. Joshua was singing—to himself? His cute little girl? She pressed her ear to the wall, sliding along it until his voice was as loud as it seemed it would get. The tune sounded vaguely familiar; it conjured memories of the religious family she had lived with when she was little. She wished she could hear them more clearly. ...*grace, how sweet....saved a wretch...me...once was lost...blind but now I...*

She shook her head in frustration as his voice grew quieter. She vaguely recognized the song and wished she could remember all the lyrics; what little she'd heard made her curious. She knew what it meant to be a wretch—killing someone definitely put you in that category. But whatever grace was, she was pretty sure it couldn't do anything for the sins of her past.

SIXTEEN

TWO MONTHS LATER

The morning sun on January 18th was blinding as it reflected off the thick layer of snow and ice that coated the landscape outside Kim's window. She pushed herself up on the bed, wincing at the sharp pain that shot through her legs and groin, and flopped over to her side, then pressed a pillow over her head to hide from the light. She couldn't remember the last time she'd slept through the night and woken feeling refreshed. Everything hurt. She was ready to be done.

Twenty minutes passed before she could stomach the thought of standing and showering. She limped to the bathroom, her robe pulled as far around her beachball stomach as it would go, and stared at herself in the mirror. Her face had grown along with her belly over the last few months. So had her hands and feet, which now didn't fit any of her shoes. Rick had finally taken her out to get a new pair of gym shoes two weeks ago—not that she used them often, since she rarely left the house anymore. Just before Christmas she'd removed her engagement ring, with the help of butter, and set it back in its box until her fingers slimmed down again. She couldn't wait to have her body back.

The shower spray did little to ease the pains that pulsed through her muscles and joints. Last night's altercation hadn't helped things, either. The fresh bruises on her legs and arms were like blueberry stains on her pale skin. She inspected each one in the mirror after her shower, cataloging her penitence and boxing the memories away, stuffing them deep into the recesses of her mind. She had other things to think about, like how to pass another day.

She waddled to the kitchen and set the kettle on the stove to make hot chocolate, then pulled out a bowl for cereal. She was so tired of eating. Her appetite had been insatiable the last couple months, despite eating seconds and thirds at almost every meal. She spent half her day eating, and most of the other half planning or cooking her next meal, or cleaning up from the last one. After two heaping helpings of cereal she dumped the bowl in the dishwasher and sipped the hot chocolate that had finally cooled enough to drink. On the sofa sat a basket of baby clothes, a jumble of Easter egg colors waiting to be folded. That would be her next chore, and by the time she got them all tucked away in the nursery she'd be ready for her midmorning snack.

While she sorted onesies and knit pants and tiny socks, she thought back to yesterday and her most recent appointment at the clinic. The doctor had pressed her for an exam, but she had refused, just as she had done for the last three months. The first time, Rick had beaten her the night before her appointment and she'd been afraid of what the doctor would say if she saw her bruises. When she hadn't consented to the exam, the doctor had made a half-hearted attempt to convince her to have one, but her reasons weren't compelling enough for Kim to risk revealing the marks on her body. She had kept her clothes on at each appointment ever since, figuring it didn't matter how dilated or effaced she was — knowing wouldn't make the baby come any faster.

Despite the doctor's prognosis that all was well, Kim couldn't shake the first-time mom paranoia that plagued her. What if all that food made her daughter an overeater? What if she didn't make it to the hospital in time? What if she turned out to be a lousy mom? It was times like these when she ached for another woman to talk to. Rick refused to let her attend the LLL meeting Jillian had mentioned, and she knew he didn't want her calling some stranger to hang out. He'd even convinced her to quit the Club, much to the girls' dismay, though she'd been secretly glad that her hypocrisy would no longer be staring her — and them — in the face.

Kim stacked the clothes in the laundry basket and carried them to the nursery. The pink of the walls made her smile every time she came in, and today was no exception. She began to hum as she tried to decide where to keep the hats and socks, the blanket sleepers and bodysuits. She rearranged and reorganized three times before feeling satisfied, savoring the decision-making process and the fact that the decision was hers alone.

She was halfway out the door when her middle tightened and took her breath away. As the tightness faded she hurried to the couch and sat down to gather her thoughts. Was that what she thought it was? She checked the clock and made a note of the time, then made herself a snack and sat, pensive, in front of the blank television.

Fifteen minutes later another tightening in her abdomen brought a nervous smile to her face. She puttered aimlessly around the apartment looking for something to keep her mind off what was happening, but when the next contraction came twelve minutes later she couldn't help but call Rick to tell him.

"So now what?" he asked.

"I don't know. I don't know how long I should wait."

"I'm almost done with this project. Can you give me one more hour?"

She laughed. "I don't think it's up to me."

He sighed. She could hear the irritation in it but she was determined not to let it bother her. "Fine," he said. "I'll be home as soon as I can. Be ready to go, okay? I don't want to sit around waiting for you."

They hung up and she watched the minutes tick away until the next contraction ten minutes later. This one kicked her into action. She grabbed her overnight bag and set it by the door, then made a sandwich to take along. A few minutes later she made another sandwich, this one for Rick, and then changed her clothes into something more comfortable. Each contraction stopped her in her tracks. She squeezed her eyes shut and panted through them, clutching whatever was near to give her support.

An hour came and went and Rick still had not come home. Kim ate the sandwich she'd made and paced the apartment, feeling like a caged animal. She called him at work again but the receptionist said he was gone. "Where is he?" Her voice was a growl that rumbled from her throat at the tail end of a contraction that came only seven minutes after the one before it. When they got down to five minutes and he still was not there, panic set in. She didn't know who to call, where to go. Joshua's face popped into her mind, but she couldn't bring herself to knock on his door. The last time they'd spoken Rick had made sure she knew never to do it again. Joshua, bless his heart, had tried to convince her to leave Rick a few weeks after her hospitalization, blurting in the middle of the parking lot that he knew Rick hit her. She'd made excuses for the noises and covered for Rick as best she could, but when she'd turned to go inside she'd seen Rick's face at the window and knew she was in trouble. She hadn't seen Joshua since.

Another contraction made her groan, and she gripped the doorknob for both support and fortification. She couldn't go to Joshua, not with Rick on the way. Hopefully, anyway. *But what if he doesn't come in time?*

She waffled until another contraction hit even more quickly than the last. Pretty soon she wouldn't be able to move herself from the apartment, much less get to the car and withstand the ten-minute drive to the hospital. She cursed Rick under her breath and lurched down the hall to Joshua's door. She pounded and called out, "Hello? Is anyone home? Joshua?"

Joshua opened the door just as she was about to move on down the hall. "Kim! What's wrong?"

"I'm in labor and I don't know where Rick is!" She began to cry, then grabbed the door frame as another contraction squeezed her middle.

Joshua took her hand when the contraction ended and led her inside. "Here, sit down. Don't worry. How close are the contractions?"

"About five minutes. But they only started two hours ago."

"Okay. Let me think." His brows knit in thought, he stared at the floor for a moment, then brightened. "Ah, okay. I remember from when my wife was pregnant with Maddie. The doctor told us to go to the hospital when her contractions were four minutes apart. So you're still okay." He smiled. "I know it's easier said than done, but try not to freak out."

She sniffed and smiled. "I'll try, but they're getting close so fast."

"That's alright. Look, if Rick doesn't come soon, I'll take you to the hospital myself, okay? Maddie can go down to Carlotta's. It's not a problem." He gave her arm a gentle squeeze. "Hey, you're going to have a baby today! Do you know if it's a girl or a boy?"

"A girl."

"Aw, that's great, congratulations. Maddie's a joy. I bet you'll have a great time with her." His face changed to one of concern. "Listen, Kim. I know what happened the last time we —"

"Kim? What are you doing in there?" Rick stood in Joshua's open door, his face dark.

Kim let out a cry of frustration and pain. "Rick! Where have you been?"

"I had to make a couple stops. It took longer than I thought it would, that's all. Come on, let's go." He glared at Joshua as Kim made her way to the door, then grabbed her arm and half supported, half dragged her back to their apartment. "What were you doing in there with him?"

"Don't yell at me!" Kim burst into tears. "I was scared and you weren't here when you said you would be. I didn't know what to do. I was afraid I wouldn't get to the hospital on time. At least Joshua was being helpful."

He raised his hand to slap her but she gripped the kitchen counter and began to groan. When she finally straightened, Rick's face was pale. "What now?"

Kim gritted her teeth. "Now we go to the hospital, you idiot." She turned and headed for the hallway, not caring what he thought of her insult. Her mind could only focus on one thing right now, and Rick's pride wasn't it.

Her contractions slowed down as they drove. Kim wanted to weep with relief, but too much of her was worried about why they were slacking off. Rick braked hard in front of the ER doors and ran inside while she hauled herself out of the car only to have another contraction hit that almost drove her to her knees. A nurse followed Rick out with a wheelchair and helped get her seated, then pushed her through to the elevator to take her to the maternity ward.

The next hour was a blur to Kim. She was only aware of her body and what it was doing without any input from her. Between the contractions she kept her eyes closed and demanded silence from everyone in the room. During contractions she moaned and swayed as she gripped the elevated foot of the bed. She forgot Rick, forgot the bruises the doctors would see, and thought nothing of the noises and words that slipped unfiltered from her mouth. All her thoughts and energy were focused on one thing, and it was the only thing that mattered.

A gasp, a shout — then a thin wail of a baby fresh in the world. Kim began to laugh and cry together. "Is it still a girl?"

The nurses laughed and the doctor placed the squirming bundle on her chest. "Yes it is. Congratulations."

Kim grasped the baby to her, oblivious to the mess. "Hey baby. Hey Anne."

Rick stepped closer and wrinkled his nose. "Wow, that's, um ..."

A nurse tucked a blanket over the squalling child. "If you're going to nurse, you can give it a try."

Kim's eyes widened against her exhaustion. "Really? Already?"

"Sure. Here." The nurse helped Kim and Anne navigate their first feeding. Kim thought of Jillian at the mall and how effortless it had looked. "It gets easier, trust me," said the nurse with an understanding smile.

Kim chuckled. "You read my mind."

"It's not hard to do when you're working with a first-time mom."

Kim smiled. *Mom*.

THREE DAYS AFTER KIM AND RICK brought Anne home, Joshua and Maddie were sitting down to eat when the wail of a baby filled the air. Maddie frowned. "Anne cries a lot."

"Well, babies do that."

"Yeah, but … she cries a *lot*."

Joshua nodded as he cut the meat on Maddie's plate. "Some babies have a hard time settling down. We should pray for her—and for Kim and Rick. It can be very frustrating as a parent to have a baby that won't stop crying."

"It can be very frustrating as a *neighbor*."

Joshua laughed. "Yes, that's true sometimes. Why don't you pray, okay?"

They bowed their heads and Maddie cleared her throat. "Dear God, thank you for our food and our house and for our day today. Please be with baby Anne and make her stop crying, and please help Kim and Rick to not get frustrated. In Jesus' name, Amen."

They were halfway through dinner when a knock came at the door. Joshua's heart sank when he saw his in-laws through the peephole. *Give me strength, God.* He opened the door. "Well hello. Come on in."

"We were in the area and thought we'd stop by since we haven't seen our granddaughter in so long," said Alisha as she stepped in.

"Gramma!" Maddie slid off her chair and ran to Alisha, wrapping her arms around her grandmother's legs.

"Hello, sweetheart. Let go, please, you're wrinkling my slacks." She caught sight of the table. "Oh, we caught you at dinner, I see." She frowned. "Not much of a meal, by the looks of it."

George nodded to Maddie's plate. "I see you're eating some macaroni and cheese. I thought she was allergic to dairy."

"Well, the pediatrician said we could try it since it's been a few years. Sometimes kids grow out of it." He refrained from sharing that he'd used raw unpasteurized milk and cheese to make the sauce from scratch. What they didn't know couldn't come back to haunt him later. "She's had a few things this week and seems to be doing pretty well."

"Hm." Alisha glanced around with the look of disdain that always came over her face when she entered their apartment, then frowned. "What's that sound?"

"That's baby Anne next door," Maddie said. "They just had a baby last week, and she cries a lot."

"Can you believe how clearly you can hear that? These walls are just paper, Joshua. Just paper."

"That doesn't sound like a baby," George said with a frown. "What is that? Who's yelling?"

Joshua's heart thunked in his chest. *Oh no, God. Please make it stop.* "Um, yeah, that's probably—"

"That's their TV," Maddie said. "They watch shows with a lot of yelling and leave it on loud a lot."

Joshua looked at Maddie. "Yes. They do, don't they."

Alisha looked from Maddie to Joshua and narrowed her eyes. "Madeline, sweetheart, will you please excuse us for a few minutes?"

Maddie looked to Joshua, confused. Joshua nodded to her room. "She means can you leave us alone for a few minutes. Why don't you go to your room and draw a picture for them to take home?"

"Okay!"

Alisha waited until the door closed before she turned on Joshua. "Are we hearing what I think we're hearing? Is there violence going on in that apartment next door?"

Joshua sighed. "I suspect there might be, yes. I've already spoken with my boss at the shelter to get her advice about what to do—"

"What to *do*? I'll tell you what to do, Joshua, you get out of this dump and away from these people before something happens to Maddie!"

"I don't think anything's going to happen to Maddie, Alisha. We almost never see them; they pretty much keep to themselves. Kim is a sweet girl who made a really bad choice, and I feel like God has put me here to help her get out of it."

He regretted it the minute he said it. Even before the words were out of his mouth he knew he shouldn't go there, but frustration rather than reason was driving his brain. To expect George and Alisha to understand compassion, much less the idea of submitting to God's will, was like expecting Maddie to understand politics.

Alisha's eyes narrowed. "Oh, I see. You put some girl who's too stupid to know she should leave a guy when he hits her ahead of your own child. She must be awfully pretty to turn your head so soon after you've lost your wife."

"I figured there was something keeping you in this slum," George said. "Makes sense now. That baby actually yours?"

Joshua closed his eyes, every muscle tensed and awaiting the order to fly into a rage. He couldn't even pray. He just flung his anger heavenward in his mind. Sucking in a breath, he counted backwards from ten, then opened his eyes.

For a brief moment, God allowed him to see his in-laws for what they really were. Wounded parents who didn't understand why their daughter was gone, who were angry at her—and him—for the path of treatment they chose, and who had no hope of ever seeing her again. To them, Maddie was the last link they had to their only child. To gain control of her would allow them the chance not only to protect that link, but to take another stab at parenting so they could fix the mistakes they'd made the first time—mistakes that led their daughter to become religious, to marry a man they deemed beneath her, and to shun the powers of Western medicine until it was too late.

Anger drained away as Joshua gained new insight into their plight. In its place grew pity and a bit of sympathy the size of a mustard seed. But it was enough.

"I understand what you're trying to do." His voice was quiet, controlled. George and Alisha looked wary. "I understand. I really do. I wish you had the hope I have of seeing Lara again. I know she tried to tell you about the belief we both shared—and still share—in Christ, and if you ever want to know more, I hope you'll ask me, because I would love nothing more than to be able to share it with you. But until you do, your bitterness and anger isn't going to go away. I know what's going on, the lengths you're willing to go to try to build a case against me so you can get Maddie, and I can't help but feel so sorry for you."

A blush crept up Alisha's neck and into her face as her features became pinched with fury. George, on the other hand, seemed to age ten years in as many seconds, his shoulders sagging and his whole face drooping. Before they could speak, Joshua continued. "Despite what you've done, and what you're trying to do, God will help me love you. But loving someone doesn't mean letting them walk all over you. I need to protect both myself and Maddie from the poison you're trying to spread. So I'll ask you not to come over without calling first and asking if it's okay. If you violate this request, or if you try to see Maddie behind my back, I *will* go to the police and file a complaint. And if you continue to spend your visits this way, then there will be no more visits. I know there are grandparents' rights laws on the books here, but I am prepared to go to court to uphold that boundary. Are we clear?"

Alisha gasped, her face nearly purple. But George just turned to the door and put a hand on Alisha's arm. "Come on," he said. "We need to go."

"Absolutely not! Didn't you hear what he just said? The absolute *nerve* he had to accuse—"

"Alisha, let's go."

"—I will *not* go. No. Not until I've seen Madeline again. Madeline!"

"Alisha!" George's shout startled Joshua as much as it did Alisha. Tears sprang to Alisha's eyes and Joshua's heart skipped a couple beats. "We're going. Now." He turned to Joshua. "Say good-bye to Madeline for us."

Joshua watched in stunned silence as George ushered his weep-ing wife out the door. He recovered and shut the door behind him as Maddie came out of her room with a pout on her face. "Where did Gramma and Grampa go? Why didn't they say good-bye?"

Joshua knelt and wrapped his arms around her. "They just had to go, sweetheart. I'm sorry."

He helped her back into her seat so they could finish their now-cold supper, his mouth making light conversation with Maddie while his heart prayed fervently for her grandparents, and for the chaos that lived next door.

DEBBIE CHEWED A NAIL AS she looked over the budget summary Joshua had emailed her. *It could be worse, right? I'm sure it could be worse.* She knew from the discussions they'd had over the last few months that things were going to be tight. Joshua had submitted grant proposals to four organizations so far, but none of them had panned out yet. She'd been so excited when all their open staff positions had finally been filled, until Joshua had reminded her that more staff meant the need for more money. Like most small nonprofits, the economy's struggles had hit them hard. *If it's not one thing, it's another. At least I'm not doing the work of three people anymore.*

Debbie didn't feel like confronting her thoughts any further, so she grabbed her purse and coat and wrote "Running errands" on the message board outside her office.

She didn't like running from things, but it was becoming a habit. Literally, like escaping her office with the excuse of errands, but figuratively in that she'd been avoiding the one person to whom she truly felt drawn.

A week after their first lunch a few months back, Joshua had asked her out again, this time for a purely personal dinner. She'd seen it coming but still didn't know how to react, and in the end she pulled the work ethics card, saying it wouldn't be right given their professional relationship. But after the gentle rebuff, she'd agonized over the decision and eventually come to regret it.

A month later they went out for lunch again, this time to discuss the shelter's operating budget. Their conversation had come easily, and she was shocked to see they'd been gone nearly three hours when they finally packed up to go back to the shelter. And just as before, a week after their lunch, Joshua had asked her out to dinner again. Once again she'd made up an excuse that left her aching inside.

Debbie drove to the bank, then to city hall, taking care of errands that really did need running, then sat in her car hating herself. She was a coward, plain and simple. She couldn't bring herself to say yes to Joshua because she was afraid she'd screw that up too, but unlike all the other men she'd dated, he sparked her in a way that made her afraid to hurt him — or worse, to lose him. It wasn't just because he'd already lost his wife, or then she'd have to face him every day at work. It was because she'd never felt so strongly about a man, especially one she barely knew. It made her want to protect him, and right now, that meant protecting him from her.

Because the truth of it was, men weren't the only ones she had a hard time trusting. She also couldn't trust herself. It had been almost five years, and she still felt the hurt as freshly now as she had then. She'd been dating Charlie for almost a year when she'd discovered he was married.

Song after song played on the radio, and three commercial breaks later she began to feel guilty for being gone for so long. She took the long way back to the shelter and snuck back to her office to avoid Joshua. Her stealth didn't pay off like she'd hoped, however.

"Come in," she called when a knock sounded on her door.

Joshua opened the door halfway and leaned in from the hall. "Hey — I thought I saw your car in the lot." Joshua was smiling, but it quickly faded. "Do you have a minute?"

"Of course." She motioned to the chair and he sat down without relaxing. "I heard it again last night. The baby was crying and Kim was screaming and …" He shook his head. "Maddie heard it too. Turns out she's heard it before, but she thinks it's the television. And my in-laws heard it too, but that's a whole different story that

I can't get into without risking punching a hole in the wall, so ..."
He shrugged. "I told you what happened when I tried to talk to her
about leaving, right?"

Debbie nodded. It was a common consequence for domestic
abuse victims, being punished for talking to someone the abuser
viewed as a threat, especially when that person was trying to pull
the victim away. She'd heard dozens of similar stories from victims
themselves, but she knew it was new territory for Joshua. He didn't
have the emotional callouses she did. "Don't blame yourself. You did
what you could. But you've got to remember that until she wants to
get out, she's not likely to acknowledge that she's even in danger.
And once she reaches that stage, chances are she'll find a way out.
It sounds like you've built a good relationship with her, shallow
though it may be. She'll remember you when she's ready."

He nodded, eyes focused on the middle distance. "I know you're
right, but it's still hard." He sighed and stood. "Thanks for letting
me talk."

"Anytime."

He smiled with a sparkle in his eyes. "I'm usually pretty chatty
at dinner. And Maddie gets tired of hearing me talk. Any chance of
you standing in for her, say this Friday?"

She let out a laugh. "You are persistent."

He spread his hands, beseeching. "A guy's gotta do what a guy's
gotta do."

She paused, not wanting to answer on auto-pilot. A little voice
nudged her. *Say yes. Come on. Say yes.*

She tried, but she couldn't muster the courage to do it. "Thanks,
Joshua. But not this time."

He stood and nodded. "No problem. But that persistence thing is
sort of a God-given gift, so ..." He grinned and walked to the door.
"Keep working on those excuses. I won't accept the same one twice."

He closed the door behind him. Debbie slumped in her seat. She
had to get cracking — the pile in her inbox was two inches deep, she
had twelve new emails, and she had to start brainstorming some
more excuses before it was too late.

SEVENTEEN

Kim's head was pounding and her arms felt like they were going to fall off. Anne hadn't stopped crying in two hours, not even for a minute, and yet somehow she had the energy to cry louder when Kim tried to put her down. So Kim continued to walk the nursery, corner to corner and back, bouncing and shushing and begging the baby to be quiet.

Through the wall she could hear the blaring television in the living room. Rick's idea of being helpful was keeping to himself and turning up the TV so he could hear it over Anne's cries. Kim tried not to be resentful—he was a man, after all, and men weren't as attuned to the needs of their babies as mothers were. Or were supposed to be. She didn't have any idea what was wrong herself.

Kim sang every song that came into her head, lullaby or not. She changed her route around the room to give them both some variety. She tried showing Anne the view out the window, tried winding up the mobile that hung above the crib, checked her diaper again, tried to nurse her again. And then, inexplicably, she began to calm down. Kim collapsed in the desk chair, singing softly and nursing her again, and watched as Anne's eyelids drooped and finally closed.

She bit back the cries of relief that bubbled from her gut, afraid to do anything that might wake her. Closing her eyes, she leaned her head back and whispered "Thank you" to the sleeping bundle in her arms.

The thought of holding Anne for her entire nap was enticing, but Kim didn't think her arms would last much longer. She waited as long as she could, then stood in slow motion and glided to the crib. Arms trembling, she lowered Anne to the mattress, then fled the room before she could do anything to jeopardize the miracle.

Kim made a beeline for the bedroom, shut the door gently be-hind her, then collapsed on the bed, weeping. She was so tired. Her entire upper body was in constant pain from the strain of holding Anne through so many crying spells. Her breasts ached from the weight of the milk that flooded them to overflowing, and her emo-tions bubbled raw beneath the surface, ready to go haywire at the slightest provocation.

And Rick just sat in the living room watching TV.

Kim sat up, gulping cleansing breaths and trying to get a grip. She shouldn't think badly of him; this was an adjustment for him too. She hadn't been able to make much for dinner the last few days, and every time the baby cried at night it woke him too. Granted, he got to go back to sleep, but he also had to go to work in the morn-ing—she at least could stay in her pajamas all day and nap with Anne. Not that she did—there was too much else to do to keep the place the way Rick liked it, laundry and dishes and cooking and cleaning—but at least the option was there.

She splashed cold water on her face and fixed her ponytail be-fore venturing back into the living room. Rick was snoring on the couch. Kim tiptoed to the kitchen and pulled cereal from the top of the fridge. She hadn't eaten since breakfast, and it was already one in the afternoon. Snack in hand, she sat at the table and wolfed it down for fear Anne would awaken before she finished.

Rick woke when the dishwasher door got away from her and banged shut. "Thanks a lot," he said, standing from the sofa. "I finally get a nap and you wake me up."

"I'm sorry, it was an accident, believe me. The last thing I want is for anyone to wake up." Her lip began to tremble. "It took over two hours for her to fall asleep. I don't know what's wrong. I didn't think it would be this hard."

"Yeah, tell me about it." Rick opened the fridge and pulled out a soda. "How long is she gonna sleep?"

"I have no idea. Two hours? Twenty minutes?"

"Alright, well—I'm going to the store. I'll only be gone an hour. It's not like there's anything I can do if she wakes up."

Kim sighed. "Yeah, you're right. Have fun."

She felt guilty for being jealous, but she hadn't been out of the house since coming home with the baby, and the thought of wandering aimlessly down grocery aisles had never sounded so heavenly. She watched Rick leave, then flopped onto the sofa and turned on the television and triggered the guide to see what was on.

The date was in the upper corner, and she did a double-take before it set in. Tomorrow was her birthday. How could she have lost track of time like that? Besides last year, it had never been a very important day, but she'd still remembered it and marked it in her own heart even though no one else had noticed. To think the day could have passed without her even remembering!

A slow smile spread across her face. Rick never went to the store for more than twenty minutes, yet he said he'd be gone an hour. He was buying her a present, she just knew it. The thought warmed her soul and made up for the last few days of frustration with him.

Anne slept for an hour, then woke crying once more. Nursing quieted her down, though, and once she was content Kim set her in the corner of the sofa and simply stared. When she wasn't screaming at the top of her little lungs, she was beautiful. Her skin was flawless, her mouth a perfect bow. Her little arms and legs were still scrawny, but her face was filling out and the rest of her was not quite so wrinkly.

"I'm trying, Anne, I really am," she said, stroking her daughter's balled-up fist with her finger. "I sure wish I knew why you cried, though."

Anne began to fuss again, so Kim picked her up and carried her to the bedroom, then laid down on the bed and placed Anne on her chest. Cradling the baby against her, Kim began to sing to her again, and soon they were both asleep.

When the front door shut, both Kim and the baby woke with a start. Kim carried her to the living room and found Rick unloading a dozen bags of food into the pantry and fridge. "Thanks for picking all that up," she said. "I appreciate it."

"No problem." He held up a package of frozen garlic bread. "Let's do spaghetti sometime this week."

"Sure." Kim scanned the counter and bags for signs of her gift, curious to see what it was but not really wanting to find it. She'd had so few gifts in her life, she didn't want to ruin this one. He must have hidden it as soon as he'd gotten in, because she didn't see it anywhere. Pleased at the thought of all the work he'd gone through for her, she planted a kiss on his cheek. "Why don't I make that spaghetti tonight?"

"Sure, that sounds great." He finished putting the food away and stuffed the bags in the trash. "Let me know when it's ready, alright?" He walked away to the couch and sat down, but this time Kim didn't mind.

KIM AWOKE IN THE MORNING to Anne crying, snow falling, and Rick still snoring beside her. *Happy birthday to me!* One-quarter of a century gone, hopefully a couple more still to go. "Hard to imagine you turning twenty-five someday," she said to Anne as she nursed her on the sofa. "Hard to imagine you even turning one!"

As she changed Anne's diaper, Kim recounted the importance of the day for her captive audience. "Today is Mommy's birthday. No one ever did anything for my birthday when I was little, but I promise your birthdays will have hundreds of balloons and dozens of little friends and a cake with extra frosting. If you turn out to be a frosting person, that is. Though last year I did have a pretty fun birthday. In fact, that's when I met your daddy. So today is actually our anniversary too!"

It took a minute for her words to sink in. "Oh no! It's our anniversary and I don't have anything to give him!" She finished Anne's diaper change with as much speed as she could muster on four hours' sleep, then grabbed some paper off the printer and three colored pens from the desk drawer, the only artlike supplies she could find. She set Anne back in her crib and turned on the mobile, then sat at the desk and thought for a moment before putting pen to paper. "Daddy is an artist," she narrated to Anne, "so he'll probably think my drawing is pretty bad. But oh well, what choice do I have?" She sketched and crafted, and a few minutes later she set down her pen with a self-depreciating laugh. "It's the thought that counts, right?"

With another piece of paper she made an envelope, then sealed the card inside with tape and set it on the table. "We'll make Daddy pancakes for breakfast," she said to Anne, whom she cradled in one arm as she puttered around the kitchen. "He'll be up in about half an hour, and then we'll all have breakfast together."

Kim had the batter ready to pour forty minutes later, but still Rick was sleeping. An hour later he was still snoring away, and Kim was famished. She gave up on the idea of breakfast together and started a few pancakes for herself, dotting them with chocolate chips. She was just popping the last bite in her mouth when Rick staggered out of the bedroom.

"Hi sweetheart," she said through a mouthful of food. "I'm making pancakes; can I get you some? I was going to wait and eat with you but I just got too hungry."

Rick waved a hand vaguely. "Yeah, sure." He nodded to the envelope on the table. "What's that?"

"Open it and see."

Rick sat down and pulled open the envelope, then read the card. "Oh, it is our anniversary, isn't it?"

She kissed him on the cheek. "A whole year ago, can you believe it? Think how much we packed into that year!"

"Yeah, a lot, huh?" He tossed the card on the table. "Yeah, I forgot all about that, Kim. Sorry."

Kim's good mood slipped a notch. "Oh—that's alright." She watched him, waiting for him to bring up the fact that he'd remembered her birthday.

After a moment he looked up at her. "Why are you staring at me?"

"Oh—no reason, sorry." She went into the kitchen to start the pancakes. A niggling fear was growing in the pit of her stomach.

No, no, he remembered—just give him some time. He's probably got some plan. She made the pancakes. He ate them. He left to shower, and when he was done she did the same. Lunch came and went, the dinner dishes were in the sink, and finally, as she sat scrubbing a pot, she said, "Okay, you're totally killing me here. You did remember it's my birthday, right?"

Rick turned around on the couch with a sheepish look on his face. "Aw man, no, I forgot."

The emotions that sat so close to the surface these days burst forth like a volcano. "You forgot? Even when I reminded you it was the anniversary of when we met, which was *on my birthday,* you still didn't remember? You mean you seriously shopped for an hour at the grocery store?" Tears spilled down her cheeks. "I can't believe you didn't remember!"

Rick rolled his eyes as he stood. "It's been a long week; give me a break."

"Give *you* a break? It's been a long week for *you?* I'm the one who gave birth less than a month ago! I'm the one who's up a million times a night! I'm the one that carries her for hours on end when she's screaming her head off. And it's been a long week for *you!*"

His eyes narrowed. "Yeah, about that birth and that baby—who's paying for those? Consider that your present, Kim. I've been a little busy working overtime trying to pay off your debt."

Kim was livid. "*My* debt? Last time I checked it takes two to make a baby. Not that you care about her—guess you're even more like your dad than I thought." She ended her tirade with a staccato-flung epithet that earned her a slap on the face. Without pausing to think, she slapped him back.

The beat of silence that followed was deafening. Then Kim gasped out the breath she'd been holding. "Rick, I'm sorry—"

His face darkened and she knew what she was in for. She closed her eyes and waited for the inevitable.

Kim sat in the desk chair in the nursery, unaware of the tears that still coursed down her face. Anne was crying as well, lying in the crib where Kim had placed her when Rick had left the apartment. She tried to calm herself, tried to rein in her anger, reminding herself that this was what she deserved and she had no one to blame but herself. It was the same mantra she chanted after every time Rick hit her. But it was getting harder and harder to believe.

When would her penance be paid? How long would she have to endure this? Years, decades — would she be crying in a room alone somewhere when she was fifty, nursing a cracked rib or a split lip or worse? How much did it take to break even, for the scales to balance and finally tip in her favor?

When she finally had control of herself, she picked up the baby, ignoring the protests from her aching muscles and new bruises, and cradled her against her chest. "Shhh, it's okay. Mama's okay, baby. Hush now." She began to nurse her, the only almost-foolproof way of calming her, and stroked her head. "You're so lucky, Anne," she whispered. "You have a mama who's going to make sure you don't turn out the way she did. You'll never be in this position, I promise. You'll never have to pay the price I have to pay because you'll never make the mistakes I've made."

The tears she thought she'd finished crying began to flow again. *I just wish I knew how long this was going to last. I thought I could bear it forever, but I can't. Maybe if I knew how long it was going to be, I could do it, but now ...*

As though sharing her pain, the baby began to cry again. Kim rocked as she murmured soothing, empty promises and prayed for an end to her misery.

EIGHTEEN

"Daddy, can we please stay outside and make a snowman?"

Joshua glanced at the clock on the dashboard. "Sweetheart, it's getting dark. It's nearly time to make dinner."

"We can eat later. I'm not even hungry. Please-please?"

Joshua pulled into his parking spot and shut off the car. "Okay, but it's going to have to be a very small, very fast snowman, okay?"

"Alright!" Maddie swung her feet as Joshua unlocked her seatbelt and helped her to the ground. She took off for the patch in front of their unit and began to form a snowball while he carried her backpack to the railing of their patio and dropped it over.

"Want some help?" he asked her.

"No, I want to make it alone. Just watch me."

"Alright then." He leaned against the building and watched as she coaxed the snowball along the ground. His ears picked up the sound of a baby crying, and he realized it was Kim's daughter. He glanced around the parking lot and saw Rick's car was not yet there. *Here I go, God. Hope you've got my back.*

He wandered towards the windows of Kim's apartment and stopped outside the one decorated with pink curtains. After one last look to the driveway and parking lot, he looked in and saw Kim bouncing the baby in her arms as she walked across the room. He knocked on the window and Kim jumped, then gave a small smile when she saw his face. He looked once more at the parking lot, then motioned for her to open the window.

"Sounds like the baby has colic, huh?"

Her eyes swept the parking lot as she spoke, her voice terse. "If that means she screams all the time and I can't fix it, then yes."

"Maddie used to do that. Have you tried swaddling her?"

Kim frowned. "Like what they do in the hospital? No, I didn't know …"

"Give it a shot. It worked wonders for Maddie. And tummy drops too."

Kim's eyebrows arched. "Tummy drops?" She laughed, though there was little amusement in it. "I wish someone had told me about this stuff before."

"Have you talked to your pediatrician yet?"

"We don't have one. We just go to the clinic, but my one-month appointment isn't until tomorrow."

"Definitely have them show you how to swaddle if you're not able to figure it out, and in the meantime, a pharmacist can help you find tummy drops at the drug store. Maddie was like a different baby when we started doing those things."

Kim's features melted into a mask of relief. "Thank you so much, Joshua. I'll send Rick to the drug store tonight."

"Great. And, um, I've been meaning to tell you, if there's ever —"

She shut the window in his face and drew the curtain over it. Headlights washed over the snow. Joshua bent down and began to pack together a snowball.

"Are you gonna make one too, Daddy?"

"Yeah, kiddo." He rolled the ball towards Maddie and waited until he heard a slamming car door before glancing up. Rick went up the walk, ignoring Joshua's nodded greeting, and let himself into the building without a word.

Please, God, don't let him have seen us talking. Joshua paused in his snowman construction to listen for sounds of distress coming from Kim's apartment, but he heard nothing. He resumed his building, much to Maddie's delight, but didn't relax until their snowmen — and their dinner — were complete and not a peep had been heard.

KIM HAD BEEN CHEERING her turn of luck — until today. The suggestions Joshua had given her at the beginning of the week had worked like magic. The first day of minimal crying gave Kim such a mental boost she found the energy to clean the bathroom before bed, as well as mop the kitchen floor. The second day was even better—it gave her hope that the day before had not just been a fluke, but that Anne had turned a corner with the help of the little pink drops and the snugly-wrapped receiving blankets. The third day she forgot to be as grateful as she had been the two days prior, and the god of calm babies snubbed her once again.

The crying started just minutes before Rick walked in the door from work. Kim almost had dinner done, but ten minutes before the roast was to come out of the oven, Anne began to wail. "Oh no," Kim said in the doting voice she found herself using with the baby. "Oh dear, oh dear, what's wrong now?" She wrapped her up and dropped a dose of the tummy medicine into her wide open mouth, then bounced her gently as she walked around the living room. Unlike the last few days, she didn't begin to calm down. Instead, she began to wail even more. Kim tried to nurse her, then checked her diaper, but neither solution helped. She tried to sing, she tried to rock. Again, nothing.

From the nursery, she heard the door slam and called to Rick to take the roast out of the oven when the timer went off. A minute later she smelled something suspicious. She walked out with the baby still in her arms and gasped. Smoke billowed to the ceiling of the kitchen. "What happened?"

"This was beeping when I came in," Rick said, his tone accusing. "The roast is charred. You ruined it."

Kim shook her head. "No, it shouldn't be too bad. It was due out at five, and it's just a few minutes past. It's probably just the outside that's blackened. We can cut it off and it'll be fine."

Rick yanked off his jacket and threw it over the back of the sofa. "Why is she crying now? What did you do to her?"

"Me? I didn't do anything. I don't know why she's so upset. She's been great the last couple days."

"Right, so you did something. What was it? Did you forget her too? Leave her in the crib too long? Forget her in the bathtub?"

Kim's lip quivered. "Of course not! I don't know what's wrong with her!"

Rick ran a hand through his hair. "You know, I work hard all day and when I get home, the last thing I want to deal with is a kitchen fire and a screaming baby."

"Well I'm sorry, I'm doing the best that I can."

"Well if you can't handle it maybe we need to change something."

"Like what? What can we do differently?"

Rick took the baby from Kim. For a blind moment hope surged through her again. *He's going to help with the baby!*

Then she saw the fire in his eyes.

"Shut up!" he yelled into Anne's face. The baby's screams escalated. "Shut up!" He shook her, then yelled again. "I said shut up!"

"No, stop!" Kim screamed and grabbed for the baby, but Rick dodged her and gave Anne another shake. Kim grasped Anne and tried to steady her in Rick's arms, and then, desperate, kicked Rick in the groin. Her aim was off, but close enough to make him groan and stagger back, releasing Anne in the process. Kim snatched her and ran for the nursery. She slammed the door closed with her foot, but Rick threw it open before she could lock it. She fell to the floor, curled around the baby, shielding her as best she could from what she knew would come next. Rick shouted a string of obscenities at Kim as his fists sought to break her. When the blows stopped falling and Rick's muttering faded into the living room, she unfolded herself and dragged herself to the door. She nudged it shut, then crawled back to Anne who lay wailing on the floor. She saw no bruises on the baby, no evidence that Rick's punches had broken through the armor she had tried to create with her arms and body. Ignoring the throbbing pain of her own injuries, Kim held Anne to her breast and encouraged her in a shaking voice to eat. Eventually she calmed enough to latch, and Kim huddled in the corner while Anne nursed, shushing and singing shakily as the adrenaline settled out of her system.

She had never suspected Rick would ever take his anger out on Anne. Anne had no sins to make amends for, no penance to pay. Kim was the one who deserved the blows, not this innocent child. How could Rick do that to his own flesh and blood?

She thought back to when she was pregnant, and Rick had beat her so badly she'd gone into labor. That night, alone in the hospital, she had decided to leave him for the sake of her baby, but he had charmed her with the nursery and she had chosen to stay. Why? Why had she decided to risk the life of her baby?

The face that haunted her dreams surfaced again in her memory. *You know why you stayed. You had to. You owe a debt you don't know how to pay any other way. The guilt was killing you— what will you do without the punishment you deserve?*

Kim stared down at the tiny person in her arms and knew she had a sacrifice to make. What was more important—her own selfish need for a way to make things right with the universe, or the life of her daughter? Could she possibly survive with the blood of yet another innocent person on her hands?

"No," she whispered. "Nothing is more important than keeping you safe. I'm your mother. I have to protect you, no matter what I have to sacrifice." She clutched Anne tighter to her breast and vowed to herself it was over.

Tomorrow. She would leave tomorrow.

Kim waited until Rick had been gone for twenty minutes the next morning before she set herself into action. She grabbed a duffel bag from the closet and shoved in some clothes for herself and the baby. Into her purse she put her social security card and birth certificate. Then she scoured the house for money, managing to scrape up a little over six dollars in bills and coins, which she placed in her wallet.

Next she packed the baby's diaper bag with the essentials and glanced over at Anne, silent in her crib. She still didn't know what

Rick's attack could have caused, but she knew if she started thinking too much about it she'd get sucked into a vortex of worry that would hinder her from doing what she needed to do.

She brought the bags to the front door, then threw together a quick lunch. She was starting to get antsy, so she ran into the nursery and put three layers of clothes on the baby, then packed her into the stroller with blankets on and around her. The diaper bag slid into the storage section beneath it. The duffel was too big, so she draped the shoulder strap over the stroller's handlebar, then pushed the stroller to the front door, pulled on her coat, opened the door, and stalked out.

But ... what if ...

Her heart was racing but her feet wouldn't move. "Just go," she said aloud. "Just go." Anne began to whimper again, and her pitiful voice was the catalyst Kim needed to finally take a step into the hall, then another, then another. She paused in front of Joshua's unit, debating. *It's the middle of the week. He wouldn't be home.* Just in case, she fired a couple quick knocks on the door, but as she suspected, no one was there. "Here we go then," she said under her breath as she pushed the stroller out the security door.

It was then that she realized she had no idea where to go. Her mind raced. She was desperate to start moving, but in which direction?

A cluster of faces popped into her mind: Bette, Suzie, Emma, Rumiko. Their offers to stay with them rang out in her memory, and she shoved the stroller onto the sidewalk and pointed it towards the salon.

In most places the sidewalk was shoveled, but there were some spots where the snow was still two and three inches thick. She rammed the stroller through the mini drifts, her feet becoming more numb with each step, eyes focused on the area ahead where the walkway was clear. Bus after bus roared past, but knowing how little money she had she couldn't bring herself to spend it on a ride. At least Anne wasn't crying.

The walk that once took her half an hour took more than twice that long, and when she reached the salon her whole body felt like it was going to fall apart. She hadn't walked this far in months, and she still had not completely healed from Anne's birth. She stood outside the salon for a minute to compose herself and calm her rattled nerves, and then she pushed open the door and went inside.

It took Bette a moment before she cried, "Kim!" and bounded out from behind the reception desk. She wrapped her arms around Kim's neck and hugged her like a long-lost sister. "I can't believe you're here! And look—the baby!" She pulled Kim to a chair. "Sit down. You look done in. Did you walk all the way here?"

Kim swallowed back the lump that rose in her throat. "Yeah, I did—need the exercise, and it looked like such a pretty day."

Bette laughed. "You're insane. It's got to be close to thirty degrees." She bent to coo at Anne. "Can I hold her? What's her name?"

Kim unearthed the baby from the pile of blankets. "This is Anne Shirley," she said as she handed her to Bette.

"Like the book!"

"That's right."

"She's gorgeous. Look at those eyes." Bette carried her back to the station area. "Girls, look, it's Kim and her baby!"

A chorus of squeals rose above the music that played on the store-wide speakers. Kim's heart melted at the sound. How had she stayed away from her friends for so long? When was the last time anyone had shown this much pleasure at her presence?

Rumiko trotted out and gave Kim a quick hug. "I've got a client, but I'm done in twenty and we can chat then. How you doing?"

"I'm good, thanks. A little worn out from the walk. I think I overestimated my abilities."

"When was she born?" Bette called back to Kim.

"The eighteenth."

Rumiko's eyes grew wide. "That's barely a month and you're out running around! Girl, you nuts." She gave her another squeeze before going back to her station. Suzie and Emma came out to give her hugs as well, then went back to their clients with promises to come hang out as soon as they could.

"How long can you stay?" Bette asked as she handed Anne back to Kim. "Oh, and she bit my chest so I think she's maybe hungry."

Kim chuckled and pulled a blanket from the stack in the stroller. "Yes, I'm sure she is." Flinging it over her shoulder and tucking Anne under her shirt to eat, Kim asked, "So how is everyone doing here? How are things? What have I missed?"

Bette sat down in the desk chair and settled her chin into her upturned hands. "Oh, let's see. They raised the rent for the stations and everyone went ballistic. But no one stepped up to organize everyone the way you did when they tried to impose tip-splitting, so ..." She shrugged. "Anyway, let's see, what else ..." She filled Kim in on all the new gossip, and while she spoke Kim felt herself getting more anxious inside. She hadn't thought at all about what she'd say to these women, how she would ask for help, and now that the opportunity to do it was here, she wasn't sure she could bring herself to admit what was going on in her life. They'd all take it the wrong way, which is why she'd never said anything to them in the first place, back when it all began. And yet, how could she ask for help, for a place to crash until she figured out what to do, without explaining why?

Emma and Rumiko came to the front to eat lunch with Bette and Kim when their clients left. Emma flashed her engagement ring for Kim to admire, and they talked wedding plans for a while. Kim hadn't touched her wedding materials in months, but made sure she didn't give them the impression that things had been called off, since technically they hadn't. But now she wasn't sure what she would do about marrying Rick. How could she when the baby would be at risk?

So many things to think about, and all of them turned upside down by Rick's attack on the baby. How would she get things right again?

Through their conversation Kim began to weed out the people

she could ask for help. Emma was trying to find someone to sublet her apartment so she could move in with her fiancé, so she was out. Bette was staying with her mom whose health was failing, so she was out, too. Rumiko already had more roommates than the lease technically allowed, so even if she invited Kim to stay with her, Kim wouldn't want to run the risk of getting either of them in trouble.

Suzie joined them just as Emma and Rumiko were going back to their stations with new clients. Kim, Bette, and Suzie chatted for a while, though the whole time Kim was only half into the conversation. As far as she could tell Suzie might be able to spare some space for her and Anne—Kim just had to figure out how to ask.

"So … you're still living in that place near the park?" Kim fished.

"Yeah—for now."

"Planning on moving?"

Suzie glanced at Bette and said through a half-smile, "Well, yeah, actually. To LA."

"What?" Kim's and Bette's voices rang out together.

"My cousin got in at one of the hottest salons in the city, and he said he'd hire me as his assistant if I wanted. He said he'd train me."

"Wow," Kim said with a sigh. "That's an incredible opportunity. You're right to go."

"Yeah—we'll be seeing you in *US Weekly* someday. 'Stylist to the stars!'"

Suzie laughed. "Not likely. But who knows, right? That's why I've got to go for it. My parents are helping foot the bill to get out there, though I have no idea where I'm going to stay."

"Your cousin won't let you crash there?"

"Eh, he would if I wanted, but I don't want to impose. He's already doing me an incredible favor. But heck, I'll sleep under a bridge for this."

That makes two of us. Kim felt panic beginning to set in. She glanced at the clock and saw it was already almost one. She had four hours to get home if she was going to give this up, and if not, she had four hours to find somewhere else to go, since Rick would certainly come looking for her here.

The urge to be home squeezed in on her so tightly she felt like she would suffocate. "Well, I should get going," she said, trying to sound casual and not as tense as she felt. "It's a treacherous walk home—half the sidewalks are still snowy—and I'm tired. This is the most I've done in a long time."

She got hugs from everyone and tucked Anne into the stroller. Despite how much she ached, she walked even faster than she had on the way to the salon, and when she got home and saw Rick's parking spot was empty, she almost sobbed with relief.

She had just taken Anne out of the stroller when the front door opened. "There you are!" Rick slammed the door shut. "Where have you been all morning? I've called here three times."

"At the salon. I took Anne over to see my friends." The simplicity of the truth felt good after all the half-truths and dodging she'd employed in her conversations that morning.

His eyes slid to the duffel hanging from the stroller. "What's in there?"

Her blood turned to ice. "It's just ... a change of clothes. For myself. In case Anne spit up on me or something."

"Looks awfully full for one change of clothes."

"I brought some for Anne too."

"Isn't that what the diaper bag is for?"

"It was full with other stuff—the diapers, wipes—"

His eyes narrowed. "Let me see."

"Let me go put Anne down first." She almost ran to the nursery, then kissed Anne and hugged her before lying her in the crib. "I love you, sweetheart. Don't worry, Mama will be alright."

She shut the door, her heart breaking when Anne began to cry. *It doesn't last forever. It's what you deserve, Kim. You have no one to blame but yourself.* The broken record played in her mind as she faced Rick, who was holding the open duffel.

"You whore." He dropped the bag. "Who did you meet?"

"What?"

"Who is he? Where is he?"

"There's no other man, Rick, I swear. I went to the salon—call them and ask!"

"With two changes of clothes?" His hand flew, catching her near her eye. "How could you think I'd just let you go?" His fist made contact with her jaw. "I own you, Kim. You are mine. No one else can have you. No one else would even want you."

He swept her legs out from under her with one hard kick. She collapsed to the floor with a shriek, then bent double and folded her arms around her head. He sank to his knees beside her and planted bruises over her arms and back. She had no control over the cries that came out of her mouth, and in her head the mantra kept playing. *It doesn't last forever. It's what you deserve. You have no one to blame but yourself.*

The punches ceased, and for a brief second she thought it was over. But then he grabbed her hair and yanked her face to his. His voice was oddly calm when he spoke. "If you try to leave me again, I'll go to the police. I'll tell them what you did. They'll take you to jail and you'll never see Anne again."

He shoved her face away and stood, cursing as he walked to the bedroom and slammed the door behind him. She heard the shower start and only then did her body began to relax.

She rolled to her hands and knees, gasping in pain, and limped into the nursery where Anne was wailing red-faced in the crib. Kim fell to her knees beside the crib and reached a hand between the bars, resting it on her daughter's face. Her shoulders began to shake. She wept—from pain, from fear, from anger. And the mantra was replaced by the little voice that grew stronger every day, asking when her debt would be repaid.

NINETEEN

Joshua closed the accounting program and pushed his chair back from the desk. "So I think if we can get one more good fund-raising return by June we'll be in good shape."

"Great—I'll get that letter out this week, then, and we'll all pray it pays off. Anything else?"

He pulled two envelopes out of his inbox. "These need your review, and I've heard great things about Chin's Restaurant downtown. Want to join me Friday for dinner?"

Debbie laughed. "Wow. Incorrigible."

"I know."

"You know what I like about you, Joshua? You don't ask with an attitude, like you just can't imagine a woman would ever say no to you."

"I've had a lot of practice dealing with 'no,'" he said with a grin.

"Yeah, you have. And yet you continue to ask."

"Well, incorrigible is my middle name and I'd hate not to live up to it."

Debbie hung her head and groaned. "Alright, look. If I go out with you, will you stop asking?"

Joshua thought for a moment, then nodded. "Yes. If you go out to dinner with me, I promise I will stop asking."

She narrowed her eyes at him but couldn't keep the smile off her face. "Fine. You win. I give up. What time?"

"Seven?"

"Okay. Let me give you my address."

He could hardly believe she'd said yes. After she left his office he started working again, but his mind kept leaping ahead to Friday night. He'd ask Carlotta down the hall if she could watch Maddie for awhile—Maddie had a great time with her kids—and he'd pick up flowers on the way to Debbie's house ...

... and she'd tell him she appreciated the dinner, but that she had to leave it at that. She just wasn't ready to be in another relationship right now.

Debbie was staring at her overflowing email inbox, but she couldn't concentrate enough to go through the messages. Her mind kept jumping ahead to Friday night—what she would wear, whether or not she'd invite him in for a predinner drink, how she would tell him that she wasn't interested in a relationship right now. Because if she didn't write the script before Friday, she'd end up saying yes to anything he asked.

The truth was, she *did* want to give in to him. She knew her mother was right, and she had to get over this assumption that under every nice guy was a demon. Her father was a great guy, so was her brother—she had to stop thinking they were merely exceptions to the rule.

And her own junk ... well, regardless of whether or not she decided to date Joshua, she had to figure out how to get past her mistakes and start trusting herself again. She wasn't the only woman in the world who had been suckered. *Get over it already. It was five years ago. Why are you still holding on?*

Because there's safety in the status quo.

The answer dawned slowly, growing more and more obvious the longer she thought about it. It was the same reason so many women stayed with abusive men—it had become their normal. Leaving it meant leaving the reality their lives were now built on. It meant accepting truths about yourself that you didn't necessarily want to accept—that you were not always the best judge of character, that you were willing to allow yourself to be mistreated. It meant breaking the inertia of your existence, jumping the rail, and forging a new path. And new could be scary.

For abused women it meant redefining the basis of their worth, the fact that they *had* worth, the fact that they could in fact survive without the person who claimed to be indispensable. For Debbie, it meant admitting she'd been foolish and prideful, that she'd let visions of a wedding and babies get in the way of common sense and discernment. It also meant giving herself a little grace and recognizing that she was not necessarily doomed to repeat her mistakes.

Her inbox forgotten, Debbie stared out the window, alternating between praying and mulling over this revelation. Shadows had shifted along the floor by the time she pulled herself from her thoughts and back to the present. A tentative peace had formed in her heart, and for the first time in five years she thought she might be able to leave the past in the past.

Which meant a relationship with Joshua was not out of the question.

"Hɪ Daddy!" Maddie bounded over to Joshua and wrapped her arms around him in a fierce, quick hug. "Guess what? Austin threw up this morning right after snack. There were little bits of fishy crackers and grapes in it because that was his snack, and it was on the floor and his chair and it was so gross!"

Joshua helped her tie her shoes and put on her jacket. "Well that's … interesting. Poor Austin, I hope he's okay."

"Yeah, we should pray for him. And for Christie, too, because she cried when Austin got sick. I think she was scared of the throwup."

Joshua laughed and led her out to the car. "I'm surprised you weren't."

She shrugged. "It was kinda cool."

"Hm. Maybe you'll be a doctor someday if you think stuff like that is cool."

"Yeah, maybe. What's for dinner?"

"Remember, kiddo? Tonight I'm going out to dinner with a friend, so I'll make you dinner but I'm not going to eat. And then you're going to Miss Carlotta's house."

"Oh yeah, I forgot!" Her feet kicked the back of his seat, a sure sign of her excitement. She launched into a list of things she wanted to do with her friends that evening, and Joshua listened with half an ear while he thought about what his evening would hopefully entail.

At six-thirty Joshua walked Maddie down to Carlotta's unit. "Come on in! The kids are so excited for Maddie to come and play tonight," she said with her usual welcoming smile. "I keep telling them she's not spending the night, but they're building forts with sleeping bags anyway. If nothing else they'll have fun, right?"

Joshua agreed with her as he gave her a house key. "Just in case Maddie wants to get something from our place—plus I thought it might be good for a neighbor to have a key. I'll give you my cell phone number too. And I promise not to be too late."

Carlotta patted his arm. "Don't you worry. I don't mind the kids staying up late, and if she wants to sleep, we've got an extra sleeping bag. Take your time and have a good night. I know you don't get many chances to get out on your own."

He gave her his cell number, then yelled a good-bye to Maddie, who had raced off to her friends as soon as they'd entered. "Bye, Daddy!" came her reply from the bedroom. Seeing how comfortable she was here made him even more excited to get out for the evening. It was a relief to not have to worry about her.

He made a quick stop to the flower shop down the street and picked up a bouquet of tulips, then pep-talked himself the entire drive to her apartment. Despite the coolness of the April evening, he was sweating in his sport coat and kicked himself for not taking it off before getting in the car. He jacked up the A/C and turned on the radio to distract him from thinking of everything he might do wrong to screw up the night. This was his one shot. He had to make it count.

"You even got flowers?" she said when she opened the door for him. "You really didn't have to do that."

"Hey, you're finally giving me a chance—I had to go all out."

She rolled her eyes but didn't lose her grin as she took the flowers into the kitchen. "Give me a minute to get these in a vase," she said. "Would you, um, like a drink?"

"So long as it won't impair my driving, sure."

He heard her chuckle. When she came out she was carrying two glasses of lemonade. "So where's Maddie tonight?"

"With a neighbor down the hall. They've got four kids, one of whom is Maddie's age."

"How old is she now? Five?"

"That's right."

"Kindergarten's right around the corner, eh?"

He sighed. "Yeah, it is. It's hard to believe. She's looking forward to it, which is good. I don't know what I'd do if she was miserable in school. Lara and I used to talk about homeschooling, but now ..." He shrugged. "But what can you do, right?" He took a sip of his drink, then shifted in his seat. *Idiot—you don't bring up the dead wife in the first five minutes! New topic.* "So tell me about what else you do."

Her brow furrowed. "What else I do?"

"Yeah—hobbies, that kind of thing."

"Oh, um ..." She shrugged. "I don't actually have any hobbies. I don't have the time, you know? I'm at the shelter seventy hours a week sometimes, so even when I am home I'm catching up on bills or sleep, or watching lame TV to relax. How about you?"

Joshua swirled the remnants of his drink. "Same as you, really, unless you count imaginary tea parties and watching countless episodes of *Blue's Clues* as hobbies."

She grinned. "Better than my sorry excuse!"

He motioned to the clock on the wall. "We should get going to dinner before we realize we have nothing else to talk about."

They managed to keep the conversation flowing on the way to Chin's, but by the time they had ordered they'd exhausted all the usual safe first-date topics. "Well, now what?" he asked.

She stared at the centerpiece for a few seconds, then said, "Tell me about your wife."

He raised a brow. "Seriously?"

"Unless you don't want to talk about it, that is. I totally understand that."

He shrugged. "I don't mind—just surprised you wanted to know." He sat back in his seat and thought for a moment. "Well, she died about a year and a half ago. She had cancer—breast first, then liver, then lymph. The third time the doctors weren't very optimistic, and I did some research on alternative medicine that Lara decided she wanted to try. But nothing worked, and by the time she decided to go back to Western treatments, it was too late."

"That's awful."

He gave her a small smile. "Yeah, it was. It's been a rough ride since then. The medical debt is just unbelievable. Maddie and I are renting a place now—I sold the house to pay off some of the bills and shrink my monthly costs. It's working, but there are still a lot of bills to pay. God's provided, though, and I don't have a lot of choices other than to just trust he's got my back."

"Do you have any family that helps? I remember you mentioning your in-laws—"

He laughed. "Yeah, Lara's parents are local. Unfortunately they're a couple of head cases." He stopped and held up a hand. "Actually, that was uncharitable. They're mourning. Lara was their only child. But they blame me for her death because I'm the one who thought of trying unconventional treatments. And now they're desperate to get Maddie because they want a second chance, per se, with Lara, and Maddie's the only option they've got."

Debbie frowned. "What do you mean, 'get' Maddie?"

"They want custody."

She let out a laugh, eyes wide. "What? Are you serious? On what grounds?"

"Oh, they're getting very creative. They think I don't know how to be a parent, that I don't feed her right, that I'm endangering her by living where we live. And it doesn't help that they heard Rick and Kim the last time they were over."

Debbie nodded. "I remember you mentioning that. They haven't been back since then?"

"I told them they couldn't come without calling first. They have a tendency to spring themselves on us, trying to catch me in the act of neglecting Maddie, I guess. Anyway—they haven't called. I'm a little surprised, actually; I didn't expect them to give up this easily."

"Maybe they finally realized you actually do know what you're doing."

"I hope so." He drained his glass, then nodded to her. "Your turn. Tell me about how you got involved with the shelter."

Debbie swirled the soda in her glass. "I was hired on as a counselor first, but after two years of that, they asked me if I wanted to oversee all the day programs. I did that for a while, and then Gloria, the head director at the time, felt like it was time to move on. She asked the board to consider me as her replacement, and they did. That was three years ago." She smiled. "Not the most exciting story."

"But what made you want to work there in the first place? It seems like a pretty emotionally challenging job. Not the kind of thing most psych majors aspire to. Private practice is a lot more lucrative and cushy, I'd bet."

"Yeah, it is." She took a deep breath. "You know, I don't think anyone's ever asked why I started working there. Except Gloria, when she first hired me."

He smiled. "I had a feeling there was a deeper story there."

She nodded. "That there is." She took another deep breath and folded her arms on the table. "So, my sister Gina was dating this guy, back when she was a freshman at MSU and I was a junior at CMU. She was always a big drama queen, so when she started moaning about the guy and what a jerk he was, we all told her to end it, then, and stop whining. No one considered that there actually *was* some drama there.

"She called me one night and told me he'd hit her. I basically said, Why are you staying with him when he's such a jerk? If you're not going to do what you need to do, then stop crying to me about it. Real compassionate, right?

"She ran away that night, took off on her bike. Her roommate said she was crying when she left but wouldn't talk about what was wrong. She got hit by a car on Sunset, over by the cemetery, and was killed."

"Good Lord. I'm so sorry, Debbie."

She gave him a small smile. "Thanks. It was … devastating. I felt horrible, of course, that our last conversation had been so awful. And then we found out from her friends that the guy had been hitting her for a while—she just hadn't told us. She'd even told one friend she was suicidal. Then I felt *really* horrendous. So I decided to change majors, go into psychology, and figure out what made a woman stay in a relationship like that and what had to happen to get her out. So that's how I ended up at the shelter."

Joshua's feelings for Debbie doubled with her story. He wanted to wrap his arms around her and tell her he understood now why she took on so much of the shelter's burdens—more importantly, wanted to tell her it was okay to let some of it go, that it wouldn't reflect badly on how much she loved her sister. But such words weren't appropriate from a colleague. Instead he simply said, "Your drive makes sense now."

"Yes, I do have my reasons."

"If I may say so," he said, choosing his words with care, "I think Gina would be honored by what you've done for her."

She smiled, and for a brief moment, he saw the wall come down. It rose again in a heartbeat, but knowing he'd said something she needed to hear gave him hope that this date with her would not be the last. "Thank you, Joshua." Then she straightened in her seat, looking around the restaurant. "Do you see our waitress? I think we need to see a dessert menu."

JOSHUA PULLED INTO HIS LOT at 10:00 p.m. He hadn't meant to stay out so late, but they had lingered over their desserts and been so caught up in conversation that he hadn't noticed the time. He was about to pull into his space when a vehicle a few spots down caught his eye.

George and Alisha's Cadillac.

He parked the car, noticing that the lights were on in his apartment, and ran up to the door, fishing for his cell phone as he unlocked the door. The voicemail icon was lit on the screen. He'd never heard it ring in the restaurant.

Groaning, he steeled himself and went inside.

Alisha was perched on the couch, but was on her feet in a second. "Glad to see you didn't intend to leave your daughter at a stranger's house all night."

Don't let her rile you. "I never heard my cell phone. I just saw that I had a message but haven't listened to it yet—is it from you?"

"No, it must be from Carla."

"Car—oh, Carlotta. Why, what happened?" He saw Maddie's bedroom door was shut. "Is Maddie okay?"

"She's fine. Stomach bug, I suspect. *Carlotta* called us at eight-thirty, saying she'd tried to reach you but couldn't. Madeline had been sick and wanted to come home, and of course Carlotta didn't want her own children getting ill." She sniffed. "Do you know they have *four* children living in that tiny apartment? You'd think someone would have explained contraception to them by now."

Steady, steady. "Thank you for picking Maddie up; I appreciate it, and I'm sure she does too. Don't let me keep you ..." He opened the door and stepped aside, the most blatant and least offensive way he could think of at the moment to tell her to leave.

Maddie's door opened and she tottered out, half-asleep. "Daddy, are you home now?"

Alisha frowned. "Go back to bed, Madeline."

"Hey, kiddo!" Joshua met her in the middle of the living room and wrapped his arms around her. "I'm so sorry I didn't get Miss Carlotta's call, sweetheart. How are you feeling?"

"I'm okay. Gramma gave me medicine."

Joshua looked to Alisha. "What did you give her?"

"Pepto-Bismol, of course." She narrowed her eyes at him. "Let me guess; she's allergic to it."

He sighed. "No, but that's not for kids. Didn't you read the label? It's got aspirin in it, so you're not supposed to give it to kids who have the flu; it can cause Reye's Syndrome."

"Well—back when Lara was a child ..." He didn't often see Alisha flustered, but she was now. He tried not to enjoy it too much.

"Daddy, am I going to be sicker now?"

"Of course not," Alisha snapped. "You're fine and your father is just trying to scare you. Go back to bed, Madeline. You should be sleeping."

"But Daddy—"

Joshua stood. "Alisha—"

"Madeline, obey your elders. I said go to bed. Don't you make me say it twice."

"Alisha!" Joshua's tone was harsher than what Maddie had ever heard him use. Face crumbling, she knelt and bowed her head to the floor, burying her face in her hands and bursting into tears.

Joshua dropped back to his knees and began to rub her back. "Aw, Maddie, it's alright, sweetheart."

Alisha scoffed. "You let her get away with that kind of melodrama? Paddle her good just once and you'll knock that nonsense right out. She's far too old to be pulling that kind of thing."

He kissed Maddie on the back of her head, then stood and walked to Alisha. His fists were balled at his sides, trying to protect both himself and Alisha from his anger. "Don't you ever talk to her like that again. And don't ever suggest again that I hit my child. I don't care what it is she's done." He pointed to the door. "Good night."

"Fine. Raise a spoiled brat if you want to. George and I will set her straight." She slammed the door behind her. He heard the baby begin to cry in Kim's apartment. He bit back the string of epithets that swam through his head on the waves of his anger and went back to Maddie to comfort her.

TWENTY

The next month was a roller coaster for Kim. Anne's ceaseless crying had abated, only to be replaced by teething that stopped and started without rhyme or reason. At her request, Rick had purchased an assortment of teething remedies, and between gels and tabs and frozen teething rings Anne seemed to improve. When things were good with the baby, things were usually good with Rick and Kim as well. When the baby's crying kept them up at night, Kim knew Rick would come after her at some point. She became an expert at managing Anne's teething, only to have it replaced after a few weeks by a rash that wouldn't go away. Kim felt like she couldn't win.

On top of that Rick thought it necessary to remind her that he wouldn't tolerate another attempt to leave him. It didn't take much to trigger him — an off-handed comment about an actor on TV, a question about the weather in the coming days. Anything that hinted at her attraction to someone else or her desire to leave the apartment would send his hand flying. Eventually she just stopped talking.

Kim thought all the time about leaving, so she figured Rick's response was the universe's way of telling her she needed to remain, to continue to pay back her debt. She tried to ignore the thought that she'd already paid enough, but the voice was getting stronger every day. If it weren't for her fears for Anne, she'd try again, and again, and again.

But she couldn't risk her daughter. If Kim were to be jailed — which she would be once Rick went to the police with her secret — Rick would have no qualms about giving Anne up. The thought of her child growing up in the foster system made Kim sick to her stomach.

But now Rick was bringing up the wedding again, reminding her of their original plan to marry in two months on the Fourth of July. She knew now she didn't want to go through with it, but what else could she do? She had no choice.

It's your own fault. It's what you deserve. You have only yourself to blame.

RICK CAME HOME ONE NIGHT in early May carrying a large cardboard box and wearing the foulest face she'd seen yet. Without a word, he disappeared into the bedroom and slammed the door. Breathing a sign of relief that she'd gotten dinner prepared on time, she strapped Anne into a bouncy seat and poured him a beer so it was ready for him when he emerged. Then she began a survey of the kitchen and living room, eyes peeled for anything that might set him off even more: dirty dishes, spills, laundry she meant to fold, mail waiting to be sorted. She walked the rooms, straightening every piece of furniture and tidying every surface, until the door opened and Rick came out.

"Hi sweetheart." She brought over the beer and set it on the end table next to the couch where he sat down. "Rough day?"

He picked up the beer and guzzled down half the glass. When he spoke, his voice seemed an octave lower. "I got laid off."

It took a moment for the implications of this to set in, but once she realized her eight hours of freedom were gone, she had to slow-breathe herself away from the edge of panic. "Oh, honey," she said, reaching a cautious hand out to rest on his arm. "Rick, I'm so sorry."

It was like standing six inches from a land mine and waiting to see what it did. She never took her eyes off him, never let her guard down. She went to the kitchen and fiddled needlessly with dinner, then came back and pulled a chair from the table towards the couch, as far from the baby as she could get, just in case.

Rick stared at the television as though no one else were there.

Kim sat still in the chair and willed the baby to stay quiet in her seat, and save for the occasional coo, she did. When the timer went off for dinner, she prepared a plate for each of them and brought his to the couch. "Would you like to eat there tonight?"

He took the plate without responding. She refilled his beer and sat at the table with her dinner, but she could barely stomach the food. He had to snap eventually. It was just a matter of when.

For the next hour she danced around him, summoning every bit of couples' clairvoyance they had developed to anticipate his needs and keep him from unraveling. But awaiting the inevitable became too stressful. She couldn't keep his anger at bay forever, so she might as well get it over with. She stopped refilling his drink. She made a little more noise than necessary as she cleaned the kitchen from dinner. She blocked his view of the television as she walked through the living room. But it wasn't until she began to hum to herself that she got any results.

"Shut up, will you? What's with you tonight?"

"Sorry."

"You don't seem very concerned."

"About your job? You'll find something else, Rick, you're a great artist."

"But what if I don't? We've got bills, we need food—or were you planning on leaving before it became a problem for you?"

"Rick, I told you I wasn't going to leave. Where would I go?"

He stood and she felt her muscles tense in preparation. She fought the reflex to run. "To whoever you were going to the first time."

She sighed, weary of this argument already. How often was he going to drag it out? "There isn't anyone else, Rick."

"Sure." He began to close the distance between them. "You were just going to head out there with the baby and hope that some kind stranger took you in, is that it?"

"No, I was going to ask one of the girls."

They froze. To hear the words slip out of her mouth startled them both. "I didn't mean ask them to 'take me in'—I meant—"

"I knew it. I *knew* it."

He was inches from her now, and the look was there in his eyes that meant she was in for it. She braced herself. "Please, Rick, it was a mistake—"

His hands shot out to her throat. She backed away, trying to escape the pressure on her voicebox, only to find her back against the wall. She clawed at his arms as he pressed his thumbs harder. "You'll never make that mistake again. Do you hear me? I won't give you the chance."

There was no air. She tried to kick but couldn't, tried to shove him back but had no strength. The edges of her vision began to go black; her chest felt like it would burst. Then Anne began to wail.

A different expression flickered across Rick's face. He blinked, then stepped back and pulled his hands from her throat and stared at them as though seeing them anew. Kim collapsed to the floor wheezing and gasping, tears running down her face. Rick spun on his heels and disappeared into the bedroom as he always did after an attack. When Kim's vision cleared, she looked over to the baby and saw her sitting content in her seat, gazing at the mobile above her, silent.

Kim crawled across the room to the baby and unlatched the bouncer seat belt with shaking hands. She rose slowly to her feet, and once her balance was established, picked up the baby and carried her to the nursery, her own post-attack recovery room. Door locked behind her, she curled up on the desk chair and sucked in deep breath after deep breath, trying to stop the shivering that shook her whole body.

In the past, the beatings had been brutal but far short of deadly. But tonight, something had changed. She didn't know what, but she knew she was living with a new threat, and it was beyond what she had ever thought she'd experience. He hadn't wanted to control her, or punish her, or even scare her. He'd wanted to kill her.

She rocked the baby on her lap and let the voice she usually tried to ignore finally speak. It convinced her that the time had come to not only protect the baby, but to protect herself as well. The rules of the game had changed, and she was justified in bailing before she found herself on a losing streak. She didn't have much to gamble with in the first place—it wouldn't take long for Rick to clean her out.

The plan began to form. She'd learned her lesson the first time—no more deciding at the last minute, no more leaving without guaranteed help. She had to know where she was going and how she was going to get there, and she had to travel light. And now that her opportunities would be even more limited, she had to be ready at a moment's notice to grab her necessities and go.

But when? And how? And who? There were still too many variables for her to feel safe.

She heard voices on the other side of the wall—Joshua and Maddie. She scooted her chair to the wall and pressed her ear to it, straining to hear. Joshua began to sing, and Kim's eyes began to tear at the words that seemed to grow clearer with each line.

"Jesus loves me, this I know, for the Bible tells me so, little ones to him belong, they are weak but he is strong. Yes, Jesus loves me ..."

Maddie's tuneless voice joined with her father's as they sang the repetitive last line, and Kim longed to break through the wall and ask them to sing the song again. She knew vaguely of Jesus from the first foster family that had wanted to adopt her, and from the few holidays she'd gone to church with the O'Rileys, but her body of knowledge was meager. The idea of Jesus being strong for the weak sounded very appealing.

Joshua began to talk, and again Kim concentrated all her efforts on picking up the words. "Help us to ... Father ... our health and blessings ... happy dreams ... Amen." A prayer. She'd never heard anyone pray outside of church or meal blessings before.

Kim leaned back in her chair and stared out the window to the darkening sky. *I guess it can't hurt to ask.* She cleared her throat, fixed her gaze on the crescent moon, and whispered, "Jesus, I need help. If you're there, can you get Anne and me out of here?" She paused, considering what else to say, then settled on the "Amen" that had sufficed for Joshua.

She kissed Anne's smooth cheek and nestled the sleeping baby closer. Eyes still locked on the sky, her mind chanted *help us, please, help us, please,* as her soul took a chance on hope.

Joshua was halfway to the shelter when he remembered what he'd left at home. He could picture right where it was too — he'd be in and out in less than a minute and only a little bit late to the staff meeting. Groaning at his mistake, he turned at the next light and began the five-minute drive back.

He pulled into the parking lot and into his space. His eye was drawn to Rick's car, which was usually gone by the time he left in the morning. *Maybe he's sick.* He tried not to delight too much at the thought of Rick miserable with the nasty stomach flu that had been going around.

Joshua quickly entered the building, then his apartment, and yes, sitting on the kitchen counter was the book he'd bought for Debbie. He was about to pick it up when he heard a door in the hallway slam. He ran to the bedroom and snuck a peek around the corner of the patio wall. Rick was getting into his car.

He's leaving. I'm here, and he's leaving. This is it!

He watched the car pull out of its spot and cruise down the parking lot to the driveway, then turn onto the street. He was torn — wait a few minutes in case he came right back, or go to Kim now?

The urge to get to Kim was so strong his feet started moving to the door before he'd even consciously made the decision. He grabbed his book on the way out, locked his door behind him, and went next door. *Let her be here and let me get her out of here before he comes back, God.* He knocked, the sound echoing the pounding of his own heart, and felt his hands grow damp. He couldn't help looking back at the security door, then doing it again. Then again.

The door opened and Joshua gasped. Two purple-blue circles

decorated her throat, and their cause was immediately clear to him. *I think we're just in time, God.*

Kim's hand flew to her throat and she blushed. "Hi, Joshua. Everything alright?"

It took him a moment to find his voice, and once he did, he didn't bother with niceties. "I work at a women's shelter, and if you want, I can take you and the baby right now."

Her eyes grew wide and seemed to light from within. "Yes. Yes!" She grabbed his arm and pulled him inside, then shut the door and locked it behind them. "The baby is in the crib. Can you get her?" She pointed to the room that sat on the other side of the wall from his bedroom. *No wonder I always hear her when she cries.* Without a word, he made a dash for the nursery and lifted the swaddled, napping child from her crib. She squirmed and began to cry. "Hey, it's okay sweetie, we're just going for a ride."

Going for a ride. "Oh no," Joshua said. Cradling the baby, he ran back out to the living room where Kim was holding her purse and a bulging plastic shopping bag. "Car seat. Is it in Rick's car?"

Kim gasped and nodded. "Now what?"

"Now we break the law and drive very carefully. Do you have everything you need?"

She nodded and reached out for the baby, then hugged her close. "This is it, baby girl." She grabbed a set of keys and followed Joshua out the door, locking it behind her.

Joshua went out the security door first, checking to make sure Rick had not come back. "I don't know how long he'll be gone," Kim said. "He lost his job, he said he was going out, but he didn't say where or when he'd be back."

"He turned right out of the parking lot," Joshua said as he helped Kim into the car. "We'll go left, just to be safe, and take a roundabout way to the shelter." He held the baby while Kim buckled the seat belt, then handed her the baby. "You see any cops, you make sure you put the baby low on your lap," he said as he got in. "I'd like to think they'd be understanding, but let's not take any chances."

He pulled out of his space and began to drive, his heart still thumping like mad as he threw exclamations up to God. *Safe! Hurry! Protection! Help! Please!*

Kim glanced over at Joshua. "I can't believe you came today. I—I prayed last night that Jesus would help us."

Thanks for the nudge, God. Joshua grinned and gave her arm a squeeze. "About ten more minutes and we'll be there."

"Can you tell me about the shelter?"

"Sure." He told her about the staff and the facility as they wound their way down residential side streets. Both sucked in a panicked breath every time a silver hatchback came into view, but soon they pulled into the parking lot behind the building and he helped her out of the car.

By unspoken agreement they both ran to the building, where Joshua swiped his key card and pulled the door shut behind them. They stood in the vestibule, panting from nerves. Then he smiled. "Welcome to Safe in His Arms."

Kim's eyes shone. "Thank you." Then she began to cry.

SHAWNEE POKED HER HEAD INTO the room where the staff meeting was under way. "Debbie? Joshua just got here, and he brought a woman with him who wants to stay here. She has a baby too."

Debbie knew immediately who she was. "Get her comfortable and I'll be there as soon as I can."

She ran through the meeting's agenda with as much speed as she could, then went out to the green room where Kim sat with her baby. Debbie reached out a hand. "It's a pleasure to meet you," she said to Kim. "Joshua's been talking about you since I met him. Is there anything I can get you—more water, something else to eat?"

"No, I'm fine, thank you."

Debbie noted the bruises on Kim's throat and thanked God for good timing. She couldn't wait to hear Joshua's side of the story.

She sat down and slid the intake forms across the table to Kim, then offered to hold Anne.

Kim smiled and lifted the squirming baby over the table. "Thank you. I can't believe I'm here. I was so scared. I still am. I know what he's going to do when he finds out I'm gone."

"It can take awhile to stop looking over your shoulder." Debbie saw the look of panic that crossed Kim's face. She'd seen it before, many times. "He can't hurt you here."

"He doesn't have to be here to do it."

Debbie looked on as Kim continued the paperwork. She wouldn't press Kim now to go into her story. She needed to give her time to get settled in, give her a chance to get to know the other women and the staff so she felt safe discussing her situation. When Kim handed her the completed papers, Debbie returned Anne to her mother's lap and opened the welcome folder, explaining the house rules and how things worked. "We don't get a lot of moms with little ones here, but when we do everyone is very eager to help with the baby, so don't hesitate to ask if you want someone to take her for a bit."

Kim clutched Anne against her. "But I can keep her with me, right?"

"Yes, of course."

Kim sighed. "Okay, good."

Debbie showed Kim around the shelter. "Since you have a baby with you, you get one of the single rooms. I'll get some diapers and wipes for you too. Is there someone who can go back to your house and get you and the baby some clothes?"

Kim frowned. "Not really. Unless Joshua wants to."

"I'll ask him when I see him next. Is there anything else you can think of that you'll need?"

Kim shook her head, lips pressed together as tears began to well in her eyes. "Forgive me," she said as she wiped them away.

Debbie smiled and squeezed her arm. "Don't apologize. It's a completely normal reaction. You've been under a lot of stress, and even though it's safe here, it's still stressful, just in a different way. I understand—everyone here does. Take whatever time you need and then you can come out to the community room when you're ready to mingle. Joshua's office is on the second floor, and if you want to go talk to him you're more than welcome to. My office is at the opposite end of the building, past the counseling rooms, and you're welcome to come see me anytime as well. Your counselor will be Tammy, though she's out this week, so I'll meet with you until she's back."

She left Kim in the room and went back to her office, a stubborn smile tugging at her lips. It wasn't until she was safe in the privacy of her office that she let herself do a little victory dance. Not because Kim was finally at the shelter—though that did make her happy, but because Joshua had taken the chance, had put himself out there for Kim, and as far as Debbie was concerned, had proven himself to be *not* just another wuss of a guy.

They hadn't gone out again since their dinner last month, but it had taken all the self-control she could muster not to extend her own invitation to him. She hadn't let on about how much she enjoyed herself—far more than she had on any date she'd been on in a long time. She hadn't told him how long she kept the tulips, and that she had actually saved a few of the silky petals after they'd fallen off and pressed them between the pages of her Bible. She'd been waiting for confirmation that he was going to be the man he said he was.

And here it was.

She jogged up the stairs, taking them two at a time, and found Joshua in his office. "How is she doing?" he asked before she could say a word.

"She's good. Shell-shocked, I think, but good. I'll check up on her in an hour or so, see how she's settling in. I told her your office was up here in case she wanted to talk to you."

"Great, thanks. Now we just need to pray Rick slinks back to his hole somewhere and disappears."

"Amen. Hey, what's on your calendar Friday?"

He flipped open his date book and scanned the page. "Phone

call with the tax guy I was telling you about, at two-thirty. That's it, though."

"Great, put me down for seven-thirty."

He frowned. "Um, I don't think I can get here that early. I can't drop Maddie off until—"

"P.M."

"Oh. Um—" he raised his eyebrows with a small, confused smile. "Are you asking me out?"

"Yup." She grinned, then went back to her office to try to be productive and not think about Friday night.

TWENTY-ONE

Kim sank onto the twin-size bed and laid Anne beside her, then allowed herself to attempt relaxation. Despite its sparse décor, the cozy room gave her a small measure of comfort. She felt cocooned and protected by its cool blue walls, and it provided the privacy she craved. It reminded her of her hospital stay during preterm labor—knowing that Rick was at home and she was protected and alone. It gave her the space she needed to finally think.

She was so conflicted. On the one hand, she felt tremendous relief that Anne was in a safe place. Since Rick had attacked her, Kim hadn't left her alone with him for even a minute. Not that she was out of the woods yet. Once Rick went to the police and she was arrested, Anne's safety might again be in jeopardy. But now that there were others involved in her life, maybe they would be able to protect her baby from Rick. When she felt more stable, she would talk to Debbie about her fears for Anne in the foster system.

But talking with Debbie—with anyone at the shelter, really—was one of the sources of her angst. How would she be able to stay here, to participate in the group sessions and individual counseling, without going into her explanation of why she had to let Rick hit her? No one here would understand that. They all thought the women were innocent and didn't deserve to be treated that way. And the other women staying here probably didn't deserve it. But she did.

Kim dried her eyes on the ends of her T-shirt. It probably didn't matter; she wouldn't be here long anyway. When Rick came home and found her gone he'd go to the police. She didn't know what would happen then—would they put a warrant out for her arrest?

If they did, and it was in the papers or on the news, then at least one of the shelter workers was likely to see it and would probably report her. Chances were she'd be in jail by the weekend.

She curled herself beside Anne, who was tugging her feet to her mouth and gnawing on her toes. Just a few days, then, of freedom. And then she'd face her fate again, this time in prison.

A knock on the door woke Kim with a start. She yanked Anne to her so hard the baby began to cry. She took a deep breath to calm her racing heart. "Come in."

Debbie poked her head in. "Oh, I'm sorry, I didn't know you were sleeping."

"That's alright." Kim heaved another calming breath and stood, swaying the baby in her arms to soothe her. "I didn't mean to. Good thing she doesn't roll yet. She could have gone right off the edge."

"I just wanted to see how you were doing, see if I could get you anything."

Kim gave Debbie a sheepish face. "I am a bit hungry."

"We can go to the kitchen if you'd like. I can hold Anne while you make something for yourself."

Kim followed Debbie down to the kitchen where two other women were fixing sandwiches. They immediately began to coo over the baby, and one tapped a finger to Anne's bare foot. "I'm Ella. Who be this sweet thing?"

"This is Anne. And I'm Kim."

"Kim, is a pleasure to meet you and sweet baby Anne. It does a heart good to see a baby so happy, don't it?"

The other woman came to them, wiping her hands on a towel. "I'm Doreen. Nice to meet you, Kim. And Anne." She smiled at the baby. "I was just making a turkey sandwich; can I make you one?"

"Oh, I can get it," Kim said.

"It's no trouble, really. Sit with the baby and relax. You're new today, right?" Kim nodded as she sat in the seat Debbie pulled out for her at the table. "Then you definitely need to just sit and relax. I know what a rough transition it can be, even when you're relieved to be here."

"So true, so true," said Ella. "I been here a week and I still looking over my shoulder. It takes time to come down from being always so tense." She shrugged her shoulders up and down as though trying to rid the tension that still resided there, and brought her sandwich to the table. "But we all here understand because we all be living the same nightmare, ya? So no one gonna fault you, you wanna just kick back a bit and take it all in."

Doreen brought both her sandwich and Kim's to the table. "Debbie, can I get you one too?"

Debbie smiled. "You're sweet, Doreen, thanks for the offer. But I'm good."

Ella took a bite of her sandwich and hummed sounds of pleasure. "Mm-mm, thank you Jesus." She shook her head. "My man set my meals for me and gave me nothing but bread and water the whole last week I be with him. Now every meal I eat is like it be from Eden itself."

Kim stared at Ella, horrified by the revelation, but Debbie merely nodded and Doreen added, "Just being allowed in the kitchen again makes me happy. My husband put a door on ours last year and kept it locked." She smirked at Kim and added, "Though I *had* tried to poison his food once. I guess I can't blame him."

Ella chuckled. "Or you!" They laughed.

"Doreen, you know he really wasn't justified in doing that, right? That's totally unacceptable, controlling behavior."

"But what if you deserve it?" The women looked at Kim and she could feel her cheeks reddening. "I'm not saying you did, Doreen, I'm just asking the question in general. Is it unacceptable behavior if you really do deserve it?"

"No one deserves to have their basic needs withheld," Debbie said. "Even killers on death row get three square meals a day and a bed to sleep in at night."

"Even they got it better than I did," said Ella. "My bed be the floor most nights." She looked to the ceiling. "Thank you Jesus for getting me out."

"Amen to that," Doreen said. "I've been here for almost a month and I still don't believe my luck. I'd have been dead by now if I'd stayed."

Ella nodded to Kim. "It look like you got out just in time too, ya? Aw no, don't be embarrassed," she said when Kim's hand flew to the bruises on her throat. "We all here have bruises and scars, even if they not be on the outside for everyone to see. You just let them remind you that you making the right choice, coming here. You and sweet baby deserve better."

Kim gave Ella a small smile, but inside she was aching. *Maybe sweet baby does. But I was right: these women will never understand.*

JOSHUA'S STOMACH FLUTTERED as he pulled into the parking lot. When he saw Rick's car wasn't there, he let out the breath he hadn't realized he was holding. "Come on, kiddo," he said to Maddie as he helped her jump to the ground. "What should we have for dinner tonight?"

"Pancakes!"

He laughed as he led her to the security door. "Pancakes for dinner? Well, why not." He opened the door and let her in, then glanced over his shoulder before passing through himself—and saw Rick's car pull in.

An arrow of adrenaline shot through him. He grabbed Maddie's hand and hustled her down the hall as he fumbled through his keys. He had the door closed behind them before the telltale squeak of the security door could be heard. He turned the deadbolt and pulled the chain, then let out another deep breath. Maddie, oblivious, dropped her backpack onto the floor and ran to her room. "I'm going to play until dinner," she said over her shoulder.

Joshua was just about to respond when he heard the security door slam. Two seconds later his door was rattled by pounding that echoed throughout the apartment and sent another shot of adrenaline through his already-jittery system. "Where is she?" Rick's holler sent a shiver up Joshua's spine. "If she's in there I'm gonna know! Where is she?"

Joshua threw his weight against the door, fearing it might be as thin as the walls. "She's not here, Rick. Go home." There was a lot more he wanted to say, but he knew the less he said the better. He didn't trust himself to keep the conversation polite.

Rick yelled a string of obscenities as he retreated to his own apartment. A few seconds later Joshua heard another door slam. In the silence that followed he dropped his head against the door and gulped deep breaths to calm his careening heart.

"Daddy?" Maddie's voice held the notes of tears kept just barely at bay.

"Coming, sweetheart."

He found her under her bed, tears on her cheeks. "That scared me," she said, then began to cry. He pulled her out and sat her on his lap, wrapping his arms around her. "It scared me too, kiddo. But he's gone."

"What if he comes back?"

"I don't think he will, honey. But if he does you don't have to worry. I'll protect you. I promise."

She sniffed and gave him a hug, then Joshua dried her tears on his shirt and planted a kiss on her forehead. "I think we deserve a treat. Why don't I put some sprinkles on those pancakes?"

She sniffed and nodded. "Okay. And maybe some peanut butter too."

He chuckled. "You've got it, kiddo." He returned to the kitchen and busied himself with cooking and fervent prayer, begging God to help him keep his promise.

ANNE WOULD NOT CALM DOWN. Kim swaddled, jiggled, and dosed her with teething remedies, but still she wailed. Kim felt awful that Anne's crying was disrupting the quiet evening for a dozen other people. A knock on her door sent a new wave of tension over her. "Come in," she said, trying to keep the exasperation out of her voice.

Doreen opened the door and leaned in. "I just wanted to see if there was anything I could do. I know how awful it is to have a baby that just won't stop crying."

Kim shifted Anne in her arms. "Thanks. Come on in, but I don't know what else can be done. I think it's her teeth again, but nothing is helping, not even medicine."

"May I?" Doreen reached out to Kim, and though she hated to give her up, her arms were aching and she just wanted the crying to stop. She eased Anne into Doreen's arms and sank onto the bed with a sniff. Doreen situated the baby in her arms and began to twist back and forth, swinging Anne in a wide arc. "My little boy was just a mess when he was teething. In the end it was washcloths frozen with chamomile tea that helped the most."

Anne's crying had downgraded to a whine, and Kim felt some of the tension leave her. "That's a good trick," she said.

"Yeah, Riley—that's my son—Riley loved to swing like this. Obviously it doesn't do anything for the pain, but for some reason it soothes them."

"I'll have to make up some frozen washcloths."

"I think there's even chamomile tea in the kitchen. If not, ask Debbie—I bet she'll find some for you." She smiled at Kim. "You look like you could use a good night's sleep. Will Anne let you go long at night without nursing?"

"Not when her teeth are bothering her, no. She'll eat every couple hours, sometimes more."

"Good for you for nursing. I know a lot of women whose abusers make them formula feed."

"Rick never seemed to care, so long as I could get her to stop crying. Nursing usually does it. Some nights I'd sleep in the nursery with her in my arms because I was so afraid she'd wake him up otherwise." Kim smiled. "I'm actually looking forward to tonight, snuggling with her in bed. Do you think they'd mind if I pulled the mattress onto the floor? She doesn't roll yet, but I'd hate for her to learn how in the middle of the night and fall off."

"I don't think they'd mind. That's a great idea. And speaking of sleeping ..."

Kim's eyes grew wide. "Is she out?"

"Like a light."

Kim laid back on the bed with a sigh. "Thank you so much, Doreen. Although I feel bad that I couldn't get her to calm down myself."

"Don't feel bad. Motherhood is one giant learning curve, and this is how you learn—experimenting and talking to other moms."

Kim sat up and smiled. "It's been a long time since I hung out with other women—and the last time I did no one knew what was going on at home, so I didn't feel like I could even let my guard down, you know?"

Doreen chuckled as she slowed her swinging. "Oh yeah, I know."

Kim pulled the mattress off the box spring and pushed it against the wall. Doreen knelt and placed the baby in the center, then stood and moved to the door. "I know it's only seven o'clock, but I'm sure you're wiped out, so I'll let you get to bed. I'm in room 4 if you ever want to come talk or anything. Oh—and I'll go make up some frozen washcloths for you, if I can get my hands on a couple."

"Wow—thank you so much."

"You're welcome. I hope you have a good night. Don't be surprised if you can't sleep—I think it took about a week before I was able to let go of the fear that my husband would find me, and I finally got a good night's rest. But I didn't have a baby to cuddle with—that might have helped." She smiled and gave Kim a little wave before closing the door behind her.

Kim changed into the pajamas Debbie had found for her and brushed her teeth with the toothbrush from the toiletries kit she'd been given when she first arrived. She turned out the light and eased herself onto the bed, trying not to wake the baby. She lay there, wide awake, staring at Anne's perfect face as her thoughts blew back and forth like leaves in the wind.

The conflicting emotions in her heart had only grown more

intense over the hours she'd been here. She was grateful for the women who had reached out to her, who had gushed over Anne and offered their assistance in whatever capacity Kim needed. She was relieved that Anne was safe and surrounded by so many people who were sympathetic to—rather than angry at—her crying. She was anxious at the thought of what Rick would do, and tense with anticipation of the time when her story would come out and she would be arrested.

And the guilt—her old, familiar companion—was back to eat away at her. But for the first time, she felt herself fighting against it. She knew that what she had suffered was nothing like what the family of her victim had suffered—possibly suffered still. But hadn't her bruises and battering made up for at least some of theirs?

Some of it, maybe—but your punishment has stopped while their loss never ends. Your penance can't begin to make up for what you did.

She closed her eyes against the tears. She couldn't win.

Another voice spoke in her heart, echoing the words she had heard sung in Joshua's baritone. *Little ones to him belong, they are weak but he is strong.* She sniffed back tears and stroked Anne's head as she reached out again to the Jesus Joshua had sung about.

I know I didn't deserve to ask you to get us out, but you did it anyway. And I definitely don't deserve to ask you for anything else, but I don't have anyone else to ask, so ... please show me what else I can do, to make up for what I did. And please protect Anne. Don't make her suffer because of me.

Doreen was right; she couldn't sleep. But it wasn't her fear of Rick that kept her awake. It was her fear of what Jesus might do to answer her prayer. She didn't know what else she could do to pay for her transgression, but whatever it was, she was willing to do it so she could finally move on.

TWENTY-TWO

Kim knocked on Debbie's door and was welcomed in. Debbie sat at her desk surrounded by piles of papers and folders. She smiled when Kim entered. "Come on in and make yourself comfortable. The floor is a little cluttered, sorry—not sure if it's a good spot for the baby or not."

"That's okay," Kim said as she sank into the sofa. "I can't get enough of holding her lately. I know a day will come when all she wants to do is crawl or walk or run, so I figure I might as well take advantage of it now while I still can."

Debbie chuckled. "Wise woman."

Kim squirmed a bit in her seat. "I've never talked with a counselor before. How does it work?"

Debbie curled up on the armchair. "It's whatever you want it to be. The idea is that over the course of your time here, you'll get to a point where you'll be prepared to go back out on your own and be armed with the skills you'll need to avoid another abusive relationship. We also want to help you identify any issues that the abuse has caused for you, help you figure out how the abuse has impacted your physical, mental, and emotional states. But we just start to scratch the surface here, really—we encourage women to continue with therapy after they leave the shelter, because it can take quite a while to really work through the issues abuse can cause."

Kim nodded, digesting what Debbie had to say, but feeling yet again like this was not the right place for her. She gnawed her lip as she bounced Anne on her knees.

"May I ask what you're thinking?" Debbie asked.

Kim quirked a smile. "I don't know if I should really say."

"You can say anything you want to here. I won't tell a soul, and there are no topics that are off-limits. Sometimes things that seem unrelated to the abuse can actually be connected in ways you just didn't see, and starting with those supposedly unrelated thoughts can help you ease into the healing process."

Dare I? She was aching to hash it all out with someone, to get all the confusion out of her head so someone else could help her make sense of it all. But she was afraid of how Debbie might respond.

Might as well. Chances are I won't be here long anyway. She smoothed Anne's thin hair and sighed. "Well ... okay, here's the thing. I don't know that I should stay here at the shelter very long. I think I'm taking up a bed that someone else could be using."

Debbie's expression gave nothing away. "What makes you say that?"

"Well ..." She bit her lip again and stared at Anne, reluctant to make eye contact with Debbie. "These other women I've talked to here—they're so sweet, they're so ... normal, you know? And they just happened to get into these relationships with these awful men and they totally didn't deserve to be treated the way they were treated. You talked a little bit about that yesterday in the kitchen, about how, even though Doreen tried to poison her husband, she didn't deserve the treatment she got afterwards."

Debbie nodded. "Right. No one deserves to be treated like property, or like a prisoner in their own home, or like they're subhuman."

"But—see, that's the thing. They didn't do anything to deserve being beat. But ... I did."

She held her breath, waiting for Debbie's reaction. But Debbie merely cocked her head and said, "What makes you think you deserve to be beaten, humiliated, degraded, and almost choked to death? I mean if you had beaten, humiliated, degraded, and almost choked someone else to death, then maybe I could see the connection. But somehow I don't think you did that."

Kim shook her head. "No, I didn't. But ..." She couldn't bring herself to say what she had done, and her unwillingness to name her crime must have been plain on her face because Debbie held up her hand.

"You don't have to tell me what you did. Honestly, it's irrelevant. Regardless of what happened, domestic abuse is not a pardonable punishment. If you broke the law, then the law should deal with you. If you hurt someone's feelings, then you and that person need to work it out. And in between those two extremes are a thousand shades of wrongdoing—but none of them are made right by what your fiancé did to you."

Kim felt tears of frustration beginning to well in her eyes. "But I don't know how else to make up for it, especially now that I have Anne. I should have made it right years ago, but I didn't, and the guilt has been killing me." She extended her arm to Debbie, pointing at the faint lines that criss-crossed her skin. "I was cutting myself, trying to deal with the pain I felt inside. And when Rick began to hit me—it was a relief. Honestly, a relief! Because I could stop hurting myself, and trying to hide it, and making excuses for it. And even though it was more extreme than what I had been doing to myself, it seemed more fitting. And when he wasn't hitting me, things were really great. I mean, I actually felt even *more* guilty sometimes, because I'd found this man that loved me so much and made me so happy. It wasn't until recently that things started to get really bad, and I think it was more because of Anne than anything else. He wasn't happy that I got pregnant." She kissed Anne's head and inhaled the sweet scent of baby shampoo that lingered there. *How could someone not love their own flesh and blood?* Rick's stories of his father came to mind. "I just don't think he knows how to be a good dad. His own dad beat him—Rick was in foster care for a bit, even. So he didn't have a real good model, you know? Same for being in a relationship, or a marriage—his mom was gone, he didn't have a model to learn from."

Debbie smiled a bit. "You're making excuses for him, Kim. You're on to something in recognizing the impact his upbringing had on how he parents Anne and how he relates to you. But that doesn't make the behavior okay."

Debbie leaned in, her posture inviting Kim to listen carefully. "Whatever you did, I know it must have been pretty serious for you to think living with abuse was a good way to make up for it. But no amount of penance would have ever made the guilt go away, because your punishment wouldn't have gotten to the root of the issue."

Rather than feeling relief, this made Kim feel even worse. "So there's nothing I can do to get out from under this? I just have to live with it for the rest of my life? The root of the issue—it's impossible for me to get to it. I can't undo what I did."

"No—you can't undo it. But you *can* face it and ask for forgiveness. You can offer to make amends in whatever way makes sense to all involved."

Kim's head was swimming. Amends meant jail. Any way she looked at it, that was the only way out. She rubbed her eyes and almost smiled with relief when Anne began to whimper. "I—I think she needs to eat. And probably nap soon too. I'm going to go feed her and put her down to sleep. Thanks for your time, Debbie." She clutched Anne to her chest and fled, eyes streaming, for the safety of her little room.

ANNE INDEED FELL ASLEEP, but try as she might, Kim could not follow suit. After half an hour of staring at the ceiling, she eased herself up from the bed and slipped out into the hall.

The kitchen was a couple doors down, close enough for her to sneak in and grab a drink and snack without worrying about Anne. But after washing an apple and pulling a couple cheese sticks from the fridge, she sat at the table instead of retreating to her room. There was too much rattling around in her brain to be cooped up in that small space. She needed room to think.

A woman teetering on the line between skinny and skeletal walked in, humming and smiling. She introduced herself as Adele, grabbed a snack, and sat across from Kim after preparing her food, and made small talk for a few minues. Seeing the troubled look on

Kim's face, she probed, "You're not rethinking coming here, are you?"

Kim sighed and shook her head as she pushed away the food she no longer had an appetite for. "Not exactly. I just had my first counseling session with Debbie, and I'm just … confused, I guess."

Adele polished off one of her apple slices. "You want to talk at me, you can. When I can't sort things out, it always helps me to just get it all out of my head, you know? But it helps when there's someone there listening and not just the walls."

"Thanks for the offer, I appreciate it." She thought for a moment, then said, "Have you had any counseling sessions yet?"

"Oh yeah, three of them. Candice, my counselor, she and I started talking about Jesus, and I felt like someone opened up a bit of my head that I'd closed off. Me and Jesus used to be tight, so when Candice brung him up I was kicking myself for dissing him for so long."

Kim sat up a little straighter, the name of Jesus conjuring Joshua's voice through the wall. "So … you know about Jesus?"

Adele laughed. "I wouldn't say I know a lot; I'm no preacher. But I went to church all the time as a kid and my mama was real spiritual, so I know some. Why you ask?"

Kim propped her chin in her hand. "I don't know much about him — but he seems to keep popping up. One of the foster couples I stayed with was some weird, fanatical kind of religious, but I don't remember a lot of what they taught me, because I was still pretty young. The one good family I was with went to a Catholic church on holidays, so I know Christmas is supposed to be Jesus' birthday, and Easter is about his death —"

"Naw, naw — his resurrection."

Kim frowned. "What's that?"

"Good Friday, which comes before Easter — that's about Jesus' death. But Easter is about when he was resurrected, when he rose from the dead."

Kim raised her eyebrows. This Jesus character was starting to sound like a fairy tale. *But Joshua doesn't seem like the type to fall for fairy tales.*

Adele dabbed at her mouth with a napkin. "You gotta get your hands on a Bible. Check your room. I bet there's one in there. It's big, right, so you don't read the whole thing right now. But what you do is you read the gospels and see what it is Jesus did. I think that might help you." She smiled, then glanced at the clock and let out a squeak. "Speaking of counseling, I'm late! I just stopped in for a snack and forgot I had to go to Candice."

Kim let out a gasp of her own. "Anne! I forgot my baby is sleeping in the bedroom!" They both hustled out the door, and Kim's chest squeezed with relief when she saw Anne lying content on the bed, pulling her feet to her mouth.

"I'm so sorry, baby," Kim said as she sank to her knees on the mattress. "I'm sorry I left you alone." She picked her up and leaned against the wall, then let her nurse while Adele's words whirled around in the blender of her mind. Her eyes went to the small nightstand, which had a single drawer. Holding Anne tightly to her, she shuffled over and pulled it open, revealing a black leather Bible with gold-edged pages. Once back at her spot on the mattress, she bolstered Anne with pillows to free up her hands and began to turn the thin pages, looking for the table of contents. She skimmed the page when she found it, and her eyes snapped to the first four titles listed under the heading "The New Testament." She flipped to the beginning of the Gospel of Matthew and skipped past the line of bizarre names until she saw an italicized heading: *The Birth of Jesus Christ.* She began to read, but the lines blurred together, her exhaustion making it hard for her to concentrate. She was about to give up and shut the book when her eyes fell on a passage set apart from the rest of the text.

Blessed are the poor in spirit, for theirs is the kingdom of heaven.

She paused, then read it again. *Poor in spirit.* She wasn't sure what that meant, but it sure sounded like how she felt. Her spirit — if that was what she thought it was — had felt downright destitute for a long time. She read more closely.

Blessed are those who mourn ...

... the meek ...

... those who hunger and thirst for righteousness ...

It started to fall apart for her after that—whatever righteousness was, she was sure she didn't have it; she didn't think she was merciful, or a peacemaker, or pure in heart. But the first few verses of that section had definitely piqued her interest.

Anne began to fuss. She dog-eared the page before shutting the giant book, then patted Anne's back to settle her. Maybe after she got Anne calmed down and occupied she'd spend some more time reading that passage. What did she have to lose?

TWENTY-THREE

Joshua had just finished tucking Maddie in when pounding on the front door made them both jump. Maddie's face began to crumple, and Joshua laid a hand on her head. "It's alright, sweetheart. Don't worry about it, okay?" He closed the door behind him and tried to maintain the illusion of calm he had conjured for Maddie's sake. He looked out the peephole and saw Rick, as he knew he would. "Please don't do that again. It scares my daughter," he said through the door.

There was a brief pause. "I'm sorry, I won't," Rick said. "Can I speak to you for a minute, please?"

Such manners. He unbolted the door but left the chain in. Opening the door as far as the chain allowed, he said, "One minute, that's it. I have work to do."

Rick fidgeted from one foot to the other and shoved his hands in his pockets. "One of the ladies down the hall said she saw Kim leaving with you yesterday. I just want to know where she went. I'm worried about her, and the baby. She hasn't called, didn't leave a note, nothing."

Obviously Rick's and Kim's little domestic secret was well-kept around here. "I don't know where she went. She saw I was home and asked for a ride to the bus depot. She didn't say where she was going." He narrowed his eyes at Rick. "But don't think for a second that I don't know why she left. You know how thin these walls are."

He watched as Rick's composed exterior developed a crack or two. "What goes on in my home is my own business."

"Not when a child is involved it isn't. Next time I hear anything like that going on again, I'm calling the cops and DHS, understand?"

A muscle jumped in Rick's neck. "I wouldn't get involved if I were you."

"Is that a threat?"

"Just returning the sentiment is all." He jabbed a finger in Joshua's direction. "I don't believe you about the bus depot. She has nowhere else to go. Now the next time you see her, you tell her to come home. We'll talk things out and patch them up, okay? You tell her I love her and miss her and just want her back safe and sound." With a final menacing stare, Rick turned and disappeared down the hall.

Joshua heard a soft knock on his office door. "Come in." He swiveled his chair and saw Kim looking into the room. He greeted her with a smile. "Kim, hi, come in and sit down. I've been wondering how you're doing. Everything alright?"

She slid into the chair beside his desk and returned the smile. He noticed the bruises on her throat were fading, though still visible. A haunted look still lingered in her eyes, which Joshua was sad to see. "Anne and I are doing pretty well. Everyone is so kind and helpful—and everyone loves Anne."

"I'll bet. She is a beautiful baby."

"And Debbie—well, all the staff, really—they're great. I came up because, well, a couple reasons actually. First, I don't think I ever really thanked you for bringing me here. I know things were getting worse, and I'm relieved that Anne is safe. And me too," she added.

"You're welcome. I'm relieved that you're here too."

She twisted her engagement ring around her finger. He was surprised she still wore it. "Have you seen Rick?"

He sighed. "Yes, I have. The last two nights, actually. He suspects me of helping you leave, and unfortunately someone else in the complex saw us leave together and told him."

"Oh no." Kim's hands twisted together. "What did you tell him?"

"I told him I drove you to the bus depot but that you didn't say

where you were going. He doesn't believe me, though." He remembered Rick's message to Kim but chose not to pass it on. Something
in her demeanor told him she hadn't given up on him.

Kim sighed and pressed her palms to her eyes. "I'm so sorry,
Joshua. I should have known he'd catch on somehow."

"Hey, Kim, don't worry about it. So what if he suspects me —
what can he do about it? It was a risk that had to be taken, and I'm
glad that I did." He gave her a reassuring smile, then said, "You said
there were a couple things you came up here for."

She sighed. "Yes. I wanted to ask you — but it's kind of personal,
so I don't know if I should ..."

Joshua spread his hands. "I'm an open book, ask away."

She gnawed her lip a moment. "Okay. One night — the night before you came and got me, actually — I heard you singing to Maddie. I think you were singing 'Jesus Loves Me.'"

Joshua chuckled. "Yeah, that's a standard at our house."

"So you believe in Jesus too?"

"Yes, I'm a Christian."

"Seems like everyone here is. I mean, I know the staff are because it's a Christian place, but even a lot of the women here seem
to be."

"Is Christianity relatively new to you?"

"Well, sort of — I mean, I know it's a religion. I know about
God, and Jesus — a little bit, anyway. Debbie told me in my counseling session yesterday that Jesus has already paid for what I'd
done, and that only through him could I be released from my guilt."
She frowned. "It's confusing, honestly. One of the other women here
talked about being part of God's family, and I do like the sound of
that, but ..." She stopped and gave him a sheepish look. "I guess I
have a ton of questions and just don't know where to start."

Joshua nodded. "When you don't have any kind of background
knowledge to build on, it can be a little overwhelming. I was raised
in a Christian family, but my wife wasn't, and there were a lot of
things that never fazed me about the faith that really hung her up

because they were so foreign to her. If you're looking for the Cliff-sNotes version, I think I can probably give it to you if you give me a minute to think."

She grinned. "I'd like that."

"Alright, let me see." *Give me the right words here, God.* He arranged his thoughts and took a deep breath. "Well, in a very small nutshell, God is perfect. People are not. God cannot abide imperfection in his presence, but he loves us because we are his creation. He wants for us to be in a relationship with him, to allow him to guide us, and to be willing to live by the laws he lays out for us in the Bible. But in order for us to be able to do any of that, we need help—we need to get our sins erased, get them paid for. A perfect life needed to be sacrificed in our place. That's where Jesus comes in.

"God sent Jesus to earth to be both fully human and fully God. As God, he was able to live a perfect life and never sin. As man, he was able to die. And so he died the death we deserve, and God made it possible for that death to cover our sins, if we are willing to admit that we're sinful and ask God to extend the benefit of Jesus' death to us, which he does as a gift, without expecting us to pay for it, which we never could."

Kim's look of concentration brightened. "Oh, I think Debbie was talking about this. There were a bunch of A words." She frowned again, thinking. "Um...acknowledge what Jesus did—that he died in our place, I guess—admit that we need help getting rid of our sin, and accept the sacrifice that was given in our place. Or something like that. Right?"

Joshua nodded. "That's the gist of it, yes. But then, in response to that gift of grace, we in turn give our lives to God, devote ourselves to living the way Jesus instructed us to in the Bible. It's not easy; God's standards are pretty high. But the grace of God through Jesus covers our mistakes, and he gives us the strength to do things we can't do on our own."

He heaved a sigh. "I'm sure there are a lot of holes there, but if nothing else, that gives you the basics. The bottom line is that God loves you and sent Jesus to die for you so you could be a part of God's family if you wanted to be."

"That was pretty impressive for being off-the-cuff," Kim said with a grin.

"Yeah, well, it's only because God gave me the words. I'm rarely that coherent."

They were both silent for a moment, until Joshua asked, "So was there anything else I could do for you?"

Kim looked about to speak, then stopped. "No—no, that's alright."

"You sure?"

"You've done enough already."

"But I'm always willing to do more. What is it?"

She bit her lip. "Well ... if you're willing—and you can totally say no—I wondered if you might go into the apartment and get some things for me?"

JOSHUA TRIED TO KEEP HIMSELF busy instead of staring out the window, but he was eager to get this over with. Kim had mentioned that Rick had been laid off, so who knew when he'd leave the apartment? Joshua had noticed, however, that Rick had been gone the last three nights that he'd come home, so obviously he was going out somewhere. He just hoped it would be soon. It was already 4:00 p.m.

He was in the middle of fixing himself a snack when he heard the slam of a door in the hallway. He paused mid-sandwich and listened for the sound of footsteps passing his apartment. When he heard them, he slapped the rest of the sandwich together and ran to the window. There was Rick, getting into his car, turning it on, pulling out of his space.

Joshua grabbed the key and a folded paper bag and walked out to the security door to double-check that he hadn't pulled back in. The spot was empty. A shot of adrenaline sent him running down the hall to Kim and Rick's apartment, muttering prayers under his breath all the way.

The bedroom on the left, the two bottom dresser drawers, and the nursery dresser. Whatever you can grab. Joshua shoved shirts, shorts, socks—and with embarrassment, bras and panties—into the bag, then scrambled to his feet and ran into the nursery. He yanked out the drawers and grabbed a handful from each, wishing he had a bigger bag, then stood and slammed the drawers shut. He opened the door and peeked out before closing the door behind him, locking it, and nearly tripping himself as he made a mad dash for his own unit.

It wasn't until he was inside, sitting at the table, that he allowed himself to relax. He'd done it. Into the lion's den and lived to tell the tale. The apartment had not been what he'd expected. The usual clutter, but less than what he and Maddie lived with. He'd expected filth—beer cans underfoot, *Playboys* on the table, dishes everywhere. He'd never considered that batterers might be neat freaks.

He finished his sandwich, packed up his laptop, and split the clothing stash between two bags before leaving for his car. Then he opened the security door, and his stomach dropped to his shoes. Rick was just getting out of his car.

Joshua gave the man a brief, silent nod as he walked to his car. *Walk normal, don't run, be cool.* He tightened his grip on the bags as they passed each other, then got in his car and forced himself to wait ten seconds before turning it on so he didn't look too eager to leave. But as soon as Rick was inside the building, he took off. His palms didn't stop sweating until he was at work.

SHAWNEE KNOCKED BUT OPENED DEBBIE'S OFFICE DOOR before hearing a response. "We've got an angry ex outside."

Groaning, Debbie shoved her chair back from the desk and followed Shawnee to the security office. A man stood out on the front steps of the shelter, pounding his fist on the door and calling for someone to let him in.

"Do we know who he's looking for?" she asked.

"Kim."

Debbie's heart sank. "Oh, no. I'm going to go tell Joshua. Shaw-nee, find Kim and keep an eye on her and Anne, just in case she hears him. Mike, go tell him to leave."

She took the stairs two at a time and arrived breathless at his office. He was unpacking his laptop onto his desk when she got there. "Rick's here."

"What?" He dropped the pen he was holding and ran a hand through his hair. "Great, now what?"

"Shawnee's gone to find Kim and Anne, in case they hear him, or hear about him. We can't stop her if she wants to go out to him, but we can try to stall her while we try to get rid of him."

"Can't you call the police and have him arrested?"

"Security will call if he doesn't heed our requests to leave. Some-one is talking with him right now."

Joshua's phone rang with the in-house tone. He picked it up with a sigh. "This is Joshua." His face clouded. "I'll be right there."

"What's wrong?"

"Rick's asking for me."

She followed him as he left the office and headed for the stairs. "What? For you? Why?"

"Apparently he saw me come in. I don't know how."

She thought for a moment. "Maybe he followed you this morn-ing. But why would he do that?"

"He's suspected me from the beginning. He confronted me twice."

"What! You never told me that." Debbie's irritation was evident, but that would have to wait.

Joshua glanced over his shoulder, apologetic but focused on the impending situation. "I'm sorry. I didn't want you to worry."

He headed for the front door. She grabbed his arm. "Wait — you're just going out there?"

"Well, yeah. He knows I'm here. Maybe I can get him to just leave her a message with me or something."

"What if he gets violent?"

"Look, don't worry, alright? I can hold my own. What's the worst that can happen?"

It was her turn to raise an eyebrow. "Seriously? You want me to tell you about the guy that nearly knifed one of our women when he came here looking for her? Or the guy that had a pistol in his pocket?"

"I don't think Rick's like that. I don't know him well, but I just get the sense. Let me try to talk to him, okay? You guys have that camera set up out there, right? You'll be able to see me and send someone out if I need help." They made eye contact once more, then he headed for the door.

Debbie made a dash for the security room so she could see what was going on. When she got there, Rick and Joshua were on the steps, talking. She cursed the fact that the cameras had no sound and studied their movements and faces to try to discern how the conversation was going.

Twice Rick tried to get past Joshua to the door. Both times Joshua muscled his way between them, hands up in a gesture of nonconfrontational defense. Rick poked him in the chest, and Debbie flinched. The figure of Mike, the guard, entered the frame, and Joshua waved him off. "Just let him take care of it, Joshua. It's his job," she said aloud.

Finally Rick took a step back. Debbie sighed with relief, but then frowned as Mike headed for the door with Joshua behind him. "That's not protocol—"

Rick lunged towards them, out of the frame. She gasped, and when she saw Joshua stagger back and fall halfway down the stairs, she told the other guard to call the police and took off running.

JOSHUA MOANED AND STRUGGLED TO HIS FEET, as Rick and Mike continued to fight it out in the vestibule. Just as he decided to hang back and wait for the fracas to end, Rick pulled a knife from his pocket, flicked his wrist, and thrust the blade into the guard's middle.

The throb in his jaw disappeared as adrenaline took over. Joshua charged up the stairs and looped his arms around Rick's, pinning his arms back as Rick stumbled away from the collapsing guard. Yelling, Rick jumped and kicked back, clipping Joshua in the knee. Joshua staggered and fell back against the wrought iron staircase railing, which caught him just low enough that his and Rick's inertia together nearly sent him backwards over it. He let go of Rick to catch himself from going over, and Rick wheeled around, knife fist flying. Joshua ducked and dodged and reciprocated with a punch of his own, which caught Rick square in the nose. Rick let out a holler as he clamped his free hand to his face, and Joshua took advantage of Rick's brief disorientation to tackle him. He sat on Rick's chest and began to pry the knife from his fist, getting a whiff of alcohol off Rick's breath as he did. Rick started hammering with his bloody fist on Joshua's side and back, but he was able to hold on until he'd wrenched the knife away and chucked it over the railing to the window well below. He then rolled off Rick's chest, fending off the blows, and scrambled down the stairs to the sidewalk to regroup. Someone had dragged Mike inside and shut the shelter door, and when Rick saw he had missed his opportunity to gain entrance, he let out a string of curses and hurtled down the stairs towards Joshua. "You took her," he growled. "You took her from me."

Joshua set his feet and raised his fists in defense. "No, I offered to help her. Maybe if you'd treated her right she wouldn't have left."

Rick swung at him, then jumped him as he ducked the punch. They fell to the pavement, locked in a bear hug. Joshua narrowly escaped being stuck beneath Rick as they lost momentum, and he scrambled to his feet while fending off Rick's fists. He bided his time until Rick was slightly off-balance, then landed a solid punch in his gut. Rick folded and fell to the ground, struggling for breath. Joshua backed away, panting, and sagged with relief when the sound of sirens could be heard in the distance.

Rick regained his breath and slowly stood, eyes locked on Joshua. Joshua raised his hands again. "Give it up, man. Cops are coming anyway."

He wiped the blood from his nose with the end of his shirt. "It's not over. Better watch your back." Joshua said nothing as he backed away towards the stairs to the shelter. "We'll see what these cops think when I tell 'em what I heard you doing with your little girl."

The words of the DHS agent came back to him. *We have to investigate every call we get.* He shook his head. "It won't matter," he said, more to himself than to Rick.

"It will when they see the bruises."

"She doesn't have any."

Rick's chin lifted just one smug fraction. "Not yet she doesn't."

It didn't matter that Rick was all talk and was hinting at a plan that was completely illogical. All Joshua could think of was Rick's violent hands on his daughter. He flew at Rick with all the force he could muster in a few short steps, knocking him to the ground. When the police pulled up to the sidewalk Joshua was unaware of anything but the satisfying feeling of his fist sinking into Rick's abdomen.

TWENTY-FOUR

Kim watched from the window as Joshua and Rick beat each other on the sidewalk. Tears rolled down her cheeks at the sight of her rescuer being led off in handcuffs. Her emotions were in such tumult she wasn't even sure which one was the cause of her crying. Rick arrested. Joshua arrested. The love she couldn't help but feel for Rick. The fear she felt for when those officers would return for her.

Or maybe it was the prayer she had just prayed with Pam in the kitchen, admitting her sins to God and acknowledging her need for a Savior.

She walked back to her room and relieved Adele from baby-sitting. She sat on the bed and let the tears come hard while she nursed her baby in her arms. "I'm so sorry, sweetie. I'm so sorry Mommy has to leave you." She covered the sweet, soft face with tears and kisses, then left the room in search of Doreen.

She and Doreen hadn't talked much, but she knew she wouldn't be totally clueless about what to do with a baby. She found her in the laundry room, scrubbing a spaghetti stain from her skirt. "Hey Kim. I heard about what was going on out there. You alright?"

"Yes ... and no. Long story." She held Anne out to her. "Can you take her for me, please?"

Doreen tossed the skirt into the washing machine and started the load. "Sure thing. Come here, cutie." She sat her up in her arms with ease.

"I checked. There are bottles and formula in the kitchen, in the bottom left cabinet. She'll need to eat again in about an hour and a half." She didn't trust herself to say more. The tears were too close to the surface and her throat was already aching to close. She gave

Anne one more kiss on the cheek, then left the room for the front door, forcing her eyes forward so she didn't lose her nerve.

After praying with Pam, they had talked about guilt, and coming clean, and doing what you could do — within reason — to make it right. Suffering under the thumb of a batterer was not within reason, but Pam had quoted the saying that confession was good for the soul. Kim knew, deep down, that there was really only one thing she could do to make up for what she did, and if she didn't do it she'd never be able to look her daughter in the eye and teach her the importance of honesty or integrity. And if she didn't do it now, who knew how Rick might embellish the story. She wanted to be the one to make the first move.

She pushed open the front door and breathed in the fresh air, savoring the faint scent of fresh cut grass and sunshine. Debbie stood talking with an officer. Rick, Joshua, and the other police and cruisers were gone. She waited until Debbie finished and the officer moved for his car. Debbie did a double-take when she saw her. "Oh, Kim — you don't need to be out here. It's all taken care of; don't worry."

Kim embraced Debbie in a brief hug. "Thank you for everything. I understand what you were talking about now, about Jesus and everything. Talk to Pam, she can tell you the story."

Debbie smiled. "Really?"

Kim gave her a small smile and nodded, but then saw the officer getting into his car. "I need to go, Debbie."

She jogged to the patrol car and waved to the officer through the door. He got out again. "How can I help you?"

She took a deep breath. *Help me, Jesus.* "I need to turn myself in."

The officer raised his eyebrows. "Oh — for what?"

She swallowed hard, then put her life in God's hands. "A woman was killed seven years ago, and the police never found out who did it. But it was me."

DEBBIE WATCHED IN CONFUSION AS KIM talked to the officer. She couldn't tell what she was saying, but once the officer opened the back door to the cruiser and helped Kim inside Debbie began to panic. She ran to the car, shouting, "Wait! What's going on?"

"She confessed to a crime, so I'm taking her to the station."

"You're arresting her?"

"Well, sort of, yes. But she's going willingly."

Debbie peeked into the window. "Kim? What's going on?"

"I have to do it, Debbie. It's the right thing to do."

"But what about Anne?"

"It's her I'm doing it for. And me. And God."

The officer got in and started the engine. Debbie backed away and watched as the car drove off. "I have no idea what just happened," she said to the empty air as she walked back to the shelter's front door. "One of my staff gets arrested for assault and one of my women admits to being a criminal. And Anne! What on earth are we supposed to do with Anne?"

She went first to her office to call the shelter's attorney on Joshua's behalf. After explaining the situation, she went in search of Doreen, eventually finding her in the common room with a group of other women.

"Did Kim tell you what she was doing?" she asked Doreen.

"No, she just asked me to watch Anne. Why, is she okay?"

Debbie sank into a chair. "She just turned herself in to the police."

The women let out a chorus of flabbergasted exclamations and asked questions over each other that Debbie was unable to answer. "All she told me was that Pam would be able to explain what happened to her. I got the sense that she finally understood salvation, and that she needed to turn herself in because it was the right thing to do."

"But what about the baby?" Adele asked. All eyes turned to the orphan gnawing on Doreen's thumb. "Where does she go now? Not back to Kim's boyfriend, I hope."

"Well, he just got arrested—" More noises of shock, and Debbie filled them in with the details since most of them had been unaware of the altercation. "So I'm guessing no, he won't get custody. But unless we can find some family for her, we'll have to turn her over to DHS."

"She doesn't have any family." All eyes turned to Pam, who had appeared in the doorway. "Kim is an orphan, and so is Rick. As far as Kim knows neither of them has any living relatives."

"This is just tragic," Doreen said as she cuddled Anne. "I can't stand the thought of the baby going into foster care."

"Pam, do you know what Kim did? Maybe she won't be arrested, or maybe the statute of limitations is up and she won't be held responsible."

Pam sat on the arm of Debbie's chair. "She didn't go into details with me, so I don't know. But I got the impression she believed it was bad enough for her to go to jail for quite a while. She knew Anne might end up in foster care. But she knew that a baby would get placed much more easily than an older child, and she wanted to turn herself in now instead of waiting to see if the police ever caught on to her, since she didn't know how old Anne might be by then. Plus she wanted to beat her fiancé to the punch.

"But we spoke for a few minutes in her room this morning, and she prayed with me to receive salvation." She shrugged. "It's all in God's hands now. There's nothing we can do now but pray."

KIM LAY ON THE BUNK in her cell and wept, but the tears were mostly those of relief. Seven years of soul-eating guilt were finally at an end. Regardless of the outcome, she felt God would take care of her and Anne. She knew next to nothing about God, but there was nothing else to which the peace she felt could be attributed. She couldn't think at all about Anne, though. Not yet. She had a feeling even God couldn't soothe her heart at the thought of losing her baby girl. At least Rick was in custody as well. When she arrived at the station, she had also named Rick as a batterer, and domestic abuse charges had been added to the list for him.

Her thoughts about the abuse and the last year with Rick made her head spin. She had a feeling she was going to need a lot of therapy. She dried her eyes on the end of her shirt and folded her hands behind her head. At least she'd have plenty of time to think through everything.

So. Kim conjured an image that was a cross between Santa Claus and a sandaled angel to serve as the face of God as she attempted another prayer. *Here I am. I have a lot of time. What should we talk about?*

I'll start with thank yous.

Thank you for the shelter, and for Debbie and Pam and all the women I met there. Thank you for Joshua. Thank you for protecting him when he was fighting Rick. Rick ... no, I'm not going to go there yet. Thank you for Anne—

She couldn't avoid the thought. She began again to weep, and her thoughts and prayers took off running, asking for all kinds of protection and blessing on the innocent baby who stood to lose more than Kim or Rick in this whole mess.

Give her a good foster family, please. A family that will love her and treat her like a daughter and not like a maid or a burden or a tax break. Let me see her again, soon. Her breasts ached at the thought of her child. Milk stained her blue T-shirt in conspicuous patches. She turned to the wall and curled inward to block out reality while she closed her eyes and fought to keep her focus on God.

Protection. Reunion. Forgiveness. Please, God. Mercy and compassion and my daughter in my arms again. Please, God. Protection. Reunion. Forgiveness ...

DEBBIE SHIFTED FROM FOOT TO FOOT in the lobby of the station. The sergeant she had spoken with had been friendly enough, but the place still made her jumpy. She'd never been in one before, and the feeling was akin to driving on the freeway with an entire city's police force behind you on the road.

Kim was somewhere in here, as was Joshua, though Joshua had

been processed already and would be released on his own recogni-
zance. The shelter's attorney had been understanding of Debbie's
fears for Kim, but because Kim was not shelter staff, his contract
did not extend to her, and Debbie couldn't afford the price from her
own pocket. She prayed the public defender was a good one.

Joshua rounded a corner, face bruised and puffy, but with a
look of calm in his eyes. Without thinking, Debbie threw her arms
around his neck. His arms circled her waist and held her tight. "Are
you okay?"

"I'm fine." He tried to smile but winced in pain. He gingerly
touched the left side of his mouth and grimaced. "Mostly, anyway.
How's Mike?"

"Alive. And lucky."

"What about Rick?"

"I haven't heard. I've been too busy trying to figure out what
happened to Kim. She turned herself in."

He frowned and winced again. "Turned herself in? For what?"

She told him the story as she led him to the car. "We don't have
a lawyer for her. I sure wish we did. She'll have to use the public
defender."

Joshua belted himself into the passenger seat and carefully
rubbed a hand over his eyes. "That's unbelievable. What about
Anne, where is she?"

"About an hour after they took Kim, someone from DHS—" Her
voice hitched as the thought of Anne missing her mother broke her
heart. She cleared her throat. "Someone from DHS picked her up."

Joshua rested a hand atop hers. "Oh man."

She blinked back tears. "A bunch of the women at the shelter
were trying to talk the agent into letting us keep her there, but it
didn't fly." She didn't mention that she'd been one of the most as-
sertive voices in that argument, begging in the end that the agent
reconsider and at least let Anne remain until her mother's fate was
determined. "And no one at the station will tell me what's going on

with Kim, either, so…" She shrugged and turned on the car. "What a day."

"You're telling me."

She looked over to him. "Back to the shelter? Or do you need a stop at an urgent care clinic?"

"No, just—" He looked at the clock on her radio and groaned. "Maddie. Her daycare is already closed, which means my in-laws were called to pick her up. I'm going to get an earful when they see me like this." He pounded a fist on his knee. "This is like handing them the rope and begging them to hang me."

"Want someone to corroborate your story?"

He looked at her with relief in his eyes. "Seriously?"

She shrugged, giving him a small smile. "It's the least I can do for the guy who saved some lives at my shelter."

She dropped him at his car and followed him to his in-laws' house, her stomach doing flip-flops the whole way. Given the stories she'd heard about them, she wasn't eager to actually meet them. Though if it meant ensuring they didn't chew him out in front of his daughter—and they'd have to be pretty gutsy to do that in front of a total stranger—it was worth it.

They turned onto a driveway that led to a gate. The guard in the guardhouse handed her a dated card to put in the window, then waved her through. She ogled the gorgeous homes and manicured lawns that lined the street. They had to be pretty big jerks to have this much money and not even help bail Joshua out of the medical debts from his wife's treatment. Her nervous energy turned to righteous indignation.

She parked behind him and they met on the sidewalk. "Listen," he said, "I apologize now for anything uncouth, rude, antagonistic, or mean that either of them says to you. They can't be predicted or trusted to act appropriately if they spot the chance to take a pot shot at me."

"Don't worry about me," she said. "Sticks and stones." She followed him up to the house and steeled herself.

The wooden door swung open a minute after Joshua had rung the bell. A middle-aged woman Debbie took to be Joshua's mother-in-law glared at him with a look that could bore holes in cement. "There you—oh my Lord, what happened to your face?"

"Kind of a long story," Joshua said. "You picked up Maddie, right?"

"Of course we did. When they called and said you hadn't shown up we went over right away. What mischief were you causing to get yourself beat up like that?" Her eyes cut over to Debbie, whom she looked up and down before narrowing her piercing blue eyes. "And who is this?"

Debbie thrust out her hand. "I'm Debbie Truman. I run the Safe in His Arms women's shelter, where Joshua works."

The woman didn't soften in the least. She gave Debbie's hand a cursory shake. "Alisha Michalson. So? Why did you tag along?"

"Alisha, can't we come in?" Joshua asked. "I'd like to see Maddie. I don't want her wondering where I am."

She looked back to Joshua, then sighed with a look of exasperation and opened the door wider. It was the only invitation she extended for them to enter. "She's in the back with George. And you still didn't answer my question. Who is this woman?"

"Why don't you ask her yourself?" He looked to Debbie. "I'll be right back, I want to go find Maddie."

"Of course, go ahead." She gave Alisha a brief smile. "I offered to come to vouch for Joshua's whereabouts in case there were any ... questions." She tried not to punctuate the sentence with a pointed look but wasn't entirely successful.

Alisha cocked a brow. "And what were his whereabouts, dare I ask?"

"We had a revenge-seeking domestic abuser trying to gain entrance to our shelter. Joshua defended an injured security guard and wrestled a knife away from the attacker."

Alisha sniffed and refused to comment. Debbie refrained from tacking "Take that!" onto the end of her explanation and instead said, "That's the second time he's been a hero to the shelter. We were on the verge of closing when I hired him, and he got us back into the black." She smiled at Alisha, then looked past her to the room beyond where Joshua and Maddie had entered, hand in hand, followed by an older, distinguished-looking gentleman. "If he's half as good at parenting as he is at everything else he does, then Maddie is one lucky little girl." *I dare you to disagree with me.*

Joshua rested a hand on his daughter's head. "Maddie, remember Debbie?" Maddie shrank back a bit behind Joshua, but a smile tugged at her mouth. Alisha frowned at the child. "Madeline, greet Ms. Truman properly. You're a big girl, don't hide behind your father like a baby."

Debbie didn't bother trying to hide her rolling eyes. "Oh please. She's not being a baby, she's just shy. I used to do the same thing, Maddie, and when I got older I wasn't shy anymore. Given some of the people in this world, I'd much rather a child be shy and cling to her father than to run out and greet every random person they run into." She avoided Alisha's indignant face and reached a hand out to the older man. "I'm Debbie Truman, by the way. You must be Joshua's father-in-law."

"George Michalson, nice to meet you, Debbie." He shook her hand and tilted his head toward Joshua. "I heard about the afternoon you all had at the shelter. I'm glad to hear everyone is alright, for the most part. It certainly could have ended a lot worse. I shudder to think of this one—" he looked down to Maddie, whose eyes were still fixed on Debbie—"being orphaned."

"She wouldn't be, George. She would have us." Alisha's tone was scolding.

"Not the same, Alisha, and you know it."

Joshua took Maddie's hand. "We should be getting along. Thank you for picking her up. I do appreciate it." He put a hand on Debbie's back, steering her toward the door, and she grinned to herself. "We'll see you later. Say good-bye, Maddie."

"Bye Gramma! Bye Grampa!"

Debbie turned and offered them the most gracious smile she could muster. "A pleasure to meet you."

Alisha said nothing, but George nodded. "And you. Best of luck with your organization. Put us on your mailing list the next time you do a fund-raising push."

"Oh, Mr. Michalson—thank you very much. I'll be sure to do that."

"George, I don't think—"

George gave her a look that silenced her. "We can discuss it later, Alisha." He opened the door for them and nodded another farewell before closing it behind them.

"Wow," Debbie said when they reached the sidewalk.

"You can say that again," Joshua said. "You really scored with my father-in-law."

"Who'd have thought?"

"Daddy, I'm hungry. All they gave me was graham crackers for a snack, and Gramma was making fish for dinner." Maddie made a face that spoke volumes on her opinion of the dish.

Joshua looked to Debbie with a sheepish grin. "I think we may have to postpone our dinner tonight."

Debbie chuckled. "Well, Maddie is hungry, and you're in no shape to cook. How about Chuck E. Cheese—my treat."

Maddie squealed as Joshua laughed. "Only met her once and you already know the way to her heart. All right, we'll see you there."

They parted ways for their own cars. Debbie slid into the driver's seat and started the engine, then noticed the light flashing on her cell phone. Her parents' phone number topped the missed calls list. She dialed them on the way out the gate. "Hey Mom. Sorry I missed you."

"Did you hear my message?"

"No, I just called you back instead. What's up?"

"We got a call from Detective Ramsey."

Debbie's stomach lurched at the mention of that name. Her family had met with him a few times during the investigation into Gina's death. They hadn't talked to him since the case went cold years ago, but she'd never forget that name. "What? Why?"

"It's incredible, Debbie. After all this time, someone confessed to Gina's murder. Some woman just walked up to a policeman and confessed. Her name is Kim Slone."

TWENTY-FIVE

Kim was just finishing breakfast when a guard stopped by her cell. "You have visitors," he said. "Debbie Truman and her family are here to see you."

The joy she felt at Debbie's name turned to confusion. "Her family? Why?"

The guard shrugged. "You want to see them or not?"

"Yes, absolutely." She polished off her oatmeal in three hasty bites, then tried to smooth her hair that was still tangled from sleep. Her heart began to pound. Maybe Debbie could tell her about Anne.

The guard led her to a room filled with Plexiglas booths. She sat in a chair and watched as Debbie entered, trailed by an older couple she assumed were Debbie's parents and a younger man who she took to be her brother. Kim picked up the phone receiver that allowed them to communicate, and Debbie sat down and did the same. "Hi Debbie! I can't believe you came to see me."

Debbie's expression was difficult to read. Kim noticed how she avoided eye contact. Her embarrassment grew. She was in jail, after all. "Hey Kim. These are my parents, Roland and Ruth, and my brother Pete."

Debbie's voice was strained, like she was trying to talk while holding her breath. Kim waved to the people standing behind her and they waved back. She tried not to stare, but she couldn't help trying to gauge their intentions from their faces. There was little she could pick up, however—though Ruth and Roland appeared to be in better spirits than Debbie or Pete. "Thanks for coming. I'm dying to know why you're here. But first, have you seen Anne? Do you know what happened to her?"

Debbie briefly met her eyes. "DHS came and got her. We tried to talk the caseworker into letting us keep her at the shelter until they knew what was going to happen with you, but they didn't go for it. I don't know where she is, though. I'm sorry."

Kim nibbled her lip and nodded. "I didn't think you would, but I had to ask."

"Of course."

"So ..." Kim shrugged. "Sorry, this is a little awkward, I'm sorry."

Debbie took a deep breath, her shoulder hunching. "I know, and I'm sorry for springing strangers on you ... but there is a reason we all came down here." She glanced back at her mother, then finally back up and held Kim's gaze. "We're here because we heard about your confession. See, the girl you ..." She stopped, swallowed. "The girl you killed was my sister, Gina."

Kim's hand gripped the receiver with white-knuckle strength. She wanted to bolt from the room, but at the same time was unable to move. She sucked in a breath and let it out in a gasp. "Debbie—I can't even ... I don't know what to say." Suddenly she couldn't stop the words. "I'm sorry. I know it means nothing, but I'm so, so sorry. It was an accident, please believe me. I didn't mean to and I didn't want to just leave her there but I had to—"

Debbie's mother tapped her daughter on the shoulder as Kim babbled, then sat down as Debbie stood. "Kim. Stop. It's alright." Her voice was soothing and held no anger or tension the way Debbie's had. Kim choked back a sob and swiped at the hot tears that stung at her eyes. "We were all stunned at the news—Debbie especially when she realized she not only knew you but that you were not at all the kind of person we had assumed you would be. But we didn't come down here today because we wanted to shame you, or yell at you, or anything like that. We just want to know what happened.

We've spent eight years wondering what went on that night, and we just want to have the puzzle finally put together for us."

Kim sniffed and took three deep breaths to regain control of herself. "Of course, of course." She stared at the table between them, gathering her thoughts. "I had been out at a classmate's house because we had a group project we had to work on. I was on my way back to my foster parents' house..."

She stopped as the memories she had stuffed down deep over the years began to surface in a rush. She remembered the house of the classmate—What was her name? Sandi—and how envious she had been of the family pictures that were scattered in frames on tables and the walls. She remembered the two other students, a jock who had always intimidated Kim with his good looks and sarcasm, and a Goth-dressing girl whose lip ring made Kim feel slightly ill. Sandi and the jock kept flirting and getting involved in their own conversations, and Goth girl kept sketching fairies on her notebook and occasionally swearing at Sandi and the jock for wasting everyone's time. Kim had felt invisible until they had begun to work in earnest, when it turned out she was the only one with any understanding at all of their assignment.

They had worked for an hour, at which point Sandi's parents had come to check on them and bid them good night. A few minutes later Sandi had assured them her parents were in bed for good, and then offered everyone a beer.

The jock and Goth girl accepted without so much as a snicker of rule-breaking glee. When she looked to Kim for her answer, she said "Yes, please," which made the others laugh, though she didn't know why. The others chugged down their first swallows as though parched, despite the two liters of soda they had already consumed over the course of the evening. She took a sip and nearly gagged at the taste. She forced another sip, then a third, only because she didn't want Sandi to ask at the end of the night why she hadn't had any of it. By the time they had finished their work, the jock's and Goth girl's cans were empty, but Kim's was still half full.

Her stomach roiled with the foul drink, and she wasn't sure if her vision was truly skewed or if she was imagining it. It was the first time she'd ever had alcohol, and she had no concept of how long it took to feel the effects or how much was needed to really make a difference. When it was time to go home she was terrified to drive, and chose a route that would take her along less-traveled streets so there was less chance of getting into an accident.

She was driving down Sunset when a cyclist a few feet ahead looked back at her twice, and then veered sharply to the left, bringing herself directly in front of Kim's car. Kim slammed on the brakes with a scream, but there was no avoiding the rider.

Ruth's eyes sparkled with tears, but her voice remained calm and controlled. "Was she trying to avoid an animal? Maybe dodge something in the gutter?"

Kim shook her head. "I didn't see anything. I don't know. But she wasn't just swerving out of the way of something. It was like she *wanted* to get in front of me."

The receiver Ruth held picked up Debbie's voice as she murmured, "Suicide." The other Trumans looked to her, shock clear on their faces. "It makes sense," Kim could hear her say. "She was running away, she'd been betrayed by her boyfriend, and no one was giving her the support she needed. And she was ... she was Gina: a drama queen, everything overdone and melodramatic. She was probably running on emotion and just wanted her misery to end. It wasn't premeditated, just done in the heat of the moment."

Kim's breaths came fast as her heart began to pound. All these years she had blamed herself for going five miles over the speed limit, blamed her reflexes, blamed the beer for slowing her down. But if Gina had meant to do it ... Well, it didn't change the fact that her actions caused someone to die, but it lessened her pain ever so slightly to know someone else was also at fault.

Ruth looked back to Kim. "What happened after that?"

"I got out to see if ... you know ... I took her pulse and it was really slow. She didn't move; she was barely breathing. I didn't know what to do, and then she just let out this sigh and ..."

Kim had felt again for a pulse, squinted up close to her face searching for her breath in the cold autumn night air. Then she'd scrambled back when it hit her the girl was dead.

She'd almost hyperventilated with panic. She'd been drinking, speeding a little—the fact that the girl had basically jumped in front of her wouldn't matter much to the police in the face of these issues, especially without witnesses.

That's when she realized—there were no witnesses. The windows of the houses along her right were dark, and to the left was a cemetery. She jumped back into the car, made a U-turn, and headed back in the other direction.

She'd inspected the car when she got home. The chrome grille was bent and one headlight was smashed. She'd woken her foster mother, telling her through her sobs that she'd hit a deer. Saundra had comforted her, shared her own story of animal encounters while driving, assured her that sometimes there was nothing you could do.

She'd heard nothing at school about a student dying. She avoided the television when the news was on, afraid hearing about the story might cause her to do something that would give away her guilt.

"She was in college. A freshman," Ruth said.

"No wonder I never heard anything. I wondered why no one was talking about it."

Everyone was silent. Kim finally offered the only thing she could. "I know it doesn't help. But I'm so sorry. You don't know how much this has haunted me, how often I've wished I could go back and change everything I did that night."

Debbie gave her a small smile. "I do know, actually. You told me in counseling."

Kim let out a strangled chuckle. "Do you understand now? Why I let Rick do what he did?"

Debbie nodded. Her mother looked between the two of them. "What do you mean?"

"Kim—I won't if you don't want me to, but if it's alright with you I'd like to tell my family what you've been through."

Her gaze dropping, Kim shrugged. "Yeah, sure."

Debbie recounted Kim's time with Rick and the reasons she let him hit her. Kim averted her eyes, feeling awkward under this microscope. When Debbie finished, Ruth turned back to Kim with a look in her eyes she couldn't decipher.

"You poor child." It was not what Kim had expected to hear. "I can't believe what you've gone through."

The sentiment tugged at her heart. She was sure Ruth meant to be compassionate, but instead she felt even worse than she had before. "What *I've* gone through? It's nothing compared to what you had to go through—losing your daughter, not knowing what happened, having to live with that mystery all these years."

Ruth shook her head. "Loss is a part of life. Losing a child rips your heart in two, I won't deny that—and from what I understand you're experiencing that yourself." Kim ducked her head to hide the strain on her features caused by holding in the sudden sob that tried to escape. "But we know we'll see Gina again in heaven. We miss her now, we grieved for the future with her that we lost, but God's peace and comfort got us through, and his Word assured us we'd see her again."

The weight of Kim's emotions bent her double. She wept, dropping her head onto her arms on the table. Ruth murmured words of comfort into the receiver that lay on the table beside her. When her tears ran out she sat up, feeling lighter in her spirit than she ever had. "Thank you," she said to Ruth. "I can't tell you how much better I feel, having told you face-to-face what happened. And your—your grace towards me..." She shook her head. "I almost can't believe you're for real. Thank you." She looked to the rest of the family and was struck by the look on Debbie's face. All the others looked at her with compassion—even Pete, whose posture had been defensive from the start. But Debbie just looked mad.

Debbie fumed all the way back to her parents' house. She hadn't expected to feel this way when she'd agreed to take her family down to the station, but seeing Kim look so unburdened and free had stirred her anger. She didn't care what her mother said about knowing the whole story—it didn't bring Gina back, and it didn't make her feel any better.

She let the door slam behind her when she entered the house. Her mother was alone in the kitchen, putting the kettle on the stove. "Tea?"

Debbie sat on a barstool and propped her chin in her hands. "Only if you don't have any ice cream."

"All out, sorry." Ruth pulled two mugs from the cabinet and ripped open the tea bags. "Want to talk about it?"

"Not really."

"Okay."

She stared at the fire beneath the kettle, watching it lap the metal. "You're happy, then?"

Ruth set the sugar bowl on the island in front of Debbie. "Happy? No. My daughter might have killed herself. What does that say about the relationship she and I had, that she didn't feel like she could come to me? I'm relieved, however, to know the whole story. I'm relieved to know she most likely felt no pain. I'm glad to know, though I'm not sure why, that someone else was there when she passed, that she wasn't alone in the middle of the road." She sat beside Debbie. "But knowing that she felt so alone that she wanted to die? Knowing she was in love with someone, and that he not only broke her heart but tried to actually harm her? That doesn't make me happy at all."

She dragged a spoon through the sugar, making patterns in the crystals. "And it breaks my heart to know that another girl her age had to go through that experience alone—had to go through her entire life alone, really, or at least without a real family, and then felt it necessary to submit herself to abuse just to make up for something that wasn't really her fault." She shook her head. "Such a broken world. Come, Jesus, come."

Debbie stared at the sugar, watching the spoon write Gina's initials and then scrape them away, over and over. Then the vision blurred with tears that fell unchecked to her cheeks. "It was supposed to be some drunk, some drunk jerk who I would be justified in hating. Not a kid who can hardly be blamed." Her mother's hand rested on her back and smoothed circles on her blouse. "Now I have no one to put my anger on but myself."

"Lay it down, Debbie. Hate and anger do you no good, doesn't matter where you direct them. Neither does guilt, and I know you've dealt with plenty of that too."

Debbie buried her face in her folded arms and let herself cry harder than she had in a long time. When she finally raised her head, a cup of tea sat steaming in front of her along with a box of tissues.

"It's time for you to take the advice you gave Kim," her mother said. "You keep saying you've forgiven yourself, that you've made your peace, but obviously you haven't. It's time to do it for good and move on."

"I don't know how. I keep doing it because it doesn't work the first time."

"Don't confuse moving on with forgetting. It's acceptance of what you've done and extending some grace to yourself for having made a mistake. And you probably can't do it on your own—that's why you need the Lord's help. Stop trying to be so self-sufficient and independent, you stubborn girl, you." Ruth smiled gently and set a plate of banana bread in front of her.

Debbie picked up a slice of bread. "Why is it I can walk other women through this kind of thing, but I can't do it myself?"

"Well, what is it they say about doctors, how they make the worst patients? Maybe it's the same idea with psychologists."

"Maybe."

"It helps to have someone else to talk to, too, instead of just letting it rattle around in your own head."

"But I talk to you all the time."

Her mother smiled. "Maybe it's time to talk to someone else."

Debbie snorted. "Like who?"

"You've talked an awful lot about that Joshua ..."

"Mom!"

"What? I'm just saying."

"Ahem. New topic please."

Her mother smiled and sat down beside her as she helped herself to a slice of the bread. "Alright then. There *is* something I'd like to talk to you about ..."

The cell at the county jail for women was just what she expected: cold, stark, and depressing. Her cell mate was blessedly quiet, her nose buried in a ratty paperback whenever they were locked in. The other women were a mixed bag of all shades of friendly and various levels of threatening. Kim mostly kept to herself.

Her attorney arranged for Anne to be brought to the prison the second day she was there. The visit was agonizing. When the social worker took her back, Kim retreated to her cell, burying herself beneath the bedsheets and sobbing into the stiff pillow. She'd thought seven years of guilt and nightmares and the recent past with Rick had been bad, but they were nothing compared to the experience of watching her baby be taken away. She tried to find comfort in knowing Anne was in good hands, but it didn't help much.

Kim quickly learned that an unoccupied mind would go instantly to memories of Anne, so she kept herself busy praying and reading the Bible Ruth had given her. Sometimes it backfired—she could identify a little too well with the agony she imagined God felt as he watched his children leave the garden—and she had to stop reading and pour out her pain in prayer. But eventually a sense of comfort would envelop her and she'd open the book once more.

On the fifth day the warden led her to a visitation room where her attorney awaited. "Discovery is completed," he said. "Your trial date is set for next Wednesday."

Five more days. "Okay."

"I talked with the prosecuting attorney. He's willing to skip straight to sentencing. There's no point in dragging everyone through a trial—you're pleading guilty, it's a straightforward case."

She shrugged. "That's fine, I guess."

He stood to leave. "Oh, and the Trumans have asked if they can speak on your behalf at the hearing."

"What? Why?"

"I don't know, but it can't hurt."

"You're sure they want to speak on my behalf and not against me?"

"They were pretty clear."

"But that doesn't make sense." She spoke aloud, though the words were meant for heaven.

"Beats me. But I'm meeting with them Monday to find out. See you next week."

THEY WERE THE LONGEST FIVE DAYS OF HER LIFE.

Anne was brought back for two more visits, and each parting was more excruciating than the last. Her cell mate was transferred, and she was alone for the last two days before her sentencing. Ruth came back to visit once, bringing with her another book, this one a hardbound Bible dictionary that was twice as thick as the bulky, leather-bound Bible. "Thank you so much," she'd told her for the hundredth time, "but honestly, you don't have to do this."

"I know I don't. But I want to." Normally cool and composed, Ruth seemed different today, more animated. She sat on the edge of the metal folding chair and fidgeted now and then. "What will you do when you're done serving your time, Kim? Where will you go?"

Kim gave a mirthless chuckle. "That's so far in the future there's no point even thinking about it. The last year has been so far from what I could have predicted—what's the point in trying to plan for the next year, let alone look ten years down the road?"

"We want to help you, Roland and I."

"What do you mean? Is that why you want to talk to the judge?"

Her eyebrows arched. "Your attorney told you about that?"

"Just that you wanted to speak on my behalf. I don't understand why, though."

"You've been dealt such a difficult hand, Kim. Such a difficult life. And it pains us to see you locked up for something that really wasn't even your fault. We just want to encourage the judge to show you mercy and compassion."

Mercy and compassion. Kim shook her head. "I don't think those words apply to my life."

"Maybe not before. But now ..." Ruth smiled. "They're the hallmarks of Christ. Your life is new in him. The old rules don't apply anymore. There's no telling what your future holds."

Kim ruminated on those words that night when sleep was elusive in the face of the next day's sentencing. Her old life held three bright spots: graduating from foster care relatively unscathed, starting her career, and having Anne. Three accomplishments in twenty-five years. With the bar set that low, God wouldn't have to work that hard to make her new life better.

KIM FOLLOWED THE BAILIFF into the courtroom and sat where he pointed. She rubbed her damp palms over her thighs as her eyes flitted from one new sight to another. What little breakfast she'd been able to eat tossed with the butterflies in her stomach. *Mercy and compassion, Lord. Mercy and compassion.*

The doors in the back of the courtroom opened. Debbie and her parents entered, and Kim's butterflies danced with apprehension. Ruth and Roland smiled at her, their countenances warm and encouraging. Debbie's face was unreadable, though she looked more peaceful than she had the day she and her family had first visited her at the jail. They took seats directly behind her, and Kim felt her courage grow just from knowing they were there.

"All rise. The Honorable Judge Fullerton presiding." Kim stood along with everyone else in the room, then settled back into her seat as the judge began the proceedings with another defendant. She paid close attention to what went on so she would know what to do when it was her turn. Her attorney had briefed her on what to expect, but his explanation flew from her head when she entered the wood-paneled room.

The judge completed the sentencing of the first defendant, then the bailiff said, "Next on the docket, the state versus Kimberly Slone." Her attorney stuffed his crossword puzzle into his briefcase as he stood along with Kim.

The judge stared down at Kim. "It always makes me nervous when a defendant decides to skip the trial. But if it's what you want, then it's okay by me. You're still comfortable being sentenced today in lieu of a trial, Ms. Slone?"

"Yes, your honor."

The judge nodded. "Alright then. Now I understand the parents of the victim wish to speak on your behalf. Are they present?"

"Yes, your honor, we are," Kim heard Roland say.

The bailiff opened the gate to admit Ruth and Roland, who came to stand beside Kim's attorney. Ruth cleared her throat. "My name is Ruth Truman, your honor. My family and I had the chance to speak with Ms. Slone and hear her side of the story. Based on what she said, and on information we learned about the days leading up to our daughter's death, we believe she committed suicide by pulling in front of Ms. Slone. There was no way Kim — Ms. Slone — could have avoided hitting her.

"Since then, Ms. Slone has been haunted by guilt, which drove her to seek punishment in an extreme fashion. Our family feels Ms. Slone has suffered enough already. Any sentence handed down to her would be, in our opinion, excessive and unnecessary. I know we're not the law, but we *are* the ones who are supposed to be vindicated by her punishment, and we feel we already have been. So, your honor, we would like to ask for mercy for Ms. Slone."

The judge shifted in his seat, eyes fixed not on Kim but on Ruth and Roland. "This is an unusual turn of events," he said. "It's not often that a victim's family asks for a sentence to be lessened." He shifted his gaze to Kim. "Ms. Slone, may I ask what punishment you sought to take care of your guilt?"

She hadn't expected this. She licked her lips, which were suddenly dry, and stood to speak. "My fiancé beat me up, your honor. A number of times. I let him because I figured I deserved it."

"How long did you submit yourself to his abuse?"

"About a year, your honor."

"And what made you decide to turn yourself in?"

She sighed. "It's sort of a long story, sir. He began to hit my daughter—"

"You have a child?"

"Yes, sir."

"Where is she now?"

"In foster care. Neither me or my fiancé have any family, and he's in jail now as well." The judge nodded. "Anyway—I left him because he began hurting her. My neighbor took me to the shelter where Mrs. Truman's daughter works ..." She explained her experience there, the things Debbie told her, and the reason why she decided she had to come forward for what she had done. "The Trumans are being very gracious, your honor, and I really appreciate their compassion. But I also understand that the law has to be followed." She fought to keep her composure. "All I ask is that I be able to see my daughter whenever possible. I don't want her growing up the way I did."

The room was silent as Kim sat down. The judge's eyes did not move from Kim's face, even as she sat down and bowed her head. Each time she peeked up, he was still staring at her.

"This is quite the story," he said after an eternity. He looked to the prosecuting attorney. "Counselor, do you have anything you would like to add?"

The state's attorney stood. "No, your honor."

The judge nodded slowly. "Please rise, Ms. Slone." Kim stood, her legs shaking beneath her. "I hereby sentence you to five years in prison, time already served."

Ruth clapped her hands over her mouth, her face frozen in surprise. Roland beamed. Kim looked to her attorney. "What does that mean?"

He smiled. "It means you're free."

EPILOGUE

Kim glanced out the window. "I think Joshua and Maddie are here."

Ruth frowned. "Not Debbie?"

"No, I don't see — oh wait, there she is. She drove separately." Kim set down the stack of linen napkins and opened the front door as the three approached. "Happy Thanksgiving!"

"Happy Thanksgiving!" Joshua and Maddie replied. Hugs were given all around; then Kim went back to setting the table while Joshua took Maddie into the kitchen for a drink and Debbie sank onto the sofa.

"How did lunch go?" Kim asked Debbie as she arranged the silverware on the napkins.

"It went well, thanks. The ladies appreciated the cookies. Thanks again for making them."

Kim grinned. "The least I could do. I'm glad they turned out okay."

"Oh — one of the ladies has a job interview on Wednesday. Would you be able to fit her in before then?"

"No problem. I'll come over Tuesday; just let me know when she's free. I don't have any appointments that week."

Debbie frowned. "I'm sorry it's taking so long to get things off the ground."

Kim shrugged. "It'll take a little time, but that's alright. I took an ad out in the little in-house newspaper that they put out at the assisted-living place I was telling you about. I've already gotten three calls from people there, and the ad has only been in for a week. And I'm going to talk to their management and see if I can do a weekly visit there, just set up in the rec room or something and take some walk-ins."

"That's a great idea."

Kim smiled and dealt out the plates. "Thanks."

Debbie looked around. "Where's Anne?"

"Sleeping. She should be up in time to wreak havoc on the dinner table, though."

Debbie laughed. "Perfect." She stood. "I'm going to get some egg nog. Can I get you something?"

"No thanks." The distant wail of a hungry baby sounded upstairs. "Speak of the devil." She jogged up the stairs to her room and lifted Anne off the mattress on the floor. "Perfect timing, baby girl!" She sat in the chair near the window to nurse her and stared down to the street where her van was parked. A conflicting mix of pride and humility welled as she read the white lettering on the rear window: *Style on the Go.* She'd splurged last week to get it done, and knowing that her little business was being advertised everywhere she drove sent a zing through her stomach. She knew it was just a matter of time before she had a full clientele. Until then she would enjoy all the extra time she had with Anne and the Trumans.

Ruth called the family to dinner awhile later, and Kim sat Anne up to take her downstairs. The others had just begun to take their seats, and Maddie dragged out a chair at her end of the table and said, "Miss Kim, can you and Anne sit by me?"

"Sure, Maddie. But I don't know how long Anne is going to want to sit."

"I'll play with her when I'm done eating."

"Thanks, sweetie, I appreciate that." Kim ruffled the little girl's hair and sat down beside her. She stood Anne on her lap as the others took their places, letting her bounce and babble at Pete, who sat across from them.

Roland reached his hands out to Pete and Kim, who sat on either side of him. "Shall we say grace?" Hands were clasped around the table and heads bowed in silence. "Father, you have showered us with innumerable blessings. Your provision and grace abound, and we are humbled by your generosity. Thank you for welcoming us into your family with open arms."

Kim snuck a peek at the others around the table, surveying the family that had welcomed her with open arms. Their offer of a home after being released from jail had changed her life in more ways than she had expected. Their wisdom, their friendship, and their assistance with her new business and with Anne not only made it possible for her to get back on her feet—they made her lifelong dream for a family a reality.

"Thank you for this meal, and for the fellowship, and for the love we feel for you and each other. In Jesus' name, Amen."

Roland squeezed her hand and gave her a wink. She smiled back, still shy in the face of his attention, but hungry for it at the same time. Beside her, Maddie hopped up on her knees and reached for a roll. "Who gets to do the wishbone?" she asked.

"You may have it," Ruth told her. Maddie squealed.

"What's the wishbone?" Kim asked her.

"It's the bone that you pull apart and get a wish for."

Joshua chuckled. "Sort of, anyway." He leaned forward to talk to Kim around Maddie. "Two people make silent wishes and then grab the ends of the wishbone and pull. Whoever gets the bigger piece is supposed to have their wish granted."

"Want to do it with me, Kim?" Maddie asked.

"That's sweet, Maddie, thanks." She looked around at the table and smiled. "But I already have everything I want."

ACKNOWLEDGMENTS

MANY HEARTFELT THANKS GO OUT TO:

Arloa Sutter, for her willingness to answer all sorts of questions about women's shelters and the nature of abuse. Thanks also for reading through the manuscript and giving my portrayal a thumbs-up—I greatly appreciated the feedback!

Tim Kaye, for helping me get the good guy and the bad guy where I needed them to be.

Brooke, for telling me about what it's like to be a hair stylist.

Matthew Filipek and Nate Heldman, for helping me with the ins and outs of criminal justice.

Wendy, Heather, and Manda from Gentle Christian Mothers, for their help in understanding the foster system.

Claudia, for being awesome, and for giving me some insights into free clinics and helping me find my way around Ann Arbor.

Joel Freeborn, for all the wine info.

Sue Brower, for your support and excellent editing.

My parents, Lee and Leslie, for their unwavering support and enthusiastic encouragement, and for making this possible. You are the most amazing people. I love you so much!

My husband, Daniel, who gives me the time and space I need to write. Without you I'd be lost. I love you so much, and always will. Thank you for how you teach me and love me.

Father, Son, and Holy Spirit—words of thanks will never be enough. May my work bring you glory.